WAR
OF THE
WORLDS.™

The Resurrection

WAR OF THE WORLDS
OF THE
WORLDS™

The Resurrection

A NOVEL BY J.M. DILLARD
BASED ON THE TELEVISION EPISODE
WRITTEN BY GREG STRANGIS
CREATED BY GREG STRANGIS

POCKET BOOKS

New York   London   Toronto   Sydney   Tokyo

Another *Original* publication of POCKET BOOKS

POCKET BOOKS, a division of Simon & Schuster Inc.
1230 Avenue of the Americas, New York, N.Y. 10020

ISBN: 0-671-67111-1

First Pocket Books printing September 1988

10 9 8 7 6 5 4 3 2 1

POCKET and colophon are trademarks of
Simon & Schuster Inc.

Printed in the U.S.A.

ACKNOWLEDGMENTS

The following is a list of those people who made this book possible, and to whom I am deeply grateful:

To Dave Stern, editor, for giving me a chance . . .

To Greg Strangis, executive producer and creator of the television series *War of the Worlds,* who wrote the script on which this novel is based, and his father, executive producer and director Sam Strangis, and the others working with them: Julie Rosenbaum, Meredith Underwood, and Tim Kirk. All were extremely helpful in providing me with everything I needed to write this book.

To D. C. Fontana, one of the all-time best writers in the business, for background on the character Sylvia Van Buren. Her scripts "Journey to Babel," "This Side of Paradise," and "The Enterprise Incident" got me hopelessly hooked on *Star Trek* . . .

To Micky, for all those walks . . .

To Kathy O'Malley and Martha Midgette, for their sage counsel . . .

To weapons expert A.B. from Barstow . . .

To Herbert, who wrote the book that started it . . .

And most of all, to George, who comes up with more useful ideas than that P.O. box in Schenectady . . .

No one would have believed in the last years of the nineteenth century that this world was being watched keenly and closely by intelligences greater than man's and yet as mortal as his own; that as men busied themselves about their various concerns they were scrutinised and studied, perhaps almost as narrowly as a man with a microscope might scrutinise the transient creatures that swarm and multiply in a drop of water. With infinite complacency, men went to and fro over this globe about their little affairs, serene in their assurance of their empire over matter. It is possible that the infusoria under the microscope do the same. No one gave a thought to the older worlds of space as sources of human danger, or thought of them only to dismiss the idea of life upon them as impossible or improbable. It is curious to recall some of the mental habits of those departed days. . . .

Yet across the gulf of space, minds that are to our minds as ours are to those of the beasts that perish, intellects vast and cool and unsympathetic, regarded this earth with envious eyes, and slowly and surely drew their plans against us. . . .

H. G. Wells
The War of the Worlds
1898

December 17
1953

PROLOGUE

The boy was dragged down into the nightmare again.

Harrison darling, get up, his mother said. It always began that way, with the sound of his mother's voice, soft and tinged with panic.

Harrison, get up—

In the dream he had been awake a long time, lying in his bed, the room dark except for the tiny night-light plugged into the wall socket opposite the bed. He listened to the growing rumble outside his window of people talking, of cars driving down the road, their headlights shining through the parted curtains, sweeping across the ceiling and down his bedroom wall. In the far distance, a strange sound . . . almost a hiss, a crackle, and the smell of smoke. Fire. A house burning, maybe lots of houses burning. Maybe the whole town was on fire.

Oddly enough, his parents were still awake and he

3

heard their urgent voices on the other side of the wall, in the kitchen. He couldn't make out the words, but he caught the higher-than-normal pitch, the fast-paced rhythm, the intonation. Almost as if they were arguing, but it wasn't that at all. They were worried about the fire, he decided finally, and soon they would come for him and tell him what to do.

The telephone rang once. His father picked it up and started speaking very quickly. A sound that had to be *all right, Clayton,* followed by the sound of his father hanging up.

Harrison groaned in his sleep, the muscles in his arms and legs twitching as he tried to run away from the dream before the bad part had a chance to begin.

Get up and get dressed, darling, his mother said in the doorway. The hall light shone behind her so that her face was hidden by darkness. Although it was the middle of the night, she was dressed herself, in a beige print dress with a full skirt. She spoke with a quiet urgency, but remained calm, controlled—she was always calm and controlled—but he sensed her fear. Underneath, she was frightened, so horribly frightened that Harrison became frightened too. His mother held a cigarette between her index and middle fingers; the ash streaked dull red in the dark as she lifted the cigarette to her mouth and inhaled nervously.

Harrison climbed from the bed and stood expectantly as his mother clicked on the light and rummaged through his dresser for clothes. She turned back toward him with a shirt in her hands. She was a pretty woman, the prettiest woman in the world to

Harrison, who shared her coloring: golden honey hair, eyes palest blue ice. Harrison would not discover the legacy of the curls until years later, when he let the crew cut grow.

Tonight her face was pale and taut; there were two deep creases in her forehead, between her eyebrows, that Harrison had never noticed before. He raised his arms so that she could pull the pajama top off him, then pull the shirt over his head. He got his arms into the sleeves without help. His mother pulled his short pajama bottoms off, then held out underwear for him to step into. Outside, a siren wailed.

He turned his head toward the window and took a step forward, clumsily stepping on the underpants and forcing them from his mother's hands onto the floor.

Hurry, she snapped. He looked back at her with surprise and this time navigated into the underwear successfully, then into a pair of pants, shoes. Tonight she did not seem to think socks important.

The instant he was dressed, she took his hand and pulled him, jerking him from the room in her haste. He whined a little. She was walking too fast for him, taking big grown-up steps, pulling him down the hallway. She had never acted this way before—so impatient, so hurried—and it scared him more than the sounds of panic coming from outside.

His father, dark-haired and stern, waited at the front door with a large suitcase; as Harrison and his mother passed by, Father paused, then clicked off all the lights.

Shouldn't we leave one on? his mother asked worriedly. *If people start looting—*

Better the place should be looted than burned down. Father's tone was curt, almost bitter. *If they see a light—*

Who are they? Harrison tried to ask, but his mother pushed him through the doorway. She trundled Harrison across the damp grass to the robin's-egg-blue Chevy parked in front and opened the door on the passenger side. Harrison paused before climbing in. The night air seemed alive, charged with electricity . . . the hair on the boy's arms and the nape of his neck rose slightly. The sky was illumined with streaks of something like lightning, but no roll of thunder followed, just the low rumble of traffic, the occasional blare of a car horn. All up and down the normally quiet neighborhood street, the windowpanes glowed yellow. No one was sleeping.

His mother stood behind him, watching the strange lightning. Harrison had never seen her afraid of anything, but now he caught the panic in her pale eyes as she gazed upward. Usually Harrison sat alone in the back of the car—he was a big boy now—but this time his mother opened the passenger door and pulled him in next to her, clutching him with a fierce tenderness.

His father threw the suitcase into the trunk, then climbed into the driver's seat and started the Chevy. They had to wait for seven cars to pass before someone let them out onto the road. *Where are we going?* Harrison wanted to ask, but the sight of his father's grim face kept him quiet.

They traveled in tense silence. All up and down the narrow street, cars full of frightened families waited to pull out of driveways. The road had filled with traffic all headed in the same direction. It was already bumper-to-bumper, but moving. Those trying to back out onto the roadway were ignored, or honked at if they dared pull in front of someone.

At the Robey's house, Harrison's father braked the Chevy and waved for elderly Mr. Robey and his wife to pull out in front of him, ignoring the blaring horns and shouted curses behind him.

Harrison's mother glanced nervously over her shoulder, then back at her husband. "James . . ."

He shrugged. "Someone did the same for us, Sarah. A few seconds aren't going to make any difference."

She nodded in agreement, but her eyes remained anxious.

Traffic remained heavy all the way through the city; it took Father fifteen minutes to get to the outskirts of town. Harrison realized then that they were headed for the highway, the road his parents took to get to work. Traffic was even worse here; the Chevy slowed to a crawl. There were people walking along the side of the road, begging for a ride. Harrison stared through the window, his eyes widening as a group of would-be hitchers headed toward the Chevy.

Lock the door, Father ordered. His mother complied, then the two of them hurried to roll up the windows. She stared at the approaching group, her eyes wide, her mouth a thin line. Harrison cringed as a man his father's age, barefoot and dressed only in a pair of dark pants, rapped his knuckles against the

7

window, then leaned close to the glass, where his breath formed a small circle of mist. Harrison could read the words on the man's lips: *Please, lady, please . . .* The man's face contorted as if he were about to cry. Others began pressing against the Chevy; the car rocked slightly.

We have a child, we can't stop, his mother cried, hugging Harrison closer to her. *I'm sorry . . . sorry . . . we can't stop.*

His father swore and blew the horn impatiently. The car in front of them had stopped. The man withdrew from the window, carried away on the tide of the jostling crowd as other desperate faces appeared in the window, other hands clawed at the glass.

And then a flash of light erupted from the sky and streaked through the crowd. People scattered, screaming. Harrison shrieked and hid his face against his mother's shoulder. When he looked out again, the people were all running away, toward the woods across the open field. Car doors flew open as those inside bolted out to join those fleeing. The earth on the side of the road was blackened and smoking; a wide, grassy strip had caught fire.

Sarah, look! His father caught her elbow and pointed at a sight beyond the rear windshield. *One of their ships! No*—three *of them!*

Harrison pressed his nose to the glass and stared. In the distant sky, three huge blacksilver ships glided in triangular formation. To Harrison, they resembled the giant manta rays he had once seen at the Aquatarium —but a filament rose from the center of each ship, and atop each filament sat a large red eye. The eye was the most horrifying part, for it turned, studying the crowd . . . and then its gaze rested on the Chevy, and on the people sitting inside. His mother made a strangled noise like a sob and pressed her son closer to her.

Harrison's father unlocked and opened his door, his hand still grasping Mother's arm. He pulled her out through the driver's side; she in turn pulled the boy with her. The three of them began to run hand in hand after the shrieking crowd. But the field was flat and grassy, and other than the distant woods, there was no place for them to run, no place Harrison could see to hide. His skin prickled, and he heard a strange hum, then a crash and the crackle of fire behind them. He swiveled his head to see the Chevy and three cars in front of it in flames.

His parents ran even faster. Someone in the crowd bumped into him, and he tripped over a grassy mound and fell facedown. The crowd swept his parents along for a ways before his mother turned and screamed.

Harrison, no—

Of all the images in the dream, he saw this one the most clearly, the way it had really happened. His mother's blue eyes wild, bulging with fear, her mouth a perfect *O,* her beautiful face aglow with reflected firelight.

No—

People ran past her, bumping her, but she fought to keep her footing, to make it back to him. *Harrison—*

His father heard her shrill cries and turned. He clutched her by the shoulders to keep from being separated. They tried to force their way back, but the crowd swept them along so that they could barely hold their ground. Someone stepped on Harrison's leg, someone else on his back; he cried out and scrunched up into a tiny ball, covering his head to protect himself. And then the crowd was gone, and he lay alone on the ground. He pushed himself up so that only his lower half was lying in the grass, and looked behind him. One of the silver ships was drawing closer, its great red eye blinking at him. The hair on the back of his neck rose until it stood on end.

His parents broke free of the crowd and began to run toward him.

A blast of heat singed the top of Harrison's head. The briefest flash of his mother's and father's bodies glowing brilliant, unearthly red imprinted itself on his eyes before he was dazzled into blindness.

Harrison hid his face and lay motionless on the ground for what might have been days . . . or several seconds.

When he looked up again, he saw two charred, smoking lumps where his parents had stood.

The muffled cries in the next room wakened Clayton Forrester from an uneasy sleep. For the split second it took him to awake, he was back in the full horror of it all, expecting to see the night sky orange with flame, imagining that in the deep shadows by the open door, something soft and unspeakable writhed, probing gently, tentatively, until it found him in his bed. . . .

The screams grew louder.

"Mahmeee!"

It was the boy, of course, having another nightmare.

Forrester sat up and drew a hand across his forehead. His palm came away damp. Good Lord, he was shaking. He drew in a deep breath and silently repeated the mantra that had kept him—barely—sane the past four months.

It's all right. It's over. It's over.

He grew calmer and lifted an edge of the curtain over his bed to peer outside at the darkness. Across the street the houses were all unlit, a reassuring sight that meant the inhabitants were asleep, that all was as it had been before. He did his best to forget that only one block away, where the pie-shaped swath of destruction tapered to a sharp point, the blackened skeletons of as-yet-unrebuilt homes remained in silent testimony to the horror that had occurred there.

He let the curtain drop. Poor Harrison was still wailing; Forrester threw back the blankets and winced as his bare feet made contact with the cold terrazzo floor. No time to find his slippers—he crossed the shadowy hall between his and Harrison's rooms in four large strides. The child's door stayed open at night. Plugged into a wall outlet, a plastic Bozo night-light provided an inordinate amount of illumination. Inside, on the bed, Harrison cowered in a small, quivering mound under his blanket.

Forrester sat on the edge of the narrow bed and reached forward to snap on the nightstand lamp. The wood and metal base formed a pistol, a six-shooter with its barrel aimed at the ceiling. It was Harrison's before the invasion; the Blackwood house was one of the few left standing, unscarred by the attack. Its inhabitants hadn't been so lucky. Before that time,

Harrison had been crazy about cowboys and Indians, had even owned a tin sheriff's badge he often tried to wear to bed, and babbled on about shooting bad guys. Lately his interest in such things had flagged. . . .

And who can blame him, Forrester thought, *after his brush with the real thing?*

The boy stopped shrieking and poked his head out to peer owlishly at Forrester. His light blue eyes were huge and far too serious to belong to a five-year-old. Harrison fought unsuccessfully to keep his lower lip from trembling, but was still too young to stop the tears that coursed down his babyishly plump cheeks. "I'm . . . sorry," he gasped between huge, gulping sobs.

"It's all right," Forrester said as soothingly as such an idiotic phrase could be said. He stroked the boy's forehead, patted the soft, dark blond bristles of his crew cut. The December night was chilly, cold enough for the ancient furnace to kick on, but Harrison's forehead was hot and moist from sobbing under the covers. "It's all right," the older man repeated.

Harrison calmed under his touch, but it was far from all right. James Blackwood—Forrester's colleague, Harrison's father—and his beautiful wife, Sarah, were dead. And at the age of five, their son was already learning not to cry. When Forrester had first taken the boy in, Harrison had called almost every night for his parents, had angrily demanded them. Now he called for them only in his sleep, and apologized if Forrester should hear.

What kind of world, Forrester thought bitterly, *demands so much of five-year-olds?*

He pulled two white tissues from the box on the nightstand. "That's better," he said as Harrison's snuffles ceased. "Think you can blow your nose for me without help?"

Harrison nodded, still with that too-adult, too-serious expression, and sat up. He looked very much like his father. He took the tissues, applied them inexpertly to the general area of his nose, and blew. Forrester helped him wipe.

"Good boy." He tossed the tissue into the trash can. "I'll bet you could use a glass of water."

"Yes," the child lisped. And then, as an afterthought, "Please."

Forrester stood. The boy tensed instantly. "I'm only going across the hall," he said lightly. "Back in two seconds."

He stepped across to the bathroom, in the dark found Harrison's yellow plastic cup, and rinsed it out before filling it up.

The screaming incidents occurred less frequently now; there was a time, only a month or two before, when Forrester felt like the father of a newborn, when Harrison had wakened terrified, yelling, not just once but two, three, four times a night. He was sure then that the boy had been permanently scarred by the incident, would never be able to sleep in a room by himself. But the child showed a remarkable resiliency —more than Forrester himself. With all his training in science, Forrester had found he was abysmally ignorant of the workings of his own mind. As long as Harrison needed him so badly, he was able to keep himself sane, sane enough to at least take care of the boy. He prided himself on his ability to stay in one piece while others around him cracked up.

But now that Harrison was recuperating, his new father was slowly falling apart. Through it all, he'd never had bad dreams. Now most nights he awakened at least once with the sensation of something huge and crushing on his chest, or, even worse, three soft, featherlike fingers being drawn lightly across the back of his neck. . . .

They're here, my God, they've come back—

He straightened at the sink and took a sip from Harrison's bathroom cup. The water smelled faintly of chlorine and plastic. There were times, such as now in this bathroom where everything was just as it had always been, when Forrester felt sure the invasion had all been a psychotic delusion. Aliens. Death rays. The stuff of a child's nightmares.

On nights like these, he came close to envying Sylvia—the woman who had endured the invasion with him, the woman he loved and had intended to marry—for her ability to forget all that had happened. He could not grieve for her, only for himself— because Sylvia remembered no loss. She was well cared for, happy, unaware that she was institutionalized, and lived in the blissful past, well before the time of the horrors she and Clayton Forrester had suffered together. On most of his visits, she failed to recognize him. Perhaps, Forrester told himself, Sylvia's solution to the problem was the best of all.

He heard Harrison sniffle and crossed the hallway into the bedroom. The boy was on his feet now, and as Forrester sat back down on the bed, he climbed on his adoptive father's lap. Harrison had grown the past four months, to be sure. The hems of his Roy Rogers pajamas, which not so long ago had dragged along the ground, edged their way up toward his ankles. But he was still such a little kid, with his head seeming too big for the rest of his skinny body.

Forrester handed him the cup. It was hard to say, exactly, who needed whom the most. He was becoming convinced that it was an equal exchange. He probably would have become as mad as Sylvia if he'd had to stay alone in this house at night.

Harrison took a few noisy slurps of his water, then paused, clutching the cup in both hands, and stared at Forrester with those pale, somber eyes. "Are you going to be my daddy now?"

Forrester smiled and stroked the boy's head. "Yes, I'm going to be your daddy now, Harrison." The child had been the one good thing to come out of all this. Forrester had already filed the adoption papers, and it was only a matter of time before Harrison would legally be his son. Even so, Forrester insisted that the child's name remain Blackwood, to ensure that James and Sarah's name would continue.

"You aren't going to die, are you?" Harrison asked suddenly, reproachfully.

Forrester did his best not to look startled by the question. "No, Harrison, I'm not going to die."

"Promise?"

Forrester nodded, realizing rather guiltily that he was making a promise he might not be able to keep. But Harrison needed some certainty in his life now, even if it meant lying a little. "I promise," Forrester answered, raising his hand solemnly as if taking an oath. "But you must promise never to forget your parents."

"I can't forget them," the boy said with sudden fierceness. "I can't forget any of it."

"I know. I can't either, son." *God, sometimes I wish I could.* He could see the father in the boy's face, could remember how, when the attack had begun in earnest, James had said, *If anything happens to Sarah and me—*

Forrester hadn't let him finish. No need to. He'd been friends with James before Harrison was born and knew what was coming next. And already he knew the child well enough to see the man: others might try to forget, but Harrison would always remember. Forrester would trust him, train him to carry on his work.

But others had already forgotten. Forrester had seen the idiocy of the government at work. He and other scientists at the Pacific Institute had begged for more money to do research, to study the aliens in detail, to discover where they had come from, why they had attacked Earth, how their ships and weapons worked. He had gone to Washington, D.C., and argued with members of Congress, with representatives of the military—all to no avail. The government wanted the "war of the worlds" forgotten. The hundreds of thousands of alien bodies remaining were stuffed into barrels and ignored. As he was now being ignored. And ignorance would triumph. The memory of what had happened would be actively forgotten, hidden from future generations, until, at last, no one remembered. . . .

Except Harrison Blackwood. Forrester patted the boy's shoulder. "Come on, cowpoke, finish your water."

Harrison took two more sips and handed the glass back to him. "Can you stay a little while?"

"Sure. But you've got to get under those covers and let me tuck you in."

"Okay." The boy's face brightened. Just relief, not quite a smile; he hadn't smiled in six months, and Forrester expected it would be at least as long before he heard the boy laugh. Here it was, the week before Christmas, a time when kids were supposed to be eagerly awaiting a visit from Santa. With the solicitousness of a new parent, Forrester had carefully wrapped and hidden away toys, even put up a five-foot pine tree in the living room. But Harrison wanted none of it. He showed no interest in helping to decorate the tree, refused to even acknowledge the fact that the holiday was approaching. Perhaps, Forrester reflected, because the boy knew that the one thing he wanted most in the world could never be given back to him. Harrison was not the only one to ignore Christmas. Not a single home in the neighborhood was strung with outdoor holiday lights this year.

Harrison jumped into the bed with childish energy and pulled the covers up. Forrester tucked him in, then got a chair from the corner of the room—a comfortable adult-sized chair put there for just such emergencies—and settled into it. "I'm going to turn the light off, but I'll still be here, even though it's dark."

Harrison seemed satisfied. "G'night, Daddy."

Forrester smiled at his new title. "Good night, son." He turned off the pistol lamp. It wouldn't be the first time he'd spent the night in this chair . . . or the last. Sometimes he sat and read Harrison stories; most of the time, the boy, with his quick, restless mind, became bored with the predictable plots and asked questions about the real world. Forrester discovered to his delight that the boy was brilliant, a born scientist, like his parents. Most of the questions were typical bright-kid questions about the color of the sky, about why it rained . . . sometimes, less often, he asked about the aliens. Why did they look so funny? How did their machines burn everything up?

And somehow trying to explain them to Harrison made talking about them possible, provided Forrester himself with a means of dealing with what had happened. Science took the scariness out of it, made the fact of the invasion more tolerable . . . until Harrison asked a question Forrester couldn't answer, such as why the aliens would want to hurt his parents.

Forrester sat in the darkness until the boy's breathing became regular. He was grateful to have a hand in raising Harrison, to have the chance to teach the child everything he, Forrester, had learned about the aliens. The world was going to need scientists like the one Harrison would become.

Because deep in his bones, Forrester knew that it wasn't over, wasn't over at all. It had scarcely even begun. . . .

October

1988

ONE

Urick sat in the tractor-trailer's cab and watched the dark landscape fly by. Next to her, Chambers held the rig at a steady fifty-five; no point in tempting the cops by speeding. There was nothing to see in the desert at night, and after Urick's initial terror subsided into restless impatience, she began to find the drive boring, to become eager to reach their destination.

The plan was in motion now. She glanced over at Chambers and thought, *What would happen if I asked him to pull over, if I jumped out of the cab and hiked my way back to town?* Would she go back to being the same person she had always been: Lena Urick, perennially broke, overage college student, always pushing back graduation another year because she had to work overtime to pay the rent? Was there still time to stop this before things went too far?

You've already gone too far. You've broken the

law—stolen a truck, carried a weapon without a license—and then there's conspiracy . . . There was no going back to the way things used to be. And there was no point in lying to herself—she couldn't back out if she wanted to. Chambers wouldn't let her go. She thought of the Uzis hidden behind their seats; an image flashed in her mind of her fleeing from the rig into the desert, of Chambers calmly pulling the Uzi from the backseat and taking aim. . . .

Would he kill you? Could he really kill you? The answer was undoubtedly yes, and in Urick's mind he would be entirely justified in killing her: she would not have respected him if he were not prepared to kill for the cause. Yet another part of her—the weaker, timid part of herself she thought of as Lena, her old self—felt the opposite.

Urick thought of her former self, Lena, as another person, no longer a part of Urick, free soldier of the People's Liberation Army, but someone else, a coward, always afraid. She insisted her comrades call her only by her last name, Urick, and Urick was cool, dedicated, unafraid, just like Chambers, who radiated perfect calm sitting there next to her. She considered for an instant that he might be as frightened as she, but dismissed the idea as ridiculous.

She'd been through their route a thousand times before, but she pulled the map from the glove compartment and unfolded it, leaving the compartment open so that she could read by its faint light. She didn't even consider asking Chambers to turn on the overhead. The less seen of their faces, the better.

She stared once again at the route underlined in red:

east, into the desert, though the map was unnecessary; she could have drawn it from memory. She looked down at her watch, the one present from her father she'd ever permitted herself to keep. She would have thrown it out the window right then if she hadn't needed it to carry out the plan. No point in anything tying her to the past, to the old Lena, and certainly not to her father. Besides, it was expensive, gold, a symbol of everything she stood against now. When Lena was fifteen, her family had left Germany to come to the United States; her father, a working-class man, a firm believer in the capitalist dream, had opened a deli . . . then two, then three, until he was a rich man who owned an entire chain. Nothing narrowed a person's mind faster, Lena learned, than the acquisition of wealth.

What would her father say if he knew what she was doing now? *You think you know it all, don't you, Lena?* She could hear him start with that lecturing tone. *So quick to judge . . . thinking only in shades of black and white. But the world isn't that way; it's all shades of gray, and you shouldn't judge a man until you've been in his position.*

I know what's right, Papa, and you'll see. Someday I'm going to save the world.

From what?

From itself. From political oppression.

A sigh, a shake of the head. *My daughter the martyr. There's more than one way to save the world, Lena.*

Lena might have listened. But Urick knew better; the only shades of gray came from those people who lived corrupted lives. She was here to cleanse the

23

world from unscrupulous men like her father . . . and from corrupt, decadent governments like the one in Washington, whose morality was dictated by the almighty dollar.

Urick registered the time. At least they were on schedule. She felt a tightness in her chest and practiced breathing slowly, methodically, then glanced out of the corner of her eye at Chambers, knowing that the sight of him would calm her. The lights on the highway reflected off the lens of his wire-rimmed glasses; they were still close enough to the city for there to be occasional traffic this late at night. He was older than she, in his early forties, a quiet man possessed of incredible determination, and he had a strange way of sensing when she was thinking about him. He caught her sly glance, tilted his face toward her—a handsome face, with compelling eyes and thick brown hair that was swept back to reveal a high forehead. The sign of great intelligence, her mother had always said. Chambers gave Urick a slight, encouraging smile. She returned it; she was not afraid to die, she decided, so long as she died with him.

A brilliant man, Chambers. A political science professor at UCLA unlike any other college professor Urick had known—for Chambers possessed strong beliefs, and he believed in acting on those principles. From the first lecture Lena Urick had been mesmerized. Yet it was more than just a schoolgirl crush—no, it was a political awakening for her, and she refused to let their relationship be cheapened by such emotions. For his part, Chambers maintained a scrupulously paternal attitude toward her. Urick thought of him as the man her father would have been had greed not corrupted him.

She forced herself to look back down at the map. They were less than an hour away from their destination, away from the line Urick knew she must cross, after which there could be no turning back.

"Damn," Chambers said softly in his deep voice. The rig shuddered and whined as he downshifted.

She looked over at him, startled. "What's wrong?" The instant she said it, she saw the flashing light reflected off the side mirror. Her heart began thumping wildly.

"Don't know." Chambers eased on the brake and pulled over to the shoulder. The rig groaned to a halt. Urick stared at the police cruiser reflected in the mirror, then at Chambers.

He didn't look at her; he was busy watching the uniformed policeman walk up to the driver's side of the cab. Urick moved to reach for the guns behind the seat. Chambers held up his hand.

"Not yet," he said softly. She drew her hand away and forced herself to sit still, to not look panic-stricken.

Chambers peered down through the open window of the cab and smiled at the policeman.

"I'll need to see your operator's permit and way-bill," the cop said with the voice of a man in his early twenties. Theoretically, Urick hated the cop because of the role he played in repressing society; personally, she had nothing against him, and was unsettled at the thought of using the Uzi this soon, against someone so young. When she thought of killing, she pictured herself killing corrupt old men her father's age, not kids barely out of school.

"Is there a problem, Officer?" Chambers was playing it just right: polite because he didn't want to get a ticket, with the barest hint of irritation at being pulled over. In the midst of her fear, Urick felt a surge of admiration for him.

The cop didn't reply; he gestured for Chambers to hand over the documents. As Chambers sighed and reached for the glove compartment, Urick caught his eye with a look that said *Do you think he knows? Shall I reach for the Uzis?* She didn't dare whisper it with the cop so nearby.

Chambers shrugged. *No. Not yet* . . . She helped him find the forged permit and the waybill. Chambers handed them down to the cop. There was a pause, and then: "Please step out of the vehicle, Mr. Chambers."

Urick held her breath as Chambers opened the door and complied. She caught a brief glimpse of the cop before Chambers slammed the door shut—a blond-haired kid who looked too young to shave and was giving Chambers that stern chip-on-the-shoulder stare. There was no reason to be so near panic. Cops always made you get out of the car. But why the hell had they stopped the rig? Chambers hadn't even been speeding. . . .

"All the way to the rear," the cop said.

Chambers' boots crunched against the gravel as he moved to the rear of the truck. Urick slid over to the driver's side and craned her neck out the window to watch. The blond cop followed Chambers to the back of the truck, where a second cop was waiting. They were going to make Chambers open it.

And they were going to get one hell of a surprise.

Urick peered into the side mirror and strained to listen; the young cop was still talking, though he and the other cop had stepped out of view. Chambers, slightly off to one side, was just visible. "Waybill doesn't list your freight, Mr. Chambers. Just says one metric ton."

Chambers sounded indignant. "Company didn't hire me to do the paperwork."

"Any objection to us having a look?"

In the flashing light she could see Chambers' silhouette shrug and pull the key from his chest pocket. There was going to be shooting. She should have scrunched down inside the cab to protect herself, but Chambers was talking. She was frightened for him, and wanted to hear what he would say.

His tone was casual as he proffered the key. "If you don't mind, I'll wait in your car while you poke around. Stuff in there's low-grade nuclear waste. They usually pack it up real good, but . . . me and the missus still plan on having a few kids." It was the story they'd rehearsed a thousand times for this very emergency, but the line about the kids and the request to sit in the cruiser were ad-libbed.

She could have laughed out loud. Perfect, Chambers! That way he could hide in the safety of the police car . . . *if* the cops still felt like poking around.

She grinned in the dark cab and waited. There was a long pause as the cops presumably took notice of Chambers' clean white jump suit and made the desired connection; then the cop's partner spoke.

"Reason we pulled you over, Mr. Chambers, you've got a short in your taillights."

"I'll check it out right away, Officer."

"Do that," the young one said. "Drive careful now, okay?"

A door slammed; the flashing light was replaced by headlights and the sound of the cruiser wheeling away at top speed. She climbed out of the cab and joined Chambers, who stood watching them leave. She wanted to gloat, to congratulate him on his cleverness, but, as usual, he was thinking only of what had to be done.

"Taillight's out," he said shortly, dropping the key back into his pocket and giving it a pat. "Check the fuse and let's roll. We're behind schedule." He headed back to the cab, slapping the rear door of the trailer as he passed by.

On the nine-foot chain-link fence that ran alongside the road, the sign read:

JERICHO VALLEY DISPOSAL SITE
AUTHORIZED PERSONNEL ONLY
Entrance 1000 Yards

A strange little song began to repeat in Urick's mind, a song she hadn't thought of in years: *Joshua in the battle of Jericho, Jericho, Jericho . . . Joshua in the battle of Jericho, and the walls came tumblin' down . . .*

Chambers downshifted and maneuvered the rig past the sign and onto the narrow gravel path leading to the first gate. They'd driven along in silence after the taillight incident. At some point, even in the darkness, Urick could tell that Chambers was nervous. For some strange reason the thought calmed her, and the closer they drew to the disposal site, the stronger her sense of unreality became.

Chambers sounded the air horn. Urick looked down at the glowing numbers on her watch: right on schedule. Two helmeted soldiers stepped out of the guard shack on the other side of the gate; one of them hit a switch, and the outer gate slid open.

Chambers put the tractor-trailer in low gear and eased it past the gate, which closed behind them. Urick read more signs on the guard shack: FEDERAL RESERVE, NO TRESPASSING ALLOWED, NUCLEAR AND TOXIC WASTES STORED HERE.

Urick didn't glance at her surroundings; she'd already memorized them. It was a tiny base, consisting of nothing more than a small barracks, a guard shack, and stack after stack of steel barrels.

One of the soldiers came up to the driver's side of the cab, and without a word reached up for the paperwork Chambers handed down. Unlike the cop, the soldier seemed satisfied with what he read; he nodded at his partner, who responded by pressing another switch. The inner gate behind the guard shack slid open. Chambers rolled the tractor-trailer past it and let go a shaky sigh.

So he *was* terrified after all, Urick thought with a twinge of disappointment. Not that it mattered; not that anything mattered, except what she had to do.

And it was almost time. She reached into the space between the seat and the back of the cab and carefully pulled out the Uzi. Chambers was already out as she climbed down, keeping the hand with the Uzi behind her back.

The soldiers had come out the rear door of the guard shack and were approaching the rig with smiles on their faces. Young corporals, clean-shaven, barely twenty years old. *This is the enemy,* Urick told herself. *These are dead men.* In every revolution, Chambers had explained, there had to be deaths. *We don't relish killing . . . but to achieve our goals we must sacrifice some on the altar of world freedom. Perhaps, if our victims knew the good their deaths would bring, they would volunteer . . .* Urick studied their leering faces and doubted it. Typical army types. Probably enlisted for no better reason than to get a free education. Suddenly, she was filled with overwhelming hatred for them.

"Got some fresh coffee in the shack," one of them said pleasantly to her, making her realize that the smiles were for her alone.

Chambers answered before she could. "Maybe later," he said stonily.

The other corporal took a step nearer. "When did you folks add women to your crews?"

"Are you threatened by a woman, soldier?" Urick asked. Her voice had a shrill edge to it. Stupid of her to argue. She should have simply killed him.

"No, ma'am," the questioner answered politely. "I just like 'em, is all."

Her hand tightened on the Uzi; Lena fled forever, leaving only Urick, and Urick realized with an eerie thrill that she was going to enjoy what she was about to do. She smiled coldly at the soldiers. "What a nice thing to say."

She drew the Uzi out for them to see and pointed it at the one who offered coffee. The effect on them was gratifying; the corporals gasped in unison and thrust their hands into the air. Out of the corner of her eye she saw that Chambers smiled. He was pleased with her performance, then; he was the one who suggested she handle the Uzi—because they'd never expect any trouble from a woman, he'd said, but she knew it was to test her loyalty. There was but one last line to cross.

"What the hell's going on?" The coffee drinker demanded.

"Liberation, my friend," Chambers told him.

One of them moved, Urick didn't know which, but her finger squeezed the trigger without her consciously deciding to do so. Because of the silencer, the burst made very little noise as it tore into Corporal Coffee, lifting him off his feet and knocking him a good yard backward and down. She looked at him lying there, the front of his uniform shredded and blood-soaked, and felt nothing.

The remaining corporal made a noise something

like a sob. He raised his hands even higher as he backed away from Urick and the gun. His face contorted. "My God, lady, why——?"

She raised the Uzi again.

"Hey, just cool it, okay?" His voice rose to hysterical pitch.

"It's okay, soldier," she told him calmly, sweetly, and smiled to herself as he relaxed a little. She was aware of Chambers' eyes on her, a little surprised that she was toying with her victim, but she didn't care. "Everything's cool."

She squeezed the trigger again. The second corporal fell back, his expression startled.

No time to think now. Only work to be done. Chambers went over to the rig and opened a side panel. He set up the rocket launcher while Urick, the Uzi dancing on a strap slung over one shoulder, ran to the back of the trailer, unlatched the doors, and swung them wide. Inside the trailer, engines revved.

Joshua in the battle of Jericho . . .

Exhilaration replaced fear. She had done it—she had killed two men for the good of the revolution, and she had not shrunk from the task. If anything, she had enjoyed it. Urick peered inside the trailer, wanting to share that feeling with her four comrades, but Mossoud, Finney, Teal, and Einhorn were indistinguishable from one another. The visors of their black helmets were already down so that she couldn't catch their eyes. Urick ran to one side, out of the way as the four all-terrain vehicles roared out of the trailer.

Standing by the side of the truck, Chambers aligned the sights on the launcher and located his target. A compact missile whined through the air; across the yard, the barracks building exploded. Urick covered her head as debris went flying, but she kept moving: what she was looking for would be on the sheltered bulletin board near the guard shack.

Behind her came the fire of automatic weapons, but she wasn't frightened. The ATVs had machine guns mounted on their handlebars. She found the duty roster neatly stapled in a conspicuous spot on the bulletin board; she tore it off and ran back toward the truck. Something she saw on her way there made her stop.

Down an aisle created by waste barrels, new ones stacked on top of ancient rusty ones, an ATV rider had been knocked from his vehicle by a soldier armed only with a piece of lumber. Two-by-four raised over his head, the soldier was moving in on the fallen rider to finish the job. If he managed to get to the weapon mounted on the ATV—

Urick dropped the roster and began to run toward the ATV, her Uzi at the ready, without even thinking about what would happen if the soldier got there before she was close enough to take aim. She hadn't taken two steps before a second ATV appeared and fired at the soldier.

The blast slammed him, mouth gaping, back against the barrels; another barrage held him there for an instant before he slid to the ground, leaving a bloody smear on the barrel behind him.

Good, Urick thought, and realized with a sudden jolt that she was smiling. It had all been so easy . . . too easy. None of it had been real, she decided. The people they had killed were not real people. She turned and picked the roster up out of the dust and brushed it off.

It was suddenly very quiet on the base; the four ATVs had returned to the truck and shut down their engines. Finney was the first one to take off his helmet, its visor spattered with blood. The others followed suit: Mossoud, tall and swarthy, not to be trusted; Teal, a short, wiry, serious man; Einhorn, with his many-times-broken nose. Finney laughed, running his fingers through his thick blond hair; he was wearing the same strange, slightly hysterical smile Urick knew was on her own lips.

She had always despised Finney.

As she approached, Finney was replying to something Chambers had asked.

"None on our team," he said, still grinning. "But Mossoud got knocked for a loop."

Mossoud wasn't smiling; his tone was more than a little defensive. "Just havin' me some fun." He rubbed his shoulder and grimaced. "Had that dude in my sights the whole time." Right. Arrogant fool, Mossoud. She knew he didn't believe in the revolution; he and Finney were doing this for the sport of it, and if things didn't work out the way they wanted, they would turn on Chambers in an instant. She'd tried to warn Chambers before about them, but he refused to listen. A pity that honest leaders like Chambers had to recruit such self-serving assholes.

She stepped up next to Chambers, trying to make her expression more serious, like his. "Duty roster lists seventeen men. One officer"—she held it so he could see it—"four noncoms, twelve enlisted." The officer would have been the one swinging the two-by-four, she decided. He'd worn a lieutenant's gold bar on his collar. The noncoms included the corporals she'd killed.

Chambers nodded. "Mossoud, Finney." His voice was serious, authoritative enough to make Finney stop gloating and listen. "Do a body count. Make sure there are no stragglers. Teal, Einhorn—set up the perimeter charges."

The others filed off, and she and Chambers were left alone. She would have liked to talk to him then about the odd metamorphosis she had undergone, how frightened, insecure Lena was gone forever and this strange new cold-blooded person had taken her place, but something about his manner held her back. Instead, she said, "Let's find a good place for the transmitter."

They were heading for the side panel when the telephone in the guard shack began to ring. She started; Chambers put a hand on her shoulder.

"Let it ring," he said. "The world's going to hear about us soon enough." And he actually smiled.

She returned the smile gratefully. *And the walls came tumblin' down . . .*

Mossoud looked down at the lieutenant's bullet-ridden body and rubbed his aching shoulder one more time. *Serves you right, you son of a bitch, thinking you could take me on!*

He bent down and felt for a wallet in the dead man's back pockets, then the hip pockets, then the pockets on the thighs. No go; maybe he had it in one of his front pockets for some strange reason, in which case any money had been shredded into confetti by the machine-gun blast. He heard the faintest noise, like a hiss: the guy breathing? Nah . . . impossible. Maybe just air seeping out of his perforated lungs.

He ignored the sound and looked at the guy's wrist. Left one bare . . . Jesus, didn't this guy wear anything where he was supposed to? On the right wrist Mossoud found what he was looking for: a watch with a gold band, eighteen karat at least, with an inscription on the back. *To Jeff, Happy Graduation, Love, Mom and Dad.* Mossoud pulled it off the dead man and slipped it onto his wrist. A nice fit. He heard Finney coming and pulled the sleeve of his leather jacket down over his prize.

"Finney. Give me a hand with this one."

"You check his pockets?" Finney nudged the stiff with his boot before stooping over to take the guy's legs. Mossoud caught the body under the shoulders.

"Guy's got nothing worth taking," Mossoud answered innocently, then groaned as they lifted the body up. "Can you believe it? All those goddamn pockets, and not a thing in 'em."

Neither noticed as, behind them, a thick, caustic liquid hissed through a bullet hole in one of the newer barrels onto an old rusted barrel beneath it. The top of the rusty barrel sizzled as the toxic ooze ate through the metal.

They were both gone by the time the three probing fingers of the alien's hand burst through.

TWO

Suzanne McCullough sat outside Dr. Jacobi's office and glanced impatiently at her watch for the thousandth time in the past twenty minutes. She'd arrived precisely five minutes before the appointed time. Coming any sooner would have revealed how anxious she was; coming any later would have reflected poorly on a newly hired employee. Of course, she'd actually been twenty-five minutes early—it'd taken less time than she expected to get Deb to school—and had wandered around the grounds to kill time. The Pacific Institute of Technology sprawled out over several acres of beautifully landscaped terrain, and at the top of one gently rising hill she'd been able to see the water. In the bright California sunshine, Ohio seemed very, very far away.

God knows, they were certainly laid back around here. Jacobi was the director, and here he was already ten minutes late. The director of Zubrovski Labs in Canton would never have been late for an appointment. Suzanne sighed and shifted on the too-soft, too-low couch. Even the receptionist was late, shuffling in five minutes before, although she was friendly and kind enough to offer coffee. Suzanne was tempted, but declined. She didn't trust herself not to spill it down the front of her silk blouse before Dr. Jacobi arrived.

If they had just told her what type of project they'd hired her *for* . . . At least then, she wouldn't be nervous *and* consumed by curiosity.

It didn't help that Debi had burst out crying at the breakfast table in the morning. Suzanne had been too busy searching for the box boldly labeled: KITCHEN/COFFEEMAKER. TOP PRIORITY! to notice the storm clouds gathering. She was now convinced that it was still in the moving van on its way to Oregon, or else sitting forlornly in the empty house back in Canton; after several desperate minutes she realized she had to give it up or be late her first day on the job. She ran her fingers through her long dark hair and sank stiffly into the kitchen chair, trying to remember where the aspirin was packed. A sniffle came from the other end of the table.

"Deb?" She had to stand to see her; the kitchen table was littered with half-emptied cardboard boxes. Miraculously, Deb had managed to find her clothes and was dressed for her second day of school. "Are you okay?"

Another sniffle. "Yeah, I'm okay, Mom," Debi said miserably into her cornflakes. "I'm just . . . tired."

And then the dam broke. Suzanne was just tired and aching enough to join her. Between sobs Deb managed to get it all out. It was her second day of sixth grade at the new school, but she didn't ever want to go back. She didn't like any of the other kids, they all dressed weird, not like home at all, and they thought she was a geek. Nobody would sit with her at lunch. . . .

"Honey, did you *ask* anyone to sit with you?" Stupid question to ask an eleven-year-old girl; she knew it the moment she said it.

*"Mom . . . I can't ask anyone I don't know. They're supposed to ask *me* . . ."*

You mustn't be so shy, Suzanne almost said, then bit her tongue. She couldn't blame Deb for taking after her mother (personality-wise, at least. Physically, Deb was the spitting image of Derek). Suzanne could still remember what it felt like; she'd spent junior high with Coke-bottle glasses, a mouthful of braces, and only one close friend, an outsider like herself. "I'm sorry, Deb." She walked over to stand next to the girl, stroked her hair, and felt a pang of guilt. Poor Deb. Today, when she got home from school, the strange new house would be empty because her mother would still be working. "It's no fun starting over; I don't much like having to start a new job myself today. But these kids won't remain strangers forever. Who knows? Maybe you'll make friends with some of them."

"I doubt it." Debi stared down into her cereal, her long blond hair hanging perilously close to the bowl; a tear dripped into the milk.

Suzanne knelt down next to her. "I'm not trying to be mean, but you have a choice: you can either sit here and cry about it, or you can tell yourself it's going to get better. To tell you the truth, I'd just as soon cry with you, but I've got to go get dressed for work."

"I'm sorry, Mom." Deb looked up at her mother; her voice rose tremulously. "I guess I'm just tired, and I sort of . . . miss Dad a little."

Suzanne gave her a fierce hug and swallowed back tears. She wasn't going to think about Derek now, or she would cry from sheer outrage at the way he treated his only daughter. She had stayed in Ohio for Debi's sake so that the girl could be close to her father . . . but most of the time Derek didn't bother to take advantage of his visitation rights, sometimes even forgot to come pick up Deb on the scheduled weekends. Debi adored him, and when he *did* show up, with his tall blond good looks, he charmed her into forgetting how he'd hurt her. *Just like he did with your mother for all those years. . . .*

She pushed the thought out of her mind and stood up, feigning cheerfulness. "Now, quit crying into your cornflakes, kid, or they'll get soggy. Eat your breakfast, and when you go to school today, be sure to notice what the kids are wearing. Maybe when I get back from work tonight, we can do a little clothes shopping."

"All right," Deb said glumly, but her expression said *Fat lot of good that'll do*. But at least she'd stopped crying and finished her cereal.

Now, outside Ephram Jacobi's office, Suzanne rose at the sight of the director of the Pacific Institute walking toward her. He noticed her, and a smile lit up his lined sun-browned face. Hale-looking and square-shouldered, there was nothing in the way he held himself or moved to indicate his age. He'd worked on the Manhattan Project forty-five years before, when he was a young man; Suzanne calculated that he had to be at least in his early seventies, though he looked more like sixty. Apparently, being director of the Institute for the past twenty years agreed with him; she took it as a hopeful sign.

As he approached, Suzanne nervously returned his smile.

"Dr. McCullough." Jacobi adjusted his old-fashioned wire-rimmed glasses as if to see her better, then gripped her hand with strong, bony fingers. "So you're finally here at last. Good. I hope the move wasn't too traumatic." He spoke with the slightest trace of an accent; she tried to identify it and failed.

"Not too," she said.

"Please." Jacobi gestured her toward his office. She entered and sat down across from him at his desk, which reminded her very much of her kitchen table back home—full of clutter. How on earth did the man get any work done in such a disorganized environment?

Jacobi settled himself into an old wooden chair on casters that creaked as he swiveled back and forth ever so slightly in it. Must be as old as he was, Suzanne decided. "It's so very good of you to have accepted our offer," he said.

Good of her? Suzanne tried not to look skeptical. They'd offered her forty percent more pay than she'd gotten in Ohio, plus all expenses incurred in the move. And suddenly she panicked. Dammit, she *knew* it was too good to be true. But she'd laid it all out to Jacobi the very first interview. Yes, she'd worked on a secret project in Canton, but it was a joint project with NASA and had nothing whatsoever to do with biological warfare, which she absolutely refused to have anything to do with. And if that was what Jacobi was offering, she'd just leave now, thank you.

He'd sworn it wasn't. *Nothing like that,* he'd reassured her. After all, hadn't he been one of the scientists on the Manhattan Project who'd later publicly denounced the use of atomic weapons, had demonstrated on the Capitol steps for peace? No, he permitted nothing like that to go on at the Pacific Institute. Not as long as he had a breath of life in him. And he spoke with such conviction that she'd believed him.

What would she do now if he told her otherwise? Quit immediately, of course . . . But then what would happen to her and Debi? She'd never be able to reimburse them the moving costs, at least not for a while. . . .

That's what you get for behaving impulsively, moving all the way to California without knowing exactly what the job was all about. Sounds more like something Derek would do.

"Dr. Jacobi," she said slowly, "I am terribly curious as to what the job entails. As I told you, I refuse to engage in any sort of research that could conceivably be used for biowarfare."

His thin lips curved upward in a smile. "Ah, yes. A scientist of principle. And that's why I hired you, Dr.

McCullough." He riffled distractedly through a stack of pink While You Were Out memos as he spoke. "But before we discuss details, I would like you to meet the man you'll be working with."

"Dr. Jacobi—" she began, frustrated. She was going to say, *I get a strong impression that you are trying to avoid answering my question . . . until you feel I'm caught too tightly in your web to say no.*

Jacobi held up his hand. "He'll be able to answer all your questions for you. Dr. Harrison Blackwood, the astrophysicist. Perhaps you've heard of him."

"No," Suzanne answered, calming down a little. An astrophysicist . . . then maybe they hired her because they were interested in space research of the type she'd done at Zubrovski Labs. "But if he can explain, then by all means . . . take me to him."

Blackwood's office was in a different wing of the building which looked like it had been constructed back in the thirties. The man couldn't be very influential around here, then, if he hadn't managed to get one of the plush new offices near Jacobi's. They stopped in front of a dark wooden door that bore the single inscription BLACKWOOD. The sign looked as old as the rest of the building; then Dr. Blackwood was no doubt as ancient as Jacobi.

Jacobi pushed open the door without knocking; catching Suzanne's raised brow, he explained: "We're pretty informal around here, Doctor. You'll get used to it." He poked his head inside, then looked back at Suzanne and put his finger to his lips. "Blackwood's lecturing. We let the local schoolchildren visit from time to time. I'm not sure who enjoys it more." He stepped inside and motioned for her to follow.

"How nice," Suzanne murmured behind him. She eased the door shut as quietly as possible. Blackwood stood speaking with his back to them; before him, a group of children Debi's age listened, wide-eyed, whether totally intent or totally lost, Suzanne wasn't sure. She and Dr. Jacobi tiptoed off to one side of the room. Neither Blackwood nor the children seemed to notice.

"Insofar as science is concerned," Blackwood was saying, "I doubt we've ever experienced a more exciting period in human history. Aided by the computer and other modern research techniques, startling discoveries are happening at an exponential rate. . . ."

The room looked more like a child-scientist's playground than an office: the ceiling was plastered with astral maps; a huge mobile of the solar system hung suspended, as did other celestial bodies, and through this makeshift cosmos sailed an inflatable plastic model of the starship *Enterprise*. About a dozen antique telescopes were aimed at the open window, and above the desk hung a framed poster of Schiaparelli's Mars, complete with *canali*.

Jacobi settled against the wall to listen. Next to him, Suzanne tried not to stare at Dr. Blackwood. She'd pictured him as looking like her old boss at Zubrovski Labs, Dr. Solomon, overweight and almost totally bald, his pale eyes magnified by the thick lenses of his glasses. She certainly hadn't pictured him looking like . . . like . . .

This. Nice-looking. Probably in his late thirties.

44

Tall, over six feet, with curly, golden brown hair. And for God's sake, dressed like a college kid in a flannel shirt, khakis, and suspenders, no tie. She realized that her mouth was slightly agape, and closed it.

"A wise man once said"—and at this point Blackwood caught sight of Jacobi and winked; Jacobi nodded back—"that a person who tries to know something about everything will eventually know everything about nothing, while the person who tries to know everything about one thing will eventually know nothing about everything."

Suzanne frowned. "Who said that?" she whispered in Jacobi's ear.

He shrugged, still smiling. "Knowing Harrison, he did."

Blackwood droned on. The kids were starting to fidget. "Of both the physical and theoretical sciences, it is crucial for you to always remember that assumptions are fraught with danger. Scientists can't function unless they can postulate theories based on assumptions. But the good scientist will always remain cautious, for to assume even the obvious is to oftentimes overlook the obvious. To help illustrate this point"— and here he withdrew a pocket watch from his khakis —"let me give you a practical example." He opened the watch and stared at its face, counting dramatically. A couple of the kids stirred and began paying attention as they realized something was about to happen.

"Five," Blackwood intoned, "four, three, two, one!"

In one of the nearby offices, a man screamed.

Blackwood's lips curved in a satisfied grin. He closed the watch and slipped it back into his pocket.

"Blaaackwoood!"

The door to Blackwood's office slammed open, and a researcher dressed in a white smock stormed in. *This* man looked like Dr. Solomon, only thinner . . . except that his shoulders and balding head were sprinkled with brightly colored confetti. The children began to titter. Even Jacobi smiled; Suzanne forced herself to maintain a serious expression.

The researcher glared at Blackwood, then realized that Jacobi was standing nearby. "I'm glad Dr. Jacobi is here to witness this, Blackwood," he snapped. "This has all the markings of another one of your infantile practical jokes!"

Blackwood took a step toward him and said in a confidential tone, "Jeffrey, you really should see someone about that scalp condition." More giggles escaped.

"You should see someone about your *mental* condition!" Jeffrey shouted.

At that, someone in the group roared; that did it. The children howled. Jeffrey did a beautiful double take. In his fury, he apparently hadn't noticed that he had an audience. His anger faded to self-consciousness, then to red-faced embarrassment.

Blackwood gestured at him like a leading man encouraging his co-star to take a bow. "Ladies and gentlemen, it is my great pleasure to introduce Dr. Guterman, the next stop on your field trip. Dr. Guterman doesn't subscribe to my assumption theory, and occasionally finds things falling down on him when he walks through doorways."

"I'll get you for this, Blackwood," Guterman thundered. He stormed from the room, slamming the door behind him.

Blackwood was nonplussed. "Why don't you look around the room for a few minutes," he told the sixth-graders, "while Dr. Guterman regains his composure?"

While the children milled around the office, Blackwood strolled over, hands in his pockets.

"Inspiring young minds is so rewarding. Morning, Ephram." He turned to Suzanne, his blue eyes regarding her curiously. "Hi—Harrison Blackwood."

"Suzanne McCullough." She felt herself frosting up. He was a charmer, just a little too glib. There was a boyishness about him that reminded her uncomfortably of Derek; he even resembled him a little physically. The fact both attracted and repelled her. But he was still too pleased with his joke on Guterman to notice.

Jacobi sensed her disapproval and quit smiling. "I really do wish you'd leave that poor fellow alone, Harrison," he chided mildly. Suzanne got the feeling he said it only for her sake.

Blackwood grinned unrepentantly. "And give up all my fun?" It was clear he wasn't in the least bit afraid of Jacobi. He turned to Suzanne. "I'm a firm believer that a person's reaction to a harmless practical joke is a window to his—or her—soul."

She eyed him coolly. If he wasn't afraid of Jacobi,

then, by God, she wasn't afraid to let him know what she thought of his childish antic. "Does that apply to whoopie cushions as well, Doctor?"

He blinked, but his cheerfulness never wavered. She got the feeling he understood exactly what she meant but didn't give enough of a damn to take offense. He went right on to the next thought without missing a beat.

"Ephram—now that I have you. Whatever happened to my request for a microbiologist?"

She drew in a breath. So Jacobi hadn't even told him about her! She'd moved across country to come here to work for Blackwood, and Blackwood didn't even know yet. . . .

Jacobi's expression was smug. "Have I ever denied you, Harrison?" He rested a supportive hand on Suzanne's shoulder. "Dr. McCullough has just joined us. She's yours if you want her."

"In a manner of speaking," she said, qualifying Jacobi's statement, then blushed to think that she had called attention to the double entendre herself.

But Blackwood politely ignored the remark. "Welcome to the Pacific Institute of Technology and Science . . . or, as we so fondly refer to it, the PITS." He extended his hand.

Without thinking, she hesitated.

His smile widened delightedly. "I gave up handshake buzzers years ago."

"Assumptions are dangerous things," she reminded him, and cautiously took his hand.

THREE

By the time dawn came, Mossoud and the others had gone to plant charges around the base's perimeter while Urick and Chambers unloaded the truck.

It had been more than twenty-four hours since Urick had any rest, but she was not in the least bit sleepy. Physically, a bit tired, and bleary-eyed, perhaps. Emotionally, she began with absolute exhilaration—they were doing it, they were actually doing it! Soon the world would hear of them; she would have a place in history. It was all too soon replaced by absolute dread—she'd gone too far to expect mercy, to expect to live if something went wrong with their plans. At weak moments she found herself doubting.

Chambers' plan had seemed so simple: overrun the base and transmit the message. They would booby-trap the perimeter to slow the army down, and the nuclear waste would provide them with more protection than any hostage could. Load some waste onto the truck, along with the explosives, and no one would try to stop them from making good their escape. The important thing, Chambers kept repeating, was to get the message to the world—to call upon fellow anarchists to bring about worldwide chaos.

It had seemed important enough to die for, or, at least, Urick had thought so then. Now despair overcame her. If the government found a way onto the base, she, Chambers, all of them, were dead, as dead as the two men she had killed. As dead as the seventeen blood-caked bodies piled into one far corner of the yard, growing stiff under the sun's first rays. *Only we just don't know it yet.*

Through it all, she worked with detached efficiency. She brought the transmitter dish from the back of the truck and knelt down in the sandy soil to adjust it. Didn't need sleep. She'd just as soon never sleep again, but she could definitely use a shower. Tiny red droplets spattered the front of her white jump suit; there were dirty smudges on the knees and pockets.

"Could you help me with this?" Chambers appeared in the back of the truck with a videocam in his arms, the tripod stuck awkwardly in the crook of one elbow and in danger of slipping out. She walked up the ramp and slid it carefully from his arms.

"Thanks," he said. He'd been quiet too, but now he gave her a long look, the way he did when he wanted to initiate conversation. He walked down the ramp in front of her with short, careful steps, and waited while she set the tripod up. It took some time to get it to stand straight in the sand.

"So how're you doing, Lena?" He carefully nestled the camera atop the tripod.

She was on her way back to work on the dish and jerked her head to look back at him. He'd never called her Lena before. At first she almost yelled at him. *Don't call me that . . . Lena is dead. Lena doesn't exist anymore. Only Urick, soldier of the People's Liberation Army.* But his expression was concerned. *Concerned about me?* she wondered.

No matter. We're all going to die soon.

"All right," she answered shortly, and went over to squat by the transmitter.

Chambers was silent. She glanced at him out of the corner of her eye; he was studying her intently. Finally, he said, "I want you to know how much I admire the way you've handled yourself through all this."

If he'd said all this sooner, maybe it would have mattered. She shrugged. "I did what I had to do."

"Which is more than most people do." He paused. "Especially when it comes to . . . killing. I know it isn't easy."

"Do you?" She gave him a hard look.

"No," Chambers said quickly, bitterly. "No, I don't really know. I've never killed anyone face-to-face, the way you did today. Doing it long distance was hard enough." Ashamed, he looked away.

She sat on her haunches, staring at him. She felt a surge of accomplishment, of pride. *He admires me. He's envious of my strength.* At the same time, it was unsettling, frightening. Chambers may have been a political science professor, but he knew no more about revolution than she did, was no more qualified than she to lead one.

He'd made her kill the guards because he was afraid to do it himself. She turned back to her work, disgusted.

He started back for the truck, then stopped. "I can get the rest of the equipment. You set up. After all, you're the mass comm major."

She nodded. He finished unloading, then came to stand beside her as she was getting the camera where she wanted it.

"The schedule calls for us to transmit in forty-seven minutes," Chambers said. He scuffed the toe of one boot nervously in the sand.

"We'll be ready." She was peering into the camera, then looked up at him. "Why don't you stand about three feet in front of me . . . here." She pointed.

He stood in the wrong place.

"No," she said, gesturing. "More to the left. I want . . ." But Chambers didn't move. Exasperated, she came around the camera and took him by the shoulders to show him. He grasped her hand and looked at her meaningfully. Forty-seven minutes. It would be a while before the others returned from setting charges around the base's perimeter.

Her expression hardened. She pushed him where she wanted him, pulled her hand away, and stepped behind the camera again. "Better. I can keep you in frame and still see the barrels in the background." She wanted the barrels in the shot to prove they were actually on the Jericho Valley site. Some of the barrels had been knocked over, no doubt during the struggle. At first she wanted to ask Chambers to set them upright, then decided it would be more effective to leave them and show that a battle had taken place.

Chambers was not offended by the rebuttal; maybe he took hope from the fact she hadn't been angered by it. He smiled at her.

"You're cheerful," she said without enthusiasm.

Suddenly he was hyper, talkative; perhaps, Urick decided, the realization hit him that he was really going to be on worldwide television.

"Something about the irony of pirating a U.S. communications satellite to broadcast our demands always makes me smile," he answered.

She was not amused. "Smile on camera and no one will take us seriously." The way he was grinning made her uncomfortable.

"If they don't"—Chambers was suddenly serious —"we'll just have to blow this place up . . . and send a big fat nuclear cloud of radioactive waste floating over their nice middle-class homes."

He smiled again. She couldn't return it; for the first time she saw everything clearly. He was a madman, this Chambers, a charismatic madman with a talent for making his insanity sound logical, even attractive, to misfits such as she. The premonition of death came over her again, this time stronger than ever, and so bitterly cold that she shivered in the early morning chill. Chambers was too wrapped up in his dream of global fame to notice. He, Urick, Finney, Mossoud, Teal, Einhorn—they were all as dead as the bodies stacked in the yard, even if they were still walking around.

Consciousness seeped back.

A long darkness. Then awareness; then sweltering, agonizing suffocation. He was trapped in some type of metal confine, and there was not enough air. He gasped, probing frantically until he found the roof of the confine. The metal was corroded there; he encountered a hole and pushed with all his newfound energy. The metal crumpled under the pressure. He was free.

Panting, dazed, he pulled himself out . . . but the light was painfully harsh. He hid for a moment in a patch of shade created by the containers, and tried to understand where he was. This was not home: the air was too rich, the gravity too heavy, the light too strong.

Memories of the battle returned. They had been successful at first, claiming victory when the sickness had overcome them. Defeat so close to success had been bitter; best for them to die here, on this alien rock, than to return home vanquished. He had been trying to maneuver his ship back to the base when the fever came upon him; around him, vessels fell from the sky as their pilots died at the controls. His transmitter reported the sad message that two of the three members of the Supreme Leader had perished. Shortly after, he succumbed himself to the pain and blacked out.

A miracle he had not been killed when his vessel crashed.

Another miracle: the sickness was gone. As confusion lifted, he remembered his duty: to find the others, especially the surviving member of the Supreme Leader, and the Advocate, and to see to it that all their efforts had not been in vain.

No doubt the others were trapped in the same type of horrible container he had emerged from. Xashron set to work.

Mossoud planted the last of the booby traps and covered it gently with sand. He'd gotten only a couple of hours sleep the day before—prebattle nerves—and had been working through the night. He stood up, dusting the sand from the legs of his jump suit, then stretched, and gently rotated the arm connected to the sore shoulder. Probably had himself one hell of a bruise . . . but then, it coulda been worse . . . he could be lying dead in the yard instead of that lieutenant.

Mossoud raised the sleeve of his jacket to peer at his most recent acquisition. It really was a nice watch, a Rolex, probably worth a nice fat wad of greenbacks. And then Mossoud chuckled to himself. If Chambers' little TV show was successful, he wouldn't have to worry about how much he could pawn the watch for. Hell, he wouldn't have to worry about dollars ever again. Not much longer to airtime. He started humming an old tune, "Act Naturally." Who'd recorded it? The Beatles? Musta been all of six when he'd first heard it.

He started back toward the truck. He hadn't made

it very far when he passed by an aisle of barrels. But something about them wasn't right. He stopped to take a closer look.

Finney appeared, stepping gingerly so as not to set off any of the charges. "Mossoud—it's almost time."

"Right behind you." Mossoud gestured for him to go on.

Finney nodded; his careful steps crunched noisily against the gravel as he left.

Mossoud drew closer to the curious scene. This was the spot where just last night Finney had killed the lieutenant. Mossoud knew that none of the barrels had been knocked over then. And no one had been there since he and Finney dragged the body away.

Yet now six barrels from the lower tier—the older rusted ones—were overturned. Didn't make any sense at all. Mossoud bent over to examine one. "What the hell . . .?"

The top of the barrel looked as if it had been exploded from the inside, as if whatever had been in there had forced its way out.

And then left. The barrel was completely empty. Question was, where the hell had it gone?

He saw with alarm that the blood-smeared barrel on the upper tier was leaking where Finney's bullet holes had punctured it. It must have dripped onto the barrel and eaten the top away. Mossoud cringed. Probably radioactive or toxic or something; and *he'd* been exposed to it! He turned to run, to warn the others. . . .

Something stirred behind one of the upright barrels, scraped softly across the gravel.

Mossoud raised his gun. "Come out! Come out with your hands up, or I'll start shooting!"

Someone, some*thing,* rose and moved into view. Mossoud stared; for an instant his mind simply refused to accept what his eyes told him.

It was an animal, he thought at first, some strange hideous beast, but it was like nothing Mossoud had ever seen. He'd grown up by the ocean, and to him the thing resembled a huge jellyfish—about five feet tall, not quite as wide—walking wobbly on its tentacles, only its skin looked like gray-brown leather, oiled and glistening. Its lipless, open mouth quivered and drooled. The worst was its eye—a huge dark thing that gazed intently at Mossoud with far more intelligence than any animal.

"Holy shit," Mossoud whispered. He took a step backward; soft, three-fingered appendages rustled behind him, wreathed themselves around his neck. . . .

He went down shooting.

Urick adjusted the sound equipment behind the camera, while Chambers smoothed his hair down in a hand-held mirror for the fifth time. Einhorn and Teal cracked off-color jokes and watched from the fringes. Chambers was becoming nervous and increasingly obsessed with his appearance, even asked Urick's opinion about whether he should wear his glasses on the air. She told him it didn't matter.

It was in the little things, her father had said, and not the big ones that people revealed their true character. She'd never believed it before; now, watching Chambers, she wondered.

He looked up anxiously from the mirror. "Could you help me with my collar?"

"It looks fine," she answered shortly, then, to give him something to do and, hopefully, shut him up: "Sound check."

"Testing," Chambers said in a deeper-than-normal voice, "one, two, three . . ."

Finney walked up and stood next to Teal and Einhorn, who were laughing and nudging each other. They were excited and happy, Urick realized; why wasn't she?

Chambers read dramatically from the smudged paper in his slightly trembling hand. "We, the free soldiers of the People's Liberation Party, have come to you, citizens of the World, with a list of demands, including the immediate resignation of the President of the United States. . . ."

She glanced at her watch and silenced him. "Perfect. Five minutes."

Chambers nodded, looking a bit green at the thought.

Five minutes and the world would be forever changed. Strangely, the closer the time for the broadcast came, the less she believed it would actually happen. It was like killing those corporals: it simply wasn't real. There was only one thing she believed in anymore, and that was the cold sensation of death's nearness that draped her like a shroud. Yet at the same time she told herself there was no reason to be so afraid now, when success was in their hands. But Urick was unable to shake the fear.

"Where's Mossoud?" Teal asked.

"On his way," Finney answered.

Chambers snapped at Finney. "You heard her. Only five minutes. Just what's taking him so long?"

Finney shrugged and began to answer, but his words were drowned out by gunfire.

"Mossoud!" Chambers shouted.

Instinctively, Urick ran to the truck and found the Uzi propped against it. She expected to hear more bursts, but after the first all was silent. Even so, the five of them spread out and headed for the gunfire's source. Urick made her way down an aisle of barrels, working her way parallel to Teal and Einhorn.

This is it, she told herself. *They've found us, and now we're all going to die.* She was sick with fear, but not at all surprised, as if she had known from the start this was going to happen.

A man screamed to her left; she whirled, Uzi at the ready, and craned her neck to see over the barrels. Two aisles down, the briefest glimpse: Finney down, back arching, mouth a rictus, being dragged by his legs by something dark. It looked like there were ropes around his thighs, but she wasn't sure even in the bright daylight. He disappeared behind a towering stack of barrels, gave one final blood-chilling scream, then fell silent.

"Finney!" she mouthed soundlessly. No gunfire; whatever had taken Finney did not use bullets. She began to follow after him, but cautiously.

On the other side of the yard, one of the barrels fell—or was knocked over.

"Chambers?" she called hoarsely, shifting the Uzi and wiping first one wet palm, and then the other, on the front of her jump suit.

No answer. Louder. *"Chambers?!"*

A rustle, this time on her right . . . muted sounds of someone struggling, a muffled cry.

"Teal!" she shouted. "Einhorn! Chambers!!" She was clenching her teeth now, the gun held tightly in both hands. Dear God, she was alone. . . .

Only a few yards in front of her came the sound of a barrel scraping across the ground, being moved aside. A shadow fell across the ground at her feet. She froze and raised the gun.

Mossoud stepped in front of her.

"Mossoud," she said, embarrassed that she had been so terrified, that she had thought herself alone among the dead. "What the hell is going on?"

There was something not right about the way he stood, the odd, unnatural angle of his head and neck. His arms dangled, useless-looking, from his body.

"Mossoud . . . are you okay?"

Mossoud didn't answer, just looked at her with eyes she did not recognize.

She screamed at him, at once furious and terrified that he would not reassure her. "Answer me, Mossoud!"

Mossoud opened his mouth and answered with a strange, unearthly moan, horrible, meaningless sounds.

She sobbed and backed away from him into something yielding and slickly wet. Before she could turn to look at it, something whiplike and incredibly strong fastened itself around her arms, her neck, and exerted crushing force on her windpipe.

Fear gave way to simple astonishment.

FOUR

"I know I chose your résumé over the others," Harrison said. They had left the older, one-story brick building and were walking in the brilliant sunshine again, cutting across the thick grass instead of taking the sidewalks that connected the buildings. The older brick structures gave way to newer, sleeker edifices. The Institute had the sprawled-out feel of a college campus, and the atmosphere was certainly relaxed. Other than Dr. Jacobi, Suzanne hadn't spotted another researcher wearing a tie; the conservative gray gabardine suit she wore no doubt marked her as an outsider. Maybe Deb wasn't the only one who needed new clothes.

Blackwood turned to regard Suzanne with those disarming pale blue eyes. "But I looked over so many. Could you remind me a little about your background?"

As the sun warmed her face, she began to understand how he had acquired his tan. "I'm flattered you chose me, but my background is pretty unsensational."

He seemed amused by that. "That's your opinion."

"Yes, well, I did my postgrad at NYU and MIT, then worked for the Smithsonian, then Rand for a few years, then a research facility in Ohio."

"I thought you worked with NASA." Blackwood watched her reaction.

"Yes . . . it was a joint project with Zubrovski Labs. I explained it all to Dr. Jacobi." Her tone was slightly reproachful. *So why didn't you bother to get the details from him sooner?*

"Ah." Blackwood nodded. "Of course; I remember now."

"And your background?" Suzanne asked. *So I can try to figure out why you've hired me.*

He shrugged cavalierly. "Oh . . . astrophysics. UCLA." He gazed at the grounds with tangible fondness and gestured sweepingly. "I've spent my whole career at this place. Even grew up here. It's almost like home."

No wonder he acted as if he owned the place and had such a casual, easy attitude toward Jacobi. "I wouldn't mind finding a home," she said, feeling wistful, then realized she had revealed too much and covered with a question. "What about your family—your parents?"

"They both worked here too." His expression didn't change, but it seemed a shadow passed over his features.

She was silent for a moment, unwilling to ask the obvious. They took several steps without speaking, then Suzanne asked, "Tell me, Dr. Blackwood . . . about your projects that need someone in my field—?"

He smiled, the darkness dispelled as quickly as it had come. "Not Doctor. Harrison. I dislike formality . . . and I *hate* titles."

She refused to be distracted so easily. "Look, Harrison, I've come all the way from Ohio, and no one has told me anything about the project we're supposed to be working on. It can't be *that* secret!"

"Close to it," he said cheerfully, and turned his head sharply to look at her. "Will there be any problem with your putting in a little overtime?"

She tensed. Dammit, she knew the job offer was too good to be true! "Yes, as a matter of fact. I explained to Dr. Jacobi—I have a young daughter. I avoid working nights and weekends. But Monday through Friday, I give a hundred and fifty percent."

"That's a mathematical impossibility," he replied, but he smiled. "A daughter. That's nice. How old is she?"

His interest seemed so genuine that she relaxed a little. "Debi's eleven. Already a sixth-grader."

"Eleven, huh? Pretty difficult age if I remember correctly. Not quite a baby but not really a teenager either."

She shook her head and smiled a little ruefully. "Difficult is an understatement . . . but then, I don't remember any age as being particularly easy."

"I suppose not." He paused. "Look, maybe we can

work something out, but I'm not going to lie to you. There could be times when we'll need you to work late. Maybe if your husband's willing to help out—"

"He's not," she snapped, and then in a calmer, lower voice, "We're divorced."

"Oh. Sorry." He looked sheepish.

"I'm not," Suzanne replied, trying hard to sound as if she meant it. They had arrived at the entrance to another building; she stopped in her tracks as he held open the glass door. "But you still haven't told me what this project is about."

He smiled and gestured her through. "There's someone I'd like you to meet first."

He led her down a corridor to a door marked COMMUNICATIONS CENTER. The instant he opened it, she was greeted by the overwhelmingly seductive fragrance of coffee.

Inside, the room was filled with enough sophisticated equipment to make NASA and SAC jealous. Consoles, computers, transmitters, and receivers lined the walls and counters; a series of photographs on the wall showed a muscular black man in a wheelchair with a racing number pinned to his jersey, and beneath, in careful hand-lettering, the legends: MARINE CORPS MARATHON, 1984; BOSTON MARATHON, 1986; LA MARATHON, 1987. In the far corner of the room a man sat peering intently at a computer monitor.

"Norton," Harrison began, "I want you to—"

His focus still on the monitor, Norton raised a coffee-colored hand in a plea for silence, but it was too late. He groaned, his concentration broken.

"Maybe we should come back another time,"

Suzanne whispered in Blackwood's ear, but he propelled her over to where Norton sat.

"Six under, one to go," Norton complained bitterly, staring into the flashing screen. "Harrison, didn't anyone ever teach you any manners? You're not supposed to interrupt a man when he's standing at the tee."

Suzanne was close enough now to see the graphics on the screen: a little golfer wearing a funny hat and checked knickers stood, his club resting on his shoulder while Norton's score flashed in the upper right-hand corner. She shot Harrison a narrow look: *Important secret project. Lots of overtime, huh?* Harrison shrugged, his expression innocent.

Norton swiveled slowly to face them; for the first time Suzanne noticed the automated wheelchair. Norton's long-sleeved shirt hid most of the muscles that showed in the photograph, but he still looked square-shouldered and strong, in his late thirties. He peered up at Suzanne with large brown eyes set in a broad, friendly face.

"Who are you?" he asked point-blank. Yet another one who had no use for formalities.

She was slightly taken aback. "Suzanne. Suzanne McCullough."

"Norton Drake." He grinned with a sudden disconcerting warmth, and extended his hand. She gave it a firm shake. "Welcome to the PITS, Suzanne."

"I've already been given the standard welcome," she answered dryly.

"Suzanne is the new microbiologist Ephram's been promising us," Harrison explained.

Norton cocked his head and scrutinized her clinically. "Doesn't look like a microbiologist. Everyone in our micro department is nearsighted and losing his hair." He shook his head. "No, she looks more like a . . . biochemist." He winked at Harrison. "Which reminds me, you *have* caught sight of the new addition to biochem, our esteemed colleague, Dr. Mona LaRue, haven't you, Harrison?"

Harrison grinned. "Later, Norton."

"Forgive me, I'm being a poor host. Coffee, Suzanne?"

"God, I'd love some. It smells wonderful."

Pleased, Norton raised a brow. "I believe I can work with this woman, Harrison." Then, in a different tone: "Gertrude—back three, right forty-five, forward ten." The wheelchair whined mechanically and started backing away from the monitor.

"Please don't bother," Suzanne began, "I can get it m—"

Norton shot her such a threatening glance that she broke off, ashamed of her patronizing attitude. "And miss the chance to show off?" he asked lightly.

Harrison was smiling, relaxed; apparently he knew Norton well enough to be completely unaffected by Suzanne's discomfort over his handicap. "Don't worry. Norton lives to show off his voice-activated dragster."

"Old news, Harrison," Norton said on his way to the drip coffeemaker on the low counter. "Got something better. Been working on the blend for months." The wheelchair rolled to a stop at the counter. Norton picked up a cup and poured steaming coffee into it.

He glanced over at Suzanne. "You like it black, I hope."

"I like it black," she answered quickly. At this point she was willing to drink it cold through a straw . . . and it *did* smell heavenly.

"Good. I'm afraid I don't stock the accoutrements. Gertrude—back three, forward ten." The chair began moving again. "None of these healthy California la-la types here touch the demon caffeine. They'd rather drink herbal teas with cutesy little names like Granny's Tummy Comfort or Sassafras Sunset. And this is a scientific institute. Shocking, isn't it? And here it is a well-known fact that caffeine improves brain function."

Harrison snickered. "Only up to a certain point, which you've definitely gone past. After that it's all downhill."

Norton sniffed at that. Suzanne forced herself to stand still and wait for him to return and hand her the cup. "What exactly do you do here, Norton?"

"You mean besides play computer golf?" Harrison quipped.

"Shut up, Blackwood. Dr. McCullough is asking a question." Norton cleared his throat and said with practiced glibness, "I collect and analyze radio transmissions from deep space, trying to separate natural phenomena from that which could be made by intelligent life."

She sipped the coffee—which tasted every bit as good as it smelled—as she listened. So . . . an extraterrestrial project. She'd been right to assume she'd been hired on the basis of her NASA project experience. "Sounds like interesting work. And this coffee is heaven."

"Thank you."

She turned to Harrison. "Now, how do I fit in?"

But he was looking down at his watch. "Gee—where's the time gone? I'm sorry, but I have a meeting with Shulman in five minutes. Should last till lunch." He glanced apologetically at Norton. "Norton old buddy, could you help me out and show Suzanne to her new office?"

"Sure. Except I don't know where it is."

"You know the one. Clayton's old office." Harrison gave Norton a brisk pat on the shoulder, then turned to Suzanne. "I really wanted to take you to lunch today to discuss the project, but I'm afraid my fiancée has other plans for me today. Maybe we can get together for a talk after lunch."

"If it's not too much trouble," she said in very clipped tones. She was furious at him for ignoring her questions as if she didn't matter, and furious at herself for actually feeling a twinge when he mentioned his fiancée.

As usual, he ignored her frosty stare on the way out. "No trouble," he said pleasantly. "No trouble at all." He left, closing the door behind him.

Norton was shaking his head and grinning. "He's not singling you out, Suzanne. He drives us *all* crazy."

She gave Harrison until two o'clock—she doubted he'd be the type to arrive back from lunch any earlier—before she wandered down the hallway and knocked on his closed door.

No answer. How on earth did the man manage to procure such a prestigious job, taking two-hour lunches and playing practical jokes on his colleagues? Working with him was not going to be pleasant.

Suzanne was turning to go when she saw the light under the door, and raised her clenched fist to knock again, then decided she might as well start practicing the local customs. She turned the doorknob and pushed.

He was there all right, with his feet propped up on the desk, crunching on a granola bar. A small pony of lite beer sat on top of a stack of dusty, stained manila folders. One of the files lay open, its aging contents scattered randomly atop the desk. But Harrison was not studying the files; he was staring intently at a yellowed black-and-white photograph with curled-up ends. Suzanne got only a fleeting glimpse of his melancholic expression before it changed back to the good-humored mask.

She glanced disapprovingly at the granola bar and the beer. "I thought you had lunch with your fiancée."

He scrambled to sit up, nearly overturning the beer onto the files, and shoved the old photo into the top drawer, then closed the folder. "Well . . ." He gave her another one of those boyish grins.

She passed over the remark, refusing to be embarrassed by him anymore. "I'm sorry," she said without making any effort to sound as if she meant it. "I didn't mean to disturb you."

"You didn't. What do you need?"

She emitted a short, frustrated sigh. Either he was so absentminded he'd forgotten, or he was having fun at her expense by pretending to forget. It was beginning to look like she would not be able to work with this man. "Direction. You never told me what I was supposed to be doing."

"Aah, right. Come in and sit down."

She sat in the uncomfortable wooden chair next to his desk and fixed her gaze on him.

He fidgeted a little nervously. "I suppose Ephram told you this project was pretty hush-hush."

"Not in so many words, but from the way everyone was acting, I assumed it was a classified government project."

"*Not* the government." He shook his head, ruefully amused. "I don't think the government would appreciate what we're doing." Her mouth fell open at that; he rushed to reassure her. "Sorry, bad joke. We sometimes work with the government; now isn't one of those times. I just meant we weren't getting a lot of cooperation from them. I'm sure you know how that can be."

She didn't. "I've worked on classified projects before. It's considered normal to brief the people involved. I can't help if I don't know what I'm supposed to be doing."

He paused awkwardly, as if searching for the right words. "Well, today I thought you could just get settled in . . . and then we'd talk about the project."

"I'm already settled in," she replied quickly. "Let's talk about the project."

He gazed out the window for an instant and cleared his throat. "Okay . . . um, you already know Norton's role in all this—"

"To analyze radio transmissions from deep space," Suzanne answered, a bit impatiently. "Searching for intelligent life."

He looked at her with those penetrating blue eyes of his and nodded. "Problem is, there's a whole lot of space to cover. A bunch of wasted space, practically speaking, since the universe is maybe ten million billion trillion times as much empty space as it is stellar material. I need you to narrow our focus."

She frowned, unable to understand what he was driving at. "I'll bite. How am I supposed to do that?"

"Simple." His eyes widened innocently—a little *too* innocently, Suzanne decided. "By daydreaming."

Confused, she blinked at him. "By daydreaming . . . ? You want to run that by me again?"

"Daydream about other worlds." He meshed his fingers, put his hands behind his neck, and leaned back comfortably in his chair. "About the life-forms they might support. Give me probables, possibles. Give me what-ifs."

She stared disbelievingly at him for a full half-minute before she found her voice. "Excuse me, Dr. Blackwood, but I know when my leg is being pulled. You can't be serious—"

"What's so unbelievable about it? You give me a what-if life-form, and I can design a model atmosphere that can support it. Then Norton can limit his intercepts to star systems containing compatible atmospheres."

"But it's ridiculously random—"

Harrison shrugged. "It would allow us to narrow our search from billions of possibilities to, oh, maybe only a few hundred thousand."

She stood up, frustrated that he would toy with her this way, furious that she had quite obviously been misled, that neither Jacobi nor Blackwood had been honest with her about the nature of the project. "Doctor Blackwood," she said, struggling to keep her tone cool and professional, "you and I both know that I wasn't hired to daydream. If you refuse to tell me why I've been hired, then I must assume that it was to do biowarfare research, in which case I am going straight to Dr. Jacobi's office to resign. I made it quite clear from the start that I will *not* participate in research of that nature—"

Harrison sat forward and sighed, his expression and tone of voice all seriousness. "I'm sorry, Suzanne." He gestured at her chair. "Please sit. I'll level with you."

She folded her arms and sat.

He looked down at his hands and fidgeted uncomfortably under her steady gaze. "We haven't deceived you, Suzanne. If I've put off telling you about the project, it's because I wanted you to feel at home before we discussed it. The nature of the project has nothing to do with biowarfare—but it's not exactly a pleasant topic of conversation, either." He looked up at her and hesitated.

"I'd like you to analyze some . . . blood and tissue samples. A thorough analysis." She started to speak, but he raised his hand. "Before you protest—I'm

73

afraid I lied about your résumé. I remember it very well. Just trying to get you to talk about yourself a little. I know you were a certified medical technician, that you worked as one while getting your graduate degrees. I also know you minored in anatomy as an undergrad. You're qualified—more qualified than anyone else who applied for this job—who *could* apply for this job. That's why I asked Ephram to hire you."

He was complimenting her to try to soften the blow. Good God, what was so horrible about this job that he couldn't even bring himself to tell her what it was?

"That's very flattering," she replied evenly, "but I still don't understand. An analysis of what sort of blood? Human? A specific individual's?"

He watched her carefully. "I've gotten hold of a sample of alien blood and tissue samples from 1953. A thorough analysis was never done. Not to mention that with the tools and techniques available to us now, our analysis can be much more exhaustive."

She stared at him for a while before finding her voice. No one had ever spoken to her about the alien invasion in years . . . since she was a girl back in Iowa. Her parents had shielded her as best they could from any real information about it, but there was no restraining a child's imagination. It didn't matter how many times her mother told her it was all over, they were all dead, they weren't ever going to come to Iowa. Suzanne used to lie shivering under the covers at night, expecting them to come for her the way they did for Uncle Matthew.

74

She'd never even been able to talk to Deb about it. After all, what was the point in frightening the child over something that could never happen again? Even now adults almost never spoke about it if the subject could be avoided. It had been briefly discussed in one or two of her college classes with that peculiar dread otherwise reserved for nuclear annihilation. Always, always with the qualification that Earth's microbial life was too deadly for the aliens, and there was no chance of their return.

"I—I thought," she stammered, "that all that had been done before. That they had been analyzed to death. From a scientific standpoint, there's not much point in rehashing that again."

"No," Harrison answered, still looking hard at her. "Any samples PIT had were destroyed by looters when people were evacuating the West Coast. And as soon as the invasion was over, the government confiscated any samples researchers had. We have only minimal information about the aliens. Not enough."

"But how did you get these samples?"

He smiled. "Want ads. There are some government workers out there willing to take some pretty big risks for the right amount of cash."

"But those samples are thirty-five years old. They've no doubt deteriorated so badly by now, there's probably very little information we could get from them."

"Whatever we can get would be useful." He rolled his chair up to the desk and leaned forward. "It's a real scientific opportunity."

"I'm not sure. It doesn't sound like much of a project. Once I've analyzed these samples, then what?"

"I want to know *how* the bacteria killed them . . . whether or not they could possibly learn to adapt, to develop defenses against our microbes."

She almost stood up. "Frankly, Dr. Blackwood, all this smacks of paranoia."

He sat back in the chair. "Maybe. But consider what *might* happen." He paused, seemed to struggle with something, then continued. "I thought *your* attitude might be different, considering . . ."

"Considering what?"

"Your uncle, Matthew Van Buren. One of the first to die in the alien attack . . . along with my parents."

She *did* stand up now. "What a cruel thing to say."

Harrison tilted his head, confused. "It *was* cruel. That's why I'm here. That's why Norton's here: he lost his entire family in an alien attack. That's why I thought you'd be interested in helping out. After all, we have something in common: Matthew Van Buren's niece—your second cousin, Sylvia—was my adoptive father's fiancée." A glint of humor shone in his eyes. "Just think . . . we're practically related." The humor faded quickly. "After the invasion, he saw to it that Sylvia was well cared for."

Her cheeks burned, even though he hadn't added *in a mental institution*. Cousin Sylvia had gone mad after the invasion and been locked away, forgotten by the family, an embarrassment which was mentioned only rarely, and then in hushed tones. Suzanne had met her only once, when she was four and Sylvia had already suffered her first of many breakdowns; Suzanne remembered little of her cousin, except that Sylvia had been quiet and withdrawn.

Harrison noticed her reaction. "Maybe I was wrong. The Midwest was safe, and you were born just a few years before the invasion. Maybe you don't care because you never experienced it yourself." His expression hardened. "You have an eleven-year-old daughter, Suzanne. Don't you want to learn something about these—these creatures, before it happens again?"

"Quite honestly, Dr. Blackwood, I think that's a sick attitude to take," she said. "The aliens can never return. Even a schoolkid knows that. They're dead the instant they're exposed to our microbes."

Harrison emphasized each word. "You don't *know* that. We've got to learn more about them. The more we know, the better off we are."

"Maybe I should have stayed in Ohio." She didn't really intend to say it, but there it was.

He rose. She could tell that under his civil veneer he was very angry. "I'm sorry. I thought because, well, never mind. If you really want to go back to Ohio, I'm sure PIT will cover your expenses."

"That's what Norton's really looking for, isn't it?" she said as it occurred to her. "Not just extraterrestrial life in general. He's looking for *them.*"

"That's right," Harrison answered, with a the-hell-with-you-if-you-don't-like-it expression. "He's looking for them. Now, are you going to work with us or not?"

They glared at each other for a while. She actually

considered packing it all up again, but she couldn't face that right now, not just yet. Maybe if she played along with Blackwood for a while, looked at his precious samples, she could find another project to work on at PITS.

"All right," she said finally. "I'll do it—sheerly out of scientific curiosity. But frankly, I think it's a waste of time and money, and the minute I can link up with another project here, I'm gone."

He sighed, relieved, and smiled, but she detected the obsession in his eyes. It frightened her. *The man's not right. Well, what do you care so long as you have a job and Deb doesn't go hungry?*

"You won't regret it," Blackwood told her. "And after all, we are paying you well."

She stiffened. "This may be hard for you to understand, Dr. Blackwood, but money isn't the most important thing I derive from my job. I like to feel that what I'm doing is . . . meaningful. Now, if you'll excuse me . . ."

His expression became serious for the first time since she'd met him. "Believe me, Suzanne, it's the most important work you've ever done, the most important work you'll ever do."

But she was already walking out of his office, and pretended not to hear. She always tried to be honest with herself, and she knew she hadn't been totally up front with Blackwood. It wasn't just that she thought the project redundant . . .

It was that she had never seen one of Them, except in her childish nightmares . . . and she wasn't sure she could stand to look at one in the flesh, even now.

FIVE

An observer stumbling upon the Jericho Valley site would have witnessed an eerie phenomenon: six humans—two in white technician's jump suits, four in black—standing shoulder-to-shoulder in three-person triangles. Around their bodies, the air crackled faintly with energy. A meditation ritual, perhaps; a communion of consciousness.

Renewed by the energy drawn up from the planet's magnetic core, Xashron stirred from his trance to peer through new eyes at his comrades. Beside him, Konar and Xeera shielded their faces and squinted at the brilliant alien sun. Their host bodies were already beginning to decay. Xeera's host bore a red gash on his forehead; the pale flesh had split open when Xeera struck him with a blunt weapon. There were still bruises circling the neck of Konar's host. Xashron's host bore similar marks, but despite its limitations, this

79

human male body was lean and young. He flexed the unfamiliar muscles, testing them. Combined with Xashron's own strength, this body would serve adequately.

Nearby, the three who formed the Advocacy broke off their communion. Xashron looked at them and felt deep hatred for those hidden inside their hosts: Xana, Horek, Oshar. Strategists from the ruling class who spouted theory, who knew nothing themselves of war, but who planned the battles, decided who would live and who would die. To Xashron, they represented the idiocy of the ruling class; their carelessness, their impatience, caused the invasion to fail at the moment victory seemed surest. Over the protests of the lower-class scientists who feared not enough was known about the new planet, the government ordered the invasion. It was Xashron's duty to prepare the planet for his people, so they might leave their dying world to start anew . . . Only, he told himself bitterly, so the ruling class can allow this planet as well to be poisoned by our technology.

And so Xashron, member of the military class, was obliged to forsake mate, carrier, children, and home, to come to this strange world. He was no lower-class servant. He was Supreme Commander, a member of the elite, in charge of an entire hemisphere's invasion . . . only to see all his soldiers perish from sickness until at last he, too, succumbed.

He wondered now how many of his people had survived . . . and how many of them had expired, torn and mangled beyond all awakening when they lost consciousness at the controls and their ships plunged from the sky. Two of the metal containers he had opened contained the decayed, mortally wounded remnants of such soldiers. Even now he mourned.

The Advocate had, of course, survived without scars, having always been protected like a carrier from all violence.

The three of the Advocate moved and opened their eyes—small, strange eyes. It would have been far more just, Xashron reflected, for them to have died instead of his soldiers.

Xana, the lone female member of the Advocate, stared at Xashron with multicolored eyes: black in the middle, ringed with blue, then white. The body she had chosen was softer, as delicate and pampered as a carrier's. He began to speak to her in his native tongue, but she interrupted, displeased. "Speak as the body you occupy would speak."

"Yes, Advocate." The strange sensation of forming unknown words, hearing them with another's ears, yet somehow understanding. "How long have we been inert?"

"Unknown at this time." She, Horek, and Oshar frowned up at the harsh yellow sun adrift in a strange blue sky.

Horek, the member of the Advocacy Xashron despised the most for his lack of intelligence, spoke. His host body was male, slightly older than the others, and his control of it was inept. He articulated the words thickly, clumsily. "But many revolutions around their sun."

"These bodies are weak," Xashron challenged, "and contaminated by negative thoughts." The brain of his

81

human host was disturbingly disorganized and undisciplined, making control of the body more difficult. The Council was correct in its judgment that the Earth inhabitants were of limited, fitful intelligence, and therefore could be exterminated without compunction. "We would more easily accomplish our mission in our natural state."

The three stared at him, then closed their eyes to consider. After a moment they simultaneously opened them again. "The consensus is," Horek said, "yours is not an accurate statement. These bodies protect us from detection."

"Until we know more," Xana added, "we will use the resources available to us."

Xashron exchanged a dissatisfied look with Konar and Xeera. These two were soldiers, like himself, although lower ranking; he knew they shared his hatred of the upper-class advisers. But they seemed unwilling to stage a rebellion at the moment.

"We surrender to your judgment as always, Advocate," Konar responded, but his tone was slightly grudging.

"Do you wish us to release the others so that our battle can continue?" Xashron asked with false helpfulness. The more soldiers revived and free, the better his chances of overpowering the Advocacy.

Xana nodded—a foreign gesture, yet Xashron understood it, just as he understood the humans' language. "Yes . . . however, the Advocacy has concluded there is no time for transmutation now," she said. "Collect our people as they are, in the metal containers."

So . . . she had detected his motive. Xana was by far

the shrewdest member of the Advocacy. Doing his best to conceal his disappointment, Xashron bowed and moved off with Xeera and Konar to do so.

Xana stood watching them for a moment; she had correctly guessed the extent of Xashron's bitterness, even before defeat and the long slumber had overtaken them. Xashron's quick mind made him a useful ally and a formidable enemy . . . and Xana preferred to keep him the former. Surely there was some way to dispel his anger before harm came to him—or to the Advocacy.

She turned back to her peers in their pale, hideous bodies, and spoke urgently. "Without the guidance of the Council, we are nothing."

"What can be done?" Horek whined. Even the human eyes of his host body managed to reflect the depths of his stupidity.

But Oshar, his new flesh white against the black clothing he wore, understood. "Once the Council is aware of our plight, it will know what to do."

"Yes," Xana replied, grateful that Oshar's mind, at least, was nearly adequate for the high office he held. "We must contact our home base. They have rather primitive equipment." She pointed with the thick, clumsy arm; the three walked over to examine the transmitter equipment.

Oshar picked up the dish and examined it. "It will be adequate if properly refined."

They set to work.

Harrison adjusted the strap on his helmet and started pedaling through the expansive parking lot.

Normally, he was in a great mood by the end of the workday; a day at the Institute left him exhilarated, ready to enjoy the rest of the evening. He realized he was one of the lucky few who got paid for doing what he loved best. But today his mood was particularly sour, thanks to Suzanne McCullough: if she quit the project, he doubted he'd find anyone else qualified to do it. The minute anyone found out what the work was all about, they turned it down. Mass denial . . . the whole world wanted to forget what had happened thirty-five years ago, and that frightened him.

He had figured Suzanne would be different because of her uncle. Matthew Van Buren's death had been widely publicized, like the deaths of Harrison's parents. Yet somehow it wasn't real to her, in spite of the fact that she had been alive during the invasion— although, he admitted to himself, not that long. And not only had she lost an uncle, but her second cousin, Sylvia Van Buren, had witnessed Matthew's death and subsequently suffered a breakdown from which she never recovered. Two relatives lost to the alien invasion . . . and yet the woman went through life trying to pretend the whole thing never happened.

He'd checked and discovered she hadn't even requisitioned the samples yet. A bad sign: she'd made up her mind not to do it, she was leaving. Or at least wavering.

Now I know why Clayton gave up . . . it's enough to drive someone insane, trying to convince people to face what could still happen.

Yet he felt that somewhere underneath all her uptightness there was a real person, someone he could work with. He was thinking, if he could just break through that anal retentive facade . . . at which point he had a brilliantly evil inspiration. It was time to find out the stuff of which Suzanne McCullough was made. He grinned to himself as he plotted—then braked the bike as he spotted her.

A few yards ahead, Suzanne was striding through the parking lot, her back to him. She must have been pretty lost in thought, because she didn't look behind her as the brakes squealed.

There she goes, 1988 working woman of the year. He glanced down at his watch and almost laughed aloud. Exactly 5:01. Incredible. She'd spent the entire afternoon killing time, *not* doing the one job she'd been hired to do . . . but she didn't dare take off one minute early. As physically beautiful as she was, Harrison reflected, she was not a pretty sight, marching like a good little corporate soldier to her car in her sensible gray suit, neatly trimmed shoulder-length brown hair, sensible leather briefcase clutched in one fist, the heels of her sensibly low pumps clicking against the asphalt like a metronome. She would grow old and sour in her little cubicle here, just like Guterman.

Not if I have anything to do with it. Immediately he was taken aback at himself. What the hell kind of thought was that? As if he cared about what happened to her, as if he had any right. After all, he was engaged to be married. He pushed the thought back and impulsively pedaled up behind her.

"Still feeling guilty about goofing off on company time?"

Startled, she jerked her head around, dark hair swinging, but managed to recover. Somehow she didn't seem as defensive now as she'd been just after lunch, but her attitude was still cautious. She slowed her pace. "Well, I've got to admit. . . . It's a little weird."

He paced her on the bike, balancing, never touching foot to ground even as they slowed. For the first time, he noticed the light freckles that covered her pale skin. Not at all professional-looking . . . which was no doubt why she tried to minimize them with makeup. He smiled at the thought. "I take it you haven't requisitioned those samples yet—"

That flustered her. She stopped and gestured apologetically with her free hand. "I'm sorry . . . It's just that—well, I kept pretty busy just settling into the office and finding out how things worked—"

"Hey," he said gently. "It's perfectly understandable; I wasn't asking for an explanation."

Back to old cautious. She narrowed her hazel eyes at him—nice eyes, Harrison thought, or at least they would be if they weren't so suspicious—and started walking again. "Then why *did* you mention it?"

"My, aren't we defensive," Harrison said cheerfully. "I asked because I thought I could save you the hassle of finding the proper requisition forms, filling them out, then trying to figure out who gets them. I can see to it that you get the remains."

"Remains?" Her eyes widened just a bit.

"I've actually managed to get hold of an undissected alien corpse. Been in someone's freezer in the garage all this time. Believe it or not, it's in pretty good shape. Was a real big hit with the neighborhood kids." He grinned at the thought. "But I thought you'd be interested in seeing one close up. And that way you can get as many different types of tissue samples as you need, including the internal organs."

She was less than thrilled. "Oh. Thank you."

"Instead of the usual two-day delay, I can get it for you tomorrow morning."

"Tomorrow," she repeated flatly. Was it his imagination, or was she looking a bit green? "That would be good. Yes. Thank you."

He smiled, secretly gloating. "No problem."

"Harrison!" A woman's voice floated over from the far end of the parking lot. "Over here!"

He craned his neck and saw Charlotte waving madly as she stood by the open door of the little Mercedes. What the hell was she doing here? He must have forgotten something . . . another one of those social functions she so adored. It was one of the few things that really irritated him about her; he loved her because she was bright and witty and had a great sense of humor, and she took very few things seriously, except these damn parties.

She was also rich, but he did his best to forgive her that.

He nodded at Suzanne. "Excuse me, I'm being paged by my fiancée. Have a pleasant evening."

He pedaled the bike over to Charlotte. Yup, a party all right; Charlotte was dressed in a slinky but somehow tasteful cocktail dress of deep emerald green, to bring out the color of her eyes. Her expertly permed blond hair was done up. He liked it down and flowing, but he had learned through experience that in situations like this one, honesty was not necessarily the shrewdest policy. "Char—you look fantastic." He eyed her appreciatively and bent forward on the bike to give her a light kiss.

"Thanks." But her forehead wrinkled as she stared past him at Suzanne. "Who was that?"

He got off the bike. "New microbiologist," he said easily, and gave her a big one-armed hug, the other hand on the handlebars. "Suzanne McCullough."

She hugged back, but he could tell by the tension in her body that she was staring over his shoulder at Suzanne. He smiled to himself. Charlotte was rich, beautiful, and intelligent, yet for all her seeming self-assurance, she could sometimes be ridiculously insecure. Not that she would ever admit to something as mundane as jealousy.

"I thought all microbiologists were nearsighted and balding." Her sharp chin dug into his shoulder as she spoke.

He broke the embrace and held her at arm's length to admire her. "Common misconception. Sounds like you've been talking to Norton."

"Not me." She put her hands on her hips and adopted a teasingly nagging tone. "We're late, Harrison. For the third time in a row."

He feigned ignorance. "For what?"

"Bleaker-Williams Industries? The Founders' Ball?"

He slapped his forehead in exaggerated repentance. "God, how could I *ever* have forgotten?"

"Freud says people don't forget. They simply

choose not to remember." She was half smiling when she said it, but he could tell by the spark in her green eyes that underneath her lightness she was honestly angry at him.

He tried to jolly her out of it. "I thought you were an interior designer, not a psychoanalyst."

"Same thing." She suddenly became all business. "I brought your clothes. Throw your bike on the rack. You can change in the car."

Good old Charlotte. Some women would have waited at home and missed the party entirely, then exploded when the offender arrived home. Not Char. She knew exactly what she wanted, and always found the most efficient way of achieving it . . . no weeping, no moaning. Just doing it. No trying to manipulate him and then getting furious when it didn't work— Char just told him the way it was going to be.

He pretended to cringe meekly. "Whatever you say, Sigmund."

Xashron worked with Xeera and Konar to load the trailer rig with flats of the rusty barrels—all words he had accessed from the host brain, along with others like forklift, *which Konar's host had known how to operate. The task kept them occupied until daylight began to fade, but not so occupied that Xashron did not manage to speak to one of them.*

"Will the Advocacy be any more successful this time than the last?" he asked Xeera as she handed him a barrel to load onto the flat. Her dark-haired human host was male, tall, and strong as Xashron's, and dressed in the same black clothing he and Konar wore.

Neither Xashron nor his host brain could read the expression on the alien face to know Xeera's thoughts, and she did not answer immediately. She had served under him, and he knew her to be slow-thinking but intelligent, and most times able to come to the right conclusion.

"I know what you think, Commander," she said at last, "that the upper class make poor military strategists. That is often true." She paused. "But will the Council be willing to support our mission if we harm the Advocacy?"

"The Council need not know we harmed them. They could simply be . . . casualties of war."

Xeera looked away. On Mor-Tax, harming a member of the ruling class meant immediate execution . . . but Xeera was wise enough to realize they were no longer on their home planet. "I would like to have Konar's opinion for a consensus."

But their task did not permit them enough time to question Konar, and then twilight came. Xana appeared alone, just as Konar had forklifted the last flat onto the truck, and Xashron pulled the rear door of the vehicle closed and fastened it.

"Go see the others," she said to Xeera and Konar, "and wait with them for instructions from home."

They bowed and left, but not without glancing at each other. Did Xana suspect their dissatisfaction?

She walked around to the secluded side of the truck and gestured at Xashron to follow. He did so uneasily.

Xana leaned wearily against the truck and gazed up at the graying sky. Certainly the host bodies were hideous to look at: thick-limbed, clumsy, most of them a revolting pale color. Some of them were decaying, but Xana's host did not seem to be degenerating as quickly as the others.

Xashron remembered, in spite of his hatred for her office, that in her natural form Xana was an exceptionally lovely female. Somehow it was reflected even in the host body, in her almost graceful movements, the timbre of her voice, her choice of words. Perhaps, he thought, after a time it might be possible to learn to appreciate the human form. His host brain recorded this female's face and body as attractive, though Xashron remained perplexed as to why. Of course, any attraction he felt for Xana was firmly controlled, since it would remain unrequited: she was a member of the ruling class, he was military, and the penalty for interclass coupling was death.

"We will hear from home soon," Xana remarked, still looking up at the sky. "You blame the Advocacy for the deaths of your soldiers, do you not?" She fixed her gaze on him, studying his reaction.

"Of course," he said. There was no point in denying something she already knew, and it was no crime simply to assign blame.

"If there is fault, it rests on the entire government, not only us three. We were not among those who voted for this early mission. We wanted further environmental tests."

"You misrepresent the truth, Advocate. You wanted further tests, but Oshar and Horek favored an early departure; the consensus rendered by your Advocacy was in favor of the latter. Perhaps you have forgotten that I was there, in the Council Chamber."

Xana sighed. "What must I do, Xashron, to prevent our Advocacy from being killed by your soldiers?"

He stared at her for a moment, impressed by her shrewd mind, her direct speech. A pity she had not been born a soldier. He reached out with a hand—how awkward, these fingers!—to make a gesture. Three fingers folded down, thumb and index finger forming a V. "I swear solemnly, Xana—whatever may happen to the other members of the Advocacy, you will not be harmed."

She mimicked his gesture and touched the tips of her index finger and thumb to his, thus forming a triangle. Their pact was sealed. "I understand." She smiled. "But we mustn't stay, or the others will talk."

The sky was deepening to black as they walked around the truck and back across the yard to where the others stood, fascinated by the video display terminal. Horek sat before it and smiled as the flashing lights reflected off his pale, dull face.

"Home," he said with reverent longing; even Xashron felt the skin of his human body prickle at the word. Home. How long had it been since he last stood on Mor-Tax? And with deep sorrow he knew he would never again return. Next to him Xana trembled.

Horek spoke again. "The Council has heard us; they agree that it is our exposure to radiation which protects us from the microbes that almost destroyed us . . . and which guarantees our mission success. To keep from becoming ill again, we must regularly expose ourselves to measured doses of radiation."

He looked up at all of them. "If we do so, we are sure of success . . . and Earth will be ours once again."

SIX

The high-rise lobby, artfully decorated in rich hues of burgundy and peach, echoed with restrained laughter and the clink of crystal champagne flutes. Charlotte sat on the low couch next to a man—Fred, Harrison thought the name was, but he found the conversation too boring to follow it very closely. He slipped a finger between his neck and the uncomfortably tight, stiff collar and tried in vain to loosen it a bit.

Fred said something witty and Char laughed, a silky, throaty sound. She was really in her element tonight: bright, witty, as sparkling as the diamonds and emeralds on her throat and ears. Harrison, uncomfortable in his new tuxedo, stood off to the side and smiled vaguely.

She turned to Harrison. "Did I mention Fred worked for Bleaker-Williams?"

"No," Harrison said with a total lack of enthusiasm. He already knew where this conversation was going.

"Mechanical engineer," Fred volunteered eagerly. Pleasant enough guy, but his only distinguishing feature were eyes set disturbingly close together. Harrison found he couldn't look at them for very long before his own eyes started to cross. "All very hush-hush . . ." Fred was saying. "We've been lucky enough to get some lucrative defense contracts. Long hours, but I can't complain about the money." He peered through thick glasses at Harrison. "I understand you're an astrophysicist."

"That's right."

"Well"—Fred leaned forward with a confidential air—"let me just say that this . . . project we're working on could certainly use someone like you."

"DOD, huh?"

"If you mean Department of Defense—well, I can't name names . . ."

Harrison caught Charlotte's dismayed look but said what he wanted to anyway. "No, thanks." He kept his tone pleasantly conversational. "I guess I'm just one of those weirdos who thinks space should be peacefully explored instead of exploited as just another arena of war and politics and crass commercialization."

Fred's round little face flushed red. "W-well," he stammered, "I suppose there's room for all kinds of opinions."

"You mustn't pay any attention to him," Charlotte soothed, shooting Harrison a dirty look. She was about to say more but was stopped by an Oriental waiter in a white jacket who proffered flutes of champagne on a silver tray.

Harrison took two and handed one to Charlotte and one to Fred, then turned and took the tray from the waiter and set it down on the coffee table.

"Sir?" The waiter, a young, earnest-looking man, seemed confused.

"Harrison Blackwood." He held out his hand to the waiter, who blushed and shyly took his hand.

"Tuan Martin." He smiled sheepishly. "People usually aren't so friendly to me, Mr. Blackwood."

"That's Dr. B—" Charlotte began, but Harrison interrupted her.

"Just Harrison." He held up an admonishing finger. "How's it going tonight, Tuan?"

"Not so bad. If there's anything I can do for you—"

"As a matter of fact, Tuan . . ." He lowered his voice. "Tell you what. I'll take that tray around for you, and you see if the kitchen has a Bud Light."

Tuan shook his head. "I can't let you take the tray. I'd get into too much trouble. But I can sure find that beer for you."

"Take your time," Harrison said. "We don't want you to get into trouble. Get it when you're finished unloading that tray."

"Thanks, Harrison." Tuan flashed a bright smile before picking up the tray and moving on to the next group.

Fred cleared his throat. "So . . . Charlotte. How is your big sister?"

"Fred used to date my sister Mimi." Charlotte tilted

her face up at him. "I never forgave her for breaking up with him and marrying that orthodontist."

"Um," Harrison said. "Tell you what, why don't I get the two of you something from the buffet?"

"Gee, thanks, Blackwood." Fred cheered visibly.

Call me Harrison, he almost said from habit, but in Fred's case he made an exception. *My friends call me Harrison, but you can call me* Doctor *Blackwood . . .*

"No problem, Fred."

Harrison wandered over to the huge buffet on the other side of the expansive lobby. Impressive spread. Char was mad for seafood, so he started heaping her plate: smoked salmon with capers, onions, and dill sauce; iced shrimp; oysters bien-something-or-other. He found the vegetables and stuck a carrot stick into his mouth.

An attractive silver-haired woman, straight and strong-looking, came up next to him, searching for a plate. Next to her stood an older man Harrison presumed was her husband. Harrison removed the carrot stick from his mouth and found a plate—real china, of course, and very pretty; Char would have been tempted to turn it over to read the name but wouldn't risk doing so in public—and handed it to her with a smile. "I hope the gentleman doesn't mind my saying so, but you're certainly looking very lovely this evening."

She put a jeweled hand to her chest and gave an embarrassed little laugh. "Why, thank you. I don't believe we've met." She took the dish from him and extended her other hand. He switched the carrot to his left hand and shook hers with his right. "Marge

Bleaker . . . and this is my husband, Howard." She nudged Howard, a portly, red-faced man who was squinting through black-rimmed glasses at a platter of oysters on the half-shell. "Howie, come meet this nice young man."

"Harrison Blackwood," Harrison repeated, gripping the man's hand, and inclined his head toward Marge. "You're a lucky man, Howie."

Howie and his wife beamed at each other with honest affection. "I certainly think so," Howie answered. "Are you enjoying our party?"

"Ah, so you're the hosts. I'm having a great time, absolutely great, thanks. Even the waiters are nice— you've got a good one working for you—Tuan Martin —who's gone to get me a beer."

"Oh, dear," Marge said. "I hope he isn't taking too long."

"Not at all; just left, as a matter of fact."

Howie blinked at him. "So, what's your line, Harrison? Frankly, I can't say I'm able to place the name right off the bat."

"There's a good reason for that, Howie—we've never met. I'm an astrophysicist at the Pacific Institute. My fiancée, Charlotte Phillipson, decorated your office suites here."

"And did a *wonderful* job, I must say," Marge gushed. "Doesn't it look gorgeous here tonight? These *colors* . . ."

But Howie was still on the same track. As he loaded oysters on the half-shell onto his plate, he said, "Astrophysicist, huh? You know, we could use someone in your field."

Harrison smiled pleasantly. "Thanks, but I'm very happy where I am now."

"I imagine so," Marge said. "I've heard of the Pacific Institute. Very prestigious."

"At least it was before I started working there."

They laughed politely. Behind them, someone in a shrill female voice called, "Howie! Marge, darling!"

Marge rolled her eyes. "Sorry, Harrison; duty calls." She and Howie turned to greet a woman who wore a tiara and looked to Harrison like the spitting image of Madame Wellington.

He stuck the carrot into the side of his mouth like a cigar and was loading a plate for Fred when Charlotte came up; her tone was one of hushed awe. "Harrison . . ." She laid a delicate hand on his forearm. "Do you have any idea who you were just talking to?"

"Yeah." He handed her the plate and started crunching on the carrot stick. "Howie and Marge."

She made a frustrated clicking sound with her tongue. "You're incorrigible, you know that? That was only Howard and Margaret Bleaker, aka Mr. and Mrs. CEO of Bleaker-Williams Industries."

He shrugged and popped the rest of the carrot into his mouth. Char's ability to be impressed by titles always amused him. Between crunches he said, "They'll always be Howie and Marge to me."

"Harrison . . ." she moaned. "Be serious."

Tuan reappeared, holding a frosted glass and a bottle. "Sorry it took so long, Harrison."

"You back already? Thanks, Tuan. You're one in a

million. All I need is the bottle." Harrison took it from him. "Charlotte Phillipson, Tuan Martin."

Char's expression was glassy. "Charmed, I'm sure."

"Pleased to meet you." Tuan bowed timidly and made his escape.

Harrison took a swig of the Bud. "Char—about the Bleakers. You know I wouldn't say anything to embarrass you."

She sighed and shook her head with affectionate disapproval. "I know that, darling. But it's not me we're talking about. Personally, I don't give a damn that you were rude to poor Fred back there, and I wouldn't give a damn if you stood on your head in the middle of the lobby right now."

"You're beginning to sound like Rhett Butler." His lips curved in a smile. "Don't tempt me, Char."

She continued, ignoring him. "But these people can be very important to *you,* if you'd ever agree to give up that ridiculous research you do and go into the private sector."

Stunned, he said, "I *like* ridiculous research." All of the sudden he got the point. He had thought they had an unspoken agreement: she was free to be Char, with all of her silly social trappings, and in return, he was free to be Harrison, with all of his idiosyncracies. For the first time it occurred to him that maybe he had misunderstood . . . maybe she'd really been trying in her own way to manipulate him after all. No wonder she was so concerned about his meeting Howie and Marge—she had probably been planning on introducing him to them tonight.

"I like rich desserts at fancy restaurants," Charlotte said a little too snottily, "but I don't make a career out of it."

"Second thoughts about marrying a man who earns half what you do?"

His bluntness made her back down just a little. This time her tone was gentler, conciliatory. "No, just trying to convince that man to live up to his potential."

It was a standoff; they were glaring at each other when a different waiter approached.

"Dr. Blackwood?"

He turned. "I'm Harrison Blackwood."

"Telephone, sir. If you'll follow me, please."

"To be continued," he said to Charlotte, and shoved the beer bottle at her. "Hold this for me?"

Her mouth pursed, but she took it with a glint of amused "I'll get you for this" in her eyes. Good old Char. Still a sport, at least.

He followed the waiter to a private telephone set up on a table in the corner. He picked up the receiver. "This is Harrison Blackwood."

"Doc!" In his excitement, Norton shouted so loud Harrison was forced to hold the receiver out three inches from his ear.

"Jesus, Norton, take it easy. What's going on?"

"I'm still at the PITS. You've got to get over here right away! Have *I* got something to show *you!*"

Thirty minutes later Harrison stood with his hands on his hips in the doorway of Norton's office. "This had better be good, Norton. Char may never speak to me again, leaving in the middle of a very important party I didn't want to be at in the first place."

Norton sat, looking haggard but animated, behind a desk draped with unfolded computer printouts. "You ever get premonitions, Harrison?" His dark eyes glittered feverishly.

"Norton, what the hell are you talking about?"

Norton gathered up one of the printouts and thrust it at Harrison. "Here . . . Got a fresh batch of radio intercepts I think you'll be interested in perusing."

Harrison took the proffered sheets. Nothing unusual he could see . . . just the usual radio wave patterns they'd been encountering all along. He frowned and handed them back. "Norton—go get yourself some sleep. I've seen these patterns before. Several times, in fact."

Norton grinned smugly. "No, Doc, you've seen *these* before." He gave Harrison a different printout. "Radio patterns collected from a point in space—the coordinates aren't important right now—off and on since we started this project." He gestured at the first printout Harrison still proffered. *"Those* patterns originated from a broadcast point on Earth."

"Earth?" Harrison blinked at him, certain he'd misunderstood. "Are you *sure?"*

Norton sniffed. "Of course I'm sure. That's why they pay me the big bucks."

Harrison sank into the chair next to Norton's desk, trying to make sense of it all. "Impossible."

"Of *course* it's impossible." Norton sounded exasperated. "That's why I yanked you from that party you didn't want to be at. Look here." He motioned for Harrison to give him the printouts; as soon as Norton had them, he spread them out, one above the other, so that both sets of wave patterns were visible. Harrison leaned closer to look at them as Norton traced a long brown finger over the repeating patterns.

"Notice the parity." He caught Harrison's puzzled frown and said, "Don't try to figure out the contents, Harrison, just look at the patterns. That's a signal—that's a response. That's a response to the first response—"

Harrison understood. "And that's a response to the second response. My God." He looked up at Norton's grinning face. "A communication. An honest-to-God communication!" His lips curved upward.

"On the money. I don't know how they did it, but those radio waves were boogeying! Talk about your subspace radio—transmission and response all occurred within an afternoon's time. Either the military is up to something we don't know about, or we've got an uncomfortably close encounter here." Norton's focus shifted abruptly. "Love your tux, by the way."

Harrison grunted. "Char bought it for me. Right now I'm tempted to let you have it." He pulled off the bow tie and loosened the collar with a groan of relief. "Norton, let's be sure we're not just hallucinating. I want to see what the SuperComputer says about this. Book time on the Cray. Priority time if you have to."

Norton raised both hands, palms out. "Whoa, Doc,

slow down. You're talking megabucks here. How're we gonna justify this to the penny pinchers?"

Harrison shrugged. "The Cray's the best computer in the world, right? So don't ask me—ask it."

"Doc . . ." Norton's tone softened. "If it's what we think it is . . . I'm not sure how I feel. Half of me is thrilled beyond belief to find something out there. But the other half—"

Is terrified as hell . . . "Don't say it," Harrison interrupted. "If it's what it looks like, Norton, it's a good thing you're not in the mood to sleep. I need you to pinpoint the location of this first transmission."

"And when I do?" Norton's expression was grim.

"Then, by God," Harrison said, "I'm going there to find out what it is."

By morning Norton's dark eyes were bloodshot. His lids fluttered; he slumped forward in his chair, his face on the verge of making contact with the map spread across his desk. Apparently, the entire pot of coffee he'd consumed at three-thirty no longer had any effect. The compass in his right hand slipped out with a faint clatter.

Hovering over him, Harrison—fading himself after the first rush of adrenaline wore off—grasped Norton's shoulder and gave it a firm shake.

Norton jerked his head up, his eyes wide, and drew a brown hand over his face. "Jesus, man . . ." He shook his head to clear the cobwebs. "Harrison, I gotta get outa this place and bag some z's." He squinted painfully at the brightening sky beyond the window. "What time is it?"

"Seven-thirty," Harrison said. "Dammit, Norton, I've missed two naps myself. But we're not leaving until you give me what I want."

Norton's lip curled. "Study your history, Doc. Slave-driver mentality never worked." But he picked up his compass and bent over the map again. *Because,* thought Harrison, *he understands that if there's any chance of it being . . . Them, then we have so very little time.*

"There." Norton triumphantly handed the plot map of the southwestern United States to Harrison. "The location of the transmissions. Now let me pass out in peace."

Harrison stared at it, transfixed. Norton had circled a desolate spot in the desert, close enough for Harrison to get there in the Bronco in a matter of several hours. It would probably take most of the day to get there; he'd need to pack a bag first, take a nap—but time was of the essence. Scrap the nap. He'd just have to try to stay awake somehow. Harrison staggered toward the door.

"You're welcome!" Norton croaked, indignant. "Anytime! No problem!"

But there was no time to respond. Harrison hurried out into the parking lot, nose buried in the map.

"Good morning," someone said.

He mumbled something into the map. It took him three full strides to recognize the voice; he lowered the map and turned to look behind him.

Suzanne McCullough was staring at him with a puzzled expression. Navy pinstripe dress today. For crying out loud, why did the woman always look as if she were on her way to an East Coast power breakfast?

"Have they changed the dress code at the Institute?" she asked, sounding amused; at that point he remembered he was still wearing the tuxedo.

"Pack a bag," he told her before he realized he was going to. "We're taking a trip." She could drive while he slept. He'd just have to make sure not to let her get too close if things started to look dangerous. And who knew? Maybe this was just the thing to convince her of the project's importance.

She blinked; her mouth dropped open a bit. "We are? Why?"

"Won't know that till we get there," he said.

SEVEN

Harrison was tossing his ditty bag into the back of the old Bronco when the little Mercedes came roaring up the driveway and stopped less than a foot behind it.

"Char." He smiled wearily and waved, then strolled over. Damn good thing she'd showed up when she did; he'd completely forgotten to let her know he was leaving town. By tonight Charlotte would have been fuming. "I'm glad you're here. I was just about to call you."

"I can't stay long," she said in clipped tones. "I'm on my way to a client's this morning."

Harrison leaned through the open window on the driver's side to kiss her, but she turned her head so that his lips pressed against carefully applied cheek blusher. He noticed then that the Mercedes' engine was still running.

"Uh-oh." He withdrew a little and rested his hands

on the car door. "Okay, Charlotte, give it to me straight. Are you *mad* mad, or just mad?"

"Harrison, how could you?" Makeup done especially well today, to enhance the performance; Charlotte whispered the words with just the right mixture of coolness and hurt. No tears, though; never tears. Char was always in control.

He didn't try to pretend that he didn't understand the question. She was too sharp for that. "I'm sorry, but it was unexpected. You know I didn't do it on purpose. We had an honest emergency at PITS—"

"I must have called your place a hundred times since last night. You wouldn't pick up the phone."

"An emergency, Char. Read my lips. I just got back from the Institute five minutes ago."

She searched his face. The day's growth of beard and the circles under his eyes must have convinced her, because she tried a different tack. "You *knew* how important that party was to me. To us."

Patience, Harrison warned himself, but he felt too weary to play this game now—and precious time was passing while God knew what was out there in the desert. "Honey, my work is important too. I've got to—"

"They want you at Bleaker-Williams. Do you have any idea how much they're willing to *pay* you there? But the offer won't last forever."

"I like what I'm doing," he said stonily. "And that's that." He tried to kiss her good-bye, give a hurried explanation, but she pulled away.

"Isn't a fiancée entitled to a vote, Harrison? Won't you even discuss it?"

"Dammit, Char—" Harrison took a deep breath and fought back his anger. In a softer tone, he replied, "We *have* discussed it. You know how I feel."

"We haven't discussed it enough." She tossed her waving blond hair back carelessly. It was an attractive gesture, one Harrison decided looked just a little too practiced. "We'll talk more tonight. Over dinner. I've made reservations at Chez L'Auberge—"

He shook his head firmly. "Can't do it. I have to go out of town."

She reacted angrily to that, and opened her mouth to argue, but he spoke quickly, forcefully, in a seriously determined tone he had never used with her before. "Just overnight. It's business. Char, I promise, I'll make it up to you when I get back. Goddamm it, it *is* an emergency and I don't have time to discuss it now."

He tried again to kiss her, but she pulled too far away; firmly, he took hold of her shoulders and brought her close enough to give her a light peck on the cheek.

"Try to understand," he said, then dashed back to the Bronco.

The Mercedes' tires squealed as Charlotte pulled out of the driveway, but Harrison forced himself not to look back.

A horn blared outside in the driveway.

Peering through the white sheers in the bedroom window, Mrs. Pennyworth said, "That would be your ride now."

"Are you sure you know where everything is?" Suzanne tucked a change of clothes into the hanging bag flung across her bed.

"I know," the older woman answered firmly. "And what I don't know, Deborah can show me."

Suzanne felt a twinge of guilt at that. Poor Deb . . . tonight when she came home, she'd find her mother gone, and a stranger waiting for her in this new, unfamiliar house. Thank God the stranger was this competent, pleasant-faced grandmother and not some seventeen-year-old kid. "I'm so sorry to do this on such short notice, Mrs. Pennyworth."

"Not one more time may you apologize for that," Mrs. Pennyworth scolded in her faint Dutch accent. "I live only two houses away. It could not be more convenient. And how grateful I am Deborah is an eleven-year-old girl and not some screaming two-year-old!"

Suzanne smiled weakly at her; a tall, strong-looking woman, Mrs. Pennyworth was near seventy, hair pulled back into a tight bun, but there were still a few golden brown strands mixed in among the silver. Suzanne had gotten her name from a list Dr. Jacobi had sent to her in Ohio; the list had also included a pediatrician, a dentist, and the name of the realtor Suzanne had purchased the house from.

"Ah." Mrs. Pennyworth looked out again at the driveway. "I see you work for Harrison Blackwood." She gave a knowing nod. "Now the short notice is understandable."

"You know Harrison?" Surprised, Suzanne glanced

up from her packing. "Did you use to work for the Institute?" In a secretarial or assistant capacity, she'd meant.

"Yes. I see Ephram told you nothing about me." Amused, the older woman turned her face from the window. "He is much like Harrison, always wanting to keep information to himself, making people guess things. I was director there of the Physics Department until I retired three years ago. My husband, William, also worked as a zoologist there before passing away."

"My goodness . . . I should be calling you *Doctor* Pennyworth, then."

"No, then I was Dr. Templaar. I used my maiden name for my work. Now that I am just an old baby-sitter, I think Mrs. Pennyworth is better. Or just Gerda for the parents."

The horn beeped again; Suzanne would have sworn at him under her breath if Mrs. Pennyworth hadn't been there. She zipped up the bag and threw it over her shoulder. "I'll at least try to call you with my location and a phone number as soon as"—good Lord, this was all so absurd—"as soon as I get to wherever it is I'm going."

"I know you will," Mrs. Pennyworth soothed. "Try not to let Harrison upset you too much. He enjoys surprising people."

This is one surprise I can do without. "Good-bye, Mrs. Pennyworth . . . Gerda . . . and thank you so much again."

"Good-bye, Suzanne. Try to relax and have a pleasant trip."

"I doubt it," she said under her breath.

She raced out of the house at top speed, trying to beat Harrison before he could press the horn again. Too late . . . another ear-piercing blast greeted her as she opened the front door.

Harrison was standing by the driver's side, about to bend down and press the horn again. He looked ready to jump on a boxcar . . . unshaven, wearing an old fedora, his tuxedo downgraded to the usual plaid flannel shirt and a rumpled pair of corduroys that obviously had never seen the hot side of an iron. As she approached, he reached for her bag without a word and tossed it carelessly into the back of the Bronco.

"You didn't have to honk so many times," she said coldly. Boss or not, he wasn't about to get away with treating her so thoughtlessly. "Maybe *you* can pack a bag in five minutes, but I have a daughter to think about. I had to get someone to take care of Debi. I hope you have a very good reason for this—"

"*Damn* good reason," he said, and she fell silent because he clearly meant it. "Can you handle a manual transmission?" The words came out slurred.

She studied him closely. He was actually swaying a little . . . not drunk, which was her first thought, but totally exhausted. Her tone changed. "When I have to."

"Good. You have to. You're driving." He handed her the keys, went around to the passenger side, and climbed in.

She took a very deep breath and released it, trying to relax, but all she wanted to do was shake him and scream at the top of her lungs, *What the hell is going on?* The thought that Mrs. Pennyworth might still be peeking at them through the window held her back. She brushed crumbs and an empty granola bar wrapper off the driver's seat, then slid behind the wheel, pulled the seat forward a bit, and put the keys into the ignition. Harrison had already reclined the passenger seat back and pulled his hat brim down over his eyes.

"It would help," she said calmly, utilizing every ounce of self-control, "if I knew where we were going."

"Map's on the dash," Harrison yawned. "Route's outlined in red."

It was there all right . . . on top of an opened box of granola bars, several scholarly astronomy journals, yellowed newspapers, and what looked like his doctoral thesis. She looked back at him to ask another question: *why,* but his jaw had dropped slightly, causing his lips to part. For God's sake, he was already asleep!

She picked up the map and found the red markings. Their destination seemed to be out in the middle of the desert . . . a several-hour drive. What on earth would they be looking for out in the middle of nowhere?

Either the man was crazy, or . . .

Or what? *There is no "or" . . . he's just plain crazy.*

Sighing, she started the Bronco's engine.

The cobra gunship hovered over the Jericho Valley Disposal Site like a noisy insect. In the co-pilot's seat, Lieutenant Colonel Paul Ironhorse leaned forward and gestured at the pilot to move the chopper in for a better look. Whatever had happened, Ironhorse knew, was not good. All communications with the installation had been cut off for more than twenty-four hours; Jericho Valley was silent as a tomb, and both the inner and outer entrance gates lay wide open. Ironhorse was not surprised to find the sentries missing.

The cobra moved past the entrance and dipped lower.

"My God," Ironhorse said, but it was drowned out by the thumping copter blades. In front of him, the pilot's head jerked back as he made a silent observation of his own.

The barracks had been blown apart, reduced to a blackened skeleton of wood and rubble. Debris littered the yard for a hundred-foot radius. A surprise attack, then, with no intent of taking any hostages. There would be no survivors among the seventeen stationed here.

The question was, where had their killers gone? Perhaps they were still here, waiting for the cobra to move in just a little closer.

The copter flew past the remains of the barracks to the far corner of the yard where stacks of toxic waste barrels stood in neat aisles. Ironhorse frowned. Strange. The barrels were loaded onto double-tiered scaffolding, but only onto the upper tier. The bottom was empty, which made the structure dangerously topheavy. Rack one up to noncom inefficiency.

And then he noticed one of the barrels down on its side, oozing. Jesus, the place was hot! Good damn thing they'd seen it in the cobra first before they sent anyone in on foot. The pilot didn't seem to react, probably hadn't even seen.

Along a farther aisle lay the bodies. The cobra lurched a bit; the pilot averted his head, sickened.

Ironhorse didn't flinch. It wasn't an easy thing to look at, but he'd seen worse in Beirut, in Kampuchea. He motioned the reluctant pilot a hair closer and tried to count. All seventeen were probably there, though the way they were stacked on top of each other, it was hard to be sure, plus the vultures were in the way. Four of them, feeding. One had a red strip of thigh muscle in its beak and was flapping its wings as it struggled to tear the meat from a corpse. What made it rough was the fact that even at this distance Ironhorse could see the vultures had already plucked out the tenderest delicacy—the eyes. They always got the eyes first.

Ironhorse had learned that as a kid on the reservation. He'd seen birds on lots of animals, once even on a man who'd gotten himself caught in a bear trap. They'd pecked his eyes out too. It was in the forests of the Blackfoot reservation in northwestern Montana, just shy of the Rockies to the west and Alberta to the north. Rugged, mountainous land, and merciless: It had taught him a lot. One survived by one's wits and accepted harshness, or one perished. The land took no excuses; it was cruel and unfair, and those who failed to learn its lessons died.

His people still lived on that land, where they had struggled vainly against the encroachment of the white man with his train—the "iron horse." Paul's family had fought against the train and lost, yet they kept the name, "one-who-shoots-the-iron horse." even though now the train and the white men owned their souls.

But not Paul Ironhorse's. He had seen too many men and women, including his own father and brother, destroy themselves on the reservation because they had forgotten the first lesson of the land: discipline, survival. If the only way for Paul to survive was to take advantage of the white man's system, the white man's discipline, then he would do it and take pride in it. He left the reservation for West Point; his first year after graduating he went to the Olympics as a decathlete and returned with a Bronze Medal.

His brother accused him of "turning white" and no longer spoke to him. His mother still wrote him but remained on the reservation in spite of his offers to take care of her elsewhere.

Ironhorse told himself it didn't matter: what mattered was that he, Paul, had survived; in his own way he had overcome his people's defeat. He had no patience with those like his brother, who whined when things were not easy, cried because life was unfair.

Of course it's unfair, Paul had shouted. *Life is always unfair, and the best anyone can do is try to even up the odds through hard work.*

That attitude had earned him a reputation in the army as hard-nosed, an ass-kicker, labels he was proud to wear.

He watched the vultures work for a while, the sight filling him with hatred. Hatred, he learned long ago, could be a good thing if you used it to motivate yourself and didn't bury it inside, where it ate at you like a cancer.

He tapped the pilot on the shoulder and motioned upward with his thumb. The grisly tableau receded as the cobra flew up and away. They landed back outside the gate, not far from the parked personnel carrier. As soon as the thumping blades slowed, Ironhorse half yelled over the noise to the pilot: "Whoever did this is long gone."

The pilot, a skinny freckle-faced kid who was still shaken by what he'd seen, blinked innocently at Ironhorse. "How can we be sure, Colonel? I mean, other than the fact no one fired on us? It could be an ambush, sir."

Ironhorse shook his head. "I'm sure. The vultures," he said enigmatically. It was true, to an extent. Vultures usually liked to wait until everything living was dead or gone. If they weren't *too* hungry.

"Wow." The kid looked so round-eyed and gullible, Ironhorse was hard-pressed to keep his own expression grim. He enjoyed cultivating what he called his "Indian mystique." The kid would probably buy it if Ironhorse pressed his ear to the ground and proclaimed that the attackers were exactly seventy-five kilometers due east. No point in mentioning the obvious clues such as the overturned barrels, which would clear anyone with an ounce of brains out of there, or the wide-open gates.

Ironhorse climbed from the cobra to call his superiors and relay the bad news.

* * *

Suzanne had been driving an hour and a half—not even enough time to leave civilization behind—when Harrison stirred and pushed back the brim of his hat with a finger.

"Feeling better?" she asked not unpleasantly. The monotony of driving in silence had worn the edge off her anger.

He brought the seat upright and rubbed his face, yawning. "Much, thanks."

"You didn't sleep very long—only ninety minutes or so."

"Ninety minutes?" His eyebrows flew up. "Jeez, I overslept. Usually I nap only one hour for every five I'm awake."

She frowned, skeptical. "You're joking."

"No, really, you should try it sometime." He meshed his fingers, turned his hands palms outward, and stretched. "Someone as dedicated as you . . . I'm surprised you're not already doing it. Makes it easier to give that hundred and fifty percent." He shot her a mischievous glance, which she ignored. "Why don't you pull over? I'll drive."

"Fair enough." She maneuvered the Bronco into the right-hand lane and pulled into an Amoco station.

"Pull 'er up to the self-serve super unleaded."

She did so. Harrison got out, stretched some more, and filled the tank. After paying up, he crawled back in on the driver's side, wincing when his knee hit the dash.

"Sorry," she said. She never could remember to move the seat back for Derek.

"'Sall right," he said, rubbing it. He got the Bronco

back out on the highway, and they rode in silence for a minute.

"All right." Suzanne turned to look at him at the first light. "I've been exceptionally good. I haven't screamed or threatened you with physical harm or burst into a flood of angry tears, but I promise to do all three if you don't tell me right now where we're going and why."

Harrison didn't answer for a beat. "Is that all?"

She stared coldly at him and waited.

A smile spread slowly over his face. "Okay, okay, I admit to being a little . . . uncommunicative. But I was preoccupied. Here goes." He took a deep breath. "Last night Norton picked up a radio broadcast signal from the location pinpointed on our map there."

She shrugged. "Out in the middle of the desert. I figure it's some type of military installation. What's so unusual about that?"

"Plenty," Harrison replied. He removed the hat, set it on the dash, and absently ran his fingers through his short, golden brown curls. "For starters, the signal was a powerful one, directed at a point somewhere in the constellation Taurus."

"But that's the same thing Norton's transmitter is doing, isn't it?" She frowned, unable to see what was so earth-shattering about the fact. "Broadcasting signals into space to see if anyone's listening?"

"If anyone else were doing this type of work out in the desert, so close to us, I'd know about it. It's hardly classified." He paused and glanced briefly at her with those intense pale-blue eyes of his, then stared back at the road. There was no amusement in his eyes or voice now. *"This* signal"—he nodded at the map on the dash—"was answered."

"What?" It came out a gasp; her first instinct was to giggle at the outright absurdity of it. "That's impossible. First, radio waves can't travel that fast—it would take *years* for that to happen—"

"I know," Harrison said calmly. "But the fact is, it happened. Norton has the computer printouts. He showed them to me. They show first a signal—originating from our spot in the desert—and then being mimicked, amplitude for amplitude, by a second signal coming from the Taurus constellation. Another signal, another mimicked response . . . then what follows looks suspiciously like a friendly little chat." He patted his breast pocket. "Norton made me a recording of the actual signals."

They traveled in silence for a while, and then she asked, "Harrison, in all honesty, what do you expect to find there? Little green men?"

"I don't know." He hesitated, then said in a quiet voice that made her shudder, "I know what I hope to God I *don't* find."

EIGHT

"Come in, Reynolds," Ironhorse said gruffly. He was seated into a personnel carrier that had been turned into a mobile command post and was in a particularly foul mood, having just shouted himself hoarse at a whining supply sergeant on the phone. Outside, within the Jericho Valley installation, soldiers wearing protective suits wandered through the yard, some of them carrying Geiger counters, some portable video packs, others with dogs on leads, policing for booby traps.

Staff Sergeant Gordon T. Reynolds, a tall man with a defensive linebacker's build, had to crouch down to enter since the vehicle was designed for sitting, not standing. Like the men in the yard, he wore protective radiation gear, except for the helmet. The dark brown skin of his forehead was puckered, his expression a mixture of agitation and concern. "You told me to brief you, Colonel, as soon as we had anything—"

"Wait a minute." Ironhorse stopped him with a gesture and peered suspiciously at him. "You clean?"

"More or less, sir." At Ironhorse's mistrustful look, Reynolds elaborated. "The tech sarge swore there's not enough radiation left on me to knock more than a few months off your life."

Ironhorse's upper lip curled slightly. "Why am I not reassured?" He nodded at his staff sergeant. "Come in, Reynolds."

Reynolds entered, crouching low, his head touching the ceiling. Ironhorse liked and trusted Gordon Reynolds, though he was careful not to show it. Maybe it had something to do with the fact that Reynolds had grown up a poor black inner-city kid, and, like his commanding officer, had battled prejudice and the odds and come out the winner. Of course, Ironhorse had no idea what Reynolds thought of him—he did not fraternize with his men; he was not in the army to be liked.

"We did a body count, Colonel," Reynolds said. "You were right, sir, all seventeen were there . . . at least what was left of them. We had to verify the number through HQ, since the roster was missing. Looks like fourteen died when the barracks were blown up—probably a rocket launcher, though no weapons were left behind."

"Damn," Ironhorse said softly. He felt a muscle in his right jaw begin to twitch. "What about the other three?"

"Shot up. Automatic weapons. The tire tracks are from an eighteen-wheeler—we're getting impressions now—and there are four-wheel all-terrain vehicle tracks all over the yard. Probably had more than one of those, from the looks of it. I figure they got the truck inside, shot the sentries, then used the rocket launcher before anyone knew what was going on."

"Killed everyone and then left." Ironhorse shook his head at the senselessness of it, then looked up sharply at the sound of an explosion outside.

"Sappers setting off booby traps," Reynolds offered helpfully.

Ironhorse ignored the comment. Reynolds had a habit of stating the obvious. "This whole thing doesn't make any sense, Sergeant. Think about it. Why the hell would someone want to overrun an installation and then *leave?* They even mined the perimeter, as if they were expecting to stay awhile."

Reynolds nervously stroked his regulation-trimmed charcoal mustache with a gloved hand. "I figure it was the punctured barrel you saw from the cobra, Colonel. Maybe the radioactivity scared 'em off. Funny thing, though, they didn't touch the protective suits in the guard house."

"Why would anyone who was going to overrun a nuclear waste dump not be prepared for such an emergency? And why choose Jericho Valley, of all places? There are other places they could overrun a lot easier—say, a nuclear power plant—and get a much bigger bargaining chip. A core meltdown of a power plant could cause a lot more havoc than some barrels of nuclear waste."

Reynolds shrugged. "Maybe they're stupid, Colonel."

Ironhorse's lips thinned. "So far, that's the best explanation I've come up with today." He paused. "Even so, I want those barrels inventoried. Low priority—just get someone on it when you can, hopefully by the end of today. Unless you have anything else to report, you're dismissed."

"Yes, sir." Reynolds turned to leave but lingered in the exit, a hesitant expression on his face.

Ironhorse raised a blue-black brow. "Was there something else, Sergeant?"

"No, sir." Reynolds seemed to change his mind, and moved reluctantly away.

"What's with you? Bodies get to you?"

Crouched in the doorway, Reynolds faced him again. "Yes, sir—well, no, sir—it's not that."

"Something else, then." Normally, Ironhorse never pried, but he got the definite impression there was something else Reynolds really *wanted* to say but simply didn't have the nerve for it. "Spit it out, Sergeant. We haven't got all day, and I can't have anything interfering with your efficiency."

Reynolds seemed truly flustered. "Well, it's uh . . . personal, Colonel. Now hardly seems the appropriate time." He gestured at the scene outside the carrier.

"I'll be the judge of that," Ironhorse answered firmly. "Say it."

Reynolds cleared his throat and fidgeted. "Permission to ask a personal favor, sir."

What the hell . . . Ironhorse frowned sternly. "Permission granted." Which did not mean that he would grant the favor, by any means.

"I'm getting married next month, sir, and I—"

Ironhorse smiled faintly, for a moment forgetting the gruesome surroundings. "Reynolds, you son of a bitch! I thought you were a confirmed ladies' man."

Apparently pleased by the remark, Reynolds smiled shyly and stroked his mustache. He didn't even try to refute the notion that women found him handsome.

"When did this happen?" Ironhorse asked.

"A couple of months ago, sir. But I wondered if you would—" He paused awkwardly, averting his light brown eyes. "If you would be my best man, sir."

Ironhorse's smile widened just a hair. "I'd be honored, Gordon."

Damned if Reynolds' cheeks didn't take on a warmer, ruddier hue—the man was actually blushing! "Thank you, Colonel. It's set for Saturday the twelfth, at 1500 hours."

"So noted. And, Sergeant—you've got one hell of a strange sense of timing."

"Yes, sir. I'm afraid Arlene's been after me—"

"Arlene." Ironhorse worked hard not to grin.

"Yes, sir. Well, she's been after me to ask you, and last night she put her foot down. With all due respect, I believe I mentioned it seemed inappropriate right now—"

"So you did," Ironhorse replied dryly. He forced every hint of warmth to vanish from his features. "Now, get your ass in gear, Sergeant, I want that remote van set up yesterday! Understood?"

Reynolds' eyes widened. He tried to snap to attention, bumping his head against the roof of the carrier. "Yes, *sir,* Colonel."

He exited the vehicle in a hurry, leaving Ironhorse to once again contemplate the grim mystery of what had happened here at Jericho Valley.

Morning faded into afternoon. Harrison and Suzanne stopped for lunch at a McDonald's before civilization petered out entirely, then drove through mile after mile after mile of rugged, sunbaked desert.

The scenery looked so much the same—rocks, sand, sagebrush—that when Suzanne opened her eyes after a short nap, it seemed as if they were still in the same spot they'd been in when she'd first shut them.

The air-conditioner droned away, causing a drop of ice-cold condensation to fall onto the instep of her foot. She moved it over to one side. Even though the air-conditioner had been blasting at full the past few hours, the temperature was barely comfortable. The sun beat through the Bronco's tinted windshield, heating the air inside.

About a mile from their destination, Harrison brought the Bronco to a halt.

Suzanne frowned down at the map in her hands, then back up at him. "We're not there yet. Why are we stopping?"

"Don't worry about it. Just stay here." He undid his seat belt and opened the door.

"Not so fast." She put a hand on his arm to stop him, then self-consciously removed it when he looked down at it, amused. "Where do you think you're going?"

"A mile down the road. When I told you to come along this morning," he said slowly, "I was too tired to think clearly. I needed someone to drive, and there you were. I've had a chance to mull it over, and I decided it would be best if I . . . checked it out alone. At least at first."

She was honestly annoyed. "I came all this way— almost *seven* hours, ran around like crazy this morning to get packed and find a baby-sitter, and now you're going to tell me to stay and *wait?* I wasn't aware the job description included chauffeur duties."

"Please, Suzanne," Harrison said wearily, staring ahead out the windshield. He wasn't teasing anymore; he was completely serious, and she wasn't at all sure she liked him better this way. "Let's not argue about this. What if something were to . . . happen?"

"Harrison . . . You're not going to tell me you think the aliens have come back, are you?"

"Yes," he answered, his tone firm. "We don't know what the hell is out there, and as you've so often reminded me, you have a daughter to think about."

"Okay, let's presume it was an honest-to-God extraterrestrial communication. How do you know it's not a group of *friendly* aliens? And if they're *not* friendly, then a mile will help me live only a little longer. I may as well get it over with now."

"Don't joke about it, Suzanne. It's not funny."

She raised an eyebrow. "You're certainly one to talk. You seem to have no problem joking about what other people take seriously. Close the door and put your seat belt back on. I'm not staying here. I can't run

126

the air-conditioner if the car's off, and besides, what am I supposed to do in the meantime? Wait a few hours, and if you don't come back, drive home? How will I know if the heat got you before your aliens did? Chances are we'll die of heatstroke."

Harrison's lips thinned; he thought about it for a moment, then sighed and shut the door. "Look, the minute we spot anything dangerous, we get the hell out. Understood?"

"No problem."

He started the Bronco up and pulled onto the highway again. They drove for another half mile when Suzanne finally spoke.

"You know, we're not going to see anything," she insisted, but the words were barely out of her mouth when Harrison slammed on the brakes.

"What the hell—"

The road was blocked. At first she thought it was a mirage produced by the heat waves rising from the black asphalt. Two helmeted soldiers in camouflage fatigues, rifles resting against their shoulders, stood in front of a wooden barricade that stretched the width of the road. On either side of it were parked two army jeeps, and behind it stood a covered personnel carrier. As they approached, one soldier stepped forward and held his hand palm out to stop them.

"Shit," Harrison muttered, and rolled down his window as the soldier approached.

The soldier's eyes were almond-shaped; his round, light brown face was flushed and trickling sweat. He bent down and looked in the open window at Harrison; his tone was friendly but firm. Suzanne liked him without knowing him. "This is a restricted area, sir. I'm afraid you'll have to turn back."

"You must be terribly hot standing out in this sun," she blurted out. "Don't your superiors realize how dangerous it is?"

The soldier grinned suddenly, crinkling the corners of his deepset eyes. "Yes, ma'am, I'm sure they do." He patted the canteen on his belt. "We've got plenty of water—not that it makes us feel any cooler." He addressed Harrison. "But you're still going to have to turn this vehicle around."

"Just a minute." Harrison reached over and popped open the glove compartment in front of Suzanne. "Get your PIT ID," he said to her, and started fumbling through the compartment's contents: credit-card slips for gas, coins, flashlight, a Rand-McNally road atlas . . . His fingers finally grasped a plastic-laminated ID card.

Suzanne found hers in the navy bag behind her seat and handed it to him. He shoved both cards in the soldier's face.

"Here. We're researchers with the Pacific Institute of Technology. Show those to your superiors."

The soldier drew back a little, then took them gingerly. "It'll take a few minutes," he said politely. "Why don't you folks pull over?"

Harrison grunted and knocked the stickshift into reverse, then backed off onto the shoulder. He turned off the ignition and opened the door. "May as well get out. Like you said, no point in staying in here with the air off."

She got out and walked around to the driver's side while he opened the back hatch and started rummaging for something. "Well," she said, "I was right. It's a military base, and they're involved in some sort of secret project. Maybe Norton's transmitter isn't the only one around."

The soldier had gone back to the barricade; now he was reading from the ID cards into a walkie-talkie and nodding.

Harrison seemed too distracted to take offense; he straightened, thermos in his hand, and stared past the barricade as if he saw something far beyond it, the soldiers, their jeeps. "It's more than that. The military doesn't set up a barricade a mile outside an installation if they're just broadcasting signals into space. No, something's happened here."

The way he said it made her frightened for an instant, but she shrugged it off; the man was clearly paranoid, in need of a good psychiatrist. Besides, if it were what Harrison suspected, it would take more than a military blockade to hold the aliens back. In the heat of the desert sun, Suzanne began to perspire under her gabardine dress. She fanned herself with her hand, a useless gesture.

Harrison noticed. "Here." He unscrewed the lid of the thermos, poured something into the top, and handed it to her. She took it eagerly; it was water, ice-cold, absolutely delicious. She drank while he pulled a couple of field stools from the back of the Bronco.

They were sitting in its shade when she saw a jeep pull up on the other side of the barricade. An officer stepped out: tall, with a broad, powerful build and square-shouldered military bearing. He emanated authority; the two guards quickly snapped to attention and saluted the instant they spotted him. He returned their salutes and strode with animallike grace through the barricades, past the wide-eyed guards, until he arrived inches short of Harrison and Suzanne.

She smiled up at him, doing her best not to be disconcerted. She despised people who enjoyed intimidating others, but mostly despised herself for being intimidated by them.

His skin was reddish-bronze, his hair jet black and close to the scalp; his eyes were hidden behind mirrored sunglasses. Above the left breast pocket of his perfectly pressed uniform was the inscription: IRONHORSE. An Indian warrior, and a formidable one at that. He didn't respond to Suzanne's smile, merely peered down at the documents he held in one large hand.

"Doctors McCullough . . . ?" His voice was deep, flinty, unyielding.

"Yes," Suzanne answered quickly.

"And Blackwood?"

Harrison rose so that he and Ironhorse stood toe-to-toe, like two sparring partners. There was coiled anger in Harrison's movements; he clearly resented Ironhorse more than the soldier resented him. "Present and accounted for," Harrison said, but there was none of his usual good humor in it. Suzanne began to honestly worry that a fistfight was about to break out, and scrambled awkwardly to her feet.

"I checked." Ironhorse sneered slightly. The lens of his glasses reflected two tiny Harrisons. "You're free to leave the area."

Harrison's expression was stony. "We don't want to leave. We want to travel east half a mile, then north another half mile."

"That's a restricted military installation."

"These are public roads." Harrison gestured, frustrated, at the expanse beyond the barricade.

Ironhorse was unimpressed. "And presently under military authority. There's nothing for you to see."

Suddenly, she shared Harrison's anger. Dammit, she wasn't going to let him intimidate them into leaving! They'd come a long way into the desert, and she wasn't going to get this far and then turn right around and head back without something to show for it. Besides, Harrison wouldn't be fit to live with if he didn't find out what lay beyond the barricade. Angrily, she blurted, "Which explains your reluctance to let us see for ourselves!"

Harrison shot her a swift, admiring glance, one corner of his mouth quirking up as he turned his face toward her, then settling into a grim line as he looked back at Ironhorse.

The military man was not amused. "We can do this one of two ways," he said. "You can turn around now and go home. Or you can force me to detain you until I've had a chance to recheck backgrounds. With the army, that's been known to take several days. Which is it, Doctors?"

She would have hit him if she'd thought it would

help things. She glanced over at Harrison, worried that he might have the same idea. But an inspiration seemed to have come to him.

He eyed the uniform casually. "Is it Captain Ironhorse?"

Ironhorse sounded disgusted at his ignorance. "Lieutenant Colonel."

"Does it matter, *Colonel,* that both of us"— Harrison nodded at Suzanne—"have Top Secret clearances?"

"Not to me, it doesn't. Around here it's 'need to know' . . ." His lips curved slightly in a coldly superior smile. "And you don't need to know. Now, if you'll excuse me . . ."

He turned to leave; Harrison reached out but stopped just short of touching the colonel's arm. Ironhorse stared down at Harrison's hand for a dangerous moment, then slowly moved his gaze up to the scientist's earnest face. Harrison's anger had vanished, replaced by good-natured cunning.

"Colonel, aren't you even the least bit curious about what it was that brought us here in the first place?"

Ironhorse turned back slowly, a muscle in his square jaw twitching; Suzanne felt the momentum of power shift to Harrison. "Officially, Dr. Blackwood, I have no authority to ask such a question."

"Last night," Harrison explained eagerly, "one of my associates intercepted radio transmissions originating from this location . . . or, more accurately, the location one half mile east and one half mile north of here."

Ironhorse's expression never changed, but a hint of

interest warmed his tone. "What kind of transmission?"

Harrison's eyes lit up. *He knows he's got him,* Suzanne told herself triumphantly, and felt herself smiling. "For the moment," Harrison said, toying with him, "let's just say they were . . . highly unusual."

Ironhorse folded thick arms across his chest and asked with something suspiciously like resignation, "You wouldn't happen to have a copy of these unusual transmissions?"

Harrison grinned and produced a cassette tape from his shirt pocket. Ironhorse reached for it, but Harrison was too quick for him and pulled it back. Tauntingly, he asked, "Is this the beginning of a negotiation, Colonel?"

NINE

Harrison's mouth was dry, but it had nothing to do with the heat of the desert. He drove the Bronco, Ironhorse next to him in the front seat, Suzanne in the back. The second Harrison had seen the barricade, he knew with an inexplicable growing excitement that *something* had happened, and the grim set of Ironhorse's jaw told him that whatever it was, it wasn't good.

He listened quietly as Ironhorse spoke and tried not to look as though he were gloating about his little victory over the colonel (thanks to Norton's tape)— which he was, of course. He'd hated the colonel the moment he'd laid eyes on him. Clayton Forrester's experience had taught his adopted son to hate everyone involved with the military/government bureaucracy. Harrison hated them for their blind, unquestioning obedience, for their narrow preoccupation with details, for their disregard for the truth. It was the military who overrode all of Forrester's suggestions for dealing with the alien remains, who made it impossible for Forrester's warnings to be heard . . . it was the military, Harrison had long ago decided, that drove his adoptive father to the verge of a complete mental breakdown.

But, much as Harrison distrusted Ironhorse, it was clear that for the moment at least, they needed each other. And it was clear that Ironhorse wanted the tape of the transmissions badly enough to start talking.

"The installation in question is the Jericho Valley Disposal Site," Ironhorse said, glancing over his shoulder at Suzanne to include her in the conversation. Harrison tilted his head to one side to hear better. Jericho Valley . . . The name sounded vaguely familiar; Harrison tried to place it, and failed.

Suzanne's eyes widened slightly. "Disposal of *what*, exactly?"

"Nuclear and toxic wastes," Ironhorse replied matter-of-factly. "Don't worry, we won't be exposing you to anything. At least, nothing significant."

"For some reason, I don't like the sound of that," Harrison said half under his breath.

The colonel paused to stare at Harrison from under his mirrored sunglasses, then continued in a detached tone. "Approximately thirty-six hours ago, Jericho Valley was attacked. Communications were cut off. When we checked it out, we found the gates wide open, and all seventeen soldiers stationed there dead. Killed."

Harrison caught Suzanne's horrified expression in

the rearview mirror. *Maybe she realizes I'm not nuts after all.* "How?" he asked Ironhorse.

Ironhorse stared out the window. "Most died when the barracks were blown sky high. I figure they used a rocket launcher. Poor bastards must have been asleep. Three were shot—automatic weapons."

Harrison wasn't exactly sure what he'd been expecting to hear, but that wasn't it.

Suzanne paled. "Terrorists?"

Ironhorse did not answer at first; he gestured for Harrison to turn. "Here it is."

The Bronco kicked up dust as it veered left onto a narrow gravel driveway. "Guess you could call them that, Dr. McCullough," Ironhorse said, answering her question. He shrugged. "But it's just a convenient label. Doesn't tell us *who* or *why*. Don't worry, ma'am, they're gone. Left fast—no threats, no demands, no calling cards. Just killed everyone and split—and left the bodies to rot where the birds could get at 'em."

Suzanne shuddered.

"And if they sent any transmissions"—the colonel looked over at Harrison—"they took their equipment with them."

"If they really were terrorists," Harrison asked, "then why didn't they take advantage of the fact that this was a nuclear waste dump?"

Ironhorse nodded. "Exactly. But they didn't. We found one barrel shot up, oozing radioactive waste. Still, it seems strange that they wouldn't have prepared for that contingency, that something like that would have been enough to scare them off after they went to the trouble of killing seventeen men."

Maybe something else scared them off, Harrison almost said but decided against it. His mind raced over the possibilities. Maybe it wasn't a return of the unfriendly invaders at all. Could it have been the appearance of a UFO that frightened them off?

"There were radiation suits in the guard shack in case of accidents," the colonel continued. "They could have protected themselves." The Bronco pulled up in front of a military base surrounded by a high chain-link fence. As Ironhorse had mentioned, the gates were swung open. Inside, men wearing radiation suits and square white hoods of heavy lead-lined material wandered around taping with hand-held cameras.

Ironhorse directed Harrison to park the Bronco outside the gate, next to a personnel carrier, and climbed out. Before Suzanne could struggle out in her impractically narrow skirt, Ironhorse was already on the passenger side, offering a helpful arm. She took it reluctantly.

"So now," the colonel said to Harrison, who climbed out of the driver's side, "you can see why I'd like to have that tape analyzed. Could I ask how it is you happened to acquire it? Or don't I need to know?"

Harrison smiled. He still couldn't stand the man, but at least Ironhorse had the good grace to poke fun at his own terminology. "It's not classified. We broadcast radio signals into space and also monitor for transmissions."

"Who were these people trying to contact?" Ironhorse seemed more confused than enlightened by Harrison's explanation.

"I don't know." Harrison feigned ignorance. "Suffice it to say we managed to pick them up because they were using some serious equipment." If he gave Ironhorse the same explanation he gave Suzanne, that would be the end of the guided tour right there. She gave him a knowing look he interpreted as meaning that she understood.

"I get the uncomfortable feeling you're hiding something from me." Ironhorse frowned but motioned them toward a large army-green van parked just beyond the personnel carrier. "If it was just the radiation," he said, "I could probably fit you into protective gear and send you in for a look. But whoever overran this installation did a very professional job of mining the area. You'll have to be satisfied with our remotes." He slid open the side panel of the van.

"I'm surprised he didn't send us out there, then," Harrison muttered in Suzanne's ear. She didn't react, but Ironhorse, who caught it, smiled sourly and thrust out his hand as Harrison moved to step up into the van.

"The tape first, Dr. Blackwood."

Harrison returned the wry smile, fished the tape from his pocket, and dropped it into Ironhorse's waiting palm. The colonel moved aside and let him pass.

Inside, a bank of video monitors lined the opposite

wall of the van. Two technicians, sitting with their backs to Harrison and the others, manned the control panels. Upon realizing that Ironhorse had entered, they struggled to rise.

"At ease," Ironhorse said abruptly. The two techs sank back down. The colonel removed his sunglasses and slipped them into his shirt pocket; his eyes were dark, almost black, and so coldly intimidating that Harrison decided he liked him better with the sunglasses on.

Harrison found it easiest to focus on one of the monitors at a time. The images were unprofessional, fuzzy, made by the hand-held cameras they'd seen wandering inside the installation. This particular soldier was aiming his camera at the bombed-out barracks. Harrison saw a jagged, blackened ceiling beam lying across a mangled government-issue cot, its mattress torn and blood-spattered.

He looked away quickly at a different monitor. Better. The camera was panning over a boring stretch of dirt that looked as if a gang of motorcyclists had roared through it, maybe popped a few wheelies. Another soldier wearing the white radiation gear wandered through the shot briefly.

A third monitor showed a puzzling scene: steel drums stacked only on the top tier of a wooden flat. "Strange," Harrison whispered to himself.

The camera pulled back; in the background, some barrels—older, rusting—lay on their sides. Something about the sight didn't seem right, compelled him to take a step closer, for a better look, but then the camera moved on abruptly to a view of what appeared to be a stack of bodies, draped discreetly with black garbage-bag plastic.

"Back up!" Harrison shouted at the monitor. The guy couldn't hear him, of course, but he was standing close enough to one of the techs to grab his mike and find the off-on switch.

"Hey!" the technician exclaimed, but Harrison scarcely heard him.

"Back up, soldier," he barked into the mike, "and focus on those overturned barrels!"

Ironhorse was at his side instantly, and grabbed his wrist, then slowly peeled the mike from his fingers. "That's it, Doctor. You've seen enough."

Harrison ignored him; his gaze was fastened on the monitor as the camera obeyed and slowly panned back to the new barrels . . . and then the older rusty ones. "Tell him to zoom in," Harrison ordered the tech. "Tell him!"

Ironhorse nodded at the tech, who leaned over his reappropriated mike. "Camera three—zoom in."

"What *is* it?" Suzanne's voice in his ear, but he couldn't answer just yet. An alarm had sounded somewhere deep in his memory, triggered somehow by the sight of the overturned barrels. He struggled to piece it together.

The camera zoomed in—on the new barrels. "Not those!" Harrison shouted. "Lower! On the ground."

The technician said something unintelligible into the mike; the image tilted, the focus adjusted and settled on the overturned barrel. CLASSIFIED 1951–1953, it said along its side. And US GOVT PROPERTY; HAZARD- OUS; DO NOT REMOVE.

Classified 1951–1953.

Harrison shivered and broke into a sweat. He had seen those markings before . . .

Twenty-one years ago, when Clayton had first brought out the files. Harrison closed his eyes and saw the photograph in Clayton's trembling hand.

Here. Clayton handed him the picture. *Those are the barrels the government stuffed the remains into. They all bear the same distinctive markings.*

CLASSIFIED 1951–1953 . . .

Hundreds of thousands of them, Clayton had said, his voice flat and bitter. *Hidden away in military installations and other secret locations all over the country, some of them only a few hundred miles from here, in Jericho Valley . . .*

Jericho Valley. No wonder it had sounded familiar. Harrison opened his eyes and stared at the monitor.

The cameraman waxed creative and pulled back, then zoomed in again, this time using a different angle.

The top of the barrel had been forced open from the *inside.* Dear God, the drum was empty . . .

Harrison's knees went weak; he clutched at the console to keep from falling, only vaguely aware of Suzanne's and the colonel's eyes on him. "Ask him" —he tried to speak louder, but his voice remained a hoarse whisper—"ask him if there are any more barrels like that."

"Camera three," the tech asked, "what's the count on barrels in this condition?"

The voice filtered through the console. "We've found six empties."

Harrison reached for the mike switch again, shouting as he suddenly found his voice. "Six empties—but how many old barrels with these markings? There should be hundreds! Thousands!"

"Only six old barrels with the 1953 stamp on them," the voice said.

Ironhorse firmly pulled Harrison's hand off the switch and replaced it with his own. "Soldier"—he leaned over the console—"how long until you've done an inventory check?"

"We're hours away, Colonel. This place has been a nuclear waste dump for nearly forty years."

"Oh, God," Harrison whispered, his gaze fixed on the monitor. "No . . ."

He closed his eyes and saw it all happening again. The sky, streaked with death rays and glowing dull orange-red from the fires that raged out of control, the air thick with smoke and screams of the fleeing. Those bodies not reduced to cinders by the rays lay crushed under debris or exposed where they were trampled to death by the terrified crowds.

He was not quite five years old, and had just seen his parents killed by the aliens' rays. The memory of it clutched at him full force, pulling him down into a dark vortex of panic.

Harrison, darling, get up . . .

He'd run screaming through the streets until his voice and legs gave out and he collapsed, sobbing, on the sidewalk. And now the nightmare was starting again. . . .

Harrison turned and ran out of the van.

"What's wrong with him?" Ironhorse asked. The gruffness was gone from his voice, and in its place was genuine puzzlement.

Suzanne was still gaping in the direction Harrison had fled. "I don't know," she answered slowly. Whatever he had seen had driven him berserk. She was shaken; she had judged him to be eccentric, perhaps slightly obsessed by the need to find the aliens who had killed his parents. Now she saw it was far worse than that. The man was in trouble, the man needed psychiatric help.

Suzanne turned back to stare with Ironhorse at the close-up of the open barrel. It was clear to her that the base had been attacked by terrorists who had stolen the nuclear waste for God knew what evil purpose, and *that* frightened her . . . as much as Harrison's panic attack. Obviously, he had been counting on finding his aliens here and now could not accept the fact that his misguided search had failed.

"Excuse me," she said to Ironhorse, and went outside to look for Harrison.

She didn't have to look far. He was in the Bronco, slumped down in the passenger seat. She walked over and bent down to peer into the open window. He was hugging himself tightly; sweat trickled from his forehead, but she knew it had nothing to do with the heat. His lips were parted slightly as he stared straight ahead into the distance.

"Harrison . . . are you okay?"

He wasn't. He jerked sharply at the sound of her voice and looked up at her. His pale eyes were bright, wild. "We have to leave."

She stared at him, unable to think of an answer.

"Now, dammit!"

She withdrew from the window. Ironhorse stood at the van's entrance, watching. She could have gone back to him then and told him Blackwood was having a mental breakdown and she was afraid to get into the truck with him. Maybe the army would get her home.

Instead, she walked around to the driver's side, climbed in, and turned the ignition key.

They rode the entire seven hours in silence.

TEN

About thirty-five miles from anywhere, the tiny burg of Brewster sat just off exit 92, smack in the middle of the Mojave Desert. The town consisted of one gas station, one Safeway, one electrical appliance store, Mae's Dress Shop, a Baptist bookstore, three churches, and four auto parts stores between there and Skylerville, the neighboring town with which Brewster shared one sheriff, his deputy, and their patrol car.

It was late afternoon, and the sun was just getting ready to slip below the horizon and take the heat with it. Inside the display window at Crutchins' Electronics, four nineteen-inch Sony color TV sets were all tuned to the same channel, a local independent station that aired mostly reruns. A rowdy group of teenagers, a couple of them with spiked technicolor hairdos, stared mesmerized at the pictures on the screens.

With Xeera and Konar by his side, Xashron stepped

up silently behind them. In thirty-five years, it seemed, the humans had made few real advances in their technology; clearly, they were still far too primitive to be a threat. Even so, Xashron was faintly amused by the drama unfolding on the television screens. It was a crude representation of a space battle between the Earthlings and some unseen enemy; the humans, vain creatures that they were, showed themselves winning the confrontation. Xashron smiled thinly at the irony of it.

On the screen, the interior of the Earth ship shuddered; consoles rained sparks. One of the actors fell, and another actor rushed to kneel over him. The camera closed in on the kneeling man's grim face.

"He's dead, Jim," one of the boys said in a shrill falsetto that was in perfect sync with the actor, who silently mouthed his line. The group laughed and nudged each other; as they did, one of them caught sight of Xashron. Soon the whole group was staring.

Someone imitated a chimpanzee, another made jungle-bird calls; a third giggled. Xashron and his soldiers shifted their attention from the television sets to the punks. The giggler fell silent. Slowly, silently, the teenagers moved on.

It was time for Xashron and the others to leave as well. The Advocate had come up with a suggestion that was actually intelligent, which indicated to Xashron that it was Xana's doing. These host bodies were deteriorating far too quickly, causing almost as much alarm as it would for them to use their natural form; apparently, their cellular structure made it impossible for them to tolerate large doses of radiation. Therefore, the Advocacy decreed, it was necessary to obtain medical information on caring for the human bodies. The method of doing so had been left to Xashron's discretion.

In the meantime, Xana and the others had work of their own.

Waller's Amoco lay south of Exit 92 outside the little desert town. It was twilight and the heat was fading; old Doc Waller was just getting ready to lock up the office when he spied Orel Ralston weaving down the road.

"Doc!" Orel spotted him and waved wildly. The action knocked him off balance, and he reacted by staggering off to one side. He had just left Nelda's Tavern a half mile down the road and was drunk as a skunk.

Doc gave up and slipped his key back into his pocket without locking the office door. Orel was running early this evening. Usually he didn't reach this particular level of intoxication until well after nightfall, after Doc had left the station, at which point Orel would stumble from Nelda's down to the Amoco and climb into one of the cars left overnight for maintenance, where he'd sleep off his drunk and leave the next morning by seven-thirty, before Doc and the customers started showing up.

Doc didn't mind, really. So long as Orel was gone before the customers got there, and didn't piss or upchuck in any of the cars, it was no problem. Doc had made it plenty clear that the night Orel puked in a customer's car would be his last.

"Doc," Orel panted, arriving at last, and grasped the old man's upper arms. Orel was a short, weasel-faced little guy, with a round nose and shiny eyes the color of the American flag—red, white, and blue—and he smelled worse than a wet dog. His overalls and the holey white T-shirt he wore beneath them were filthy, as was the greasy red-brown hair he brushed forward in an attempt to hide a receding hairline. "Doc, how are you?" His breath was sour from beer.

"You're early tonight, Orel." Doc pried Orel's dirty hands loose and put an arm under his shoulders to prop him up. "C'mon over this way. I got a nice '79 Ford LTD with some real cushy seats."

Orel balked. "Don't wanna sleep," he slurred. "Ain't tired. How 'bout you bringing us a coupla beers?"

He was referring to the cooler Doc kept hidden behind the counter in the office. Doc kept it stocked with Pabst Blue Ribbon in the can, or Coors, if it was on special that week at the Brewster Safeway. Sometimes, when things got too slow, Doc would pop open a can for himself and sometimes, if he was feeling especially generous, for the part-time mechanic, Luis Ortega. 'Course, he never dreamed of doing it when there were customers around.

"Cooler's empty," Doc lied, though he knew there were a couple of Pabsts still left in the melted ice. "C'mon, Orel, let's check out that LTD."

Orel yielded and wobbled along with Doc's help over to the four-door LTD. It was unlocked, of course; in forty years, Doc had never locked a car or truck on his property, and none of them had ever been stolen or vandalized. The LTD was white with a black vinyl top that was starting to peel away from the metal in a couple of places; otherwise, it looked pretty good for a '79, though Doc couldn't say the same for the transmission.

Doc opened the heavy rear door—Lord, they didn't make 'em like this anymore; now they had those little tinfoil Japanese cars that crumpled if you looked cross-eyed at 'em—and eased Orel inside.

Orel curled up on the rear seat—real leather, nice and cushy—with a contented sigh. Doc had parked it in the shade and kept the windows cracked so the air inside would be fresh and not too hot. Luis had given him a hard time about it that morning, but Doc felt sorry for old Orel.

Orel's seventeen-year-old daughter Sally had died of leukemia four years ago, and afterward, Orel's wife, Minnie, had gone off the deep end. They said she was still in some kind of mental hospital off in Riverside or somewhere, but Orel wouldn't talk about it anymore. A lot of kids had died of leukemia around here, and the old folks of one kind or another of cancer— enough to make folks suspicious. All that nuclear testing back in the fifties, everyone said, and when that group of families decided to sue the U.S. government, people in Brewster talked of joining the suit, or starting their own. Of course, after those folks lost the case, people here gave up talking about it.

Doc's own wife, Lucy, had died of breast cancer twelve years before, when she was only fifty-one and he was fifty-eight. Since then he'd just been marking time, minding the station and having an occasional beer when the waiting got to weigh heavy on him. Just his damn luck he turned out to be long-lived. Without Lucy, life seemed flat and dry and endless, like the desert.

He made sure Orel was clear of the door, then closed it and headed back to the office to lock up. He'd just turned the key in the lock when he heard the tractor-trailer rumbling down the exit ramp.

"Shit," Doc sighed, but he opened the door, switched on the lights, then walked around the counter to switch on the diesel pump. Business wasn't so good that he could afford to turn down big rigs like the one pulling into the station. Shiny and new it was, not a scratch on it. No writing on the sign, neither, and when Doc saw the guy in the white coverall climb out and start pumping diesel into one of the tanks, he became a tad suspicious. A worker at one of them nuclear dump places, for sure; he bet if somebody took a Geiger counter and aimed it at that rig, the needle would go clear off the scale. Doc hated those places, and the people from them who stopped by; in the back of his mind he blamed them for Lucy's death.

Still, business was business. Doc walked out of the office and ambled on over to the island. The guy in the coverall had his back to him and didn't notice him.

"Whyn'cha let me do that, fella?" Doc inquired cheerfully as soon as he was in earshot. "This here's a full-service station."

Without turning around, the man shook his head very slowly.

"Have it your way," Doc replied pleasantly. "Where ya headed?"

The man still didn't speak, but inclined his head back toward Route 15, going east.

Luis came in four mornings a week, and was gone after lunch; the rest of the time Doc spent pretty much by himself, especially the evenings at home, which sometimes got rough. He enjoyed talking with his customers every chance he got—felt it was his right. He refused to be discouraged into silence. "I see. Where ya comin' from?"

The man nodded west.

"Talkative, ain't ya?" Doc said, a little disgusted. "Here, I'll finish that up." He crossed over the island and reached out for the nozzle. Startled, the man turned toward him. Doc caught a whiff of something rotten.

"Jesus H. Christ on a raft," he whispered, feeling a sudden strange tingle of fear. The man's face was deathly pale, a sick, graying color, and there was a huge oozing sore on his cheek that for some reason made him think of Lucy. Cancer, Doc thought, horrified; the poor fool's face was eaten away by it. And such a young man too.

"Son," he said kindly, "you best start being a heap more careful standin' out in the sun like this without no hat."

As he spoke, two others—a man and a woman—stepped down out of the cab. As they moved closer, Doc was struck by that same cloying, sickly sweet smell of vomit and decay and things too abominable to mention. There was puke down the front of their white coveralls, he realized, and dark streaks down the legs that he didn't even want to guess at. Their

151

faces were covered with weeping sores, just like the guy at the pump, but it couldn't be that they all had the same type of cancer progressed to the same stage; Doc had had enough experience with the disease to realize it wasn't contagious. No, there was something else wrong with them, something even more horrible than the big C. Nervously, Doc took a big step backward.

"You folks got some type of commutable disease or somethin'?"

No answer. Maybe they *couldn't* talk, Doc thought frantically, because their tongues had rotted off in there. Silently, the two began to move toward him while the third continued to fill the big rig's tanks. The vile stench grew stronger; there was an evil purposefulness in the movements of the two that made him tremble. In a brilliant, horrifying flash, Doc realized they were *corpses* . . . walking corpses, much as Lucy had been in those awful final days.

"No," he cried feebly, raising his hands in a pitiful attempt to ward off death. "Not like this." True, he took no joy in living anymore, but he'd planned on going quietly—dying in his sleep in his own bed, or maybe slumping over one day at the station—and the thought of joining these three, of becoming as they were, *here, now,* terrified him.

They kept coming, and he kept shrinking away, until at last he stepped back against something firm and moist and inhumanly strong.

Orel stirred inside the big LTD. He was powerfully thirsty, and the drunk was beginning to wear off a bit, so that he remembered where he was. He grabbed onto the top of the backseat—really was nice leather, some far away part of his brain realized; there was no better, kinder person in the world than ole Doc Waller—and pulled himself up. Eyes still closed, he slowly peeled his cottony tongue away from the inside of his cheek—damn, he was dry; but no point in asking for water, which would just sober him up again—and croaked: "Hey, Doc, what say we head over to Jed's for some moonshine?"

Doc had actually gone with him once, not long after Lucy died, and they'd both gotten stinky drunk. Orel's memory wasn't too good these days, but he never forgot a detail when it came to drinking.

It didn't come out loud enough for anyone to hear, so Orel cleared his throat and tried louder.

"Doc?"

He opened his eyes, forced them to focus, and peered out the back windshield. What he saw sobered him up fast. Orel blinked and shook his head to clear it, but the horrible scene remained.

He sucked back a sob and sank soundlessly down, out of sight.

Griff Kelsey slipped his shoes off and sat down in the black leather La-Z-Boy recliner—the one Elaine had bought him for his fiftieth birthday two years ago—in front of the television set. From the TV tray beside him Griff removed the small plastic square marked "physician's sample" and pushed two Empirin number four through the foil, put them on his tongue, tilted his head back, and washed them down with a sip from the large old-fashioned glass filled three-quarters of the way with Jack Daniel's.

Years of alcoholism had left their mark in the broken veins on his nose and cheeks, in the extra weight. He still took two number fours every evening around this time, even though the migraines he started taking them for had stopped nine months before when Elaine left him for that lawyer in Palm Springs.

Now he took them because the money was gone and there was some young bastard over in Cadiz who'd set up what they called a "family practice" nowadays and was stealing all his patients. He also took them because Elaine had taken the Lincoln Towne Car and the poodle (good riddance, actually) and the entire goddamn savings account. She'd left him only the Grand Wagoneer (though he never used it for house calls anymore) and the house.

It was a nice house, the ritziest one in Brewster, a sprawling Spanish villa with an authentic red tile roof and two dying palm trees out front. It was near the center of town, and he kept his shingle prominently displayed.

GRIFFITH W. KELSEY, M.D.
General Practitioner
→

The arrow pointed around to the side, where the office entrance was.

Used to be Griff was the only doctor for miles around, unless you wanted to drive the forty-five minutes or so to Barstow or Hinkley. When he was growing up in Brewster, that's exactly what people had to do if they needed to see the doctor. Griff vowed to change all that. He went off to Arizona State, then to medical school—which he barely made it through, graduating dead last in his class—and came right back to Brewster the minute he finished his residency at a Las Vegas hospital. After all, he figured the only doctor for thirty miles around was bound to make potfuls of money. Which was exactly what he did until Elaine took him to the cleaners and that new doctor in Cadiz stole all his patients.

On bad days, when there were no patients or only one or two, he took a Valium along with the Empirins. But today actually hadn't gone too badly. Nine patients, and all but one paid cash. Griff celebrated by putting his favorite Swanson's in the oven: turkey with dressing and apple crunch for dessert, though he wished there were some way to keep the cranberries from getting so hot they burned his tongue.

Waiting for the kitchen timer to go off, he settled back in the recliner and pulled the lever so the footrest came out, then picked up the remote control on the padded armrest and flicked the TV on to the cable news channel. He sipped the Jack and listened with vague interest. An item from Atlanta: blood mysteriously seeping up through the floorboards in an elderly widow's home. Police mystified . . . Three more Palestinians killed on the West Bank. Slow news day.

They were talking about the bond market rally when he heard the noise. Not the kind where you have to ask yourself if you really heard something or not, but a *boom*, the sound of someone breaking the door down, and it had come from the other side of the house, where the office was.

Griff pushed the footrest back and struggled to his feet, spilling Jack down the front of his white professional smock. He set the glass down on the tray. His heart was thumping so wildly in his chest that he couldn't catch his breath. Someone had broken into the office.

The fear was nauseating in its intensity. It was a possibility that had always worried him: a thief or an addict searching for drugs. A few years back he'd talked to Elaine about getting a fancy security system for the house, especially the office. She'd scoffed at him. *There aren't any junkies in Brewster—present company excepted.*

No, he'd answered, but there were plenty of them traveling between L.A. and Vegas.

And they're going to bother to take the exit and come all the way out here, to the middle of goddamn nowhere to look for excitement? Dream on . . .

She talked him out of it, of course. The money he would have spent on the expensive system now belonged to her and her precious attorney. It was just one more reason to hate her.

Griff ran softly back to the bedroom and pulled the .44 Magnum out from under an unfolded pile of underwear in his top dresser drawer. He always kept it loaded; now he took the safety off and held it close to him as he picked up the phone and dialed 911.

Someone came on the line, and he gave his name, address, and said, "A burglar's just broken into the house. Get the sheriff out here fast . . ." But the sheriff could be anywhere in San Bernadino County right now, and although the 911 operator promised twenty minutes, Griff knew better. He kept the Magnum held high as he walked, perspiring, down the dim hallway. Maybe it'd be best to just stay put until Sheriff Deak got there, just let 'em take whatever they wanted. After all, he was fully insured . . . but then, there were thousands of dollars' worth of samples in the supply cabinet in his office. And all his Empirin and Valium. He'd be damned before he'd let them wipe him out.

The door to the office wing was closed, but Griff thought he could hear someone two rooms down, in the waiting room. He turned the knob noiselessly and slipped inside the darkened back room he used as his private office. The supply closet was just off this room; Griff felt a twinge of relief. So far, the samples were safe.

Beyond the office lay a short corridor that led either directly across to the examination room, or out to the tiny foyer he used as a waiting room.

Footsteps; a thump. Sounds of someone— some*thing*. Sounds not necessarily produced by a human body. Maybe it was some sort of animal.

But what the hell kind of desert animal was capable of breaking down the door? Griff thrust the Magnum forward at arm's length, held his breath, and tiptoed out to the corridor. Beyond, in the waiting room, something moved in the shadows. He crept to the room's entrance and cried in a voice that cracked and shook: "I've got a gun, dammit! Get the hell out of there or I'll start shooting!"

Silence. It was getting dark outside, but there was still barely enough light for Griff to make out a human form standing between himself and the wide-open door. And then a voice—low, harsh, a man's, and yet somehow inhuman.

"We're ill. We need . . . help." The words were articulated clumsily, as if the man's mouth were filled with pebbles, or part of his tongue were missing. Something the size of a mastiff, black, thick-bodied, skittered behind the intruder, off to one side. An attack dog, Griff thought, but he didn't hear any panting or growling.

"Need help, my ass," he said. The fact that the man sounded ill and weak gave him a small amount of courage. "You need help, use the goddamn doorbell." He fumbled with his free hand against the wall and found the switch. "I'm going to turn on the light. Make one move and you're dead."

He snapped it on. He had been a doctor for twenty-five years, could drain an abscess or stitch up a cut between bites of a sandwich without losing his appetite, but the sight of the man made him cry out, a voiceless gasp.

The skin on his face had degenerated into one huge open weeping sore. Griff had seen enough photographs of victims of radiation sickness in Hiroshima to know what was wrong with the man, and his first thought was *Too far gone. He's been exposed to a lethal amount* . . . The second thought was that there'd been some sort of terrible catastrophe at a nearby nuclear power plant—the man wore a white technician's jump suit, which was stained with vomit and diarrhea. Griff's third thought was that anyone at this stage of radiation sickness should have been far too weak to force the door open.

"We need your help," the man repeated in the same gravelly voice. His eyes sparkled with fever.

"All right, buddy." Griff gestured at him with the Magnum. "We'll talk about that in a minute. Where'd the dog go?"

The man stared uncomprehendingly at him and took a step forward. Griff compensated by moving back. The guy was probably hot with radioactivity himself.

"C'mon," he said impatiently. "Where's the dog— or whatever it was you brought with you?"

The man took another step toward Griff.

Griff took aim again, tightened his finger on the trigger. "I *mean* it." His pitch rose. "*Stop* or I'll shoot."

Another step.

He backed away and was about to pull the trigger when something whiplike whistled through the air and fastened itself around his neck once, twice, and squeezed like a boa constrictor. Griff gasped as the air was forced out of him. The Magnum went off, sending a bullet into the thick pile carpeting.

There was a hot searing pain that covered his face, his torso, as if he were drowning in acid—that made Griff scream. It was followed by the sensation of something moving inside him, pressing against his internal organs, moving up inside his head. Pressure, horrible mounting pressure inside his skull, increasing beyond his ability to bear it, until he was sure his brain, his skull, would explode. He felt his mind dimming, like a flame dying for lack of oxygen, smothered by a flood of strange thoughts not his own.

"We need you," the man said again.

ELEVEN

The scars of destruction in the quiet old neighborhood were gone now, buried under tract housing, but Harrison's mind saw them still. The darkness had taken on a nightmarish quality; in every shadow, every unlit doorway, he imagined he saw dark, ominous forms writhing.

Harrison pulled the Bronco up into the concrete driveway in front of the modest one-story house and turned off the headlights. After dropping Suzanne off, he had headed there without even realizing where he was going. In a way, the sight of the old house comforted him; yet at the same time, it added to the illusion that he had moved backward in time some thirty-five years. Harrison switched off the ignition and rested his head gently against the steering wheel, taking deep, measured breaths in an effort to regain some measure of control.

The kitchen lights filtered through faded yellow-checked curtains; as usual, Clayton was still up, even at this late hour. Like his adopted son, Forrester was troubled by insomnia which, instead of easing as time separated him from tragedy, steadily worsened. After Harrison was old enough to move into his own place, Clayton wandered fully dressed from room to room most nights, with all the lights on, catching an occasional catnap. No matter what time Harrison stopped by—even after a late date with Char, sometimes three in the morning—there was Clayton, fully awake, with the television blaring whether he was watching it or not. There was a time when Harrison visited him every day, then work and Charlotte kept him busy, so that he stopped by only every few days, then only once a week, then every two weeks. Work and Charlotte—and the fact that he could scarcely bear to see his idol sliding deeper into idleness and despair.

Harrison got out of the Bronco, went to the side door, and let himself in with a key. The kitchen was filthy: garbage bags piled up by the back door, dishes covered with moldy food stacked up in the sink, crumbs on the counters, the floors—everywhere. Clayton had been a meticulous man, at least until depression had seized him; when Harrison moved out, it got worse. Harrison realized guiltily that now that he no longer needed a father to take care of him, Clayton had lost his purpose, and was simply waiting to die.

Harrison walked through the kitchen into the hallway. The smell of aging garbage gave way to a familiar, musty old-paper smell that Harrison found nowhere else except this house, one that he associated immediately with Clayton Forrester and his beloved files. In the living room, the old black and white Motorola was tuned to Johnny Carson with the volume at full blast. Six feet away, Clayton Forrester sat snoring on the sofa, his slippered feet propped on the coffee table, head thrown back, mouth open. His cheeks were covered with a several-day growth of silver beard, which meant he hadn't been out for a while. He wore the beige cardigan Harrison had given him last Christmas, and while it fit him then, now he seemed swallowed up by it. He looked frail, bony, shrunken under his clothes. On the end table next to the sofa were three plastic prescription bottles—two of Clayton's heart medicine, one of Elavil for the depression.

Harrison sat down in the sagging green armchair with the broken spring and watched Clayton sleep.

Clayton, I need your help—

The thought pulsed in his mind so strongly that he almost expected to hear it. He wanted to reach out, shake Forrester awake, force him to listen.

Clayton, it's happening again. I need your help—

He actually leaned forward and reached a hand out to touch the old man, but something stopped him.

Look at him—he's a beaten old man. What more can he do to help? What right do you have to expect anything more from him? Harrison realized that he had come for reassurance, a terrified child running to his father for protection, for comfort. He rubbed his face with his hands.

Why did I come here? What am I, crazy? Clayton

163

doesn't deserve this. He's tired, old, not well—he's been through enough already, and this would kill him. What possible good would it do to tell him?

Nothing, Harrison knew, except make himself feel better. He was behaving like a selfish child, running to his parent for comfort and reassurance, thinking only of himself. He sat in the armchair and stared at Clayton, unable to move.

On the television the audience roared at some off-color *double entendre* Carson had made to a comely guest. The sound of raucous laughter struck Harrison as offensive. He rose, leaned over toward the set, and snapped it off, intending to leave. Clayton could sleep—he had already given Harrison all he needed by way of the files. There was nothing more to be gained by terrifying the old man with the news of what had happened at Jericho Valley.

The screen went gray, then black; Clayton stirred. "Harrison?" Looking disoriented, he raised his head. There was a frightening vagueness in his dark eyes where there had once been brilliance. Harrison looked away, unable to meet that gaze for long.

"Sorry, Clayton." He tried to smile, tried to keep the fear from showing in his eyes. "I didn't mean to wake you."

"My God." At the sight of him, Clayton sat forward on the couch and rested a hand on his chest. "What time is it?"

"Almost midnight." Harrison walked over to the side of the couch, but didn't sit. "Did I startle you?"

Clayton grunted and shook his head. "Supposed to

take my pill a half hour ago. Dammit, I guess I slept through my watch alarm—" He fumbled with one hand for the glass on the end table. His tone was carefully casual, but Harrison detected the shortness of breath.

"Let me get you some water." Harrison scooped up the glass and hurried into the kitchen across the creaking wooden floor. As he held the glass under the tap, he saw that his hands were shaking.

Jesus, I've damn near startled him into a heart attack just by turning off the TV. I can't tell him what's happened—it'll kill him. What the hell was I thinking of, coming here tonight? What did I expect him to do?

His own breath was coming in short gasps, but there was no time to calm himself—Clayton needed the medication *now*. He returned to the living room so fast, water sloshed over the side of the glass.

Clayton was sitting with his eyes closed. His skin looked gray and waxy.

"Clayton? *Dad?*" Harrison leaned over him.

Forrester opened his eyes and tried unsuccessfully to smile. "You haven't called me that in a long time." He took the glass, sipped some water, then tilted his head back and swallowed. One of the medicine bottles was uncapped; apparently, he'd already put the pill into his mouth. "Thanks," Clayton said. He drank some more water and set the glass down with an unsteady hand.

"You okay?" Harrison crouched down, holding on to the armrest of the sofa.

"Sure." Forrester coughed, then turned his head to

stare innocently at him with soft brown eyes. "Just forgot to take my pill, that's all." He paused. "Out with Charlotte again tonight?"

"Yeah," Harrison lied. Clayton despised Charlotte, but it was as good an excuse as any. "Just wanted to see how you were doing."

"Fine," Clayton answered with total sincerity, despite the evidence to the contrary. "So you and she are still planning on getting married?"

"Well . . . yes . . . actually, we're having a little disagreement right now." Normally, Harrison would never have mentioned it, since it only gave Clayton more ammunition for his anti-Charlotte campaign— but Forrester might accept it as an explanation for Harrison's agitated mood. "It's work related."

Clayton nodded. "Let me guess. She wants you to get a higher-paying job. Go where the money is." He lowered his hand from his chest; the color seemed to come back to his face. Harrison relaxed a little.

"Speaking of work . . . Ephram finally got me that microbiologist. Remember the one we talked about?"

Clayton did. "Sylvia's cousin?"

"Second cousin," Harrison corrected him.

"Does she look anything like her?"

Harrison shrugged. If there was any resemblance other than the fact that both were brunettes, he'd missed it, but to please Clayton, he replied, "A little."

"Married?" Clayton asked innocently.

"Divorced." Harrison's lips thinned. "Not that it's any of your damn business."

Clayton smiled faintly. "I'm sure it's not. But I'll

bet she has more in common with you than Charlotte Phillipson does."

Harrison shook his head. "I'm afraid our theory backfired. She's not as interested in working against the aliens as we thought. Instead of wanting to deal with the reality of what happened, she's running away from it."

"So she's refused the job?" Clayton seemed disappointed.

"Not yet. She's at least willing to listen, to look at some tissue samples, though——" Harrison broke off. He had almost said, *though after what happened today, I'm not sure she'll stay . . .*

"Harrison," Clayton said softly. His voice was suddenly stronger, his eyes lit up by a spark of his former brilliance. "Something happened today, something you're not telling me. I may be a forgetful old man, but I'm not that stupid. I can tell when you're upset. You should see your face."

Harrison rose and stared down at the worn carpet covering the terrazzo floor. "It's nothing, really. Like I said, I had a fight with Char."

Clayton shook his head gently. "It has nothing to do with Charlotte, I'm afraid. I've seen you after fights with girlfriends, Harrison. No, this is something far worse."

Harrison looked back up and cursed himself for being so transparent; he tried to think of a better excuse, something Clayton might believe, but his mind was a blank.

"When you first came in," Clayton said slowly,

"your expression—God, I'm not sure I have the words to describe it." He hesitated, thinking. *"Haunted,* maybe. I haven't seen that look on your face in a very long time."

Harrison stared at him. My God, the old man knew . . .

Forrester's eyes were still focused on Harrison, but he seemed to see beyond him, at something, someone else in the distant past. "I think the last time I saw that expression on your face, you were six years old. When I woke up and saw you, for a minute, I was back in 'fifty-three . . ."

"You're right . . . I think the aliens are back." Harrison nodded, amazed. "How did you know?"

Forrester managed a slight smile. "I didn't—until just now." He patted his chest. "You didn't tell me because you were worried the shock would kill me. But I've already had my scare, son, and I'm all right now. Why don't you tell me about it?"

Harrison sank down on the couch next to him and leaned forward to cover his eyes with his hands. "Norton picked up a transmission," he began wearily. "It was directed toward a point in the constellation Taurus. It originated from the Jericho Valley disposal site—"

"Jericho Valley," Clayton echoed. "I remember. One of the first storage areas. Everyone who worked with the project was furious about it because it was only hours away from the Institute itself, not to mention the most populated areas of the West Coast."

"Six barrels are empty, and the rest—hundreds—are missing." He glanced unhappily at Forrester. "I saw it with my own eyes. The military already knows about it because all the soldiers on the base were killed. They're trying to blame it on terrorists, of course." He leaned forward again to rest his head in his hands. "I don't know what to do, Clayton. I don't know what to do. I'm so scared, I can't think—"

The news had the completely opposite effect that Harrison expected; instead of becoming agitated, Forrester seemed to grow stronger, calmer, younger. "Six barrels," he said, his voice soothingly rational. "We're very, very lucky. They have no weapons, no shelter, no ships . . . and without those, the odds are greatly in our favor. This time we can stop them even if for some reason the bacteria doesn't."

"God, I hope so," Harrison whispered. "Because Norton's the only one I can count on. I'm not even sure Suzanne, the microbiologist, will believe me."

Clayton's tone was firm as he reached out to rest a hand on the younger man's shoulder. "Harrison, sometimes I think I did you a disservice raising you as I did, exposing you to all of this. You feel the fate of the world rests solely on your shoulders. But this isn't something you and Norton can solve by yourselves. You've got to get help—"

"Where?"

"The government."

"The *government?*" Harrison straightened abruptly; Clayton pulled his hand away. "I can't believe you, of all people, are telling me this. After what they did to you, you expect me to *trust* them?"

"There's no reason to make this a personal vendetta," Clayton answered coolly. "They didn't single me out—and what they did affected the entire world. We're talking right now about the fate of every man, woman, and child on this planet. You can't afford to let what happened in the past stop you from getting every shred of help you can—because if you don't, you put all our lives in jeopardy. Who knows? Maybe now the government is willing to try to correct what it did."

"I can't trust them," Harrison said.

"I didn't say you should." Forrester sighed. "You can take advantage of their help without trusting them. There are some names of Pentagon contacts in the files—I can't remember them off the top of my head anymore. You might want to see if any of them are still alive. If not, maybe Jacobi can help you get in touch with the right people."

"All right," Harrison agreed grudgingly.

"And do what you can to convince that microbiologist," Clayton added, his face alert, responsive. "Getting a thorough analysis on paper is critical if you're going to get the government to believe you. You're going to need all the help you can get."

"I'll try," Harrison said with a sinking feeling, "but I don't think it's going to be easy."

TWELVE

Suzanne leaned over the ancient IBM Selectric in her office, squinting at the line typed on white bond paper:

> Doctor Blackwood:
>   I am hereby tendering my resignation.

There was definitely more she wanted to say, but she was so angry, so exhausted, so confused that she couldn't sort it all out. Certainly she hadn't been able to get to sleep after arriving home at eleven-thirty. She'd tossed and turned, too furious to relax and then, finally, left Debi and Mrs. Pennyworth to slumber peacefully while she went to the Institute to type up her resignation letter. Now it was one-thirty, and Suzanne had it all planned: she'd leave it on his desk tonight and never have to see the man again. She felt sorry for him in a way, sure, but that didn't alter the fact that he was suffering from paranoid delusions and utterly impossible to work for. She'd be filling in Jacobi too; a prestigious place like the Institute didn't need a nut like Harrison Blackwood giving it a bad name.

She reread the sentence for the thousandth time. Oh, the hell with it! She yanked the paper from the carriage, signed and dated it, folded it, and slipped it inside the envelope already addressed: "Dr. Harrison Blackwood." If he wanted an explanation, he could just ask poor old Jacobi, who would get an earful from her tomorrow. She glanced at her watch and groaned. Today, that is. Maybe she'd be able to talk Dr. Jacobi into a transfer; but if not, she promised herself grimly, then, by God, she'd quit and she and Debi would be on the next plane back to Canton.

The thought caused tears to sting her eyes. She had wanted to come someplace totally new and different, someplace where she could start a new life, where there was nothing to remind her and Debi of Derek and all the pain he'd caused.

So much for that bright idea . . . Feeling very tired and very defeated, she laid her head down on the desk and prepared for a good cry.

The door opened suddenly. Startled, she jerked her head up and saw Blackwood, uncombed, unshaven, with dark shadows under his eyes. Apparently, he'd come straight here without stopping home; he hadn't even changed his clothes.

"I saw the light under your door," he said quietly. His mood was still as somber as it had been on the drive home, but at least now he was capable of rational speech. "Didn't mean to disturb you. I'm sorry."

"I'm not," she snapped, no longer caring if he saw just how angry she was. "I'm leaving." She licked the flap on the envelope, sealed it, and handed it to him.

He took it gingerly, holding it by the corner with two fingers as if it were something obscene. "What the hell is this?" But he was frowning as if he had already guessed.

She pressed her palms flat against the desktop and pushed herself into a standing position. "My resignation, Dr. Blackwood. I'm quitting."

Harrison winced as if she had slapped him. "You can't quit *now.*" He slipped the envelope into his shirt pocket and stepped closer to the desk. "There's something I have to try out on you first."

She laughed, a sharp, bitter sound. "There's *more?*" You're not satisfied with having dragged me off to the middle of nowhere chasing after God knows what? Or with having me drive all night—seven hours without a stop, without you uttering a single word?" By now she was shouting at him. *"What more could you possibly try out on me?!"*

"I'm sorry—" he began, but she waved him silent, leaning forward over the desk to vent her anger on him full force. "I worked hard, Blackwood, damned hard to get where I am. Being mistreated was *never* part of the job description." She walked around the desk and tried to get past him to the door, but he blocked her way.

"Suzanne, please . . ." His tone was conciliatory. "I need your help now more than ever. What would you say if I told you I could prove the aliens have come back?"

She considered this for a moment, then looked him in the eye and said, "Read my letter."

Anger darkened his features. "I'm *serious,* dammit!"

"All right, then," she replied with heated sarcasm. "First get a psychiatrist. Then read my letter."

He tried again to launch into an explanation; again, she refused to let him. "Harrison—" She hesitated, seeking the right words. They didn't come, so she blurted it straight out—still angrily, but without the nasty edge to her voice. "I'm *sorry* you lost your parents, Harrison. I'm *sorry* Norton lost his family. But you two are feeding each other's paranoia, trying to get revenge for something you simply can't. And you were looking to make it a trio. But I can't pretend, I can't play along!"

Whatever hurt flickered in his eyes vanished quickly, replaced by resignation. "Okay, Dr. McCullough. You seem to think I'm irrational. I'd like to show that *you're* the one who's not thinking clearly. Let's do this logically then, like scientists."

She raised an eyebrow skeptically. "I can't wait to hear this one."

"No, really," Harrison persisted. "Logically, there are two types of mistakes one can commit when making assumptions. One kind of mistake is to assume that something is true when, in fact, it is false. This is not a particularly serious error. For example, if I assume the aliens have come back, but they haven't really, what harm is there in that?"

"Just an enormous waste of time and effort and money," she said coldly. She already saw what he was getting at, and was frustrated that she did not have a rebuttal for him.

"All right." He spread his hands. "I'll grant you that. An enormous waste of time and effort and money. But what about the more serious type of logical error—to assume that something is false when, in fact, it's *true?* If we assume the aliens haven't returned when they actually *have,* we lose far more than just time and effort and money. We lose an entire *world.*"

She stared at him without answering.

"All right, Suzanne." He raised his hands in an infinitely weary gesture of surrender. "I can see that no matter what I say, you're not going to listen. I give up. I've upset you; I was thoughtless; I was wrong. But there's no need for you to quit the Institute. Let me talk to Ephram. I'm sure we can get you transferred to another department."

"Well . . . all right." She blinked at him, surprise replacing anger. She had not expected this calmly reasoned response after the incident at the army installation.

"And I promise," he continued, regarding her soberly, "to make an appointment with the resident

psychiatrist today. Now"—in the same soothing tone
—"could I please just show you that proof I was
talking about? It's in my office."

She wavered for an instant. An alarming thought
popped into her head: *He's crazy . . . he's dangerous
. . . if he gets you alone in his office he might . . .*

He might what? *Good grief,* she scolded herself, *he's
not going to do anything there that he wouldn't do here,
in your office.*

"I'll give you two minutes," she told him firmly.
"And then I'm going home to get some sleep."

He seemed relieved. "Fair enough." Reluctantly,
she followed him down the hallway back to his office.
Inside, his desk and the two chairs next to it were
covered with dusty cardboard boxes stuffed full of
yellowed file folders. The room was filled with an
unpleasantly moldy, musty smell. He bent down and
transferred the boxes from the chairs to the floor and
motioned for her to sit. She did so warily.

He sat behind the desk, resting a hand on the side of
one of the boxes. "Permission to give a little background first," he said, eyeing her askance.

"Go ahead."

Harrison ran his fingers through his light brown
curls and turned his face to stare at the dark window-
pane. A muscle in his lean jaw twitched as he spoke.
"My parents were killed when the alien invasion was
only three days old. They were colleagues of Dr.
Clayton Forrester. In fact, this was my father's office."
Which explained the ancient nameplate on the door.
Harrison turned to glance affectionately at his sur-

roundings, then patted the cardboard under his hand. "Clayton Forrester was practically my second father anyway; after my folks died, he raised me. I grew up smothered in this research, listening to Clayton's theories . . . seeing how broken he was when nobody took him seriously. He said that if the aliens invaded once, they could do it again. No one wanted to hear that."

"But the bacteria—" she interrupted.

Harrison smiled hollowly at her. "Ah, yes, the famous bacteria. Clayton led a team of scientists whose intent was to do exhaustive research on the aliens, learn everything possible about them. The microbiologist and zoologist working with him both noted that the alien remains—even the tissue samples —didn't show any decomposition. They suggested that perhaps the aliens weren't dead—at least, not death as we know it. Forrester released their preliminary report to the government. It begged for more funding so that an adequate investigation of this phenomenon could be conducted." He pulled a thick document out from under a box and handed it to her.

She took it somewhat skeptically and glanced through it. It seemed to be what he said it was.

"The government's response to this report?" Harrison asked, his voice full of irony. "They didn't like what Forrester and his people were saying. Instead of expanding the research, the government cut Forrester off, then confiscated all alien remains and sealed them in steel drums. Out of sight, out of mind. What you've heard—the party line that we know everything there is to know about the aliens—is an outright lie, Suzanne. You wouldn't be repeating any research that's already been done; after all these years, we know virtually *nothing* about them." He leaned forward with such urgency that Suzanne, still scanning the report, jumped a little. "But you saw those barrels at the Jericho Valley site."

"Yes, I saw them," she said gently. "That's where my charge of paranoia comes in. I admit, the government was wrong to ignore Forrester, and maybe you have some reason to be a little paranoid after all. But as far as Jericho Valley's concerned, it seems clear to me that terrorists removed those barrels for their own purposes. To think that aliens popped out of them . . . well, I admit, the barrels were old and rusty—they even had *1953* stamped on them. But that doesn't mean *they're* the barrels that contained alien remains."

His ice-blue eyes shone with such fierce intensity that she thought, *He is mad . . . at least a little.* "Can you remember what was stamped on those barrels? It's important, Suzanne. Can you remember?"

She closed her eyes. She had an excellent memory for visual detail, and as the image of the monitor close-up of the rusty, overturned barrel coalesced before her, she read aloud: "CLASSIFIED: 1951–1953. That's all."

She opened her eyes to find him grinning hugely at her. "Very impressive, Dr. McCullough. You've just made proof very easy."

"I'm waiting. It's already been two minutes." But

her tone was kinder; maybe he was a little nutty, but he was somewhat justified in it.

Harrison jumped up and riffled through one of the cardboard boxes on the desk, found what he wanted, and presented it triumphantly to her. She took it from him and squinted at it.

"This," he said emphatically, "is what the barrels looked like when they were new. Clayton tried his best to document for history's sake what the government did with the remains. Most of *those* records were destroyed by the government . . . but this picture remains."

It was an old black and white photo, fading and curled at the edges. On the back, a date was stamped in red ink: 10/23/53. The front showed a stack of shiny, unpainted steel drums, all bearing the same legend across their sides:

CLASSIFIED: 1951–1953

She stared at it silently for a long time.

Harrison was watching her keenly. "Those barrels are *empty* now, Suzanne, and they looked as if they'd been forced open from the *inside* . . . remember?"

She remembered. An old terror welled up inside her, clutched at her throat, the same terror she'd felt as a child after Uncle Matthew's death, as she waited in bed beneath the covers for the aliens to make their way across the country and come for her too. When she could speak, she whispered, "My God. Oh, my God . . ." She put her hands to her face. "It can't be true . . ."

"I wish I *were* crazy," Harrison said sadly. "Six of

these same barrels are now empty, and the rest of them are missing. *Hundreds* of them, gone." He came around the desk and crouched next to her chair to gaze up into her face; she could see his concern about the effect this revelation was having on her.

"That's why I hired you," he told her. "To help me continue Forrester's research. To try to find out if it's possible the aliens aren't dead, but forced by the bacteria into a state of estivation or suspended animation or anabiosis. But something has happened to bring them out of it. The whole way home I was trying to figure it out, and I think I've got an idea. I wanted to bounce it off you."

She nodded, still stunned, and with that one little gesture she felt as if she had somehow stepped over an invisible line, that from now on things could never go back to being as safe and familiar and comfortable as they had always been.

He put a hand on the arm of her chair and leaned forward, his face excited and alive, suddenly free of fatigue, the face of a man doing what he was born to do. "Jericho Valley was hot with radioactivity, right? Maybe that did it. Maybe the microbes that infected the aliens were wiped out from the exposure." He paused, and when she didn't answer immediately, asked: "Well? You're the microbiologist. Am I way off base?"

She found her voice at last. "I suppose it could be possible, depending on the circumstances." She paused. "Have you ever heard of the African lungfish?"

He shook his head.

"The lungfish can survive without water for at least four years and maybe as much as ten. It goes into such a profound state of anabiosis that the average person would think the fish was long dead. But if you pour water over it, it's like a resurrection. The fish is alive and swimming again."

His eyes lit up hopefully. "So you *don't* think I'm a nut case."

"Definitely a nut case," she answered dryly. "But that doesn't make you wrong. Still, the radiation would have to have been extremely intense to kill off all the microorganisms inside those steel drums. Far too intense to permit those soldiers to wander around inside that base, even with their radiation suits."

"The barrel I saw looked corroded, as if something had eaten away at it. Ironhorse said one of the new barrels was leaking radioactive waste. If it leaked onto one of the older barrels . . ."

"That sounds like a real possibility. That alien corpse you want dissected—we could irradiate that and see what happens. Now, *that* would be ironclad proof—"

"I'm afraid not." Harrison shook his head. "Remember, it's been frozen for years . . . and its head—or the area that should correspond to its head—was crushed somehow, probably in a collision when it became ill and lost control of its ship. I doubt we could get a rise out of it."

"Damn," she said softly. "Then where do we start?"

"We'll think of something." Harrison stood up. "We've got to figure out a plan of action to stop them quickly. They don't have their ships and their weapons this time, but they're organized—and they're intelligent."

"Any specific suggestions?" She got up from the chair and put the report under her arm, intending to take it home, then yawned, surprising herself. She clamped a hand over her mouth. "Sorry."

"Don't apologize—we're both tired. In terms of specific recommendations, I think we'd better start by getting some rest. I'm about three naps behind, myself."

"I can't just go home and go to sleep without knowing we've got some kind of plan to stop them."

"We'll figure something out." Harrison shrugged. "Time may be of the essence, but I'm frankly too tired to think straight right now—"

She kept talking without hearing him. "We've got to contact the government and get help on this."

He sighed and nodded reluctantly. "I know. I hate doing it because they're the ones responsible for this mess in the first place, but I was going to look through Clayton's files and see if I could find a name, someone, anyone to contact at the Pentagon— But I'm afraid they'll all be retired or dead by now, in which case we have to start at the bottom." He shook his head, frustrated. "Dammit, it's all going to take too much time."

The idea descended on her full-blown. "Wait a

minute. I know a *very* important general back east at the Pentagon. He'd be more than willing to do me a favor."

He raised a sardonic brow. "And now you're going to tell me he's just a good friend, right?"

"Of the family," she snapped. "Let's just say he knows my father *very* well. He could be of enormous help to us. General Wilson. His job is to cut through red tape."

Harrison sighed and rubbed his face wearily. "Only if he's a good enough friend to keep from getting us caught up in the bureaucracy. I want free rein in this. If it looks like a government agency is going to tie our hands, I'll run the other way."

"I believe I could get *us* free rein," she replied, correcting him.

"All right then. Get in touch with him."

"Just give me time to make arrangements with the sitter and get some sleep. If we could leave tomorrow night—I mean tonight—" She broke off, suddenly overwhelmed by it all.

"That's the spirit." He put a hand lightly on her shoulder and glanced pointedly at the report. "I take it you're not still thinking about that transfer?"

She pulled the envelope from his shirt pocket and, smiling, ripped it in two.

Suzanne got back home at three A.M. The hallway was an obstacle course of half-unloaded moving boxes, so she snapped on the light in order to get to her bedroom without waking the entire neighborhood. At least she'd be able to unload the boxes with a greater sense of finality now: this was home after all. She would stay in California and she would work with Harrison Blackwood. The certainty brought with it a sense of relief.

She slipped her flats off and held them in one hand as she tiptoed past the guest room. The door was cracked open; a strong, wheezing snoring came from inside. Mrs. Pennyworth. Suzanne smiled. Apparently, the elderly woman was a sound sleeper.

A few steps down, the door to Deb's room was ajar. The hall light was shining right into Deb's face, but the kid never stirred. Took after her dad, who always slept like the Rock of Gibraltar, regardless of the circumstances. Suzanne had always envied them that particular talent. She leaned against the doorway and watched as Deb breathed through parted rosebud lips in regular little sighs. The girl was sprawled on her side, clutching her pillow, her forehead puckered into a frown, her hair, glinting gold where the light caught it, spilling over her face.

Suzanne was overcome by enormous guilt at the thought that by the time Deb woke up, she'd find out her mother was going to be leaving again that night . . . but then the guilt was counterbalanced by a stronger, more savage emotion. She thought of what Harrison Blackwood must have been like as a kid. Young, so much younger even than Deb. And what it must have been like for him . . . so young, and all alone.

It'll never happen to you, kid, she promised Deb silently. *If I have to spend the next year traveling around the country in cars and planes, I swear, I'll never let it happen again.*

It was a very long time before she finally got to sleep.

THIRTEEN

The tracks at the Jericho Valley site matched up with those of a vehicle stolen from a trucking company warehouse two days earlier. A missing employee, Lena Urick, was suspected. It wasn't reported stolen until the next day, but amusingly enough, the police had stopped it shortly after it was stolen, before the bulletin was released.

And then just a few hours ago, HQ had monitored a call in to the San Bernadino County Sheriff's Office: The big white rig had been spotted at a gas station just off Route 15. The attendant was missing, presumed kidnapped.

A hostage, Ironhorse decided as he rode in the jeep alongside Reynolds, who drove silently while the colonel leaned back and felt the cool night air on his face.

The jeep was followed by a troop carrier full of

soldiers; not his own men, not Delta force, but they would have to do. Might as well relax while he could; there would be no sleep for any of them tonight. But Ironhorse's mind remained restless; he couldn't quite pin down what the terrorists were up to. His best guess was that they had taken the nuclear waste to either (a) contaminate the drinking supply of a large city, or (b) threaten to release it somewhere near the center of a large town.

The Nevada state police were ready and on the lookout: there was no way the rig was going to make it across the state border on any of the main roads without being stopped at a checkpoint, but there had been no sign of it yet. Which made no sense; surely they realized by now that they had the entire military, the state police, and every sheriff within a radius of two hundred miles ready and waiting for them. They'd missed their chance.

That was what bothered him so much about the attack on Jericho Valley. If the terrorists had any brains—and obviously, these folks' combined IQ was a match for a head of iceberg lettuce—they'd have stayed put in the Jericho Valley spot and made their demands from there. Transporting that much highly radioactive material was an unnecessary risk; if they wanted to grandstand, they could easily have done so from Jericho, especially if that nut Blackwood had been right about their having sophisticated transmission equipment.

The tape was being analyzed now, and Ironhorse was impatient for the results, though regardless of whether a message had been sent or not, the whole scenario still didn't make any sense. And if there was one thing Ironhorse hated, it was an unsolved riddle.

A weird bird, Blackwood. After the man's hysterical departure, Ironhorse decided to dismiss the whole business about a transmission. But then, once inventory was taken on the barrels, it turned out Blackwood was right. Three hundred twenty of them *were* missing; the terrorists obviously had packed them into the rig. And something about the sight of the empty barrel had terrified Blackwood enough to send him running. *Just a nut case,* Ironhorse told himself again.

But instinct told him there was something wrong about this whole incident, something he definitely didn't like. He shook his head silently; next to him, Reynolds kept his focus straight ahead on the flat stretch of road illuminated by the jeep's headlights.

The headlights swept to the right as Reynolds maneuvered off the highway onto the graded curve of the exit ramp. The troop carrier's lights reflected off the rearview as it followed suit. The tiny gas station— four gasoline pumps, one diesel—lay just off the exit, in such easy view the owner hadn't invested in a neon sign. Next to the gas island, under the fluorescents, the sheriff and his deputy were interrogating a seedy-looking witness who gesticulated wildly to punctuate his story.

Reynolds pulled the jeep up just behind the sheriff's cruiser.

"Get me a reading with the Geiger counter," Ironhorse ordered, and climbed out of the jeep without waiting to hear Reynolds' faint, "Yessir, Colonel." Reynolds was tough, disciplined, command material;

if Ironhorse trusted anyone in the world other than himself to get things done, it was Gordon Reynolds.

Both the sheriff and the deputy regarded Ironhorse and his soldiers with a mixture of mistrust and awe. The man they were interrogating—a greasy-looking little alkie who reeked of stale booze and well-aged sweat—folded his arms triumphantly. "See? See what I tole ya? They've sent the army in."

"Evening, Sheriff," Ironhorse said without offering his hand. "Lieutenant Colonel Paul Ironhorse." He didn't address the deputy, a slight, weak-chinned individual; this was business between two superiors.

"Colonel." The sheriff nodded, tilting the brim of his Stetson slightly downward. He was a husky man with a broad face and shrewd, narrow eyes. "Sheriff Bobby Deak. This here's my deputy, Ernest Jenkins."

Ernest touched the brim of his hat; Ironhorse ignored him. Where he came from, a grown man would have called himself Robert or Bob, not Bobby, but this sheriff did not seem a stupid man. Perhaps the name and the casual good-ol'-boy demeanor were tactics to make others underestimate him.

"What brings the army out this way?" Deak asked with a trace of surprise.

"Your report that a stolen truck was sighted here," Ironhorse answered plainly. He would have said little more, except to start questioning the old drunk, but Reynolds came forward to scan the area. The Geiger counter in his hands buzzed loudly as he moved closer to the fuel pumps.

"They've been through here for sure, Colonel," Reynolds announced.

Ironhorse grunted. "Go ahead and scout the area."

"Yessir." Reynolds moved back to the parked troop carrier and started barking orders at those inside. The soldiers jumped out and began scattering.

"That doesn't really answer my question, Colonel," Deak said pleasantly, watching a dozen different flashlights swinging as the troops fanned out into the darkness surrounding the station. He was smiling, but there was an edge to his words. "If I can be of any help to you, I'd like to know."

Ironhorse relented. The guy seemed sharp enough; maybe it'd be best to work with him rather than around him. "We've had an incident involving suspected terrorists," he said finally. "There's a good chance they've been through this area."

"Terrorists!" the alkie exclaimed, taking a step closer to Ironhorse. The colonel caught a whiff of his breath—sour, putrid, reeking of booze. Ironhorse hated the smell of liquor; he was particularly sensitive to it, since he never touched the stuff himself, but had been exposed to it as a kid too damn many times on the reservation. He wanted to turn his head away but restrained himself in Deak's presence.

"Hot damn, I knew it!" The alkie's eyes glittered feverishly. "There's something strange going on here, Colonel, and I'm glad to see they've called the army out."

Deak rolled his eyes skyward. "Orel Ralston here says he was a witness, Colonel, but . . . I'm afraid even *he* admits he wasn't too sober at the time."

Orel pointed a scolding finger at Deak and shook it

with gusto. "I may have been drunk at the time, Sheriff, but you're leaving out something very important—what I saw sobered me right up!" He hung his head, his sharp features contorted suddenly with grief. "I saw Doc Waller, my only real friend in the whole world, killed." He covered his face with yellowed bony hands. The fingernails had black dirt under them.

"You can't believe anything Orel tells you," the deputy interjected, his tone one of contempt. "He's just an old drunk—"

"Go to hell, Ernie Jenkins," Orel said, peering up between spread fingers. "I know you. You went to high school with my daughter, Sally. She used to tutor you in English, remember? You woulda flunked right out of eleventh grade if it hadn't been for her."

Ernie's face colored, and his thin lips pursed so tightly they almost disappeared. He fell silent.

Ironhorse folded his arms; quietly he stated, "I'd just like to hear what Mr. Ralston has to say . . . without any interruptions. From the beginning, please, Mr. Ralston."

Orel looked up gratefully, his dirty face streaked with tears. "Thanks, Colonel. I was sleepin' over in that Ford over there"—he pointed to a large white car parked over in a corner of the station—"and I woke up suddenlike. See, Doc—he's the station owner here—he lets me sleep . . . usedta let me sleep in one of the cars on the evenings I was too . . . inconvenienced, you might say."

"Drunk as a skunk, you mean," Deak interjected.

Orel ignored him and went on. "Anyway, I woke up suddenlike because I heard this big truck pull up to the station. Don't ask me why, but I looked up to see what was goin' on . . . and I seen this big truck at the pump, fillin' 'er up with diesel."

"Describe the truck and any passengers," Ironhorse said.

"Well . . ." Orel gazed up and to the right, remembering. "It was a big tractor-trailer. White, I think—at least the trailer was. I couldn't see the plates."

"What was the name on the truck?" Ironhorse asked. A trick question; so far the guy had the description down pat.

Orel thought. "Weren't no name. Just a plain white trailer."

Bingo. A perfect match for the police description, except for the California plates. Orel Ralston may have been drunk at the time, but he'd remembered all the important details. Ironhorse persisted, pleased with his luck so far. "What about the people?"

"This is the terrible part. There were two men— one of 'em wearing a white overall thing, one of 'em all in black. And a blond-haired woman, dressed in white. They were walking toward Doc like they were fixin' to kill him. It was awful . . ."

Orel grimaced and made a noise like a sob, then ran a shaking hand over his red, rheumy eyes. "They looked . . . awful. Awful sick. Pale. Like they was dyin'. I thought maybe they worked at one of them newkewler dump places and there'd been an accident or somethin'. And . . . well, I don't like to mention this, but . . ." He gave the colonel an embarrassed glance, ducked his head, and lowered his voice. "The folks in white, I could see—looked like they puked or shit all over themselves. Woulda puked myself at the sight of 'em if I hadn't been scared to death for poor Doc."

Good God, a description. And of people suffering from radiation sickness to boot—it had to be the terrorists who overran Jericho Valley. This was better than Ironhorse had expected. He leaned forward with interest. "Three people. Can you describe them in more detail?"

"Uh . . . yeah. The woman had blond hair. Reckon I said that already. Young, maybe thirty. Actually woulda been pretty if she hadn't been so sick. The two men—one had kinda brown hair, and one was kinda dark—like you. Only not an Injun. Not Mexican either, I don't think. Somethin' foreign, maybe Italian." Orel shook his head.

"But I haven't told you the awful part yet. They were comin' toward Doc, and he put his hands up, trying to get away from 'em . . . but there was somethin' awful that came up behind him and got him, picked him right up by the throat and throttled him like he was an old rag doll." Orel grimaced again at the memory.

"Some*thing?*" Ironhorse prompted. "What exactly do you mean?"

"*This,*" Deak said cynically, folding his arms, "is where it gets good."

"It's true," Orel burst out, a fresh tear streaking

down his face. "I seen it. It was . . . an awful-lookin'
thing. An animal, I guess. About the size of . . . hell, I
don't know, about the size of a gorilla, maybe. Except
it didn't have no hair or real arms or legs. It was like a
big ugly leather sack, wet-lookin', and it walked on
these skinny ropes for legs. It musta come outa the
truck, because the people helped it; they backed Doc
right up to it. And that thing put one of its rope-legs
around Doc's neck and—" Orel buried his face in his
hands.

"Fuckin' drunk," the deputy muttered, and shook
his head.

Which was Ironhorse's impression as well, but there
was something about the old man's story . . .

As a child, he'd been told tales about the strangers
who came from the stars to visit judgment upon the
white man, to steal the land from the whites the way
they had stolen it from Ironhorse's people. The man
had described the creatures in remarkably the same
way as Paul's grandfather, except that his grandfather
had called them "bears-with-three-arms," or "star-
bears." The bears-with-three-arms had spared the
reservations, attacking only the whites' cities; and
then they had all died, killed not by the white people,
but by their own greed. Unfortunately, the whites had
not learned from the star-bears' example during the
past thirty-five years . . .

And, of course, there was the very brief reference in
history class at West Point. The invasion of '53, they'd
called it, and tried to blame the whole thing on the
unpreparedness of the American military. That was
when young Ironhorse learned he could not dismiss

his grandfather's story as legend, that the star-bears really had come and laid the white man to waste . . .

Coincidence, Ironhorse told himself. Just coincidence. The old guy's brain was pickled. A lucky thing he'd been able to identify the truck, though.

"And then they took Doc's body with them?" Deak prompted Orel gently, but with no small amount of skepticism.

The old man nodded without looking up, his wrinkled face contorted with horror at the memory of what he described. "It was awful what that thing done to him . . . it went all liquidylike, and covered Doc's face and chest . . . and then, suddenly, it just seemed to seep right into him. And Doc, poor dead Doc . . ." Orel sobbed loudly and trembled. "He opened his eyes again and got up, and it was just like he wasn't dead no more. Only I knew better."

While the old man spoke, Deak narrowed his eyes to glance sideways at Ironhorse and shook his head. Ironhorse did not respond.

"Well," Orel continued, "then I hid back down in the car. I was afraid they were gonna come for me next. I think I musta stayed in the backseat, scared to death, for an hour before I got the nerve up to come out. When I did, Doc's body was gone."

That strained Ironhorse's ability to believe a bit too far. The old guy must have been pickled for sure. So much for the theory of the star-bears.

"Interesting thing." Deak addressed the colonel while Orel wept into his cupped hands. "Nothing ever happens in Brewster, except for an occasional shooting at the local bar. But there was another incident tonight—might be related to this. A doctor kidnapped right out of his house. He kept his medical office there . . . worked out of his home. There were signs of a struggle: someone broke the door down, came in, and got him. We found a handgun that had been fired on the floor. We're pretty sure he fired it at the intruders." Deak paused. "Frankly, Colonel, I'd like to know why these people would stop through here and take these two hostages—that is, assuming both men are still alive."

"You and me both," Ironhorse replied grimly. "Believe me, Sheriff, if I knew more about what they were doing, I'd let you know." Kidnapping the doctor made some sense, at least, in light of what Orel had said about radiation sickness—but the gas station owner was a mystery. The nuclear waste they were hauling provided enough of a bargaining chip for them; why take more precious time to pick up unnecessary hostages?

"Poor Doc," Orel sighed, drawing a finger under his nose and sniffling loudly. "He didn't deserve to die like that."

Deak leaned over and said into Ironhorse's ear, "You know what it's like. Ever since 'fifty-three, all the drunks have seen aliens instead of pink elephants."

"I wonder," Ironhorse said in a way that made Deak look at him sharply. There was something about the old drunk's story, something about the way Blackwood had run terrified from the van that made Ironhorse decide there was much more to this incident, a much deeper mystery than appeared on the surface.

And he wasn't at all sure he was going to enjoy the act of discovering what it was all about.

The big rig shuddered to a halt as it arrived at its destination. Inside the trailer, Xashron sat with his back supported by a barrel and listened to the wind howl outside while he waited with Xeera and Konar. They had come to a consensus during the long journey: soon the process of freeing the others would begin; soon Xashron would command hundreds of soldiers instead of two, and the Advocacy would fall.

On Mor-Tax, Xashron and his followers would be executed for daring even to speak of harming a member of the ruling class, but this was a new world, with new rules. What mattered now was that the invasion was successful, that no more soldiers died needlessly. And time was also a crucial factor: in its enthusiasm, the Council had launched a shipload of carriers the second day of the invasion, after Xashron had reported to his superiors that victory was theirs. The delicate carriers would arrive on Earth within a matter of a Terran year; Xashron would see to it that their mission to populate the Earth with Mor-Taxans was fulfilled.

The rear door of the rig rumbled upward. Outside, in the night wind that mercifully obliterated any tire tracks, stood Xana and Horek; beyond them, a large white house and a structure Xashron's host brain identified as a barn sat on a vast stretch of uncultivated but fertile-looking terrain.

Xana's host body appeared exhausted; her voice faltered as she addressed Xashron as one superior to another. "The Advocacy wills the others to be revived."

*She glanced meaningfully at Xashron as if to remind
him of his earlier promise. "We will do so here. But first
we must take a few days to rest and feed, and the
physician will tend to your host bodies so that the
effects of the radiation will be minimized."*

*Xashron rose on wobbly legs. His white coverall was
damp and smelled of bile and other excreta from the
host's body. He and his companions had been violently
ill during the journey, retching until nothing more
came. He had surrendered some control of the host's
nervous system so as to avoid feeling the pain: this
human body burned with fever, and the sensation
brought back unpleasant memories of the plague that
had defeated them. If the body became much weaker,
Xashron would be forced to abandon it.*

*"As you wish, Advocate," he answered with difficulty,
supporting himself against a steel barrel.*

*Xana nodded weakly, the wind ruffling her short
golden hair. She and Horek turned and headed back
toward the front of the truck.*

*"You heard the will of the Advocacy," Xashron said
to the others as he stepped outside into the windy night.
The sky above them flashed with heat lightning; there
came a distant rumble. "Let us go to the physician first,
so that our host bodies will be made stronger."*

*They would need all their strength for the struggle
ahead.*

FOURTEEN

Why do I love her? Harrison asked himself the next evening, pausing in the midst of his packing to gaze at Charlotte Phillipson again. She sat on the tie-dyed cotton bedspread of the narrow twin bed in his spartan little bedroom. She'd once referred (with no small amount of disdain) to his decorating scheme as early-American college-student/hippie. There was still no carpet on the floor, and no furniture out in the living/dining area except for the heavy mahogany dining room set his parents had left him. Char had tried to pick up the hippie theme by giving him an original Peter Max print which Harrison despised but left hanging in the living room for her sake.

Now Charlotte sat on the bed, looking gorgeous and leggy in a short pink cashmere dress and a long strand of pearls; clouds of Giorgio perfume wafted toward Harrison every time she moved. But her beauty was compromised by the fact that she sat stiff, erect, so disapproving and withdrawn that the universe seemed to curve inward near her. She gripped herself tightly and stared with cold, reproachful eyes at Harrison.

At the moment his question really had him stumped. He'd known earlier—just a few days it had seemed—why he loved her, but he seemed to have forgotten. *Because she has a good sense of humor?*

He studied Char's baleful expression. Hunh-uh. Scratch that one.

Because she never tries to manipulate me?

Correction. You *thought* she didn't try to manipulate you . . . until that damn party, where you found out she was hoping you'd be impressed enough to want to work for that company.

Because she's attractive?

For now it seemed the most promising explanation he could come up with.

Since the threat of the aliens had become real once again, Char and all the things she cared about dwindled in importance for him. She seemed so petty sitting there, and he realized with surprise that in the back of his mind he'd been comparing her to Suzanne McCullough and finding Char lacking (which would have thrilled Clayton no end). Maybe if he swore Char to secrecy and explained what was going on, she would understand.

Yet part of him was certain that if he did explain, Char would argue with him that the things *she* cared about were still more important. Char, with her silly parties and her social life, somehow made the ugliness

200

of what the aliens had done, of what they might do, seem very unreal.

Perhaps that was why he loved her . . . or thought he did. Maybe he didn't love her seriously at all. He'd kept the relationship light and airy on purpose—William Powell and Myrna Loy reincarnate—possibly because he was afraid of losing anything really precious to him. He stared at Char and thought, *If she left today, I would survive* . . .

He knew that somehow wasn't right.

"I can't believe you're doing this," Char said in her carefully cultivated, throaty voice while Harrison stuffed a few pairs of Jockey low-rise briefs into the zippered pouch of the hanging bag in his closet. He'd packed a navy jacket and khaki pants; he figured that would be fancy enough for the uptight folks in D.C., but he wasn't sure. Normally, he would have asked Char's advice on what to pack—he had no patience figuring out such things—but it didn't seem appropriate at the moment.

"After dashing off from that party night before last, then taking off for God knows where," Char went on, "you expect me to believe you can't take an hour right now to talk to me. Frankly, Harrison, I'm beginning to think you're avoiding me on purpose."

"Don't be ridiculous, Charlotte," he said curtly, zipping the pouch up. He'd taken a two-hour nap, but fear and exhaustion still left him on edge; at the moment he didn't have the patience to soothe her hurt feelings. "You know I'd never do that. Something has come up at work."

"Look at you." She gestured at him with perfectly

manicured hands, the nails hot pink, long, sharp. "You're spending twenty-four hours a day working for that damn Institute, yet they pay you peanuts. Don't you realize that at Bleaker-Williams you could quadruple your salary and work reasonable hours?"

Harrison felt his face harden. "Char, don't ever mention that place again. You know how I feel about what they do. And you know I don't give a shit about working nine to five."

"I went to a lot of trouble to get you that job offer!" she blurted angrily.

Stunned, he gaped at her. From her tone of voice, it was clear she considered him an ingrate. "So . . ." he said softly. "It wasn't *their* idea, after all, was it? I'm amazed at you, Charlotte. Amazed." He shook his head in disgust and went back to packing with renewed energy. "I'm not going to discuss my choice of career with you or anyone else. Case closed."

"Dammit!" she cried, jumping up from the bed so that the strand of pearls swung, clicking. "Your career affects *us,* Harrison. It's *us* we have to talk about."

He glanced at his watch and very coolly replied, "The plane takes off for Washington in forty-two minutes. I barely have enough time to pick up Suzanne and make it to the airport. The discussion is going to have to wait." It was a lie—the plane wouldn't leave for another ninety minutes—but he'd had enough of this particular argument.

"And that's more important than *us?*"

There was a spoiled, whiny note in her voice that he found irritating. She was trying to force him into an either/or situation, and no way in hell was he going to let her do it. He turned his back to her and started rummaging through the closet to choose a tie; he had no idea what would match the navy and khaki, so he pulled out the closest one, a yellow silk Dior she'd given him. He waited until he could keep the anger from his voice, then said, his back still to her, "It's not that cut and dried, Char. What I'm doing right now is crucially important to you, to me, to everyone. It makes all this"—he gestured expansively with an arm at the room, the world around him,—"seem very irrelevant."

"Irrelevant!" she gasped. "*We're* irrelevant?"

He faced her. "Don't twist what I said. I can't tell you why I have to go yet, but when I do, I know you'll understand." He zippered the bag up and pulled it from the closet. "I've got to leave."

"I want to understand *now*," Char said petulantly.

He shook his head. "There just isn't any time to talk about it now."

"No time—!" She turned away for a moment; when she faced him again, her expression had darkened. "Harrison, I swear—" Her tone was dangerous, threatening. "If you leave like this, it's over for us."

It was all so melodramatic, so petty that he half laughed, shook his head in disbelief, and spread his hands. "Charlotte . . ." he began helplessly. This wasn't the woman he knew; this was someone else, a spoiled brat that he didn't like very much. "Look at you, Char, you're positively seething. This is all so ridiculous."

The laughter made her even more furious; her green eyes narrowed. "Dammit, I *mean* it!"

"Ultimata don't become you," he said in a feeble attempt at lightness. "We can discuss it when I get back."

She trembled and clenched her fists. "You *ass*hole!" Why, she was having a temper tantrum! Just how skilled an actress was she, to have hidden this side of herself from him for almost two years?

She was gasping with anger, frowning so hard her brows were touching, her face contorted; at any moment he expected her to start stamping her feet. For some perverse reason, her overly childish reaction struck him as outright funny, and he snickered before he could stop himself. It was the worst possible thing he could have done, of course. She wheeled around on one hot-pink heel and headed out.

Harrison dropped the bag on the bed and followed, reaching after her. He caught her gently, firmly, by the wrist and walked around to face her. "C'mon, Char, be reasonable."

For a moment he thought she was going to claw his eyes with those sharp pink nails, but then she relaxed in his grasp and looked sulkily at him. "No, *you* be reasonable." Translation: Do it my way.

The laughter had eased his anger; now he was merely disgusted with her, but in control of himself. One of them had to play the adult here, and it obviously wasn't going to be Charlotte. Harrison turned her palm up, kissed it, then let go of her hand. "Looks to me like we're having a major disagreement here. But there simply isn't time to resolve it now. I'll call you when I get to the hotel." He leaned down and tried to kiss her, but she pushed him away, her expression so cold and hateful it took his breath away.

"Don't bother." Her tone was clipped, icy. "Good-*bye, Harrison.*"

She strode out, the strand of pearls dancing from side to side. This time he didn't try to stop her but stood staring at the empty doorway, not quite able to believe that she had really been serious.

"Well, *shit,*" he said finally. He picked his bag up from the bed and went to catch his plane.

Already bathed and in the long Minnie Mouse T-shirt that served as pajamas, Deb lay sprawled on her stomach in front of the TV watching a rerun of *Three's Company.* The volume was turned up to an obnoxious level; Deb stared sullenly at the screen without seeing it, chin resting on one hand, which rested on a clean college-ruled page in her open three-ring binder. A paperback edition of *Macbeth* stood spine side up atop a hardcover volume of *An Introduction to Algebra.*

Behind her, Suzanne staggered into the foyer and eased the heavy suitcase down by the front door, then frowned in the direction of the blaring TV. Mrs. Pennyworth was expected momentarily; Harrison, in about fifteen minutes. She'd finally wakened around noon, feeling as if what had happened last night were all part of a horrible dream. The shock of it had faded, leaving her with an odd sense of unreality. Even after Harrison had called with the travel arrangements, she still had trouble believing it was really true, that

Harrison's paranoid fantasies were neither paranoid nor fantasies, that somewhere only a few hundred miles away, the aliens were making plans for a new attack.

It was especially hard to believe now, here, watching the *I Love Lucy*–type antics on the screen in this all-too-normal domestic setting. Deb had been thrilled to see her mother at first; then, after the announcement that Suzanne was leaving again, she'd settled into a protracted moping session. The TV, with its ridiculous volume, Suzanne knew, was a none-too-subtle display of hostility. Deb hated that particular show and never watched it.

"Deb," she said, walking into the living room. No response; Debi was pretending not to hear. She spoke louder, enough to make herself heard over the roar of the laugh track. "Deb! Turn that down, please."

Deb rose languidly and complied without looking at her mother.

"Doesn't look to me like you've done your homework."

"No," Deb murmured. She was a lousy liar, like her mother, and therefore usually didn't attempt it.

"You know the rule," Suzanne said firmly, doing her best not to look surprised. She hadn't invoked the TV rule in at least a year. Deb was an A student (one way at least that she did *not* take after her father) who did her homework cheerfully, without being told, then read voraciously in her free time; her appreciation of television was limited to *Jeopardy* and *National Geographic* specials.

Deb muttered a little as she clicked off the TV. Blessed relief.

"What was that, young lady?"

Deb faced her mother grudgingly, face tilted down, hair falling in her eyes. "I don't understand. Why do you have to leave again so soon? You just got back."

"I'll be home day after tomorrow, chicken." She moved over to the sofa near Deb and sat down. *Chicken* wasn't an accusation of cowardice, but a term of affection she'd picked up from Derek. She'd forgotten its origin . . . maybe it had had something to do with Suzanne being an old mother hen. *I will* not *feel guilty, dammit.* But it was too late, even though she'd gone over this a thousand times in her head last night and this afternoon. There was no cause for guilt . . . she *had* to go to Washington, pure and simple. It was the best thing she could do for Deb . . . and for herself and Harrison, for everyone.

"And *then* when will you leave again?" Deb whined.

She felt a minor surge of irritation at her daughter's petulant attitude, but the question caught her off guard. "I don't know. Maybe they'll let me stay home for a while after this."

Deb's tone was snotty, entirely unlike her. "You still didn't say *why*."

"You can knock off that tone of voice right now, Deborah Anne," Suzanne warned. "I'm not leaving because I want to. I'd much rather stay here with you. But it's my job and I have to do it. I can't discuss it with you because it's a secret, like my job in Ohio. You're grown-up enough to understand that. And frankly, I already feel rotten about having to leave you with Mrs. Pennyworth like this. I wouldn't do it unless what I had to do was very, very important."

"More important than *me*?"

Suzanne stood up; somehow, she managed to keep her voice calm. "Deb, you *know* that isn't true. You're the most important thing in the world to me. But that's a cruel thing of you to say. If you're going to keep trying to make me feel worse than I already do, maybe it'd be better for you to go pout in your room before you say something to make me lose my temper."

Deb looked up at last, stricken, and said in a wavering little voice, "Mom, I'm sorry. I don't mean to make you feel bad too. It's just that . . ." The corner of her trembling mouth quirked down; a tear slid down the side of her nose.

"Poor old chicken." Suzanne held out her arms. "Come over here."

Deb came over and clutched at her; Suzanne sat down and situated her daughter in her lap. "Poor old chicken," she soothed, giving Deb a big hug and kissing the top of her head. The girl's hair was soft and fine and smelled of baby shampoo. "This has all been too much for you, hasn't it?"

Deb nodded, her face buried in Suzanne's shoulder.

"Were things any better at school today?"

"It's okay," Deb murmured. "There's one girl who's nice."

"I'm glad," Suzanne said. "That's a start. And I haven't forgotten about those new clothes. I promise you'll get them when I get back."

Deb sat up and shook her head. "I don't care about the clothes anymore," she said, her voice miserable but no longer accusatory. "I'm just tired of being alone, that's all."

"You'll be with Mrs. Pennyworth."

Debi sighed with the exaggerated disgust of an adolescent. "It's not the same, Mom. She's nice and all, but . . . she's *old*."

"So am I," Suzanne answered lightly. "What's that got to do with anything? She's a very interesting person. You ought to get to know her better."

"I guess I'll get the chance." The corner of Deb's mouth twisted up wryly in a feeble effort at good humor. She wiped the tears from her cheeks.

"That's my girl." Suzanne hugged her, overwhelmed with affection and a sense of panic. *If anything happens to me . . . good Lord, who would take care of Debi?* Suzanne's father was dead, her mother near seventy and living in a retirement community in Florida, too old to take care of a child, and Derek couldn't be trusted to do right by his own daughter. *That's it, McCullough,* she told herself. *You're simply going to have to stay alive.*

"I'll get it," Deb said with abrupt cheerfulness when the doorbell rang, and wriggled out of Suzanne's grasp to dash into the foyer. Suzanne watched her as she stood on tiptoe to peer through the peephole, then opened the door to let Mrs. Pennyworth in.

Please, God, she prayed; she was not a religious person, but there were times when she became so out of sheer desperation. *If we could just stop them in time . . . so Deb doesn't ever have to know.* More than anything, she wanted to spare her daughter the terror she had experienced as a child, waiting in the dark.

Mrs. Pennyworth stepped into the living room carrying a small tan overnight bag. Her silver-blond hair was wound around her head in thick braided coils, giving her a distinctly Old World look from the neck up, which was immediately contradicted by the faded Levis and bright yellow Reeboks she wore. Suzanne rose.

"Let me take that to your bedroom for you, Mrs. Pennyworth," Debi offered gravely, thrusting out a hand. Suzanne smiled at her daughter. Such a good kid, after all she'd been through.

"Why, thank you, Deborah." Mrs. Pennyworth beamed as she handed Deb the overnight bag, then took the proffered seat next to Suzanne on the couch. "What a sweet daughter you have, Suzanne."

"She certainly is," Suzanne remarked as Deb scampered off with the bag.

"And now . . . will you be calling me from Washington to let me know where you are staying?"

"This time I've actually got the number of the hotel where I can be reached. The Crystal City Hyatt. I left it on the pad next to the kitchen phone. The flights are there too." She sighed, suddenly exhausted and overwhelmed by the thought of the journey ahead. "I should be back day after tomorrow, in the afternoon. Three forty-five I think is when the flight arrives."

Mrs. Pennyworth's light gray eyes regarded her with concern. "You seem very tired. I hope your trip is an easy one."

"Thanks." She ran a hand over her forehead; it was

warm, and the coolness of her palm was soothing. "So do I. I'm afraid this has all been a little rough on Deb, though; she's pretty upset that I'm leaving again. I hope she isn't any trouble."

"A bright child like Deborah is never trouble." Mrs. Pennyworth rested folded hands beneath her ample bosom. "Soon she will understand why you must take these trips."

"Dear God, I hope not," Suzanne whispered without thinking, a hint of fear in her voice.

Mrs. Pennyworth gave her a sharp look. After a pause she said, "I think you should know that Clayton Forrester was a colleague of mine. I also know Harrison very well. When I saw all this traveling in the middle of the night, all this urgency—well, it is enough to make an old woman like myself frightened."

She knew. Suzanne stared down at her own lap, feeling a curious mixture of relief and shock at the fact. She turned to face her. "I wish I could tell you something reassuring, Mrs. Pennyworth, but I can't." She propped her elbows on her knees and lowered her forehead into her hands. "It looks bad . . . very bad."

Mrs. Pennyworth bowed her head for a moment. "I see." She seemed to come to a decision, then looked back over at Suzanne. "If things get too dangerous, you call me, yes? That way, I can be sure to get Deborah to someplace that is safe."

Suzanne nodded, unable to speak.

"Mom?" Debi asked quizzically as she came back into the room. "Why are you crying?"

FIFTEEN

All of it—the flight, the taxicab ride to the hotel in Crystal City, an ugly patch of urban high-rises that sprouted up near the Pentagon, the restless night, the ride the next morning to the Pentagon with its endless parking lot, the waiting to get inside, the wait once inside to see General Wilson—all of it blurred into one hugely frustrating waste of time for Harrison. Everything was taking far too much time—and in the meanwhile, the aliens were free to roam the country-side, to make what plans they could.

And now, at approximately eight A.M. Eastern Standard Time, a bleary-eyed Harrison found himself staring across the polished sheen of the government-issue desk at Brigadier General Henry J. Wilson. This was it—quite literally, do or die. If they couldn't convince Wilson, then it was the three of them—he, Norton, and Suzanne—against God knew how many revived alien forces. Not good odds at all; and, for one of the very rare instances in his life, Harrison felt truly nervous. It didn't help matters that he hated the general instantly, and the way he figured it, he had at least three very good reasons to do so. First, because of the harm done Clayton Forrester and his project by the military; second, because Harrison had tried all last night and this morning to call Charlotte and kept getting her answering machine; and third, because the general's face had lit up like the Fourth of July at the sight of Suzanne. He'd climbed out of his chair, the smug bastard, and given her a bear hug right in front of Harrison. Then Suzanne had shocked him by giving Wilson a chaste (hah!) peck on the cheek. Oh, they tried hard enough to make it look like an affectionate sister-brother, haven't-seen-you-in-a-long-time sort of embrace, but Harrison knew better.

And then Wilson had introduced himself without even having the decency to look embarrassed at his lechery. Obviously, the man wasn't one to give a damn about appearances. A wonder he'd ever made it this far in the military.

And so, Harrison narrated silently, glancing at Suzanne in the chair next to his, *the staid, upright Dr. McCullough reveals the truth about her less-than-upright past.* And he resented Wilson for it. Resentment, or jealousy?

Oh, hell, Blackwood, knock it off. Who cares that he's old enough to be her father? None of your damn business. Besides, you've got another woman you're supposed to be worrying about at the moment.

Wilson *was* old enough to be her father, of course,

with his salt-and-pepper hair and bushy eyebrows, and his pipe. He was a stocky, meticulous man in his starched uniform, and he had an air of importance about him—not arrogance or conceit, exactly, but the easy confidence of a man who is used to his every order being obeyed.

"So . . . Dr. Blackwood. I'm very interested in hearing what you have to say." His expression one of pleasant attentiveness, Wilson pulled a package of Borkum Riff from the top desk drawer and stuffed tobacco into the bowl of his pipe, then tamped it down with practiced skill. On the wall above his head, a boldly lettered sign proclaimed DESIGNATED SMOKING AREA. "I'm willing to listen because Suzanne here speaks very highly of you." He winked fondly at her. "Er . . . do you mind?" Wilson nodded at the pipe and looked questioningly at them.

"Not at all," Suzanne said; Harrison shook his head. Actually, he *did* mind, but for the time being, he wanted to stay on the general's good side.

"Nasty habit, actually," Wilson said cheerfully. "I've tried several times to quit, since the army's going to be smokeless by 1990, but not with much success. I may be forced into early retirement." He chuckled at his own humor.

Harrison cleared his throat, ignoring the curious look Suzanne was giving him—surprised to see him nervous, no doubt—and ran a finger under his collar. Damn tie. How could anyone think with one of these stupid things cutting off the blood flow to the brain? He never wore the torturous things, and had a good notion to pull it off right now. What the hell difference would it make? A lousy tie wouldn't be the deciding factor on whether or not the general believed what he had to say. Still, insecurity held him back.

"I had hoped you would listen, General, for the simple reason that what I have to say is vitally important to all of us . . . and to our national security." Harrison managed to say it respectfully enough so that the general didn't take offense but raised an interested brow.

Wilson struck a match, held it to the bowl, and sucked in. "Go ahead," he said between puffs. "You've certainly got my attention."

"All right." Harrison paused, choosing his words carefully. "Have you ever heard of the Forrester Project, General?"

Wilson drew on his pipe, one elbow resting on his desk, and furrowed his brow. "Forrester . . . that was a long time ago, wasn't it? Back in the fifties?"

"Nineteen fifty-three, to be exact." Harrison leaned forward, encouraged that Wilson should remember.

"We're talking about the invasion, then."

"The alien invasion, yes. I don't see why everyone in the military is so reluctant to say that word."

Wilson narrowed pale blue eyes behind a puff of smoke. "For a scientist, you have a tendency to overgeneralize, Doctor. I'm a military man, and I'm willing to say the word *alien*. But if the military is reluctant to use it, perhaps it's because of the hysteria that followed." He glanced from Suzanne to Harrison. "I'm sure you're both too young to remem—"

"*I* remember," Harrison interrupted hotly. "I was there." Suzanne shifted uncomfortably in her chair.

"I see." Wilson's teeth clicked against the stem of his pipe. He held two fingers to the pipe bowl to steady it as he spoke. "Well, I'm sorry to hear that. You must have been terribly young." His tone was sympathetic, but matter-of-fact. "Yes, I remember the Forrester Project. As a matter of fact, I'm old enough to remember it well—I had just enlisted. Forrester was the one who went around scaring people, saying the aliens weren't really dead. The army interred the aliens at great cost to the government to prevent a full-scale panic. I was on clean-up detail."

Out of the corner of his eye Harrison saw Suzanne cringe. "I kept my parents' surname," Harrison said, "but I'm Clayton Forrester's adopted son." His tone was heavy with repressed anger. "And he was right."

The pipe clicked against Wilson's teeth again as he digested this without any outward reaction. "That's a very startling claim. I trust you brought proof."

Harrison smiled thinly and reached for the brief-case by his feet. Handsome oxblood leather, another expensive present from Char he almost never used, like the yellow silk tie around his neck. He set the briefcase on his lap, snapped it open, and pulled out a file that he tossed onto Wilson's desk. "I'm glad you remember the Forrester Project; it saves me a lot of explanation. But there's a copy of the report issued by Forrester's research group in there, just to refresh your memory."

Wilson opened the file and began to glance through it.

"To summarize," Harrison continued, "Forrester was worried about the fact that the alien bodies and

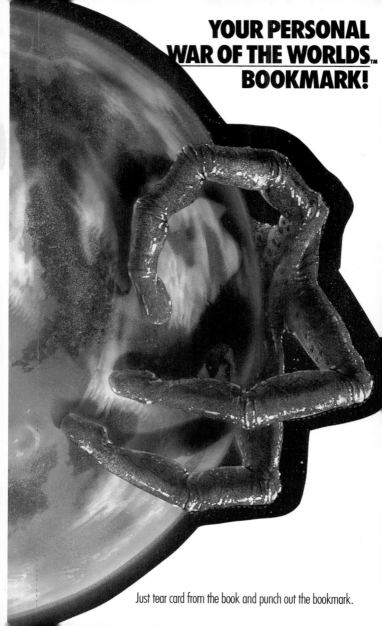

YOUR PERSONAL
WAR OF THE WORLDS™
BOOKMARK!

Just tear card from the book and punch out the bookmark.

DON'T MISS THE NEW WAR OF THE WORLDS. TELEVISION SERIES.

Printed in U.S.A.

They never left!

WAR OF THE WORLDS™
The Resurrection

Beginning Fall, 1988
Check your local television listings for time and channel.

tissue samples simply didn't demonstrate any deterioration as dead, decaying tissues should. It seemed as if they were in a type of"—he decided against using the scientific term for Wilson's sake—"suspended animation, so to speak. Forrester asked the government for funding to do more research, more analysis so that we'd know enough about the aliens to stop them the next time—"

"The next time?" Wilson asked with gentle surprise, and tilted his broad, jowly face up at Harrison.

Harrison smiled wryly. "I should have said, in the event of another alien attack." He shut the briefcase and put it back down by his feet. "It's not a particularly popular topic; Dr. Forrester and I have become used to being labeled paranoid." Next to him, Suzanne squirmed guiltily. "Why don't you just take a look at the old photographs in there, General?" He nodded at the file in Wilson's hands. "The ones of the barrels stamped 1953. I'll bet you can even tell me what's inside them."

Wilson riffled through the file and found what he was looking for. "I can," he said cautiously, scrutinizing Harrison. "But it's classified."

"Maybe," Harrison's tone became confidential, "you've also heard of a place called Jericho Valley."

Wilson put the file down and stared at Harrison with his full attention. "What do you know about Jericho Valley, Dr. Blackwood?"

Harrison and Suzanne glanced triumphantly at each other. So he'd finally struck a nerve. "It's a long story," Harrison began. "One of my colleagues intercepted a very unusual transmission emanating from inside the Jericho Valley installation. One that was answered—"

"By whom?" Wilson leaned forward across his desk.

"A resident of one of the star systems in the constellation Taurus. That's as much as we know right now. I gave a recording of that very transmission to a Lieutenant Colonel Paul Ironhorse—I suspect he's having it analyzed right now. A copy of the computer runs are in there for you." Harrison nodded at the file. "If you let your people look at it, they'll come to the same conclusion we did—that a bona fide communication took place."

Wilson unfolded the printout onto the desk; he studied it for a long time before he muttered, "Incredible." He addressed Harrison. "But I fail to see how this proves anything about your aliens."

"Unfortunately, I don't have pictures of the barrels I saw at Jericho Valley. Colonel Ironhorse let us have a look." At Wilson's sharp glance, he hastily explained. "Both Suzanne and I have the necessary security clearance to do so. Anyway, I noticed something very alarming. The barrels—the same barrels you see in that photo—were gone. Hundreds of them, vanished . . . and six of them were on their sides, empty —as if whatever was inside forced its way out."

"It's true," Suzanne volunteered. "I saw them too. I can verify that the markings on the empty barrels at Jericho Valley are identical to those on the barrels in the photograph."

"And if you don't believe us," Harrison added, heartened by the fact that Wilson actually seemed to be listening thus far, "you can check with a Lieutenant Colonel Paul Ironhorse to get the markings stamped on those barrels. The point of all this is, there was a nuclear waste spill at Jericho Valley. The place was hot with radiation. I believe the level was high enough to kill off the bacteria in the aliens' systems, which in turn brought them out of their suspended state." He stopped and anxiously searched the general's face for a reaction; Wilson's expression was one of concern but otherwise unreadable.

The general took his pipe from his mouth, set it in an ashtray, then leaned forward and folded his hands on top of his desk. "That," he said slowly, "is the most fantastic story I think I've ever heard."

"It's not a story," Harrison said desperately. God, he couldn't afford to be turned away now! "It's a scientific theory, supported by a body of fact, presented in a logical and reasonable fashion. I'm a respected astrophysicist"—he shook his head—"not some kook spouting stories about UFOs."

"I didn't mean to suggest otherwise, Doctor." Wilson paused to choose his words carefully. "The fact that you were brought here by my niece gives you more credibility than you realize."

"Niece?" Harrison did a double take, frowning first at Wilson and then at Suzanne. "I thought you said he was a friend of your father's." Why the hell hadn't she said anything? Here he was, thinking that she and Wilson were . . . well, anything but familial in their relationship. And he would have worried far less about their chances of getting help from the general if he'd known the guy was Suzanne's uncle.

Suzanne smiled sweetly at Wilson. "Uncle Hank is my father's favorite brother."

Wilson beamed back. "And you're my favorite niece."

Old home week. Encouraged, Harrison began to smile himself. "So you're willing to help us, General?"

The warm smile vanished; Wilson was all military again. "Unfortunately, Doctor, I'll need some hard evidence before I can act on your theory." He reached into the In box on one corner of his desk, fished out a thick manuscript, and started flipping through it. "Just this morning, as a matter of fact, I received a report on the incident you make reference to"—he broke off to scan a page—"which suggests the work of a terrorist group. Ah, here it is." He touched a thick stubby finger to the paper and squinted at it. "Can't read this damn small print without my glasses. The People's Liberation Party."

Harrison felt himself sink from triumph down into despair. He sat forward on the edge of his chair. "General, I've already given you evidence. And I'm trying to warn you about something a lot more dangerous than terrorists. Terrorists didn't leave with those barrels—the six revived aliens did."

"Just because those barrels were empty doesn't mean the aliens *walked* out, Doctor," the general replied patiently. "What real proof do you have that the aliens are alive? It's far more likely that the terrorists stole them."

"What possible use would terrorists have for them?" Harrison asked him angrily.

"To instigate panic, for one thing."

"And what about the transmission, General? How are you going to explain *that* away?"

"Try to look at it from my point of view, Dr. Blackwood—"

"No, look at it from mine!" Before he knew it, Harrison was on his feet bent over the desk, shoving his face into Wilson's. He was vaguely aware that he was shouting and that Suzanne was going through paroxysms of embarrassment, but he didn't care. In the back of his mind, a phrase kept repeating: *Clayton was wrong. I should never have wasted my time coming to Washington. Goddamn military, they'll kill us all through their stupidity. Goddamn military, they'll kill us all . . .*

"Please take your seat, Doctor," Wilson was repeating calmly, but Harrison ignored him.

"These creatures are completely ruthless, General, without mercy! They see us as something less than animals, an inconvenience to be done away with. Thirty-five years ago, they tried to take over the world, killed millions of people—and no one wants to remember! Well, I can't forget. They killed my parents —and, General, this time they won't stop until we're *all* dead. You, me, Suzanne . . ."

Wilson blinked at him and picked up his pipe again. "I'm sorry, Doctor." His tone was gentle.

Harrison stopped, slightly dazed by his own outburst, but unrepentant. Still leaning over the desk, he glared at Wilson. For a moment no one spoke.

"Bring me something concrete," Wilson said finally. "I'll see that it gets to the proper people. You have my word."

"There isn't time," Harrison told him bitterly. Concrete? Jesus, what more did the man want? Feeling defeated and furious, he wheeled around and strode out of the office, afraid if he stayed a second longer he'd say something to the general that even his niece would be unable to smooth over.

Yet, as furious as he was, his mind was already racing to find a solution to Wilson's challenge. *The son of a bitch wants hard evidence, huh? Then by God, I'll find a way to give him that if it's the last—and it probably will be—thing I do.* He didn't break his rapid stride until he was back out in the waiting area. It was devoid of people, save for a lone receptionist who was busily fielding incoming phone calls.

Harrison tore off the tie—*good riddance*—tossed the briefcase on a chair, opened it, and pulled out the portable phone. He dialed the Institute number, then checked his watch as he remembered the three-hour time difference. It was eleven-thirty here in D.C., which meant there was about a fifty-fifty chance that Norton would be there this time of the morning. Probably just setting the coffee up now.

The Institute switchboard operator answered.

"Extension 5900," Harrison said. Behind him came the sound of heels clicking against the uncarpeted floor at top speed . . . Suzanne. She walked up beside him, her scowl fiercely disapproving, her posture rigid, tight, angry.

"If you expect people to help you," she began in a low voice that rose in volume, "you'd better learn to be a hell of a lot more gracious. You were impossibly rude to my uncle back there."

222

"The world doesn't have time for graciousness," he snapped, so vehemently that she recoiled slightly. "The general wants concrete proof, does he? I suppose that means depositing a live alien on his desk! Well, by God, I'll get him one if that's what it takes! But we're giving them time, Suzanne, time they can use against us—we're giving them too much time!"

"Harrison!" Norton's voice came over the receiver. He was shouting in an effort to interrupt. "Harrison, did you call me just so I could listen to you and Suzanne arguing?"

He took a deep breath and forced himself to speak calmly. "Sorry, Norton."

There was a pause, and then Norton said, "Doesn't sound like things are going too well for us."

"They're not." Harrison met Suzanne's worried eyes and shook his head. "The army's decided our proof isn't enough. Looks like we've got some work to do."

Back at his desk, Wilson puffed thoughtfully on his pipe for a moment before reaching out to press the button on his intercom. "Ms. Underwood? See that I'm put on the President's afternoon calendar. Then connect me with Lieutenant Colonel Paul Ironhorse."

SIXTEEN

At eight o'clock the next morning, Suzanne, clutching an oversize mug of coffee she'd stolen from Norton, stumbled bleary-eyed down the corridor toward her office. She and Harrison had returned from the visit with Wilson the night before, and Suzanne hadn't been able to sleep well afterward; her mind had kept rehashing all the possible ways they could provide Uncle Hank with the evidence he'd requested, and as a result she was exhausted again this morning.

She pushed open the door to her office, reached to flick on the light switch—and frowned to find it already on. Odd. Someone must have been in here while she was gone—she never forgot to turn off the lights in her life. She turned and took a step toward her desk—and froze.

There was a strange man sitting in her chair, drinking a cup of coffee.

She headed for the door, her first impulse to call Security, but unfortunately, her phone was on the desk next to the stranger's right elbow.

He set his cup down on the desk, rose, and smiled disarmingly at her. "I'm sorry if I startled you. You must be Dr. McCullough."

Suzanne hesitated in the doorway and studied him suspiciously, not quite able to decide whether to head back down the hall in search of the guard. The visitor certainly didn't seem threatening: he was a lean, silver-haired gentleman who looked to be in his late sixties, clean shaven, affable, with an easy charm and rather handsome features. He was casually dressed in a blue cotton shirt and a pair of khakis.

"Yes, I'm Dr. McCullough . . ." she answered cautiously. "Just whom were you looking for?"

"No one in particular." The stranger picked up his coffee and came around the desk toward her; instead of feeling threatened, she got the odd impression that there was something very familiar about him. "I used to work here. This was my office before I retired, and, I have to admit, I was indulging in a bit of nostalgia. My apologies. Usually, the place is deserted until eight-thirty, nine o'clock." He paused. "You must be a very dedicated worker, Dr. McCullough."

She frowned, curious. "Do I know you?"

"I don't think so." He extended a hand. "Clayton Forrester."

"Dr. Forrester—" she repeated, surprised. No wonder he seemed familiar; Harrison had a picture of a much younger Forrester on his desk. She barely managed to stop herself from saying, *But I thought you were dead* . . . though, come to think of it, Harrison never had actually come right out and said as much. She took his hand; his grip wasn't very strong, and when she looked at him closely, he did seem rather pale. "I'm very honored to meet you, sir, but Harrison never mentioned that you would be coming."

"Harrison didn't know." Forrester gestured her toward her chair. "Please, sit. You don't mind if I rest a moment?" He sounded a little breathless.

"Not at all." She took her seat behind the desk and eyed him with concern, but Forrester already seemed recovered and was casually sipping his coffee. "Was this really your office, Dr. Forrester?"

He waved a hand at her. "Please . . . call me Clayton."

"Clayton," she repeated a little awkwardly. Now she understood where Harrison got the first-name habit from—as well as the khakis. "And my name is Suzanne."

"Yes, I know, Suzanne." He nodded. "Harrison has nothing but good things to say about you."

The corner of her mouth quirked cynically before she had a chance to stop it. "Really?"

He looked up from his cup, his soft brown eyes shining with faint amusement. "You sound surprised. You shouldn't be."

"Well . . . uh, I'm not, really. I have a lot of admiration for Harrison . . . professionally speaking, of course."

"Of course," Forrester agreed, his tone carefully

noncommittal. "Harrison is quite impressed with you. So am I. When I saw your résumé, I told Harrison he should hire you immediately." He paused. "Actually, I've come today because I was hoping to hear from Harrison last night, after he got back from Washington . . . and he's not answering his phone. Has a nasty habit of unplugging the damn thing when he's sleeping or doesn't want to talk to anyone. I'm assuming the worst—that you didn't get the help you were hoping for."

The mere mention of it reminded her of how tired and discouraged she felt. She took a large swallow of coffee and stared down into the cup, clutching it tightly as if to draw strength from it. "No," she said flatly. "But we're hopeful. The military wants proof, and we're going to find a way to give them just that."

"I see." Forrester nodded gravely; he stared at her so intently that after several seconds she fidgeted self-consciously in her chair. He noticed, and shook himself out of his reverie. "I'm sorry." He smiled apologetically and stared down into his cup. "It's just that—" He looked up at her. "You know, you remind me very much of someone who was close to me."

She felt herself starting to blush, but at the same time she was genuinely touched. "I do?"

He nodded, smiling wistfully. "Your cousin—your second cousin, I suppose. You're very much like her."

Sylvia, she realized, and tensed at the thought.

Forrester noticed her discomfort and said, "Sylvia was a very brilliant, warm woman. A very brave woman who went through more than anyone should

227

have to." His face darkened for an instant, but it passed quickly, and then he was smiling up at Suzanne again. "You must forgive me, Suzanne. I'm an old man, and old age brings with it a certain amount of freedom—such as the freedom to speak one's mind. I don't have time to beat around the bush anymore."

"Sorry?" she whispered. She couldn't quite follow, and assumed that he was rambling, a little bit senile. The thought embarrassed her even more.

But Forrester seemed quite cognizant of what he was saying. "Let me say what I've come to say. Harrison is an incredibly good, caring man—I know, I raised him. But you must be patient with him. This joking facade of his is just a big cover-up; underneath, he's a very serious young man. Too serious to be wasting his time with the likes of that Phillipson woman." His lip curled slightly at the thought.

"Um," she said, by this time blushing furiously and far too startled to say anything intelligible. Why, he was giving her his blessing to go after Harrison!

"Wasting his time," Forrester repeated, shaking his head. "He has absolutely nothing in common with—"

Clayton broke off at the sound of someone clearing his throat. Suzanne glanced up to see Harrison, his arms folded, leaning in the doorway, his expression one of utmost disapproval. He was looking only a little less haggard than he had last night, and was dressed in the flannel shirt and khakis again.

"Forgive me for interrupting the heart-to-heart. Clayton—" His tone was one of disapproval, embarrassment, and honest surprise. "What the devil are *you* doing here?"

Brown eyes wide with innocence, Forrester smiled up at Harrison. "Why, hello, Harrison," he said smoothly, not in the least bit disconcerted by the timing of the interruption. "We were just talking about you."

"So I heard," Harrison answered dryly. "How did you get here?"

"I took a taxi."

Harrison seemed somewhat dazed by this information, but said, "Well, look, Clayton, Dr. McCullough—"

"Suzanne," Clayton corrected him, and took a casual sip of his coffee.

To her surprise, Harrison actually blushed. "Yes, well, Suzanne has a lot of work to do. Come with me and I'll fill you in on what happened."

Clayton stood up and said graciously, "I enjoyed meeting you, Suzanne."

She rose and took his hand. "It was a pleasure, Clayton."

Harrison straightened and stepped inside the room. "You know where my office is, Clayton. Catch up to you in two seconds."

"Right." Forrester turned to give Suzanne a wink, then headed out the door.

Harrison rolled his eyes at her, then closed the door behind him. "Suzanne—I apologize if he embarrassed you. I hope he didn't say anything that—"

"Actually," she interrupted, "I thought he was charming. A little too direct, maybe, but perfectly lucid." Which was all true. Forrester had seemed very aware of the effect his words had on both Harrison and Suzanne.

Harrison relaxed noticeably, but shook his head as if unable to believe what had just happened.

"Frankly," Suzanne said, and hesitated, then decided to say it anyway. "I thought he had passed away a long time ago, from the way you spoke about it. It was sort of like talking to a ghost."

"I suppose it was," Harrison answered softly, and looked away. "I guess in my own mind I think of the man who raised me as dead. He's been crippled by depression for years; in fact, this is the first time he's been out of the house in weeks . . . and the first time he's been to PITS in years."

"I didn't realize . . . he seemed perfectly well to me." Suzanne saw it all suddenly from Harrison's point of view, what it must have been like to lose both parents to the aliens, and then to watch a third slowly destroyed by them over the years. The man wasn't paranoid or eccentric at all. "I'm sorry, Harrison. That must be very difficult for you."

Harrison shrugged. "It's been harder on Clayton. But it's funny . . . it's almost as if—" He paused. "I thought knowing about what's happened with the aliens would be the straw to break the camel's back, but it seems to have the opposite effect."

"I'm glad for that, at least."

Harrison still wouldn't meet her eyes. "So am I. And I'm amazed to find him here." He turned to leave but glanced back at her awkwardly. "Well, again, I'm sorry if he embarrassed you—"

"Speak for yourself," she said lightly.

He grimaced at that and left.

Harrison caught up with Forrester in the hallway. The anger and embarrassment he felt about what Clayton had said to Suzanne was eclipsed by his joy at seeing his second father up and around and looking interested in his surroundings. Clayton actually seemed—well, not his old self, but certainly better. He'd shaved, combed his hair, and put on clean clothes, and he wasn't shuffling, but walking with something very much like a sense of purpose toward Harrison's office.

"Clayton, I'm really surprised to see you here."

Clayton seemed rather amused by the stir he was creating. "You didn't call," he replied good-naturedly. "I was concerned. I figured the government turned you down." He looked sideways at Harrison. "I came to see if there was anything I could do to help."

Not really, Harrison almost answered, but stopped himself at the last minute. His gaze traveled over the older man. *Look at him—he came all this way after all this time. You can't just send him home and tell him he's useless.*

As they paused at the door to his office, Harrison reached out and laid a hand on Forrester's bony shoulder. "Actually, the government didn't exactly turn us down—but they're demanding evidence. I could really use another brain to pick. Let me fill you in on what we're doing . . ."

Clayton's eyes brightened.

SEVENTEEN

Insistent jazzlike percussion was blasting at full volume from the stereo speakers mounted on the ceiling of Norton's office. Harrison stood in the doorway with his hands clapped over his ears and felt his teeth vibrate.

"Norton!" he yelled.

No response. Oblivious to Harrison's presence, Norton was navigating in his chair over to the computer, squinting at a sheaf of papers in his hand.

"Dammit, Norton, turn that *down*!"

Norton glanced up just as the chair lowered him in front of his computer console. "Oh, hi, Harrison. Volume *down*." The noise eased to a tolerable level.

"Whew." Harrison entered, shaking his head to clear the ringing in his ears. "What the hell are you listening to?"

"You like it?" Norton moved the upper half of his

body to the beat, shoulders and muscular brown arms swaying as he snapped his fingers in time.

"Frankly, no," Harrison answered flatly. He was not in a particularly good mood—by midmorning, Clayton, though interested in discussing Harrison's strategy for providing Wilson with his "hard evidence," had become physically exhausted, and Harrison had sent him home in a taxi. Nothing serious, Clayton had assured him, just not used to getting out and around anymore, but Harrison was still worried.

"Surprised you don't recognize it," Norton retorted. "It's our alien boys. I personally think it beats the hell out of the Muzak they play around here. Did I tell you I was in the cafeteria the other day with Suzanne and heard the elevator rendition of Prince's 'Let's Pretend We're Married'?" He sighed. "The bastardization of art. I almost lost my lunch."

Harrison ignored him and peered over his shoulder at the numbers on the terminal screen. "Anything new?"

Since the meeting in Washington, Harrison had been overwhelmed by an anxious restlessness. Every minute lost trying to dig up evidence to please Wilson was another minute the aliens had to regroup and locate their ships and weapons.

It was worsened by the fact that there was nothing he or Clayton could really do at the moment to produce that evidence: it was up to Norton and Suzanne now. Since Clayton had gone, Harrison had been pacing up and down the halls the rest of the morning, poking his head into Norton's office and generally irritating the hell out of him. This was probably the fifth time he'd been by to see how Norton was doing, although after the embarrassing scene with Clayton earlier, Harrison had avoided Suzanne. Maybe the loud percussion was Norton's way of discouraging further visits.

"Zip, zed, zero, nothing." Norton's head rocked from side to side. "You know I'll call the minute I've got something. The bad guys are maintaining radio silence." He reached out and touched Harrison's arm. "Catch this riff . . ." He beat on the edge of the terminal, using both index fingers as drumsticks. "Don't know what it's all about, but you gotta admit —those aliens sure got rhythm."

Harrison groaned and nodded at the terminal screen. "Anything from the Cray on this?"

"Still computing. Like you, it's definitely not into music appreciation." Norton tapped a few keys, then watched the screen as old information scrolled upward and new data appeared. "Care to know how much 'plutonium' time the computer has cost the department so far?"

Harrison shuddered and covered his eyes with his hands. "I'm too poor to ask."

"Good answer," Norton said dryly.

Harrison parted his fingers and peeked anyway. The Cray had been churning away for the past 3.54 hours —and at the rate things were going, it would probably take twice that to reach the solution. He sighed and dropped his hands. "Ephram's not going to appreciate this."

"Damn right," Norton said cheerfully, "and there's not a thing we can do about it—unless you feel that saving department funds is worth letting the bad guys take over again." He angled in the chair to get a better look at Harrison. "Look, why don't you be a good researcher and run along now? You're starting to get on my nerves. Go bother Suzanne for a while."

Harrison sighed. "She won't appreciate it. I've already been to see her once this morning." At Norton's nasty look, he added, "Visit Suzanne, huh? Great idea. Maybe I'll do just that."

Harrison opened the door to Suzanne's office and poked his nose inside. Damn. Forgot to knock again —and now she'd jump down his throat for it.

Even though she'd moved in three days before, the office showed no signs of personality. The shelves were neatly filled with her reference texts (probably in alphabetical order, Harrison decided) but the walls were bare except for a plain Lucite clock. The only indication of human life sat on the desk: the gold-framed photograph of a young blond-haired girl.

Suzanne hunched over a computer terminal perpendicular to the desk, glancing at a page in an enormously fat reference book. Nearby, some of Forrester's old files lay neatly stacked. She was completely absorbed in whatever she saw, and didn't hear him enter.

Harrison cleared his throat delicately. He'd been purposely avoiding her since the Washington trip; they'd been spending a lot of time together, and while he was actually beginning to enjoy her company, he didn't want anyone, including Suzanne, to get the wrong idea. Especially not after the humiliating episode with Clayton this morning. Besides, the fact that he was beginning to get along with her made him feel vaguely guilty about Charlotte; he resolved to see her tonight, to try to patch things up.

She looked up from the terminal and over her shoulder at him. A deep crease between her eyebrows had developed from squinting at the screen. "Oh, hi," she said distractedly, and turned back to the computer. He got the feeling she would have done the same had the Archangel Gabriel appeared in the doorway. If she had been at all offended by anything Clayton had said, it certainly didn't show now. In fact, she seemed to have completely forgotten.

He ambled up to the side of the desk and half sat on its edge. She didn't seem to mind; hell, she didn't even seem to notice. For the first time, he was grateful for her ultraprofessional demeanor.

"Tell me something," he said to her back. "*Any-thing.*"

Keeping her gaze fixed on a column of figures in the reference book, Suzanne answered, "Almost good timing. Give me one more minute . . ." She typed a number with one hand. She seemed to be focusing on a point between the terminal screen and the book. She paused without looking at the screen, then pressed the enter key. "Okay. We'll have it in a minute."

"How do you *do* that?" Harrison asked.

"Hmm? Oh, you mean look at the book and the screen at the same time?" She watched the screen now as her answer appeared. "Easy. It's more efficient for microbiologists to develop independent vision in each eye. I learned how to look into a microscope with my

236

left eye and watch my right hand take notes. It's not that hard."

Suzanne swiveled in her chair to face him. "Okay. Using Dr. Forrester's notes about the most likely strain of bacteria to infect the aliens . . . and then exposing them—on paper, of course—to a level of radiation consistent with that at the waste disposal site . . ." She trailed off and swiveled back to check something on the screen.

Harrison leaned toward her eagerly, scarcely able to contain himself. "Yes—?"

She turned to him again and stated in the dispassionate manner of a scientist, "No bacteria could have survived the exposure. That's assuming you were correct about the nuclear waste corroding that one barrel, so that exposure was direct."

"So I'm *right*!" He slapped the top of the desk and leapt to his feet.

"I didn't say that," she answered soberly, a little taken aback by his excitement. "I'm saying that statistically, your theory is *possible*. And if you are right, it's hardly cause for celebration . . . given the outcome."

"You don't understand." He grinned at her. "You've just given Uncle General Hank another reason to listen to us—to help us fight the aliens. Now, we just need Norton to pinpoint their location for us. Suzanne, you're great!"

Impulsively, Harrison bent down and took her face in his hands. He meant to plant an enthusiastic kiss on her cheek, but she twisted her head to one side, startled, and the kiss caught her full on the lips.

He dropped his hands and drew back, horrified at what he had done. Here he'd behaved so circumspectly on the trip, and now . . . good Lord, she probably thought he was making a pass at her. She probably thought he'd put Clayton up to saying those things about Charlotte.

"Sorry," he began, trying to sound casual and airy and failing utterly. "That was an accident. I didn't mean to, uh . . ."

"It's all right." She retreated to the icy professionalism of her first day at the Institute, but her cheeks were flushed. "You needn't explain."

"Well." He paused awkwardly. "You've done your part today. Why don't you call it quits and go spend some time with your daughter?"

She glanced at the wall clock. "Debi's not home from school until four. It's not even lunchtime. And as you pointed out yesterday, time is the one luxury we can't afford right now. I thought I'd take a look at those alien remains you acquired. If they really have remained free of decay the way Forrester indicated, that ought to impress Uncle Hank."

"Let me arrange it," Harrison replied so quickly that she frowned suspiciously at him. He shrugged, his expression all innocence. "You and Norton have all the work to do. I'm going nuts around here with nothing to do but pace. Why don't you take a break—take a nap or a long lunch, or both—and let me take care of it? I know the procedure; I can reserve a lab faster than you can."

"All right." Suzanne squeezed her eyes shut and

rubbed at the crease between her brows, trying to smoothe it away. "Thanks."

"No problem. Just go to the Medical Complex after lunch. I'll tell the receptionist which lab."

Harrison left in a hurry, guiltily reflecting on the fact that when he had kissed her, she had not pulled away.

The PIT Medical Complex was the newest building on the Institute grounds, a two-story hexagon of sleek white marble and reflective silvered glass. The interior smelled faintly of sawdust mixed with fresh paint; the carpet was still plush and unstained. Incongruously enough, the lab the receptionist led Suzanne to was cheerful and sunny—the entire south wall was one-way mirrored glass, so that those inside could see out but still have privacy—in stark contrast, Suzanne decided, to her frame of mind about the task she now faced. The glass wall overlooked the playground of the PIT Daycare Center; at the moment, a group of four- and five-year-olds were playing catch with an oversize ball, the soft plastic kind with the sparkles in it. The glass muted their laughter and excited cries only slightly. Suzanne watched them for a second before beginning her task; the sight made her think about spending the afternoon with Debi.

Enjoy it. Could be your last chance to spend time with your daughter . . .

Oh, hell, why was she being so morbid? *You've got a job to do. Just do it.*

The dissection table was the same kind found in a

coroner's office: stainless steel, slanting down on one side into a sink, with a hand-held spray for rinsing the table clean. She doubted she'd need the spray . . . after thirty-five years in a freezer, the alien couldn't be expected to have much fluid left in him.

She stared at the lifeless lump on the table, covered by a black plastic sheet. The sheet was a weird touch; she was a microbiologist, not a mortician, and at first she attributed it to Harrison's sense of drama, until it occurred to her that it might not do to have an alien body sitting out where someone could see it. Only there was something wrong with it; the body seemed far too small, about the size of a human toddler. Perhaps Harrison had been able to get only *part* of a corpse. Certainly the aliens wouldn't have brought any of their young along for the invasion.

She took the corner of the sheet in her hand, began to lift it up.

And stopped.

Suddenly she was a small kid again, pulling the covers up over her head. *I can't do it. I can't.*

It had never happened to her before. She'd always been proud of her iron stomach, of the fact that even as a kid she hadn't flinched when the doctor gave her a shot. Hell, she'd watched to make sure he was doing it right. As an undergrad she'd dated a medical student, and he'd snuck her in one night to see the half-dissected corpses. He was so disappointed when she looked at the pickled body with clinical interest and remarked, *So this is the spleen?* When Debi was six and fell off her bike onto hard gravel and her knee broke wide open, she and Suzanne had both stared fascinated as the emergency room doctor who stitched her up irrigated the wound and said, *See, Deb, that's your kneecap.* Derek had turned green and rushed out in search of the men's room. But the last thing you could call Suzanne was a coward.

Get a grip on yourself. For God's sake, you're a scientist.

She straightened, took a deep breath, and started to remove the sheet again. Immediately, she felt dizzy and wobbled back a few steps, putting a hand to her head. She closed her eyes and took a few more deep breaths.

Suzanne, you are going to do this. It's dead . . . or near as dammit. Either way, it can't hurt you.

Outside, the children cheered. Suzanne opened her eyes. A little girl held the ball with pride in her chubby arms.

For Deb's sake—

She squared her shoulders and went back over to the dissection table, then resolutely threw back the sheet.

Faceup on the stainless steel, a plastic E.T. doll smiled innocently at her.

She gasped. For a moment she stood stunned; then seething fury overtook her. She stalked over to the phone on the wall, yanked the receiver off the hook, and mashed down the numbers of Harrison's extension. He answered on the first ring, his tone amused and expectant. He'd been waiting, the bastard.

"Blackwood, you son of a bitch!" she began, and

stopped, not knowing what else to say. Several seconds of silence passed between them; she could have sworn she heard him grinning on the other end of the line.

"You—you—" She tried her best to maintain her anger, but in the end, she lost, and burst into soft, helpless laughter.

EIGHTEEN

After she thought about it, Suzanne decided she was grateful for Harrison's little joke—although she'd never let *him* know. It broke the tension and made the real task a little easier. Afterward, she called him from the lab.

"Well?" His good humor had vanished; he sounded a little edgy.

"Very interesting. This thing was fairly well-preserved after all those years in the freezer. I shouldn't call it a thing really. Very impressive cerebral cortex–type structure. It's a highly intelligent creature, probably more intelligent than we are."

"Speak for yourself, Suzanne."

"Very funny. I thought you'd be glad to know I can verify the anatomical information in Forrester's files. One interesting point, however. The zoologist who made the notes dissected a couple of males. But he made certain incorrect presumptions here about the female of the species. The alien I just dissected was female."

"I'll be damned," Harrison said. "An equal-opportunity invasion force."

"Apparently so, but it gets even more interesting. The egg produced by the female is similar to that produced by a human female in that it isn't viable outside the body. However, the female has no womb."

"Physical abnormality? Or a hysterectomy?"

"Doesn't look like it. My guess is these creatures lay eggs like reptiles or amphibians. That's what Penny-worth suggested in his notes. But our female had no means of producing a protective outer layer . . . at least, not that I could see. It'd be like a chicken laying eggs without the shell. And no place for the embryo to incubate in either sex." She paused. "When I read over Forrester's report, it mentioned that the number *three* seemed to be important to them and—"

"Wait a minute," Harrison interrupted. "I think I see what you're getting at. Are you suggesting that it takes three of them to tango? A ménage à trois?"

"Exactly."

He whistled softly into the receiver. "Guess we haven't examined all the sexes yet."

"Guess not." Her tone lightened. "So . . . did I pass the test?"

"Test?" He sounded confused.

"Your practical-joke test, remember? 'Window to the soul' and all that? So did I pass, or are you going to write me off as another Guterman?"

"Guterman should be so good-looking," he said quickly, and hung up.

In a small cul-de-sac in the swank residential area known as Hampton Hill, Harrison sat in the darkness of the parked Bronco and gazed across the street at a row of town houses. He was looking at the second-floor window of one in particular. Light filtered through the curtains of Charlotte's bedroom, which meant she was home. Harrison looked down at the glowing numbers of the cellular phone in his hand and hesitated. The benign hum of the dial tone ceased and was replaced by a recorded message:

If you'd like to make a call, please hang up and dial again. If you'd like to make a call, please hang up—

Harrison pressed the hook down with his thumb.

Dammit, either dial her number or go home.

If he went home, of course, he'd never see her again. But then, he wasn't exactly sure he *wanted* to. He didn't ever want to talk to the Charlotte who'd done her best to manipulate him into giving up the work he loved, who had refused to answer the twenty-four messages he'd left on her answering machine, who finally let it slip that she really *did* take her wealth and social status seriously. Harrison had trouble believing that woman actually existed. He wanted to talk to the *real* Charlotte, the one who laughed at his jokes, who tolerated his attempts at individuality with wry humor, who loved to display him at parties with the tolerant pride of a parent showing off a precocious child.

If that Char were gone forever, if she had been a sham, he had to know. He dialed her number again.

The machine answered on the first ring, just as he had expected.

Hi, this is the answering machine at five five five oh three seven four. We can't come to the phone right now—Char always said "we" because she was terrified of strangers learning she lived alone—*but if you leave your name, number, and message, we'll get back to you. Don't forget to wait for the tone. 'Bye!*

Harrison waited for the tone, then said hurriedly, "Charlotte, I know you're there. This is my very last message. I'm across the street and very shortly I'll be knocking on your door. If you don't open it, I'm going to drive the Bronco right the hell into your living room and track mud all over your Oriental rugs. Do you understand?"

He half hoped she would pick up the phone, even if it were only to tell him to go to hell, but the recorder beeped again and the dial tone came back. Harrison folded up the phone and shoved it back into his jacket pocket, then took a deep breath, climbed out of the Bronco, and marched up to Charlotte's door. The porch was dark; he had never used the doorbell before and had to search for it. He jabbed it with a finger.

He waited for a full minute. No reply. He pushed the bell again, and this time he held it down. "Charlotte!" He bellowed it at the top of his lungs. "Come down here!" Char had to wait a year before she could purchase this particular town house; the neighbors were very particular about who they allowed in, and there were all sorts of codes and restrictions about what color paint you could use and what landscape scheme you used in the tiny patch of front yard. The neighbors were going to love this.

The upstairs curtains parted. Char cried out, "Go away!"

He took his finger off the bell and took a step back to try to catch a glimpse of her, but she remained invisible behind the curtain. Cupping his hands around his mouth, he cried, "Not until I talk to you first!" Good. The more of a disturbance he created, the better his chances of getting inside to talk to her.

"No! For God's sake, keep your voice down!"

"Not me." He shook his head and upped the volume even more. "No, I think I'll just stand right here and discuss it with you now. That way, the whole neighborhood can listen in!"

There was a pause, then the sound of a screen being slid up. Charlotte leaned out of the window and rested delicate hands on the ledge. He'd been gloating up to that point, but when he caught sight of her, he drew in his breath. She truly was a beautiful woman, and tonight she wore a low-cut red silk robe that looked like it might slip off her shoulder any second. She tossed her hair back, then in an abrupt change of tactics, called down in a low voice, "Harrison . . . do you really love me?" She was half smiling, teasing him, the old Char again.

He smiled back gratefully. "You know I do, Char."

"Why?" She rested an elbow on the ledge and propped her chin against her hand, her expression coquettish.

Shit, a test. Harrison cast about desperately for a

second, then started talking in the hopes inspiration would come. Too long of a pause now would not be well received. "That's easy . . . because you're smart." *That's it—tell her you love her for her mind first. But don't forget anything important . . .* "And beautiful. And you've got a great sense of humor." *Used to, anyway.* "And an even greater pair of legs."

She seemed pleased, but there was a hint of warning in her tone as she asked the next question. "You love me more than your work?"

That threw him. Flustered, he stammered, "Char, that—that's not a very fair question."

"Yes it is!" She withdrew immediately from the window, her voice trembling with hurt and wrath. "And you've already answered it! Now, if you don't leave, I'm calling the police!"

"Go ahead," he dared her. He was getting weary of this little game. If she wanted it to end like this, then so be it. "Go right ahead. I'll put up a good fight and embarrass the hell out of you in front of your neighbors." Perfect timing; as he said it, the porch light of the next door neighbor came on.

"You—!" she began, but was far too furious to finish. The window slammed shut. Char would either call the police as promised or come open the door; Harrison was betting on the former.

"Oh, the *hell* with it," he said, disgusted, and headed for the Bronco, but before he had taken two steps, the phone beeped in his pocket. He pulled it out, set it on Talk and said into the receiver, "Whoever you are, you've got damn lousy timing."

"Wanna make a bet?" Norton asked at the other end of the line. "I've located our bad guys, Doc. You've got to come right away."

"I'll be right there." He folded the phone shut, ran to the Bronco, and roared off down the street. He'd resolve things with Char later, when there was time.

By the time Charlotte made it down to the front door, all she could see were the Bronco's taillights receding into the darkness.

For some reason, this time Deb didn't seem so upset by the idea of her mother leaving again. Maybe, Suzanne decided, it was the fact that they'd spent the afternoon together. Suzanne took her shopping at the Rialto Plaza, a cluster of small shops that opened onto a beautifully landscaped atrium. Deb picked out a jump suit and two miniskirts; Suzanne noted that her daughter's taste in clothing was changing, becoming more adult. Outside in the little park, Debi ate an ice cream cone while her mother watched and listened to the sixth-grader blithely rattle on about her classes, the cute (male) math teacher, and her new friend, Kim Song, who had this gorgeous black hair all the way down to her waist. Suzanne listened with feigned interest, trying her best to enjoy her daughter and the quiet sunny afternoon while there was still time.

Dear God, whatever happens in the future, please let Deb be all right. So long as Deb's okay, what happens to me isn't important. For an instant Suzanne allowed herself to think what might happen, and became terrified beyond all reason.

"Mom?" Deb stopped chattering and licking her ice cream cone and eyed her mother with concern. "Are you okay?"

Suzanne blinked back tears. "I'm fine, chicken. Just fine."

Later, when the phone rang after dinner, Deb raced to pick it up, hopeful that it was Kim, the new friend. But she handed the receiver over to her mother. "For you," she said, deflated. "A Norton Somebody-or-other." She lingered to listen to Suzanne's side of the conversation, and when her mother hung up, said, sounding very weary and very adult: "You go pack, Mom. I'll call Mrs. Pennyworth."

Suzanne hugged her then, and held her for a long time.

Now, as Suzanne stood, overnight bag clutched in one hand, in front of the door to Norton's office, she was once again overwhelmed by fear. The aliens existed, were a part of the here and now, and she and Harrison would have to find them to get the proof Uncle Hank wanted. She drew a deep breath to compose herself and opened the door.

Norton was at his desk, poring over a U.S. map that covered the entire surface. He didn't look up as she entered.

Harrison, on the other hand, scowled up at her from the video equipment he was packing into a case. "What the hell are *you* doing here?"

"I called her," Norton murmured distractedly, and marked on the map with a red felt-tip pen.

"Some welcome." Suzanne set the bag down on the floor next to Norton's desk and put her hands on her hips. "I was under the impression that I was part of this project too."

Harrison shrugged, still frowning; he was in a foul mood, which confused her. Earlier today he'd been elated at the prospect of locating the aliens.

Norton spoke, addressing his remark to Harrison, much to her irritation. "The transmission was only a few short bursts, but that's all I needed to nail them." He folded the map so the area marked in red was in the center, and proffered it to Harrison. "Drive like hell and you might make it there in about eleven hours."

Harrison straightened and went over to take the map from Norton. Suzanne stepped behind him and peered at it over his shoulder. Norton had scribed a neat red circle in the southwestern corner of Alpine County. Far from any big cities, it appeared; probably farm country up there. "Eleven hours is too damn long. Besides, who said anything about driving?" Harrison asked. "I'll charter a helicopter."

Norton rubbed his eyes. "Easy, my friend. You got any idea how much that's gonna cost? Ephram mentioned today that someone on the board got wind of this and already chewed his ass out for all the time we spent on the Cray."

"How much does a new world cost?" Harrison waved the map angrily so that the paper crackled. "And where do you go to buy one?"

"If we're right about this," Suzanne said to Norton,

"it's all academic anyway. You can tell Jacobi I said that." To Harrison she said, "Let's go."

He wheeled around to stare at her. For the first time, he seemed to notice the overnight bag in her hand. "Wait a minute, Suzanne—you're not going." His tone indicated that there would be no more discussion on the subject, but she caught the uncertain glance he shot Norton, who shrugged innocently as if to say *leave me out of it.*

She remained perfectly calm. Let him have a temper tantrum; that was fine with her, but the outcome would be the same. He was talking foolishness, and they both knew it. She'd been thinking all day about what she'd do when the call came that Norton had located the aliens, and her mind was made up. "Don't waste any more time, Harrison. You know as well as I do that without a witness any evidence you bring back is going to be debunked."

He tried at first to pretend anger. "Dammit, Suzanne, I'm not going to argue with you about this!"

"Very convincing, but it won't work." She folded her arms and let it roll off her to let him see that an outburst wasn't going to work.

Exasperated, he continued. "If the aliens *are* there, as we believe, then it's too dangerous. We went through this once before, Suzanne, remember? What happened to the single parent who only worked weekdays?"

"The world has changed since I said that. You need *me.* General Wilson isn't going to believe such fantastic evidence unless he hears it from someone he trusts—yours truly."

"I can get proof all by myself." Harrison pointed at the video equipment on the floor. "I don't need an eyewitness. That's what the camera's for."

"A videotape can be altered very easily. I doubt Uncle Hank will take your word alone that it wasn't— but I know he'll take mine."

He sighed in silent frustration. "This isn't the time to be cute, Suzanne." He lowered the map and looked at her, his tone passionately serious. "Good Lord, what would happen to Debi if you were killed? Do you think I could ever allow that to happen to her?"

"Amen," Norton said softly.

She was slightly taken aback and at the same time touched by his honest concern. She could see he was just as frightened at the thought of going as she was; maybe the bad mood was his way of covering it. As much as she hated the idea of going, she answered, "If we spend much more time arguing, it will happen to a lot more children than Debi. It makes more sense for me to go with you; and if two go, chances are increased that at least one of us will make it back. Besides, I don't know about you, but *I* certainly don't plan on doing anything foolish."

He started to speak, but she kept talking. "What's so dangerous? The aliens don't have their weapons anymore, and the camera has a telephoto lens, right? We'll film from a safe distance."

"With them, there *is* no safe distance." Harrison's voice was very soft.

"Bottom line: I go or you don't get in to see Wilson again."

Harrison regarded her stonily; Norton shook his head. "I think you're being jammed, Doc."

"I *know* I am," Harrison replied without taking his eyes off her.

"I can always charter my own helicopter." She took the map from Harrison's hand; he was startled enough to let her take it at first, then tried to grab it back.

"Too late." She smiled at him. "I've memorized the location. Now, shall we save the department some money and charter only one helicopter?"

"Dr. McCullough," Harrison said heavily, emphasizing each word, "if you get yourself killed, I will never forgive you."

While the process of freeing the others continued, Xashron crept up into the dark forest. The process of movement in the weakened host body was still tiring, though the symptoms of radiation sickness had eased due to the ministrations of Rashon, the skilled medic who now inhabited the human physician's body.

While the vegetation in the forest was familiar to his host's eyes, Xashron found it amazing, awe-inspiring. The variety of plant life was the one thing about Earth which impressed him—especially the huge growths called trees, *living wood and greenery so tall, they stretched into the sky. In the darkness Xashron thought them intimidating. Back home such a living creation would fetch an entire ruling-class family's wealth. Xashron laid a gray, decaying hand on the round trunk and ran it along the rough surface, wincing at the surprise of splinters in his palm. Incredible texture, color, and the smell . . . Xashron gingerly brought his*

254

nose to the bark. Astringent, almost medicinal . . . and yet oddly, gloriously fragrant.

He rested against the tree and watched the religious tableau in the valley below him. By the light of three flickering bonfires, those already freed from the hideous metal containers were forming pyramids with their bodies, drawing energy up from the ground to aid them in the struggle ahead, while a handful of soldiers worked to release more of those imprisoned.

The sight of his soldiers emerging into the fire glow from their thirty-five-year sleep filled Xashron with grimly determined pride. They were not dead, the soldiers of Mor-Tax, not defeated after all this time. They would still emerge victorious.

There came the heavy, awkward sound of human footfall, of movement through the underbrush, but Xashron was unafraid. At the sight of Xana in her host body, he drew closer.

"Xashron." Even her human voice, with its curious pitch and timbre, was pleasant to him. His host eyes appreciated her human form as having once been comely. It still had not degenerated as rapidly as the others. "I came to speak with you alone because I know the time is near. Soon, all your soldiers will be set free."

"There is time yet," he answered, wishing only for both of them to be free from these cumbersome bodies, so he could see her once again as she truly was.

In the darkness of the forest, he reached out and did a socially unthinkable thing: he touched her arm. Beneath the fabric, her skin felt warm. She did not pull the arm away as he expected, which gave him great hope: for she was ruling class, and for a soldier such as himself to touch uninvited was to risk severe punishment. And for the act Xashron now contemplated, the penalty was death.

"Things are different here," he told her. "The laws that bound us on Mor-Tax no longer have meaning for us. Who can touch us? Home is almost forty Terran years distant. Here, we can make our own laws." He drew his hand up her arm. The sensation was strangely thrilling.

She focused intently on his eyes and said carefully, "I agree. When will you strike against the Advocacy?"

"When all my soldiers are free . . . and Xeera and Konar have communicated my intent to them. Certainly before daylight comes again."

"Some will refuse to harm the Advocacy. Some will turn against you."

"I expect that," Xashron answered confidently. "But most will feel as I do. They have suffered much at the Advocacy's hands."

"And what of me?"

He moved closer until their host bodies touched. "Have you no faith in the promise I gave you, Xana?"

"I believe you will not harm me." Her fever-bright eyes were hard, defiant. "But will the military respect the voice of only one *member of the Advocacy?"*

"It will . . . if you accept two members of the military to complete the triad. The soldiers will understand it is a necessary emergency action. But you must agree to convince the Council."

She was silent for a moment. "I accept—provided you are one of the members of the triad."

"Agreed." He pressed her to him. Her body was warm, an unfamiliar but not unpleasant sensation. "Let us leave these bodies for a time, Xana. Let me see you again as you really are."

She laid her hands on his shoulders and whispered, "But you are a soldier, and I a ruler. If we are found together—and with the added scandal that no carrier is present—we will be killed. Even your own followers would not accept—"

"These are new bodies, Xana, and a new world." He began the slow, painstaking process of exiting the host without destroying it. When he was free, he let the body fall away. The relief, the surge of strength, was intoxicating. He looked up, pleased to see that Xana had done likewise. As her human form fell away to reveal what lay beneath, Xashron gasped at her dark, shimmering beauty.

The host body twitched as it lay on the ground. "Still alive," Xana explained, following his concerned gaze. "And very spirited. A nuisance, sometimes, but at least she is strong and the body will last longer than if it were dead."

"Xana," he sighed. He pulled her to him, and she did not resist.

Urick woke to find herself in hell.

Total disorientation . . . total agony. Raging fever, chills that locked her muscles in spasm, nausea so intense that she lay on her back retching, though nothing came. She opened her eyes to peer up at a bright full moon shining down through the branches of tall pines. In her delirium she could remember nothing of the past few days, nor understand where she was or how she had come to be there. In the periphery of her vision she saw something—someone lying next to her in a shaft of moonlight. It took a great effort to turn her head toward it.

Finney. She tried to say his name, wanted to ask what had happened to Chambers and the others, but managed to emit only a weak croak. Finney's dull eyes bulged, and there were huge sores covering the gray, waxy skin of his face. As she watched, a fly lit on a sore on his cheek, then walked across the bridge of his nose, down and up again onto the open, staring eye, pausing on the blue-gray iris to clean itself. Finney blinked once, and flinched.

Urick looked away and wept soundlessly, without tears. She was dying in this strange, remote forest. Bits of memories floated back to her . . . Jericho Valley, setting up the transmitter . . . the thrill of fear when they noticed Mossoud was gone, then heard the gunfire. Their message was never broadcast . . .

Though to Lena the cause no longer mattered. There was only pain and suffering—punishment for killing the corporals, her fevered brain told her. All she wished for now was death, an end to misery. She groped weakly at her side, searching for her weapon, but the Uzi was gone. She probably wouldn't have been strong enough to aim and fire it at herself anyway.

Something dark and shapeless stepped into her line of vision, blotting out tree limbs and blue sky. Strange alien forms, the last things she remembered seeing at

Jericho Valley. As one of them reached out for her, Urick opened her mouth to cry out, but no sound came except a low moan. At the same time, she hoped—prayed—it would kill her.

She was not to be so fortunate.

NINETEEN

Jimmy Smith, age seventeen, squinted at the small patch of forest illuminated by his and Jake's flashlights. The trees seemed to hover over the two like dark, watchful living things; occasionally, something rustled in the branches to add to the illusion, causing Jake's old hound dog, Emmy Lou, to run ahead and circle with her nose to the ground and her crooked tail wagging. Jimmy wasn't really scared, but there was something creepy about the woods at night. Maybe it was all those times as a Boy Scout (not so long ago) when he'd camped with the troop in the woods, everybody trying to see who could tell the scariest story. There was one Donny Ramirez used to tell about the windigo—the evil spirit that turned humans into hungry cannibals who wept blood instead of tears—that still gave Jimmy the shudders. He sure wasn't gonna start thinking about *that* one now.

"Jake?" Jimmy tried hard not to sound like he was tired or complaining, but they'd been at it since eleven o'clock last night and it must have been close to three in the morning right about now. Jimmy wanted Jake to like him; Jake was married to Jimmy's oldest sister, Susan, and Jimmy worshipped his brother-in-law. Jake knew everything, like how to hunt deer at night: First you get Emmy Lou to chase it until it was tired out, then you shine the light in its eyes and blind it. That way, all you had to do was take aim, and presto! Venison chops. And Jake had decided it was high time Jimmy bagged his first deer—a young doe, except that after Jake shone the flashlight in its eyes and Jimmy was all set to pull the trigger, the doe turned her head and looked right at Jimmy. Of course, he knew it was just coincidence . . . but she kept staring at him, her ears twitching, her chest heaving, and it seemed to Jimmy she trembled just a little.

He lowered the rifle. Jake got disgusted and tried to pull it from him, but the noise scared the doe and she got away. Jake didn't talk for a while after that—he was real mad, but after a while he got over it and said, "Happens to everybody the first time. What you've gotta remember is you can't think. You've just got to do it. Once you start thinking, you wind up in trouble." And then Jake went back to being cheerful, and Jimmy didn't feel quite so bad.

But now he didn't care if he ever bagged a deer in his life; all he wanted to do was get off his feet for a while. "Jake?" Jimmy whispered again. "I'm beat. How much longer?" Like a fool he'd worn new boots, and they'd rubbed raw spots on the backs of both heels. At this point he was ready to go home.

Jake was a couple paces ahead; he stopped and pulled a flask from the pocket of his down vest. "Been watching you limp the past couple miles now and wondering when you were finally going to say something." He said it nice, so that Jimmy felt like a real fool for not complaining, but Jake smiled and unscrewed the cap on the flask. "Here—for medicinal purposes only. This'll help those blisters. It's only about a half mile, maybe less." He offered Jimmy the flask.

The boy smiled and took it with his free hand. "Good," he said casually, trying to sound grown-up. "If I don't get some rest soon, I won't be able to bag a deer if it walks up and kisses me." He appreciated the fact that Jake always treated him like an adult, which made Jimmy all the more eager to behave like one. He put the bottle to his lips and leaned his head back, taking a big pull. It was whiskey, Jimmy supposed, but it smelled the same as his mother's nail polish remover. He held it in his mouth for a second, then swallowed reluctantly; the liquor burned like battery acid going down, and when it hit his stomach he wheezed noisily, sucking in air. Not too cool . . . but Jake didn't laugh, didn't even grin, just took the flask from him and helped himself to some, then wiped his mouth on his sleeve and belched, frankly satisfied.

"Kinda strange," Jake remarked, sweeping the flashlight beam first along the tops of the trees, then along the ground. "You notice how quiet it's been the past few minutes? Haven't heard a sound—not even an owl hoot."

Jimmy wished Jake wouldn't talk spooky like that —but he thought about it and decided his brother-in-law had a point. Maybe that's why the woods had begun to seem so eerie. Even old Emmy Lou had quit her whining and was sticking pretty close to Jake's heels.

"Well, don't matter," Jake said casually, maybe realizing the unsettling effect his words had on his young companion. "We're almost there—the old farm's just on the other side of this rise."

Jimmy didn't much care for the thought of sleeping in an old abandoned building, but he was too tired to argue and certainly too tired to make it back to the jeep without a little shut-eye. He struggled to follow Jake and Emmy Lou up the incline. "You sure nobody'll be there?"

"Been camping there five years now, and haven't run into a soul, except maybe a raccoon or two," Jake answered. Ahead of him, Emmy Lou dashed to the crest and looked down into the little valley.

Whatever she saw wasn't good. The hair on her back rose as she stiffened and growled low in her throat. It was the most evil, vicious noise Jimmy had ever heard her make, and the sound of it sent a chill through him that made him shudder.

"What is it, girl?" Jake crept up next to her and went down on one knee; Jimmy came up cautiously behind the two and looked down into the valley.

Somebody was at the abandoned farm, all right.

Two huge bonfires were going out in front of the ramshackle house with the peeling white paint. In the orange glow cast by the fire, shadowy forms writhed.

Jimmy gaped and dropped the flashlight. He wasn't near enough to see all that clearly, but what he did see convinced him not to come any closer. There were *things* down there—dark, hulking things, dozens of them, some of them swaying in groups of three, some of them moving around. They looked like big black crabs perched on skinny tentacles, and a group of them were carrying metal cans out of a big truck parked off to one side of the house.

The crab-things were bad enough, but what really frightened Jimmy most were the people. They stood by the fire, three groups of three, and they reminded Jimmy of the time he'd gone as a zombie for Halloween . . . only these guys weren't pretending. Their skin was all gross and puffy-looking, with shreds of flesh rotting off in places, and their faces were covered with gooey, crusty sores. No two ways about it, Jimmy decided. These guys were *dead.* He trembled and made a small whimpering sound.

Being the fastest thinker of the three, Emmy Lou turned tail and ran. The other two recognized inspiration when they saw it and followed.

The white truck was sighted once more thirty miles shy of the Nevada border by a lone state trooper who radioed for help, then promptly vanished, leaving his patrol car abandoned just off a deserted stretch of Highway 15. Ironhorse alerted the police and the

Clark County Sheriff's Office, expecting the truck to continue east toward Vegas. Roadblocks were set up; there was no way the big rig could make it across the state line without being stopped.

That was two days ago. Either the truck had veered north toward Death Valley or headed south for Arizona or Mexico; in any case, the sightings ceased. Ironhorse requested more troops, so a massive search fanning in all directions could be launched, but it was all taking too much time.

Another puzzle: within hours after being exposed to such a strong dose of radiation, the terrorists should have been dead or dying, certainly far too ill to have made it as far as the Mojave.

Then word came from Alpine County, just south of Tahoe. Two witnesses had escaped with a fantastic story: the white truck was stopped at an abandoned farm, where huge crablike creatures were seen unloading steel barrels.

Ironhorse stood in the glass-partitioned office and watched as, a few cubicles down, a uniformed deputy offered coffee to a couple of disheveled hunters. The older man took the cup gratefully, but the younger, just a high school kid, shook his head and stared back at Ironhorse with wide, haunted eyes. The colonel turned away and took a sip of hot black coffee from the styrofoam cup in his hand.

Reynolds was talking. His dark eyes were bloodshot from the recent lack of sleep. "Frankly, Colonel, I never heard such a crock of bullshit in my life. Those two good ol' boys musta been drunk as skunks."

Ironhorse crossed over to the map spread over the vacant desk in the tiny office. He trusted Reynolds as much as anyone he knew, but even with his staff sergeant, Ironhorse liked to keep his cards close to his chest. He still hadn't bothered to mention the "gorillas" the old alkie at the gas station had seen to anyone.

"They seemed more tired and frightened than drunk," the colonel answered, turning back to take one more glance at the boy's pale face. "And they gave a perfect ID of the truck we've been chasing."

Reynolds seemed a little taken aback by his answer. "I know, sir, but you have to admit the rest of their story sounds like one-fifty–proof delusions—or worse."

"Maybe," Ironhorse conceded cautiously. Or maybe, like the old drunk, they were one of the few permitted to gaze upon the star-bears and live. With the alkie, he was willing to write it all off—but the fact that aliens had been mentioned twice in connection with the white truck had to be more than sheer coincidence.

He turned to Reynolds. "Team briefing in fifteen minutes, Sergeant. I want everyone at one hundred percent. We move out in an hour."

"Whatever you say, Colonel." Reynolds' tone was entirely dutiful, but as he exited the cubicle, Ironhorse caught the sergeant's dubious expression.

No matter. The colonel turned his attention to the shakily scrawled X the older hunter had marked on the map. Whoever, whatever was hiding there was about to receive a visit from Delta squad.

* * *

266

It was early afternoon when the helicopter deposited Suzanne and Harrison two miles from their destination.

"This is better than the desert," Suzanne commented as they carried the equipment the rest of the way. It was beautiful mountainous country, rugged and forested with tall pine. Oddly, the closer they came to the object of their search, the more everything took on a sense of unreality, and the less her fear became.

Harrison looked up from the map in his hand and grunted. "At least you've learned to dress more sensibly." He nodded at her khakis.

She shrugged. "If you can't beat 'em . . . Frankly, I'm beginning to think the job calls more for a professional camper than for a microbiologist."

They grew quiet as they approached the location marked in red on Norton's map. "Here," Harrison said, his voice almost inaudible, and eased the camera equipment to the ground near the crest of a rocky ridge.

Suzanne lowered her own case and together they crouched near a clump of bushes and peered down into the valley. Binoculars dangled from a strap around Harrison's neck; he raised them to his eyes.

"All quiet," he whispered.

She could see nothing but a couple of run-down buildings. She nudged him and gestured for the binoculars, which he handed over.

She peered through them. Just an old dilapidated farmhouse built of hand-hewn planks that had silvered with age, and a barn covered with faded, peeling red paint, both nestled in a quiet valley; it must have been a lovely place years ago. Even now it looked peaceful, benign, incapable of housing anything evil. Someone had recently set a couple of bonfires. She handed the binoculars back and glanced over at the map still in his hand. "Are you sure this is the right place? I didn't see the truck or any barrels."

Harrison shrugged. "They could have ditched the truck or hidden it somewhere. The barn looks big enough. And it looks like someone had themselves a little barbecue recently." He turned back to paw through the equipment case, then pulled out the Geiger counter and began monitoring. The counter emitted a few healthy clicks.

He looked over at Suzanne. "They're around, all right. Wait till I take this thing closer." He yawned. "But not now. We should wait until it gets dark." He walked, still crouched down, behind the bushes, found a comfortable hollow, which he padded with pine needles, and settled into it.

Suzanne stared back at him, stunned, and followed. "How can you sleep at a time like this?"

"It's very simple," he answered, pulling the brim of his fedora over his eyes. "I need my one hour out of five. And I'm exhausted after the past few days. Aren't you?"

She sat on the ground near him. "Well, yes, but that doesn't mean I can go to sleep just like that. Especially considering our situation. Good Lord, I think I'd have nightmares. Frankly, I've been having them anyway lately."

He pushed the brim up with one finger and looked at her. "Why do you think I sleep only an hour at a time? You should try it. Helps keep them from starting."

That gave her pause. Considering what he'd been through as a kid, it was no wonder. "Maybe I'll rest in a while," she said, "but don't you think one of us ought to stand watch?"

Harrison pulled his hat back down and snickered. "Suzanne, based on my own personal experience, I can safely say that if they spot us, watching is about all we'll be able to do about it."

She sighed. "Well, I won't be able to sleep for a while anyway." She picked up the map where he'd dropped it, found a comfortable spot against a boulder, and nestled against it. "So you're *sure* this is the right place, huh? Just seems too quiet."

"This is it." His voice was already sleepy and fading. "Rattlesnake Ridge."

"Rattlesnake Ridge." She sat up. "How'd it get *that* name?"

Harrison grinned but didn't answer. In a few seconds he was breathing regularly, and Suzanne was sitting perfectly straight, her eyes open wide and on the lookout.

She had a wooden pointer in her hand, the kind teachers used to use years ago, and she was explaining to Mrs. Pennyworth and Debi the anatomical structure of aliens, pointing at the E.T. doll on the steel dissection table.

"Wake up," Harrison said.

"What?!" Suzanne sat up with a start, heart pounding.

"Take it easy." He put a hand on her shoulder while she caught her breath. "It's starting to get dark, that's all. Time to get moving."

She looked up at the rising moon as it traveled past wisps of clouds, then down at the deserted buildings. Both the house and barn were unlit and empty-looking.

Harrison patted her shoulder awkwardly, then took his hand away. "You okay?"

"I'm fine," she said a little coldly, then nodded back at the farmhouse. "You're still sure they're here?"

"You hear that?" he asked.

"Hear what?" She strained, but could hear only silence.

"No crickets." Harrison gave her a knowing look. "They're here all right." He continued in the same soothing tone. "We're not trying to get ourselves killed, okay? I'm only going close enough for some instrument readings. You stay back and record everything with the camera."

At first she considered arguing with him about it, accusing him of gallantry, but as long as there seemed to be no real danger . . . She nodded and reached for the video camera while Harrison found the Geiger counter and made gingerly for the slope.

She didn't feel frightened, exactly . . . only very cold, so cold that her teeth began to chatter even though she wore a light jacket. The air was cooling off rapidly. Embarrassed, she gritted her teeth so that Harrison wouldn't hear.

Before he made it very far down the hill, the Geiger counter began to buzz in earnest. "See," Harrison hissed at her. "What'd I tell you? They're around. But we'd better not get too much—"

She didn't hear the rest of what he had to say. Something clamped itself over her mouth and pulled her backward, off balance.

TWENTY

A great force struck Harrison in the back, hurling him facedown into the grass. The Geiger counter went flying. A heavy weight pressed down on him, keeping him pinned. He tried to call Suzanne's name and couldn't; the wind had been knocked out of him. He could hear her muffled cries as she struggled.

Shit, this is it, he told himself, feeling more frustrated than frightened, and damn awful about the fact that he'd let her come along. And her poor daughter . . . at least Norton would figure out what had happened, but would he be able to get proof to Wilson in time?

"Promise not to scream, and I'll take away my hand." A man's voice, low and soft, and very far away. Suzanne's moaning stopped. At the same time, the pressure against Harrison's back disappeared, leaving a dull ache. Slowly, Harrison rolled over and sat up, holding the injured spot with one hand, not knowing exactly what to expect next.

He squinted at the vaguely familiar, sneering face looming over him in the darkness. These were no aliens. "Well, I'll be goddamned," Harrison said with something less than pleasure. "Ironhorse. What are you doing here?" Nearby, Suzanne glared at a large, formidable-looking soldier dressed in battle fatigues, his face smeared with black camouflage paint.

Ironhorse straightened. "No, Doctor, that's my line. What are *you* doing here?" He extended a hand and jerked Harrison to his feet.

Harrison groaned and rubbed the offending spot in his back. "Jesus, I think I bruised a rib. That is, *you* bruised it." He scanned the ground quickly, in search of the Geiger counter. "Dammit, Colonel, if you hurt any of our equipment—"

"The army will pay for any damages." Ironhorse's black eyes glittered with amusement, making Harrison hate him all the more for his damnably smug attitude. "You still haven't told me what you're doing here."

Harrison ignored him for a moment, stepping over toward Suzanne and her war-painted assailant. "Suzanne, did this joker hurt you?"

"Only my dignity," she answered dryly, and gave the camera a pat. "Fortunately, this is still in one piece."

Harrison turned back to the colonel. "I'm not going to answer your question, Colonel Ironhorse, because you wouldn't believe us if we told you."

Ironhorse considered this and handed Blackwood

back the still-buzzing Geiger counter. Harrison brushed the dirt off it; it seemed to be okay. "You're right," the colonel said, "I probably wouldn't. I had the tape you gave me analyzed. Remember the one? With the transmission supposedly made by the terrorists? Twenty minutes of the *Best of Buddy Rich.*"

Harrison smiled coldly. "It's not my fault your people couldn't do their jobs, Colonel."

Ironhorse narrowed his eyes and started to speak, then seemed to remember something. He glanced down at his watch and addressed the soldier. "It's time, Sergeant."

The soldier nodded and disappeared quickly into the dark forest. Harrison watched him go. "Where's he headed in such a hurry?" He had a dreadful premonition that he hoped was wrong.

"Good thing we stopped you before you made it down or you would have been right in the middle of the fireworks," Ironhorse said casually. "We're about to secure the area."

"You can't do that!" Both he and Suzanne spoke at the same time, almost crying it out.

Ironhorse smiled with irritating superiority. "Ah, but we *can,* Doctors. You're both very privileged; you're about to witness a rare event—and live to tell about it. Delta squad in action. Anytime, anyplace, any objective—my men are the best."

Harrison had heard of them, all right, but he shook his head. "If you value your men, Colonel, call them back. You have no concept of who or what you're dealing with."

Ironhorse cocked his head and shot him a curious

look. "Just a few terrorists, with small arms . . . and a poorly defended perimeter. I figure my men are overprepared."

Suzanne moved closer, leaning toward the Indian to hiss: "You don't understand . . . it's not just terrorists you're fighting—"

Harrison put a hand on her arm to silence her. After their last encounter, Ironhorse no doubt thought him crazy, and any explanations would be considered the ravings of a couple of lunatic scientists. The man would see soon enough for himself.

She turned toward him angrily. "And what happens when all his men are *killed?*"

"Excuse me, Dr. . . . McCullough, isn't it?" Ironhorse asked politely; Suzanne glanced up at him. "It doesn't matter to my men whether they're fighting terrorists . . . or something else." His expression was enigmatic.

Jesus, Harrison thought, *he knows.* Perhaps the colonel wasn't as dull-witted as he'd first believed. Harrison and Suzanne exchanged surprised glances.

Ironhorse was still talking, this time to Harrison. "I still remember the look on your face when you saw those empty barrels, Blackwood."

Harrison raised a brow at that and said cautiously, "And just how experienced are you at fighting those things, Colonel? How much do you know about the *first* time they did battle with us?"

Ironhorse shrugged. "Enough. I know they don't have their ships or their weapons. Without those, my men will make mincemeat out of them."

"And have your men been told *who* they're fighting?" Suzanne's tone was cold.

"The terrorists had weapons," Harrison pointed out. "They overran an army installation, killed every soldier in there—and the aliens overtook *them.*"

Ironhorse sighed as if weary at having to explain such elementary things to such ignorant people. "You have to remember—we're engaging in pure speculation here. *I* won't believe they're really aliens until I see it with my own eyes. I'm certainly *not* going to say anything crazy to my men, particularly something crazy I can't back up. I keep my suspicions to myself. Otherwise, my men would lose faith in my judgment."

"And knowing the shock and confusion they'll experience when they find out *who* they're fighting," Harrison retorted, "you expect them to be able to win?"

"Absolutely. You obviously don't know jackshit" —he glanced at Suzanne—"excuse my language, Doctor—about Delta squad, Blackwood. Aliens or not, whoever, whatever's down there doesn't stand a chance."

"You're making a horrible mistake," Harrison said softly, feeling helpless as he thought of the young soldier who had just left. If there were only something he could *do* to stop it. . . .

Ironhorse checked his watch. *"Now,"* he said.

Behind the shelter of a tall pine on the outskirts of the farm, Reynolds stood silently gazing at his watch. At the instant the digits changed to 19:00:00, he motioned right and left for his men to move forward.

276

He was aware of a sense of exhilaration, of the rapid-fire drumming of his heart, of the thought of Arlene, and a sudden panic: How would she feel if something happened to him? But Reynolds, though still young, had seen enough combat to ignore such sensations. Like his role model the colonel, Reynolds had long ago adopted the motto, *Don't think—act*. At the moment his mind was too focused on what came next to worry about analyzing his own feelings.

He dashed to a vantage point from which he could see both the farmhouse and the barn, to be sure his men were in position. They were ready; the entrances to both buildings were covered by soldiers wearing gas masks. Reynolds raised an arm to signal two riflemen several yards in front of him; they fired off canisters of tear gas into the house and barn.

Within seconds, thick white clouds of gas began billowing out of both structures. The men positioned near the entrances followed the gas up with a couple of well-aimed concussion grenades. The ground vibrated with the explosions; a pane of glass still left in one of the farmhouse windows shattered, sending glass flying onto the porch.

Those who weren't wounded were due to come rushing out, coughing and gagging, any second now. It was time. Reynolds blew three short blasts on the whistle around his neck, then dropped it and pulled down his own gasmask. He charged forward. Meanwhile, the soldiers began storming the buildings, some jumping through windows, others kicking down doors.

Clutching his M-16, Reynolds ran to the barn

entrance. The tear gas was beginning to clear only slowly; it was still too thick inside the barn for him to see anything except the backs of his men as they disappeared into the fog, and the vague outline of the tractor-trailer. Reynolds smiled grimly. They were here, all right, and he'd like nothing better than the chance to get even with those sons of bitches, after seeing what they did to the soldiers at Jericho Valley. But there was still no sign of anyone fleeing the house or barn, no sound of gunfire . . . just a strange vibrating, humming sound, as if someone were chanting.

Reynolds raised the rifle and waited.

Xashron climbed up the ladder into the gray shadows of the loft, where most of the recently revived soldiers rested against bales of hay. The Advocacy and their attendants camped inside the warmer, more spacious accommodations of the old farmhouse, but Xashron, though he could have remained with them in comfort due to his high rank, preferred to camp with his soldiers.

Flanked by Xeera and Konar, Xashron stepped forward where he could be seen. There was a rustling as some of them tried to rise at the sight of their supreme commander, sounds of surprise from others who did not recognize and did not trust Xashron in his human form.

The Supreme Commander raised an arm in a clumsy approximation of a Mor-Taxan gesture. "Rest," he told them in their native tongue, for none of them had yet taken host bodies. He paused to look them over. At least thirty dark forms—no more than that, Xashron had insisted, for he would not release more soldiers than he had adequate supplies for, despite his desire to overthrow the Advocacy—were huddled on beds of straw; some of them rose on their thin appendages, to show respect, regardless of Xashron's order.

Feeling a deep sense of pride at the sight of them, Xashron said, "I have come not as your commander, but as a fellow soldier, to seek a consensus. I am proud you have survived, for this allows us a second opportunity to secure Earth before our colonists arrive. Yet I grieve because you, and your brothers and sisters who died, have suffered much at the hands of the Council. The sight of my soldiers falling beside me has made me bitter. We require enlightened leadership if we are to succeed."

He paused to judge the response; all listened quietly, without dissension so far, which gave Xashron the boldness to speak candidly.

"The current Advocacy is unenlightened," he said. "We must have a new Advocate."

There were murmurs. A female standing in a far corner of the loft said, "Such talk is dangerous, Commander. You put yourself at risk."

"I put all of you at risk as well." Xashron eyed her calmly. "You could be punished merely for listening to such talk. All of those who do not wish to hear what I have to say are permitted to leave without fear of punishment."

The female was silent; no one moved. One of the males reclining against a bale of hay asked, "What do you suggest we do, Commander?"

"I suggest we retain one member of the ruling

279

class"—he did not mention Xana's name, for fear that someone had seen them slip off together into the forest; best to seem impartial at this point—*"and replace two members with soldiers: myself, and whomever you select by consensus."*

Whispers. Some silently considered, others looked pleased; but Xorr, the commander of a squadron, spoke as he reclined on his bed of straw. *"Supreme Commander—I have always bowed to your will. But the Advocacy would never agree to such a thing, nor would the Council. Such an action is unheard of— letting the military rule side by side with the upper class. . . ."*

Next to Xashron, Konar came to his leader's defense. *"Our situation is unheard of. The Supreme Commander merely wishes to avoid the errors of the past, errors which came close to destroying us all . . . or have you so quickly forgotten, Commander Xorr? The military needs a voice in this new world, for this is strictly a military operation. There are only three members of the upper class on Earth—yet they rule us all. Should they continue to do so—those three who recommended the invasion be launched before our scientists even knew of the danger that awaited us here?"*

"It's true," someone said clearly, amid echoes of agreement. *"The Advocacy thought only of its own glory."*

Xorr rose angrily on unsteady appendages. *"And what do you, Supreme Commander, suggest we do with the two deposed members of the Advocacy? We all know they will not surrender peacefully."*

Xashron studied the group. Xorr was misguided in his loyalty, but shrewd enough to force Xashron into admitting he must kill the two Advocates, words that on Mor-Tax would have earned him immediate death . . . and which, on Earth, would offend those who were undecided about Xashron's plan.

"I leave their fate to a consensus," Xashron said evasively. "Let all of you decide what is best—I can do nothing without the assistance of the majority. All I ask for now is that you consider my words. This is a new world; old laws, old taboos are no longer relevant here. What is important now is ensuring, at all costs, that no more mistakes are made." He paused. "Through a miracle, I have my soldiers back; I will not lose them a second time to please the egos of our rulers."

Xorr took a step forward. "And as members of the military, Supreme Commander, you and I are sworn to protect the ruling class with our lives. This is the highest law . . . or have you so conveniently forgotten the oath you took?"

Xorr's statement created an almost palpable tension in the room, for each soldier had taken the same pledge to protect the ruling class; some murmured their agreement with Xorr's proclamation of loyalty, others looked silently to the Supreme Commander for guidance. With disappointment, Xashron realized that it would take both time and political maneuvering to overcome Xorr's opposition—and time was the one commodity the invading forces could no longer afford to squander.

"I have not forgotten my oath," Xashron replied. "I, too, am loyal to the Advocacy . . . but my loyalty

to my entire world, to the survival of my people and my fellow soldiers, runs much deeper. Your focus is too restricted, Xorr. We are speaking not of the survival of two members of the ruling class, but of the survival of our entire race."

Xorr had no answer; Xashron could sense the momentum of opinion shift in his own favor. Perhaps there was still a chance of convincing the majority, in which case he would have to assassinate Xorr and his followers as soon as it could be arranged—a pity, since Xorr was a competent military leader—before Xorr could kill him.

He was about to ask for an immediate consensus, but there was no time. Xeera, glancing over the edge of the hayloft, cried out.

"Commander, we're under attack!"

Xashron rushed to her side to see just as billowing clouds of gas filled the barn.

On the hillcrest, Harrison and Suzanne watched helplessly as the men swarmed into the abandoned buildings. "Colonel, please," Harrison began, "for the sake of your men—"

But Ironhorse ignored him totally, staring transfixed through a pair of field glasses. Finally, he lowered them and swore softly. "Damn . . . they're not even here!"

"Thank God for that," Harrison said fervently, at the same time it dashed his hopes of getting Wilson's proof.

That was a split second before the shooting started.

* * *

The humming grew louder, then stopped. Expectantly, Reynolds flattened himself against the termite-damaged wood near the entrance; but instead of hearing the sounds of surrender, he detected a sharp, brief whistle coming from inside. He drew closer to the door's edge and peered into the barn. Someone cried out; the sounds of struggle . . . and then through the wisps of gas, Reynolds saw chaos: Dozens of huge, shapeless black forms dropping from the rafters onto the soldiers below. In the melee, guns fired, and the whistling sound came again. And whatever was happening didn't look too good for Delta squad.

Reynolds was about to rush in to help out when he saw something—someone—coming at him through the mist. A man, a stranger. Reynolds stepped back and took aim.

The man saw but kept coming. He held an odd-looking object in his hand that Reynolds decided was a weapon: a length of thick wire, weighted at the ends with what looked like mechanical gears. The man staggered, but there was no blood on his dark clothing, only vague, indescribable filth.

"Halt!" Reynolds barked, but the man kept coming. Even in the darkness Reynolds could see there was something horribly wrong with him; his face was swollen and covered with pus-filled sores and flies. The man started to slowly swing the cable. Revolted, Reynolds fired.

The terrorist fell straight onto his back two feet from the entrance, and then, to Reynolds' wide-eyed horror, the man's skin began to bubble and pop, releasing small sprays of pus. It was as if someone had poured strong acid on the body; the skin melted, leaving dark red muscle and bone and gleamingly slick internal organs. Something black and gelatinous had wound itself all around the skeleton and the organs, and when the fizzling stopped, a smoldering pile of bones and nasty-looking black scum remained.

Reynolds was still gaping, stunned, when he heard the whistling sound again. Strong wire wrapped itself around his legs and arms, forcing the rifle from his grasp as he dropped to the ground. He flailed in vain, then tried to worm his way toward the M-16. He actually managed to get a hand on it, but his arms were pinned so that he couldn't raise it and take aim. From the side of the barn, another man appeared, his face as ghastly as the other's, an Uzi balanced on his hip.

It was the last thing Reynolds saw before the world exploded.

"Reynolds!" Ironhorse dropped the field glasses and dashed down the slope seconds before the burst of automatic gunfire.

"No, Colonel, don't—" Harrison reached for him, but Ironhorse was already gone. Harrison squeezed his eyes shut as the man with the Uzi fired at Reynolds.

Ironhorse tore down the hill and made his way toward the barn, but he was too late. Reynolds' body was a twisted heap, tangled in wire and old rusted gears, a makeshift bola. "Reynolds," the colonel whispered, crouching over the young soldier. At the sight of him, Ironhorse closed his eyes. The Uzi blast had caught Reynolds in the right side of his face, now a bloody, unrecognizable mass.

"You *bastards*—" Ironhorse stood up. At the same time, the roar of an engine sounded behind him as a rider dressed all in black came speeding out of the barn on a four-wheel ATV. A machine gun was mounted on the handlebars, and the rider aimed it at Ironhorse.

Ironhorse roared with fury and fired his M-16. The rider was knocked from the ATV, which flipped onto its back, wheels spinning crazily. The rider's body began to dissolve, bubbling and fizzling, the same as the one Reynolds had killed. But there was no time for Ironhorse to watch—a man and a woman in grotesque, decaying bodies were approaching from the direction of the farmhouse. He fired again, missed; the two fled into the safety of the barn through a side entrance.

The colonel peered into the barn as the remnants of the tear gas stung his eyes, making tears stream down his face. The barn was quiet, except for dark, inhuman shapes . . . if anyone from Delta squad was still inside, they weren't alive. Damn Blackwood for being right! It no longer mattered to Ironhorse if he lived or not. The way he saw it, he deserved to die with his men. He reached for a grenade on his belt, loaded it onto the attachment on his rifle, aimed it straight into the barn, and fired.

The blast made Ironhorse stagger backward; the old

building groaned and shuddered as wooden rafters gave way and collapsed to the floor, carrying other dark alien forms with them.

That's right, you bastards, DIE. . . .

He slipped another grenade onto the launcher and began to take aim again, when his legs went out from under him, tangled in one of the makeshift bolas. An old man approached from behind the far side of the barn—not as badly deteriorated as the others, but definitely eaten away by radiation. The old gas station owner, some detached part of Ironhorse's mind realized calmly. What the hell was going on?

Was the gas station owner, he corrected himself grimly. At least his hands were still free. He fired the grenade right at the guy's chest when he was still several yards away.

The old man caught it in his bare hand like some martial arts expert. Ironhorse knew then he had to be hallucinating. This whole thing was some weird, unbelievable dream—the grenade should have torn the man's hand off, or at least taken a few fingers with it—but here the guy was holding it. The old man studied the grenade curiously, as if he'd never seen anything like it before.

The colonel covered his head with his arms and turned away just before the explosion.

"Wait here," Harrison said to Suzanne. He couldn't stand by and watch Ironhorse get killed too.

"Oh no you don't." She shot him a dangerous look. "You're not going down there. And you're not leaving me alone."

"Look at him!" Harrison pointed; Ironhorse was struggling to untangle his legs without success.

"But you don't even have any weapons." She hesitated, then said, "I'm going with you."

"No way. One, you've got the kid to think about; two, you've got the camera. You alone can convince Wilson, and you know it. You've got to survive or we can all kiss our asses good-bye."

"Harrison—"

But he was already making his way down toward the battle.

"God damn you, Blackwood!" But at least she stayed put.

He had just made it to the bottom of the hill and was headed for the barn, watching as Ironhorse finally managed to free his legs. But at the same time, the colonel was entirely unaware of another man—grotesque, rotting—coming from the barn. The man aimed an Uzi right at Ironhorse.

"Colonel!" Harrison shouted, falling to the ground. "The barn!"

Ironhorse wheeled around and fired just in time. The man staggered backward and collapsed inside the old building. Harrison started toward the barn again; before he had taken three steps, the colonel was on the ground again, tangled not in one, but two of the aliens' weapons, unable to raise his arms to fire his weapon. A man and a woman were coming toward him out of the barn; a second man approached from the side near the farmhouse. All three were armed with automatic weapons.

Harrison swallowed hard. He didn't consider himself a particularly heroic individual, and at the moment it seemed like retreat was the sanest solution. But he couldn't watch another human being—even if it was the despicable Ironhorse—be killed without doing something. He looked around desperately, and spotted the ATV resting on its handlebars.

He dashed for it without realizing he'd already made the decision to do so. His heart was hammering so hard he couldn't get his breath, but somehow he managed to heave the thing upright and get it started.

Ironhorse was still flailing in the tangle of bolas. Harrison roared up beside him, painfully aware that the three ghouls had spotted him and were slowly taking aim.

"Cut me loose!" Ironhorse bellowed, but Harrison didn't bother to respond, just hooked the weighted end of one of the bolas over the back of the ATV and took off. Ironhorse screeched curses behind him as the terrorists fired. Harrison never looked back, not even when the bullets whined past his ears, until they made it up to the top of the incline, back into the safety of the forest.

"God almighty," Ironhorse swore after they'd stopped, and held still while Harrison cut the wires restraining him with a jackknife. "My backside is bruised to Kingdom Come and back."

"Then we're even," Harrison answered grimly, cutting the last strand and helping Ironhorse free.

"Look . . ." The colonel put a hand on Harrison's wrist. "Bruised or not . . . thanks for saving my ass."

"Forget it." Harrison shrugged and did his best not to smile. "Doesn't mean we have to be friends or anything. Come on, we've got to find Suzanne." He ran back toward the place he'd left her.

The colonel rose stiffly to his feet and followed. Harrison ran through the forest until he found the area he remembered: there was the boulder Suzanne had sat against; there was the hollow where he'd napped . . . but there was no sign of life. "Suzanne!" he called.

Ironhorse came up behind him and unhooked a flashlight from his belt. Harrison turned to him worriedly. "This is the area, isn't it? It's gotten a lot darker since we left, but I could have sworn—"

"This is it." Ironhorse switched the flashlight on and swept the beam over the area. "There," he said suddenly.

Harrison looked. The light hovered over the Geiger counter and the video equipment, smashed and lying in pieces atop a blanket of pine needles. Fighting off a sickening sensation of fear, he cupped his hands to his mouth and shouted. *"Sue—!"*

Ironhorse clamped a hand firmly over Harrison's mouth and looked anxiously behind them. "Easy! You'll give away our position."

Harrison did not struggle; slowly, cautiously, the colonel removed his hand. "Come on, Doctor, we can't risk hanging around here. They're probably following. We've got to put some more distance between ourselves and them."

"No." Harrison shook his head stubbornly. "We're not leaving without Suzanne. She *has* to be here somewhere."

Ironhorse looked hard at him. "Blackwood, you saw

what they did to my armed, trained men. If those things have her, there's nothing we can do. Dying ourselves won't help to bring her back." He reached out to grab Harrison's arm, but the scientist pulled back. "Come on!"

"For God's sake," Harrison cried as desperation filled him, "we can't just leave her!"

"Forget her, Blackwood!" the colonel snapped, and then, more softly: "She's had it." He caught hold of Harrison's upper arm with a viselike grip.

This time Harrison let himself be led away, looking back over his shoulder the entire time for any sign of Suzanne.

TWENTY-ONE

The next several hours spent hiding and shivering in the cold, dark forest were as nightmarish as anything Harrison had ever experienced. He and Ironhorse kept moving, pausing at times to hold perfectly still as the aliens passed by with soft, slithering rustles and the clumsier sound of human yet inhuman footfalls crashing through the underbrush. Without Ironhorse, he would not have made it, in his near delirium, unable to distinguish alien forms from the ominous black shapes of the bushes. The colonel remained calmly watchful, and somehow managed to keep Harrison moving long after he wanted to give up.

By dawn their trackers had given up and passed out of the forest, and Harrison realized Suzanne, too, was nowhere to be found in the woods. Ironhorse had circled back and led them to the place where they'd left her, but there was no sign of her. Discouraged, they rested, Ironhorse crouching on the ground but keeping one eye open, Harrison sitting on the rock where Suzanne had sat. He was exhausted beyond reason from fear and chill and exertion, and his back ached where Ironhorse had struck him the night before.

One scene played over and over like a B-grade melodrama in his mind: Mrs. Pennyworth with one arm around a fair-haired girl, and Harrison, the heavy, saying: *I'm sorry, Debi, but your mother . . .* He couldn't find the words, but it didn't matter; Debi understood all too well. *You killed her! You killed my mother!* the girl screamed, clawing at him while Mrs. Pennyworth did her best to hold Debi back. But the girl broke free and grabbed hold of him.

Someone shook his shoulder. Harrison opened his eyes to see Ironhorse standing over him. Amazingly, the colonel looked no worse for wear. "They're still gone," Ironhorse said. "I'm going down to the house and check for survivors."

"Suzanne—" Harrison began and broke off, confused, not knowing exactly what it was he meant to say about her. He rubbed his face.

Ironhorse removed his hand from Harrison's shoulder and glanced down into the valley. "It's possible she decided to go down there," he said, but Harrison heard the doubt in his tone.

He knows she's dead. He just wants to see if any of his men are still alive. Harrison got shakily to his feet. "I'll go with you."

Ironhorse stood up, raising a coal-black brow. "No offense, Blackwood, but you don't look up to—"

"I'm going with you," Harrison repeated firmly, shaking his arms and legs to get the stiffness out.

"Then we'd better do it fast, before they figure out where we are and head back this way."

Harrison nodded and took a few staggering steps. If Suzanne wasn't down there, at least he'd know for sure that the aliens had her, and that she was dead . . . or worse. He limped down the hill behind Ironhorse, every step aggravating the pain in his back.

Down in the valley, the air was still faintly acrid; the house and barn still smoldered.

"Here." Ironhorse paused to remove the rifle that hung on a strap around his back, and offered it to Harrison. "I'll use this." He patted the pistol in his side holster.

Harrison shook his head. "No thanks." He disapproved—in theory anyway—of the damn things, and right now he didn't feel he deserved to protect himself.

Ironhorse pushed it at him. "Don't be stupid. There might still be some of them down here."

"No," Harrison said more firmly, and walked ahead of him. Ironhorse shrugged and grasped the rifle in both hands, following.

The grass gave way to dirt near the barn. The colonel apparently saw something; he moved quickly to the entrance and crouched down in the sand.

"What is it?" Harrison followed as quickly as he could.

"Gordie," Ironhorse whispered, then said aloud, "Sergeant Reynolds. His body was here . . . now it's gone."

"What?" Harrison blinked down at the tangled mass of cable by Ironhorse, then peered uneasily into the barn. All was quiet darkness.

Ironhorse picked up the alien weapon and studied it, then dropped it to one side. There was a deep red, congealed spot on the ground; still sitting on his heels, the colonel reached with one hand, not quite brushing his fingers over the spot where Reynolds had fallen.

"Gordie . . ." he said, without looking at Harrison. "Damn them." His voice dropped to a whisper. "Damn them to hell."

Harrison stood back quietly, feeling a tug of sympathy for the man. Beneath the tough-guy exterior, there was a real human being . . . and as horrible as it was for Harrison to lose Suzanne, how much worse must the loss of so many men be for the colonel?

Ironhorse crouched silently with his back to Harrison for a while, then raised his head and said, "And over there . . . look at that." He pointed to two blackish, evil-looking masses near the barn entrance. "One of those was the man Reynolds shot, and one of those was the ATV rider who tried to waste me." He looked questioningly at Harrison. "What the hell *is* this?"

"I don't know," Harrison answered honestly.

"Unbelievable." Ironhorse shook his head, then rose. "I'll check out the barn. Think you're up for the house?"

"Sure." Harrison wasn't really, but he left the colonel where he was and walked over to the old farmhouse. The front door had been kicked off its hinges and lay in the middle of the doorway, half in, half out. Harrison stepped over it gingerly. In the front room, the walls were charred; plaster lay scattered on the floor, and the wooden ceiling beams hung down in long, thin shreds. A faint trace of gas remained, stinging his eyes and making them tear. He circled around the first floor through the kitchen and dining room, until he arrived back at the entrance, near the staircase. "Suzanne?" he called out timidly.

There were signs of struggle everywhere, but, amazingly enough, no bodies. Harrison climbed the rickety stairs with some trepidation; in one of the second-floor bedrooms he found purplish stains spattered across a wall, and realized it must be alien blood . . . but excitement faded quickly to disappointment. There was no way to get a sample; all his instruments were smashed, useless up on the hillside. "Suzanne?" he called again, this time louder as desperation began to take hold of him.

There was no denying it—she really was gone. He stumbled down the stairs, through the front doorway, and out into the brightening daylight. He stood on the front porch and leaned heavily against one of the remaining posts. Let the damn house collapse on him—he didn't care.

He remembered his words to her and shuddered. *Dr. McCullough, if you get yourself killed, I will never forgive you.* Fat lot of good that had done. He thought about the things he had forced himself to ignore while she was still alive, like how beautiful she was. As lovely as Charlotte. No, dammit, even prettier because, unlike Char, Suzanne seemed totally unaware of her good looks. Okay, so maybe she'd been an uptight person, but she had her priorities straight.

Once she was convinced the alien threat was real, she'd been a trooper, hadn't complained once about the trips, about the danger . . . had even insisted on coming when she knew the risk involved.

And, in some crazy way, he felt he had been able to get over Charlotte so easily because he had hoped that somehow, Suzanne and he . . .

He didn't even let himself finish the thought. Wouldn't have worked anyway. No two people were less alike. He rested his forehead against the post, ignoring the ominous creak, and didn't look up when Ironhorse walked up and said, "Nothing. You?"

Harrison shook his head. *"Damn* it," he whispered, swallowing hard to keep back tears. He wouldn't cry here, now, especially not in front of the poker-faced colonel. "I shouldn't have let her talk me into bringing her along."

To his surprise, Ironhorse's tone was sympathetic. "It wasn't your fault, Blackwood."

"Then *whose* was it?" Harrison jerked his head up angrily. "All right, so she was the most uptight person I've ever met—but at least she believed me! Where else am I going to find someone like . . . her?"

A violent sneeze coming from underneath the porch caused the worn wooden planks under Harrison's feet to shudder. He dashed off the porch and stood next to Ironhorse, who raised his rifle as the grate under the porch began to move, then fell forward onto the grass. Suzanne, her face smudged and dirty, peered out.

"It's me! For God's sake, don't shoot!"

Ironhorse grinned and lowered the gun. He and Harrison knelt down as Suzanne struggled from the crawl space on her stomach; they both helped her to her feet. She was filthy, her jacket and khakis covered with dirt and cobwebs, but to Harrison she looked absolutely gorgeous.

He was grinning so hard his cheeks hurt; impulsively, he grabbed her and squeezed her tightly, not giving a damn anymore what the colonel thought. She responded gratefully, hugging back with enthusiasm at first, but then something caused her to stiffen in his embrace. She wormed free. "I'll have you know that I am *not* uptight!" she said indignantly, brushing at the spiderwebs in her straight, dark brown hair. "I am a pro*fess*ional!"

He laughed at the realization she had been honestly insulted by his remark. Still giddy with relief, he said, "A professional who doesn't know how to take orders. You were supposed to stay hidden back in the forest, remember? I spent one hell of a night looking for you."

She bristled a little at that. "You neglected to tell me that those things—aliens—were going to be crawling all over. By the time I slipped away and worked my way down here, you and the colonel were doing your off-road routine." She pointed at the crawl space. "This seemed like a good place to wait things out. You think *you* spent a hell of a night. I was down there trying to negotiate with the rats and the snakes! And it was *freezing* last night—I'm still shivering." She rubbed her arms in an effort to warm herself, and craned her neck to peer anxiously around. "The aliens—where are they?"

"Hard to say now," Ironhorse replied, stooping to

retrieve one of the makeshift weapons from the ground. "From their tracks, I'd say they split up in a dozen directions." He held the weapon up, letting it dangle. "This is some weird stuff we're dealing with here. A bola made from what looks like baling wire and old gears. I saw a stripped-down old tractor behind the barn." He looked over at Harrison. "The truck was parked in the barn, all right; there are tire tracks in there that came from an eighteen-wheeler, along with more empty barrels—I counted thirty-six. Truck's gone now, and they must have taken the unopened barrels with them."

Harrison closed his eyes and turned away, sickened. He had hoped to stop them while there were only a handful free, before they'd had a chance to release any of the others.

"If they made these, they must be pretty intelligent," Ironhorse continued. "But the weirdest thing about all this are the terrorists who don't act like terrorists . . . who don't *die* like terrorists. At first I thought that maybe there were human beings behind all this. Then I thought maybe some strange cooperation between humans and aliens. But now . . ."

Harrison turned back to look at him. "Whatever they were, Colonel, they weren't human."

"Agreed." Ironhorse shook his head as if unable to believe what he had seen. "If I tell my superiors, they'll give me a Section Eight so fast my head would spin. But I know what I saw. A body dissolved after I shot it—the same way it happened with the guy Reynolds shot just before he was killed."

"I saw it too," Harrison told him grimly.

"So did I." Suzanne nodded thoughtfully, once again in scientist mode. "I've been thinking about that. Did you notice how clumsily they moved, almost as if . . ." She faltered, then continued. "As if they weren't used to their own bodies?" She glanced at Ironhorse. "Maybe you'll think *I* qualify for a Section Eight after this, but it seemed to me that the aliens were *controlling* those bodies, the way one would a puppet. Either mentally, or, more likely, from within."

Harrison gaped at her, astounded. "You mean an alien *inside* a human body? Come on, Suzanne, we both know that's impossible!"

"Is it?" she responded coolly, arching a delicate brow at him. "Where's your much-touted imagination, Dr. Blackwood?"

Ironhorse seemed interested. "Shut up and listen," he told Harrison. "She's got a point. When that guy dissolved, it seemed he had something black inside— something that didn't belong. Hell, you've got the remains of three of them around here . . . all you need to do is take a look." He turned to Suzanne. "But they dissolved . . . just like something out of a grade-B horror flick."

She nodded. "This is all pure conjecture, but maybe, in order to exit the human body, the alien secretes a strong acid. It would destroy the host, of course."

"And the alien, too, if it was hurt or couldn't make it out in time," Ironhorse finished, stroking his chin.

Harrison frowned. "Like you say, Suzanne, it's all pure conjecture. But at least we've got the concrete proof Uncle General Wilson wanted. If we can just figure out a way to transport some of those bodies with us."

Ironhorse removed his jacket. "You can use this," he said as Suzanne grimaced and Harrison looked uncertain. The colonel shrugged. "But whatever we do, let's do it fast before they come back."

Within a matter of hours they were face-to-face with General Wilson in a borrowed office at Vandenberg Air Force Base. Wilson stood contemplating the sunny fall morning beyond the window, one loosely clenched hand resting against the small of his back, the other holding the bowl of his pipe.

Seated behind him were his niece and Harrison, who slumped wearily in the straight-back wooden chair and tried to ignore his throbbing back, aggravated by the hours spent sitting in the helicopter and then waiting to see Wilson.

Suzanne looked far better than Harrison felt. She sat upright in the chair, hands folded in her lap, and her damn-the-torpedoes expression combined with the determined tilt of her chin gave Harrison comfort. Clearly, she and the general were made of the same stern stuff. During the past few days, Harrison reflected, she'd given more like three hundred percent than a hundred fifty. He shot her an encouraging look. She saw, but was too focused on what Wilson was saying to acknowledge.

Her uncle was still staring out the window. "What you're telling me, then," he said in response to Suzanne's extended monologue, "is that you failed to get the sort of hard evidence I asked for."

Harrison and Suzanne gasped simultaneously, but she got the first word in. "Failed to get *proof?*" Her voice was shrill, indignant. "For God's sake, I just showed you my figures on the radiation levels at Jericho Valley—"

"Theory," Wilson countered without looking at her.

"What about the partially dissolved body we recovered?" Harrison retorted, impatient that Wilson seemed to be playing some sort of game with them. "How much more concrete can we get?"

Wilson sighed. "There wasn't much left . . . hardly identifiable. I'll take your word that it's what you say it is, but, frankly, anyone could dissolve tissues with acid and claim they're alien remains."

Harrison watched with interest as a bright red flush spread across Suzanne's cheeks, the bridge of her nose. Her brows flew together. "Surely you're not suggesting that we *tampered—*"

"I'm not suggesting any such thing, Suzanne." He turned his head to regard her from the corner of his eye. "I'm telling you the kinds of things my superiors will say to me."

Harrison came to their defense. *"Three* eyewitnesses, General," he said emphatically. "And one of them an army colonel. What more do you need?"

"Lieutenant colonel, actually," Wilson corrected him, turning his short, stocky body toward them. "And as yet he hasn't officially backed your story."

"That son of a—" Harrison muttered darkly. Wilson ignored him and walked over to the small government-issue desk to empty the contents of his pipe into a glass ashtray, then refill it with fresh tobacco.

"So." Suzanne sat, a coiled spring, hands clutching the armrests, knees and ankles together, posture unnaturally stiff. "Our word—mine and Harrison's—counts for nothing, then?"

Wilson looked up from the ashtray and gestured apologetically with the pipe. "I didn't say that, Suzanne. But it *is* hearsay."

"Hearsay!" Harrison blurted. Exhaustion magnified his frustration, and he began to rise from his chair until Suzanne reached out with a restraining arm. He sank back with a sickening sensation of defeat. "How can you call it that?"

"When I tell my superiors, that's what they will call it."

"A whole squadron of soldiers were killed!" Suzanne exclaimed.

"Missing," Wilson said, spreading his plump hands. "AWOL. No bodies recovered."

Harrison lowered his head into his hands. He saw it all clearly now: Wilson wasn't going to help, then, had never intended to help them. The general had come all this way only to find out about his missing squadron, and didn't believe them for a minute, had permitted these meetings only to placate Suzanne. He understood now how Clayton had felt during his nervous breakdown. *Dear God, I've failed. Failed Clayton, Mom, Dad, everyone . . . and after all that I've done, it's going to all happen again.*

He felt Suzanne's hand on his arm and forced

himself to look up. "Why won't you believe me when I tell you what I *saw?*"

"What we *all* saw!" Suzanne jumped to her feet, fists clenched. "Dammit all, Uncle Hank, talk to your colonel! If he won't tell you that he saw his men killed, then—well, then bring him here and let me have a word with him!"

"Calm down, Suzanne, and have a seat," Wilson answered firmly, gesturing for her to sit. He waited until she reluctantly did so, then sat behind the desk. "Actually, I talked to the colonel at length very early this morning. He hasn't made an official report of what happened and he isn't going to." At Harrison's angry expression, he hastened to add, "At least, not an unclassified one. But he did admit that something incredible took place last night."

"What did he tell you?" Harrison demanded bitterly. "That the Russians have some super-secret device that made us all hallucinate?"

"Hardly." Wilson paused to relight his pipe and drew on it, his sharp blue eyes scrutinizing them from behind a fresh haze of smoke. "I didn't mean to upset either of you. I'm trying to explain why—considering the . . . uncertain nature of what we're dealing with— it's vital that this whole affair be kept top secret." He rested his elbows on the desk and leaned forward. "When Delta squad is defeated, captured, the army sits up and takes notice." His tone was confidential. "So do I . . . and my superiors. Very *important* superiors. Suzanne knows who I mean."

Harrison glanced first at Wilson, then at Suzanne,

scarcely daring to believe what he'd just heard . . . but he saw hope light up Suzanne's pale, drawn face. The President? So he'd been right the first time—the general had just been toying with them.

Wilson sat back, obviously pleased with the effect his words had. "These same people are very eager to keep this matter hush-hush."

Harrison sat forward with a sudden surge of energy. "Hold it right there, General. Keeping this quiet *won't* make it go away. I remember what happened to Clayton Forrester thirty-five years ago when the army decided to hush things up."

To his utter amazement, Wilson nodded sympathetically. "I understand. What happened to your adoptive father was an unfortunate mistake, Dr. Blackwood. For all of us. I think we've come far enough along not to make the same mistake again. The Pr—" He corrected himself. "My superiors would rather this didn't become a political issue. They want it kept quiet, but that doesn't mean they want it ignored. I've been asked to offer you a job."

Harrison gaped at him, unable to believe what he had just heard.

Wilson's expression was somber. "Find the aliens, Dr. Blackwood. Stop them before they do more harm."

A surge of relief washed over Harrison, a sensation so sweet tears stung the back of his eyes. He closed them and wished Clayton were sitting there with them. "Pinch me," he whispered, looking over at Suzanne. "I'm dreaming."

This time they reached for each other at the same

time, their laughter sounding suspiciously close to sobs. Suzanne gave him an awkward squeeze, then withdrew into her chair again. She shook her head, smiling warmly. "You're not dreaming," she said huskily. "I told you Uncle Hank would come through." She gazed affectionately at her uncle.

Harrison's exhilaration faded as a sudden suspicion took hold of him. "Wait a minute," he said to Wilson. "I want a guarantee I can do things *my* way. No red tape."

"Guaranteed." Wilson nodded. "Your own people, your own methods, whatever you want."

"Now I know I *am* dreaming."

"Naturally," Wilson continued, "we'll have to establish certain security procedures—"

Harrison's grin faded as he became defensive again. "What kinds of procedures?"

Wilson's gaze was innocent. "To protect you and your colleagues. And to protect the secrecy of the project. Nothing you wouldn't do yourself, I assure you."

Dammit, Harrison thought, *I* knew *there had to be a catch* . . . but at this point he knew he had already gotten more than he'd hoped for. No point in alienating Wilson while he was feeling generous.

Wilson went on. "Aside from that, you have a blank check."

Harrison and Suzanne looked at each other with wide eyes. "How big a check?" Suzanne asked coyly.

Wilson shrugged cavalierly, doing his best not to smile as he spoke, but surrendering at last. "I think the Federal Reserve can cover any check you choose to write." He hesitated. "Of course, you'll need a co-signer . . ." He reached across the desk for the intercom, pressed down a button, and said, "We're ready now."

"Oh, Lord," Harrison muttered, understanding everything.

The door opened and Lieutenant Colonel Paul Ironhorse entered, wearing a freshly laundered uniform and the barest trace of that aggravatingly smug sneer.

Harrison put his head in his hands and groaned; Suzanne emitted a gentle sigh.

"Well," Wilson said brightly, rising, "I believe you all know one another."

"Hello?" The connection was full of static, and Forrester's voice sounded weak and breathless.

"Clayton?" Harrison asked excitedly. "Clayton, I'm calling from Vandenberg Air Force Base. They *believe* us; they're actually going to help us!"

Silence for a few seconds and then Clayton breathed, "Thank God. Thank God. Harrison, I knew you'd do it."

Harrison laughed, feeling exhilarated and giddy. "Suzanne and Norton did it too. Listen, they're going to take us somewhere safe—and I've told them I want you to come too. Someone from General Wilson's office will be contacting you."

"You don't need me, Harrison," Clayton said, but Harrison could tell from his voice that Forrester was pleased. "I'd just be in the way."

"Bag the old-and-in-the-way excuse, Clayton. I

don't have time for arguments. We're leaving tonight."

"Tonight? That's a bit soon, don't you think?"

"The sooner the better," Harrison stated emphatically.

Forrester hesitated. "I'm an old man, Harrison. I can't be rushed. I'll come—but there are some archived papers at the Institute—"

"Good Lord, *more* files?"

"More files," Clayton stated firmly. "Perhaps not as vital as the ones I've given you, but we can use every scrap of information we can get our hands on. I'll get Jacobi to help me; just give me a day or two."

"Tell it to Wilson's office when they call. But they aren't going to like it."

"That's their problem. And, Harrison—"

"Yes, Clayton?"

"I love you, son."

TWENTY-TWO

A full moon shone eerily above the remote expanse of desert. Traveling with its headlights off, the eighteen-wheeler slowed as it approached the gate. Posted along the nine-foot-high, seemingly endless chain-link fence were warnings

DANGER
NUCLEAR TESTING SITE
KEEP OUT

along with yellow and black radioactive-fallout symbols.

The truck groaned to a halt, and a Delta squad soldier leapt out. He ripped away the chains securing the gate with an easy, fluid motion, then swung the gate open and let the big rig through. It rumbled past, then stopped again to give the soldier time to close the gate and hop up into the cab.

The rig began moving again. It drove through miles of lifeless, rocky desert and tumbleweed, past a rise where a shelter was built into the ground so that those inside could witness the above-ground detonations that had occurred here some thirty-odd years before.

The rig continued a few more miles, until it reached a ramshackle hangar that was used these days as a makeshift toxic waste dump. The soldier jumped down from the cab and slid the hangar door open wide; the truck pulled inside.

All that remained now was to unload the contents of the trailer and convey them to their permanent base, whose existence they had learned of from their Delta squad hosts: a cavern deep beneath the desert surface, created by an underground nuclear blast . . . a place where no living human would dare to venture.

"I am here at your request, Advocacy," Xashron said humbly, though he burned with anger at what he perceived to be betrayal. He stood in the dark belly of the cavern; before him, the three comprising the Advocacy reclined in their human forms against a ledge hewn from the rock.

Prior to the summons, Xashron had been supervising the release of the last of his soldiers from the barrels, and silently planning his strategy against Xorr and his followers. As Xashron's inferior, Xorr was morally bound to keep silent of the Supreme Commander's plan, for he was sworn to protect his Supreme Commander with one exception: if the Commander harmed a member of the ruling class. Since Xashron had not yet committed the deed or even stated that he intended to do so, Xorr could bring no charge against him but was free to take what measures he could to protect the Advocacy.

Which was clearly what Xorr was doing now as he and another member of his unit stood, armed with the human soldiers' firearms, guarding the three. Xashron had expected as much, and did not fault Xorr for doing so, but the fact that the Advocacy had summoned him, Xashron decided, meant that Xorr had broken his oath of loyalty and had told the Advocacy that Xashron was plotting their murders.

Perhaps such treachery should not have surprised him; for, in the event of Xashron's death, Xorr, also a brilliant military strategist, was most likely to be chosen by consensus to be the new Supreme Commander.

It was Xana, back again in her human form, who replied first. Xashron carefully noted her expression, her movements, the cadence of her speech, but could detect no anxiety, no fear there, only the faintest hint of warning. "We have called you, Xashron," Xana said, "because we wish to discuss a . . . problem."

Horek, using a gesture borrowed from his host brain, nodded. "Xorr has informed us that there is a plot among some in the military to harm the Advocacy. This, of course, cannot be tolerated."

Xashron looked at them and said nothing.

Oshar spoke. "Therefore, we require your assistance.

*Speak to your soldiers, Xashron. Rally them together.
Xorr has suggested we commence battle against Earth
as soon as possible in order to unite the military. Oshar
has used the primitive transmission equipment to
activate the homing beacons on our vessels. We have
already located one triad of ships nearby, and so we
have already informed the Council of our intent to
retrieve them tomorrow."*

"Tomorrow?" Xashron took a step forward, relieved
that Xorr had kept silent as to the instigator of the
unrest, yet disturbed by Oshar's words. "Advocate, my
people are recovering from their long sleep . . . and the
others from the last battle with the humans. My
co-pilot, Konar, was injured. I cannot go to battle
without a member of my triad—"

"Then find another co-pilot," Horek said flatly. "We
will tolerate no delays."

Xashron struggled to hide his fury. Tolerate no
delays, will you, Horek? This is the same brand of
idiotic haste that almost killed us once before— *And
at the same time, Xashron was bitterly disappointed.
He could not refuse to lead his men into battle, yet
there was no time to organize an uprising against the
Advocacy so quickly. Xorr was truly clever. He knew
that ordered to do battle Xashron would concern himself with seeing to it that his soldiers were prepared, and
would do nothing rash—such as risk a number of them
in a fight against supporters of the Advocacy—to
jeopardize the success of the mission or his soldiers'
welfare.*

"Very well," he said. "Perhaps Konar will be suffi-
ciently recovered by tomorrow to serve with me." He

311

paused. "But I would like to discuss one concern, if possible."

"Speak," Xana told him.

"If we retrieve three ships—it would be best to do so using the cover of human host bodies."

"Agreed," Horek allowed.

"However, flying three ships will require a minimum of twenty-one soldiers. We have but seventeen, excluding the three host bodies occupied by your Advocacy."

"You may have this body if you require it," Xana said. Horek and Oshar were not so generous.

Horek scowled at him. "Then you must go find more, Commander, along with a means of getting into the military installation where our ships are held. You can consult the human soldiers' minds—and, as always, we rely on your talent for strategy."

Xashron bowed his head. "Thank you, Advocacy," he replied stiffly, and promised himself that he would deal with Xorr and the Advocacy as soon as his mission was accomplished.

Harrison stood in front of the open door of his house and was assaulted by the smell of rotten banana peel, a less-than-subtle reminder that he hadn't been home enough lately to take out the garbage. And more than that greeted him: on the foyer tile lay a pale pink envelope. He felt a surge of hopefulness: Char! For a moment he forgot all that had happened, remembered only that he missed her and wanted to bury his face in her soft, perfumed hair. He bent down to pick the envelope up; it was addressed in Char's oversized, elegant calligraphy, in violet ink, to H. Blackwood.

"Shit." Not a good sign. With sour disappointment he recalled their last few encounters. He was not one to hold grudges, always quick to forgive and forget hurts, and he kept making the mistake of assuming that everyone else was like him. Clearly, it wasn't the case with Charlotte. There was something heavy sliding around inside the envelope—his housekey. *Dammit, I don't need this right now . . .*

He slipped it, unopened, into his shirt pocket. He'd pack first and read the letter later tonight, after they got to where they were going.

"All clear," Ironhorse called from inside, and Harrison walked into the living room. The colonel had insisted on "securing the area" before permitting Harrison into his own house; Harrison tolerated it with faint amusement, but at the same time he wondered just how long he and Ironhorse could work together without coming to blows. For now, his ultramilitary approach to everything was something to make fun of; after a while it was bound to become aggravating in the extreme. Ironhorse no doubt thought the same thing about him.

He walked past the colonel without looking at him, into the bedroom, and dug three bags—one suitcase and two shapeless nylon tote bags—out of the closet, threw them on the bed, and stared at them. Now, what did you pack when you didn't know where you were going and you had no idea how long you were going to stay? He finally emptied his underwear and sock drawer into the suitcase, then pulled every clean pair of pants from the closet and packed them in too. By the time he stuffed his shirts in, the suitcase was full and he pressed hard on it to get it snapped shut. His ditty bag was in one of the nylon bags, and he gazed at it: only enough toiletries for a weekend, really.

Ironhorse stuck his scowling face into the bedroom. At the sight of him, Harrison asked, "Hey, just how long are we gonna be there?"

"As long as it takes to stop them," Ironhorse said grimly. "Could be weeks . . . could be months."

Harrison nodded and picked the bag up, intending to head for the bathroom, but the colonel blocked the doorway and thrust an overstuffed white plastic garbage bag at Harrison like an accusation. "Which way to the dumpster?"

Harrison backed away from the rotten odor. "You don't have to do that—"

Ironhorse's gaze was dangerous. "I do. I have orders from Wilson to see to your well-being. You leave for three months and come back, this thing'll be lethal. Besides, the damn thing is gassing me out."

Fighting an urgent need to hold his nose, Harrison pointed. "Out the back door and hang a right. It's at the end of the walkway."

Ironhorse disappeared immediately; Harrison called after him, "You know, when this is over, I could really use someone to come in twice a week—"

The back door slammed in response.

He went to the bathroom and threw extra toiletries into the bag: shave cream, toothpaste, shampoo. By the time he went back into the bedroom, he realized he had packed everything except the most important stuff, back at the Institute. He sat wearily on the bed and looked around. He wouldn't miss the little house; it was just a place to sleep—but leaving the Institute was going to be rough.

He became consciously aware of the letter in his pocket; it seemed to press against his chest with tangible weight. For an instant he struggled against the impulse to pull it from his pocket and read it . . . then yielded.

He tore it open and shook it so that the key dropped into his hand, then put the key in his pocket and slid the neatly folded page from the envelope.

It took him a second to work up the courage to unfold it, even though the key already told him what he wanted to know.

Harrison—
(No "dear" or anything. Damn, she was mad.)
Am returning your key. Mail me mine. If you show in person, this time I *will* call the police.

That was it—not even a signature. Mostly he felt numb, but under the layer of numbness was an undeniable hurt. Impossible to believe that she could really stop loving him—turn it off like the kitchen faucet—because he didn't make enough money. Refused to make enough money. He let the letter drop into his lap and picked up a framed photograph on the nightstand. It was a picture of himself and Char mugging for the camera at some party or other, Harrison in a tuxedo with his index fingers hooked into the corners of his mouth, pulling it into a wide gaping grin while his tongue hung out; Char self-consciously photogenic, wearing that tolerant smile of hers. He stared at her, his feelings oddly mixed: he hated her for misleading him, letting him think she loved him for himself . . . and at the same time, he loved her—or, at least, the person he *thought* she had been—funny, bright, carefree, all the things he pretended to be and knew he could never really be because of the burden bequeathed him by Clayton and his parents.

Clayton, at least, Harrison mused ironically, would be glad to hear about the breakup.

Ironhorse appeared in the doorway again and nodded at the suitcases on the floor. "All set?"

Harrison nodded and set the photo back on the nightstand. "Yeah, but we'll need to stop by the Institute. There are a thousand things there I need—"

"It's taken care of."

"But those things are more important than anything here," Harrison protested. "I need my instru—"

Ironhorse silenced him with a bronze hand. "I said it's all taken care of, Doctor." He crossed the room to pick up the suitcase and one of the bags; on his way out he paused to glance at the photograph of Char. "Pretty lady."

"Yeah," Harrison said dully, sliding the letter back inside the envelope. He was about to put it back into his pocket but changed his mind and set it down next to the picture.

Where he was going, he wouldn't be needing either of them.

The station wagon threaded its way behind the Bronco, which was packed so full Suzanne couldn't make out the three men inside, only suitcases pressing Norton's chair against the rear windshield. The Bronco kicked up so much dust on the unpaved road, she had the windows rolled up and the vent turned on. In the front seat, Deb leaned against the passenger door, sourly watching the landscape roll by, right elbow on the armrest, cheek against her hand. If she withdrew any further, Suzanne decided, she would fall right out the door.

"All right," Suzanne said calmly, trying to play the rational adult. A real challenge at this point; her eyes were burning with fatigue, and an hour ago, her rumbling stomach communicated to her that in her excitement she had neglected to eat anything that day. "You can stop pouting now, Ms. McCullough."

"I'm not pouting," Debi muttered into her hand. "How much longer?"

Suzanne sighed. "I don't know. They didn't tell me. I'm not enjoying this any more than you, Deb."

"Why do we have to move?" Deb whined, sitting up. "They already moved us *once*—isn't that enough?"

"It's only for a little while." There were times such as this one when Suzanne wished she could explain everything to Debi, so she could understand the urgent necessity of her mother's absences, of the second move. Yet at the same time, Suzanne felt relief that the project's secrecy precluded her from telling Deb about the aliens. *So young,* she thought, glancing over at her daughter's sullen face. *She deserves to stay a kid a little while longer.*

"Deb, you know this is secret work, like the work I did in Ohio. Except that *this* project is even more secret . . . and important." She paused, trying to decide whether or not her next remark would frighten Deb, then went ahead anyway. "We're going to a place because we have to be protected. It's important that *no one* find out what we're doing."

The girl's eyes brightened a bit. "You mean like foreign spies?"

Feeling triumphant, Suzanne shrugged nonchalantly and kept her eyes on the Bronco. "Something like that. I can't say exactly, of course."

"Ooh, neat." Deb settled back, looking somewhat satisfied. "The Russians are after my mom."

"I didn't say that. And remember, it's top secret."

"You can trust me." Deb scrutinized her mother's face carefully. "So that's why I couldn't stay in school?"

"Mmm," Suzanne said noncommittally. "You'll have a private tutor here."

"That's nice." Deb sighed and nestled her cheek against her hand again. "But I already miss Kim . . . and Mrs. Pennyworth." Her blue eyes suddenly began to cloud up.

"It's for the best, chicken," Suzanne soothed.

"Maybe you'll make some new friends where we're going."

Debi turned her face toward the window again. "I hate making new friends."

She rode the rest of the way without speaking.

"How much farther?" Harrison asked as he navigated the Bronco down the uneven dirt road. Much longer, and he'd have to ask Ironhorse to take the wheel before he nodded off.

The colonel leaned forward in the backseat to answer. "We're almost there."

"Thank God. I might make it."

"Amen," Norton echoed next to him in the front seat. "My ass is sure tired of this bumpy road."

Harrison frowned at him. "Quit complaining. *You* didn't spend the night being chased by aliens. Besides, I thought your ass didn't feel much of anything."

Norton lifted a humorously scornful brow at him. "Typical scientist. Doesn't recognize figurative language when he hears it."

Ironhorse shifted in the backseat, apparently uncomfortable with the direct reference to Norton's handicap. Harrison smiled faintly to himself. Maybe some time around Norton would loosen him up. "I know relocating is an inconvenience," the colonel said, "but it's only short-term . . . until we've neutralized the problem."

Norton glanced over his shoulder at Ironhorse. "I like the way this man talks. In fact, my ass is feeling better already. Harrison, you feeling any better?"

Harrison grinned. As a matter of fact, he was, and

the closer he drew to their destination, the better he felt. He might even risk three or four hours of sleep tonight. "A whole lot better, Norton, thank you for asking." He looked up in the rearview mirror at the colonel's stern but puzzled face. "What makes you think neutralizing—gee, I like that word—the aliens will be that easy, especially after what we saw last night?"

Ironhorse's expression shifted to that of someone who knew he wasn't being taken seriously yet at the same time knew he was right. "You saw what they did to my men, Blackwood. I don't care how many of those things are out there. Without their ships or their weapons, they don't have a chance. We'll track them down and kill them."

"If you don't mind, I'll just stick with tracking," Norton said softly.

The colonel frowned at him. "If you're not prepared to take this operation seriously, Mr. Drake—"

"Oh, man, I'm serious." Norton's brown eyes widened innocently. "Whatever made you think I wasn't serious? I'm *always* serious. Harrison, tell the man just how serious I am."

Straight-faced, Harrison said, "When it comes to keeping that unfeeling ass of his safe, Norton is *very* serious."

"Serious," Norton intoned solemnly, "is my middle name. Norton Serious Drake."

Ironhorse shook his head, disgusted, and raised a muscular arm to point at a barely visible dirt path. "This is it."

Harrison steered the Bronco left onto the path, then

minutes later pulled to a stop before a closed electric gate. "Very impressive. Now what?"

In answer, the colonel removed a small remote control from his shirt pocket and punched a combination into the number pad. The gate swung open. "Welcome to Federal Government Property Number 348, a/k/a The Ranch. Without proper authority no one comes in . . ."

Harrison drove the Bronco past the gate, checking in the outside rearview to make sure Suzanne followed. She did, and behind her the gate closed automatically. Ironhorse continued. ". . . And no one gets out."

Harrison blinked, trying to focus his weary eyes. He wasn't sure what he'd expected, but it certainly hadn't been this. Sprawled out on the rolling grassland lay an honest-to-God ranch: a graciously imposing manorial house, freshly whitewashed, sat in front of wooden stables that opened onto a huge fenced-in corral, complete with horse, which paused in the midst of munching hay to eye the newcomers. Harrison emitted a low whistle. "Not bad."

"It's landed-gentry time," Norton said approvingly. "Seriously speaking, Colonel, I think I could get used to this."

"Oh," Debi breathed worshipfully, her nose and hands pressed against the car window, "you didn't tell me about a horse."

"I didn't know about a horse." Suzanne frowned. She had never been near an animal that size, and wasn't so sure she liked the idea of Deb getting close to one. She pulled the wagon to a stop behind the Bronco. "Besides, I thought you hated making new friends."

"Oh, Mommm . . ." Deb groaned, meaning: Surely you knew better than to take the remark seriously.

"Be careful," Suzanne warned, but Deb was already out of the car and dashing toward the corral. Deb ran right up to the fence and called out to the handsome chestnut-colored animal, who, much to Suzanne's relief, remained at a respectable distance, studying her warily as he took another mouthful of hay. Satisfied that her daughter was in no imminent danger, Suzanne opened up the back of the station wagon and started to unload luggage.

A familiar voice came from the porch. "Leave those, Suzanne. Tom and the colonel can take care of them for you."

She looked up and gasped. Mrs. Pennyworth stood smiling on the front porch, the usual braid wound around her head, and wearing the usual jeans and Reeboks. She was wiping her hands on a yellow-plaid dish towel as if she'd just come from the kitchen.

"Mrs. Pennyworth! How on earth—"

The Dutch woman's smile went from welcoming to mysterious. "Ephram said you would be needing someone to tutor Deborah and to cook . . ."

"But you were sitting with Deb only a few hours before we started packing." Come to think of it, Mrs. Pennyworth had been the *only* baby-sitter on the list Jacobi had given her. No wonder the woman had never questioned Suzanne's constant "emergencies."

"You might say this is my home away from home," the older woman said enigmatically, "so there was no need for me to spend any time packing."

Debi came wandering back, looking frustrated by her inability to establish communications with the horse. "He's awfully shy—" She broke off at the sight of Mrs. Pennyworth and sped like a bullet toward the porch. Her hug was so enthusiastic, Mrs. Pennyworth staggered backward a step. "Mrs. Pennyworth—how did *you* get here?"

Mrs. Pennyworth hugged back, dish towel in hand. "Well, I explained to your mother's employer that I was good friends with you and so had to come along. Besides, I heard you needed a teacher."

"That's great!" Deb stepped back and gazed wistfully in the direction of the corral. "This place won't be so bad after all."

"And here is Mr. Thomas Kensington." Mrs. Pennyworth gestured at the man approaching from the direction of the stables.

Dressed in riding breeches, suede jacket, and a felt hat, Kensington was gray-haired, lean, and walked with a slight limp. As he joined the group, he nodded unsmilingly at them. "Tom Kensington," he said rather stiffly.

"Thomas is responsible for the maintenance of everything here," Mrs. Pennyworth said. She was apparently the only one not taken aback by the man's cold demeanor. "The house, the grounds . . . and Deborah will be interested to know, the stables. He is the owner of the horse, Spirit."

"Oh, Mr. Kensington." Debi fastened her adoring gaze on him. "Please, could you teach me how to ride?"

Kensington coughed nervously and shrugged. "I think that depends on your mother and Mrs. Pennyworth, young lady."

Suzanne sighed. "If it's all right with everyone else, I suppose it's all right with me."

Mrs. Pennyworth nodded. "So long as you finish your lessons first." She gestured with the dish towel at Harrison and the others as they approached. "Is anyone here hungry? I have a roast with potatoes and carrots in the oven." And at the grateful sounds of appreciation that followed, Mrs. Pennyworth smiled. "Come in, then, so we can all get acquainted."

TWENTY-THREE

By the time Norton finally made it out of his bedroom the next morning, Colonel Ironhorse was waiting for him.

Poker-faced, the burly colonel stared down at him. "You didn't come down to breakfast, Mr. Drake. Frankly, I was beginning to get concerned."

Norton curled his lip sourly at both the realization he'd missed breakfast and the patronizing remark. The colonel was just another typically ignorant non-plege (Norton's own term for anyone who walked on two legs and blithely assumed everyone else did too). Without help, it'd taken Norton a full hour to wash up and get dressed, even though the facilities here were great: a private toilet and shower designed for a paraplegic, just off his bedroom. It was now only nine o'clock; Norton had risen at eight, and after the sleep he'd missed lately, that was pretty damn good, even for a military type.

"Wasn't in the mood for breakfast anyway," Norton snapped. Even Harrison had the good grace not to bother him before he'd had his first cup of coffee. "Did it occur to you I might be tired, Colonel? Excuse me. I'm on my way to a date with a cup of coffee."

"We'll get you some—" Ironhorse began.

"I'll get it myself, thank you," Norton replied rather nastily. This guy was laying on the "help-the-crip" bit just a little too thick this morning. And still wearing his uniform—was he expecting a surprise inspection, maybe? "Gertrude—full speed ahead."

The colonel followed him. "I was going to say, we'll get you some when we get to where we're going. But you're headed in the wrong direction."

"Gertrude, stop," Norton ordered, then scowled up at the colonel. "I thought the kitchen was that way."

"The coffee is this way—toward the elevator."

"Elevator?" Norton's frown deepened. "You're hallucinating, Ironside. This is a one-story hacienda."

"It's Iron*horse.*" The colonel's black eyes regarded him humorlessly. "I was going to show you to your office, Mr. Drake. If you'll come with me, please." The colonel gestured for him to follow.

Norton balked. "I don't need an escort, thanks. I'll find my way around."

"Do you know where the elevator is?"

"Well, no, but . . ."

"I was going to show you your office as a common courtesy," Ironhorse said patiently, "the way I did for Dr. McCullough and Blackwood."

"Oh." Norton became vaguely aware that he might have overreacted. "Well then, let's go."

But Ironhorse stood staring at him. "And I wanted to be sure you had the equipment you needed. It's my job, after all."

"All right, all right." Norton waved an impatient hand at him. "Just get me to the coffee first."

Ironhorse turned and headed down the hallway.

"Gertrude, full speed ahead." The chair followed the colonel. At the end of the hallway, back by Norton's bedroom, was the elevator.

"Handicapped access." A snideness crept into Norton's tone, one he really hadn't intended. "Very considerate of you. Gertrude—ahead three and rotate one eighty."

The chair carried him into the elevator. The controls were low, easy for him to reach, and he blinked at the three choices: DOWN, UP and OPEN DOORS. No top floor, so he pressed the DOWN button, and tried to ignore the fact that Ironhorse was watching him. "Chip on your shoulder, Mr. Drake?"

So there it was. The colonel was just looking for a polite way to get even for the razzing Norton had given him the other day. If Norton and Harrison had anything in common besides their hatred of the aliens, it was their hatred of uptight, regulations-spouting military types, but Norton wasn't prepared to take him on without any caffeine in his system.

"I'm tired." Norton drew a palm down over his forehead, eyes, cheek. "And Harrison will verify that I'm not known for my cheerfulness before my first cup of the day." He paused, then tilted his chin up defiantly at Ironhorse. "Besides, Colonel Ironass, what's it to you? Bet you have a few chips of your own."

To his astonishment, the colonel didn't take offense. In fact, Norton thought he saw a glint of humor in those inscrutable black eyes. "Just call me Chief and find out," Ironhorse said softly.

Norton looked the Indian's powerful build up and down and swallowed. "No thanks."

The elevator came to a smooth stop; the door opened. Ironhorse stepped out. "As you can see, the elevator directly accesses your office." He turned to glance at Norton. "More consideration."

Norton directed the chair out of the elevator and closed his eyes as he sniffed the air. "My God, I'm having an olfactory hallucination—that's my own private blend of coffee I smell. How did you—" He broke off as he opened his eyes and caught sight of the room around him. A slow smile spread over his face.

The office was huge. Not only did it contain the same transmission equipment as his office at the Institute, and then some, but over in one corner— now he knew he was hallucinating—sat a Cray supercomputer operator's console, complete with laserjet printer. "Gertie—rotate forty-five left, ahead ten." The chair rolled him up alongside the computer console, which he stroked lovingly. "Colonel, pinch me if I'm dreaming, but am I to understand that this is my *very own* Cray?"

The barest hint of a smile crossed Ironhorse's thin lips, then vanished; obviously, the colonel was pleased with Norton's reaction. "The computer engineers didn't have much set-up time," he replied nonchalantly. "But this baby can still access the DDN—the Defense Data Network."

"Where are you hiding the CPU?"

"In the next room," Ironhorse replied. "I understand it's pretty noisy . . . and I figured you might not enjoy working at a constant fifty-five degrees. Like I said, if you find there's anything else you need, more memory, more peripheral storage—"

Norton grinned and shook his head. He'd clearly underestimated the man. So he was an uptight military asshole, but there was actually a working brain hidden beneath that ultratough exterior. "This'll do fine for now. I don't think anything else has been invented yet. What'd you do? Read my Christmas list?"

The colonel crossed the room as Norton spoke, picked up a Melitta glass pitcher and poured coffee into a mug. "You can't be expected to do the job if you don't have the equipment." He set the pitcher of coffee back on a hotplate and walked over to Norton and the Cray.

"Keep up that attitude, Colonel, and I might even get to like you."

Ironhorse handed him the cup of steaming coffee. "If I can offer this as a common courtesy, Mr. Drake—without adding to that chip of yours."

Norton hesitated only for a split second before taking it.

Ironhorse stepped across the hallway to Dr. McCullough's office. There was something he liked about Drake in spite of the guy's smart mouth. Maybe it was the fact that like the colonel himself Drake had overcome the odds, had come out the victor in an impossible situation. He'd read Drake's dossier: born into a poor family, which, like Blackwood's, had been killed in an alien attack that left the three-year-old child orphaned. After that he'd lived in a children's home, then a couple of foster homes . . . but instead of turning sour, Drake had harnessed his bitterness and set it to work for him. The kid had been a National Merit scholar, had won math scholarships to the best universities. Ironhorse had to admire him.

Learning about Blackwood's tragic past had eased Ironhorse's contempt for him somewhat, but he doubted he'd ever come to like the guy. Dr. McCullough was a different story. Now, *there* was a responsible, hardworking individual who would have done well in the military. Ironhorse peered into the doorway of her office and did his best to assume a pleasant expression—something he was quite unused to doing. "Finding everything you need, Doctor?"

The windowless office was about two-thirds the size of Drake's. Glossy black-topped counters ran the length of two interior walls; above them, glass-front cabinets displayed every conceivable type of lab equipment: beakers, test tubes, petri dishes, and a lot of instruments Ironhorse didn't recognize. The exterior wall was a bookshelf stocked with reference volumes; next to it, in one corner, stood a computer terminal and leather ergonomic chair. One of the cabinet doors was open, and McCullough had unloaded some instruments onto the counter and was studying them. At the sound of the colonel's voice, she looked up with a distracted expression.

Give her horn-rimmed glasses and a white smock instead of the blue jeans and red checked shirt, Ironhorse decided, and she'd be the perfect caricature of the absent-minded scientist. Brains and looks, the whole package—yet the lady seemed quite unaware of it.

"Yes, thank you," Dr. McCullough answered blankly. "There are things here *I* don't even understand. Somebody must have spent a fortune."

Ironhorse squared his shoulders, proud that his work had not gone unappreciated. "The government wants everyone happy."

McCullough sighed and frowned down at the mysterious instrument before her. "I'm happy enough, I suppose. Now all I have to do is find a bacteria harmless to man, impervious to radiation, and lethal to the aliens." She shook her head. "Maybe I should just cure the common cold first."

"If anyone can do it, ma'am, I'm sure you can," Ironhorse answered encouragingly. He withdrew and headed down the corridor for Blackwood's office.

The door was closed; Ironhorse rapped on the wood with his knuckles. At the muffled "Come in," the colonel entered.

Dressed, as usual, as if he were about to embark on a hike rather than research, Blackwood stood in the middle of the room, hands on hips, craning his neck back to admire the ceiling. Of all the offices, Ironhorse was particularly proud of this one; it was a virtually exact replica of Blackwood's office back at the Pacific

Institute, right down to the inflatable starship *Enterprise*.

"Basement window's too high, and the view's wrong," Blackwood murmured, still surveying the ceiling. "And the room's bigger. But when I close the door, I can forget that I'm not at the Institute." He gave the colonel a curious look. "Someone obviously wanted to make me feel right at home."

"A perfect copy, isn't it?" Ironhorse asked, swelling with pride.

Blackwood nodded and stared up again. "As if my life before this thing didn't matter"—he looked back at Ironhorse with an expression of wonder—"or never existed at all."

"It never existed," Ironhorse said with conviction. "Not for any of us."

After dinner that night Suzanne sat on the living room sofa with Debi snuggled next to her and watched as Kensington carefully added two more logs to the blaze in the fireplace. The room looked as if a family had lovingly decorated it with simple country furniture, even a handmade quilt draped across the back of the couch.

"More coffee?" Mrs. Pennyworth gestured with the coffeepot at Suzanne's empty cup on the table.

"No, thanks." Suzanne shook her head. She was sinking into luxurious drowsiness here in the fire's warm glow, surrounded by a circle of friends: Harrison a circumspect distance away on the couch, Norton nearby in the wheelchair, Ironhorse settled into a leather wing-back chair, obviously the seat of authority. And in two days, Clayton Forrester would be arriving. It was very hard not to feel a sense of . . . family, of belonging, and very easy to feel safe, to forget the terror hidden somewhere outside the haven of the ranch. She reached out and idly stroked her daughter's hair, but Debi was far too enthralled by the tale Ironhorse was spinning to notice.

Even the colonel seemed affected by the mellow setting; as unfeeling and unapproachable as he seemed in his military persona, now he leaned forward in the wingback as he spoke, a cup of coffee balanced on one thigh, clearly relishing his role of storyteller. "Actually, it's short for 'one-who-shoots-the-iron-horse.'" He was explaining the origin of his family name in response to Deb's question. "I'll bet you can figure that one out."

Deb wrinkled her forehead. "Iron horse? I don't get it. Sounds like a car or truck."

Ironhorse shook his head. "Nope. Think back about a hundred years or so."

Deb thought for a minute, then burst forth with: "I got it! A train!"

Norton, who'd been close to dozing off, jerked his head up sharply. Suzanne laid a gentle hand on her daughter's arm to quiet her.

"Excellent," the colonel said approvingly, his black eyes dancing with firelight. "Your daughter's very sharp, Dr. McCullough."

"I'm afraid she knows it already," Suzanne answered, smiling, and reached out to fondle a lock of Debi's blond hair.

"Oh, Mommm . . ." Deb batted at her mother's

hand with adolescent disgust and asked the colonel, "Your family fought the trains?"

Ironhorse nodded somberly. "As the railroad moved west, it pushed my people off their land. Unfortunately, you know how it comes out. The Blackfoot tribes were spread all over Montana, Utah, up into Alberta. And now we're crowded onto a few tiny reservations."

"That's awful!" Deb's eyes were round with dismay. "Is it really true?"

Ironhorse's bronze features hardened. "It's true all right. I grew up on a reservation." He shifted the topic abruptly, as if it were too painful to consider for long. "But where were we in the story?"

"Your great-great-grandfather," Debi prompted.

"That's right." Ironhorse's expression warmed. "Anyway, since my great-great-grandfather was shaman of the tribe—"

"What's a shaman?"

Suzanne clicked her tongue. "If you keep interrupting Colonel Ironhorse, Debi, he'll never be able to finish his story."

Ironhorse smiled indulgently at the girl. While telling the story, he was transformed into a completely different person. *Why,* Suzanne thought, amazed, *he really is a kind-hearted man.*

"That's all right, Dr. McCullough," the colonel replied. "I enjoy answering her questions. A shaman is the tribe's spiritual leader, Debi, sometimes called a medicine man. He was the most respected person in the tribe, more even than the chief. The shaman used his magical powers to enter the bodies of animals and learn their wisdom."

"Neat. You mean, like if I entered Spirit's body to try to find out what it was like to be a horse?"

"Something like that. Anyway, the warriors brought their strange discovery to my great-great-grandfather to find out what it meant."

Deb was on the edge of the couch. "What was it? The discovery, I mean."

"It was a flat rock"—Ironhorse drew one hand, palm down, horizontally through the air to indicate just how flat—"covered with drawings no one had ever seen before. And they were very, very old too."

"How old?"

Suzanne frowned. "For goodness' sake, Deb, let him finish the story." She was actually becoming rather interested in it herself.

The colonel continued, unfazed by the interruption. As he spoke, his tone became increasingly dramatic, that of a real storyteller. "Older than the nearby cave drawings, or the drawings on ancient pieces of buffalo hide passed down through generations."

"What kind of draw—oops." Deb clamped a hand over her mouth and looked guiltily at her mother, who shook her head with a tolerant smile. There was no controlling Deb's curiosity.

"What kind of drawings?" Ironhorse intoned melodically, tilting his head. "Well now, I'm glad you asked. They were of a man wearing a bowl that covered his entire head. His eyes glowed, and he carried a wand."

Suzanne shifted, unsure as to whether or not she liked the direction this story was going.

"A magic wand?" Deb breathed.

"It seemed like magic because the wand threw out great bolts of light." The colonel paused to take a sip of coffee. Suzanne shot him a warning glance, now certain that she didn't like this particular tale at all. Surely the colonel realized that Debi had no idea about the nature of the Blackwood Project . . . and that stories about aliens were bound to scare such a young girl.

But Ironhorse continued, seemingly oblivious to Suzanne's disapproval. "My great-great-grandfather took this rock and went out into the desert for one moon—that's about a month. When he came back, he gathered everyone in the tribe together." Ironhorse set his cup on the coffee table and acted out the part with sweeping gestures and a booming voice. "'We know that our people were the first people ever to walk this earth,' the shaman said in a strong voice, even though he was weak and hungry. 'But others came before us.'"

"Wow!" Deb grinned. "What did they do then?"

Ironhorse finally seemed to catch Suzanne's warning look; he picked up his cup and said offhandedly, "They fired him and got themselves a new shaman."

The adults snickered, except for Norton, who stirred from his reverie and looked about, disoriented.

Debi groaned with disgust. "And *I* really thought they'd been visited by a space man. You made that all up!"

Ironhorse's expression became serious. "Only that last part."

"Bedtime," Suzanne said quickly. Actually, it was way past Deb's usual bedtime, but Suzanne had so enjoyed having Deb around that she hadn't had the heart to send her daughter to bed. But now she wanted a word with Ironhorse before any more stories about alien visitors were told.

"Aw, Mom . . ."

"Complain while you get ready for bed." She gave the girl a playful swat on the bottom as Deb rose. "Now, scoot."

Deb sighed. "Okay. Good night, everybody. And thank you for the story, Colonel Ironhorse."

"You're welcome, Debi. Good night."

The other adults murmured their good-nights as Debi padded off to her room.

Kensington, who'd been squatting, back poker-straight, by the fireplace, spoke up for the first time that evening. "You folks going to be here long?" A strangely cold little man, his question came out sounding more like a challenge than a casual, friendly inquiry.

Harrison looked up from contemplating the fire. "We hope not, Mr. Kensington. No offense intended."

Mrs. Pennyworth spoke up from her place in the armchair farthest from the fireplace, her tone as warm as Kensington's had been cool. "And none taken, Harrison. You stay as long as you have to." She shot Kensington a dirty look; from the familiarity of her disdain, Suzanne assumed the two knew each

337

other very well. "And what kind of question was that, Thomas?"

Kensington sniffed and replied, his tone defensive, "We might need to restock the pantry, that's all."

"I take care of the pantry." Mrs. Pennyworth jabbed at herself with a thick finger. "You take care of the grounds."

Kensington sighed as he rose from his place by the fire. The corner of his mouth quirked up; it could have been the beginnings of a smile, or a sign of irritation. "Then I guess I'd better check the security system and turn in. Good night, all." He walked off stiffly in the direction of the kitchen.

"To check my pantry, no doubt." Mrs. Pennyworth shook her head.

"Colonel—" Suzanne began.

Ironhorse didn't give her a chance to speak. "I'm sorry, Dr. McCullough. I didn't realize when I started that the story was so directly related to what we were doing. A subconscious slip-up. I take it Debi has no idea—"

"Of course she has no idea," Suzanne said, feeling a twinge of irritation. "I'm not in the habit of informing my daughter about the secret government projects I happen to be working on."

"I'll be careful about my choice of stories next time, Doctor," Ironhorse promised, his expression contrite.

"Colonel . . ." Norton was suddenly completely alert. "You believe that story?"

Ironhorse shrugged. "Indian folklore, if you ask me. Nothing more, nothing less."

"Funny thing about folklore," Harrison said, rising. "Almost always there's an element of truth in it."

He paused to give Suzanne a look that seemed to go right through her. "I agree that your daughter doesn't need to know what we're doing, but it's hardly fair to try to protect her from history, from what really happened. Good night."

They watched him leave in silence. That night Suzanne dreamed about the mysterious drawing on the rock.

TWENTY-FOUR

The next morning at eight, a taxi deposited Clayton Forrester at the entrance to the Institute. From there he walked to the cafeteria and got himself a cup of coffee. He wasn't allowed caffeine, and the walk was longer than what he was used to, but it left him pleasantly winded. Besides, old habits were hard to break. For thirty years Forrester had arrived at the Institute every morning at precisely eight o'clock, walked to the cafeteria for his coffee, then headed to his office almost a full hour before anyone else arrived. It was his favorite part of the day, the quiet time when he could contemplate the tasks ahead without interruption, the time when he got three-quarters of the day's work done.

As he walked along the sidewalk through the cool morning air and stared out at the sprawling grassy landscape, he realized with mild surprise that he,

Clayton Forrester, was actually enjoying this walk, enjoying the taste and smell of the forbidden coffee, enjoying the familiar scenery, enjoying the fact that there was important work to be done. It was his closest brush with pleasure in years, and there was a faint smile on his lips.

All this in spite of the totally sleepless night he'd spent. He'd lain on the living room sofa for his customary nap during Johnny Carson—and the second he drifted off he was awakened by the screams of a frightened child. Heart pounding, he'd dashed through the shadows to Harrison's old room before he remembered that the boy had moved out years ago. He forced himself to settle back on the couch with the admonition that he needed rest.

The second time he was roused by the roll of thunder. He ran to the window to see heat lightning redden the dark sky, and for an instant he'd panicked at the sight, thinking it was the aliens' death rays. After that he resigned himself to staying awake. Yet, at the same time, his horror that the aliens had returned was mixed with genuine excitement at the thought of working again. And in this morning's sunlight, the terror was gone, replaced by a genuine sense of purpose.

By the time he made it past the security guard and into his building, Forrester was puffing a bit. The heart was, of course, bad—had been bad for some time. The first attack had come at age sixty, and a few years back, when the pacemaker was installed, the doctor (just a kid Harrison's age) made it clear in no uncertain terms that Clayton was living on borrowed time. Which suited Forrester just fine. It was only the memory of his promise to the boy

You aren't going to die, are you?

No, Harrison, I'm not going to die.

that kept him from finishing off an entire bottle of sleeping pills at once and being done with it. Harrison had suffered enough for one lifetime, and Clayton refused to add to the boy's grief. Harrison already had enough guilt at being a survivor.

Forrester walked silently down the hallway—the carpet was a new addition since he'd retired—into the older wing, and finally arrived at his old office. It felt right being there, even though the plastic imitation woodgrain plaque on the door read MCCULLOUGH now. The door was unlocked, as Forrester had known it would be—everything of value belonging to its current occupant had been removed a day and a half ago. He turned the doorknob and entered.

Clayton had packed his belongings at the house yesterday, and was ready to go, but it had taken Archives a full day to come up with the files. And here they were, covering the entire desktop, in topless cardboard boxes stuffed full of manila folders. Clayton walked around, behind the desk. A box rested in the seat of the swivel chair, but there was no sign of Suzanne McCullough's things; even the photograph of her daughter was gone. Clayton had noticed it a few days before, and it had reminded him of the photograph of Harrison he'd kept in almost the same spot. It made him sympathize with Suzanne all the more; he knew the horror of trying to raise a child with the specter of the aliens hanging over one's head like the sword of Damocles.

He set the coffee on the one clear spot near the desk's edge, then bent over and started going through one of the boxes. It was tedious work, and the angle made his back ache. After about fifteen minutes of it, he straightened, put his hands against the small of his back, then stretched backward. This would never do. He eyed the formidable-looking box resting in the chair. He wasn't supposed to do any heavy lifting, but then, Jacobi wasn't coming for another half hour, and Clayton refused to stand all that time. Besides, Jacobi was older and smaller than he was. Forrester bent down, slid his hands under the bottom of the box, and lifted it with a grunt.

It was even heavier than it looked. Red-faced, gasping, Clayton slowly lowered the box. About four inches from the floor, he let it drop onto the carpet with a muted thud. Clayton went back and sank into the chair with a sigh, then picked up his coffee and took a small sip. Some thick-headed, muscle-bound college student who worked part-time as a gofer must have thought himself brilliant to set the heavy carton in the chair, where someone else would obviously have to—

Pain blotted out the rest of the thought. Heavy, crushing pain that squeezed his chest until it pushed all the air from his lungs in one startled, frightened gasp. Forrester panted and waited for it to lessen, but instead of easing, it bore down harder against his chest while it swept down his left arm.

His grip on the cup eased; it fell, spilling scalding hot liquid down the front of his cotton shirt, into his lap, down his legs. Clayton scarcely felt it. He was too busy struggling to breathe, to hold back the growing blackness that loomed threateningly along the periphery of his vision.

In the midst of the fear and the struggle, he was vaguely conscious of the irony of it all—that this should happen today of all days, when, after all these long years, he finally felt like living . . . and yet, as he looked out at the familiar surroundings as they began to gray and dim, it somehow seemed good to have it happen here, in the place he loved best.

With his other attacks, the pain had gradually eased, then faded, but this was nothing like the other attacks. The agony mounted until it reached truly unbearable intensity. Forrester raised a hand to his chest. "Harrison," he whispered.

And then the darkness took over, and there was no pain at all.

TWENTY-FIVE

At nine o'clock that same morning, Harrison watched through his office window as Kensington led Spirit, with Debi aback, for a slow walk around the corral. After checking out the new yet familiar office yesterday, Harrison had come to the conclusion that there was very little for him to do until (a) the aliens broke their radio silence, or (b) Norton somehow managed to break the code.

Harrison sighed and walked back to his desk to shuffle through the Forrester Project files. He'd read every scrap of paper in them at least a thousand times, but he picked up the folder succinctly labeled "Three" and slumped down at his desk to go through it again.

A whirring sound in the hall caused him to glance up. Norton sat in the doorway looking uncharacteristically vexed, his brown forehead puckered.

"I take it you haven't come to tell me you've cracked the code," Harrison said.

Norton shook his head glumly. "Doc, I'm getting nowhere fast. Forward seven, Gertrude." The chair rolled forward and parked a short distance in front of Harrison's desk.

"I thought you said if you could just spend enough time on the Cray——"

Norton interrupted him. "Without more information, all the supercomputers in the world can't decipher those alien radio signals." He folded his strong arms in a gesture of finality, as if to say: *That's all I can do about it. Now what?* They stared at each other unhappily for a moment.

"Then," Harrison said at last, "we'll simply have to reconceptualize our approach."

"Hey," Norton scoffed, "you're talking to the king of reconceptualization himself." His tone softened. "What I need, good buddy, is a clue. The archeologists had the Rosetta Stone before they could figure out how to read hieroglyphics. We've got diddly-squat."

Harrison closed the folder in his hands, put it on top of the other aged files, and reached across the desk to proffer them to Norton. "We've got Clayton's old research. We even have photocopies of alien maps found in the wreckage of ships. Maybe your Rosetta Stone is in here."

Norton's expression wasn't particularly hopeful, but he took the files. "I guess it's worth a try. Home, Gertrude." The chair did a 180-degree turn and headed out.

The vaguest outline of an idea began to form in Harrison's brain; he stood up suddenly. "Norton—"

"Hold it, Gertie. One eighty." Norton turned to face him again.

Harrison felt a dawning excitement. "Does the number three mean anything to you?"

Norton shrugged. "Should it?"

"It meant something to the aliens. Think about it. Their ships flew in groups of three, their optic devices were divided into three units, they attacked all their targets in three directions. Even those weapons they made, the bolas, had three weighted ends. Three, Norton . . ." His voice rose with enthusiasm. "Think number three. Just a hunch, but the answer's there, I know it is."

"Number three, huh?" Norton stroked his chin, then said a little more cheerfully, "Hey, I'll think of it. A hunch is the best thing we've got right now. What've we got to lose?"

Just a world, Harrison thought, but he didn't let himself say it.

By late that afternoon Harrison was sitting with his feet propped on his desk, staring out the basement window with the usual ennui, when he heard the shout.

"Bingo!"

It came from the direction of Norton's office, and Harrison knew instantly what it meant. He scrambled to his feet and dashed out the door. In the corridor he almost collided with Suzanne as she came running out of the lab.

"What on earth—" She broke off as he clutched at her to keep from losing his balance.

"Yes!" Norton's voice ranted on. "Absolutely, undoubtedly, *yes!*"

"Sounds like we've got a breakthrough," Harrison told her; together, they made it down to the communications center. Ironhorse was already inside, staring quizzically at Norton, who sat over at the Cray console, pressing a computer printout to his chest in a display of ecstatic affection. His eyes were closed, his dark face lit up by a beatific smile.

"Norton!" Harrison grinned at him. He'd expected results, of course—after all, Norton Drake plus a Cray supercomputer were an unbeatable combination, but he hadn't expected them this *fast*. "Norton, you son of a gun, you did it, didn't you?"

Norton opened his eyes and smiled sweetly at Harrison. "I did it all right. Me and the Cray."

Ironhorse's voice rose with frustration. "Did *what?* Will someone please tell me what the hell is going on?"

Norton gave him a who-is-this-imbecile? stare. "Cracked the alien lingo, of course, Colonel! What planet have you been stationed on?"

"Well then, let us see it," Suzanne said, putting a hand out.

Norton pulled it out of her reach and held it up with a grand flourish so everyone could see.

Ironhorse bent down to squint at it, then began to read aloud. "One, two, one, one—" He rose. "Doesn't make any sense to me." He glared at Norton, then Harrison. "Is this somebody's idea of a joke?"

"No, no, no." Norton clicked his tongue with disgust. "The top line is two to the seventh power." He pointed at the page with an index finger. "Bottom line's two to the third. Two to the seventh is a hundred twenty-eight. Two to the third is eight."

"We can all work the math, Norton," Harrison said impatiently, bending over to look at the columns of numbers himself. A math-based code? Seemed too easy. Maybe the aliens were trying to mislead them.

"Some of us, anyway," Norton muttered, casting a contemptuous sidewise glance at Ironhorse.

"Have you worked out what the numbers stand for?" Harrison asked.

Norton seemed to deflate a little, apparently disappointed that no one shared his elation. "Come on, Doc, you expect me to do everything around here? How should I know what they mean? I focused on one part of the transmission—" He cheered up again at the thought. "That 'think number three' stuff really helped. These are all base three." He drew his finger along a horizontal column of numbers and shook his head in appreciative awe. "Beautiful. Anyway, this is what I came up with."

"A coded message?" Suzanne asked.

To Harrison's surprise, Ironhorse straightened and shook his head. "Too easy," the colonel said. "Even primitive codes use large prime numbers as their key."

Apparently impressed, Norton raised his eyebrows

at Harrison. "When the soldier's right, he's right. This is no code. This is pure."

Ironhorse grunted. "The question is, pure *what?*"

Harrison took the printout from Norton's hand and studied the rows of numbers. It was all right here, staring him in the face. Maybe if he just stared at it long enough . . . "We're overthinking this," he said distractedly, "digging too deep. We're giving the aliens too much credit."

"You mean we're assuming the obvious . . ." Suzanne began.

Harrison nodded. "Thereby overlooking the obvious." He began to pace, staring down at the paper in his hand, making his way around Norton's desk, swamped with mounds of printouts and old file folders, past the counters of transmission equipment, to the doorway and back. Somehow, the pacing freed his mind to wander, and he tried to lead it gently along the most obvious paths.

"I'm missing something," Ironhorse said in a low voice.

He heard Suzanne chuckle softly. "What it all means is that you'll get to go on one of Harrison's famous—or should I say infamous—field trips."

Harrison registered the exchange without letting it break his concentration. The information was all there if he could just see it. It was *all there.*

He stopped pacing and looked up at Norton. "Have you loaded all of Clayton's material into the Cray?"

Norton nodded. Now that his excitement had faded, his voice sounded tired. "Damn straight. Spent all morning and afternoon doing it. Tedious work. I bet my eyes look like little pinwheels." He scrunched them shut and rubbed them.

"So *that's* why you missed breakfast again," Ironhorse muttered.

Norton's eyebrows rushed together. "Tell me, Colonel, does General Wilson make you take attendance at every meal? I bet you've got a little rollbook with all our names in it."

Harrison refused to be distracted. "Norton, how long to run a basic substitution program—those numbers against the material in the alien documents?"

"Ah." Norton's eyes gleamed as he understood what Harrison was getting at. "Now you're talking, Doc." He gave the Cray an affectionate pat. "With my friend here—maybe twenty seconds."

"Well then, do it," Harrison told him.

They gathered around the Cray as Norton cracked his knuckles, then poised over the keyboard and wiggled his fingers like a concert pianist preparing to play.

"Enough showmanship," Ironhorse groaned.

Norton's fingers flew over the keyboard, typing in the names of files and programs faster than Harrison could follow. He drew in his breath and counted.

Approximately eighteen seconds later, numbers and symbols began filling the screen, scrolling by too fast for human eyes to read. Suddenly, the numbers stopped coming—and on the screen was something Harrison recognized: a representation of an alien topographic map complete with three-dimensional mountain ranges. Along the vertical and horizontal axes were numbers—the alien equivalent of longitude and latitude. On each axis a number was highlighted and blinking.

Norton squinted at them. "First group of numbers in the paradigm appear to be a date—tomorrow's, as a matter of fact. And the rest—"

"Coordinates on their map?" Suzanne interrupted.

A grin spread over Harrison's face as he stared at the monitor screen. "Exactly. Norton, can you get us a hard copy?"

Before he finished the question, Norton had already pressed a button and the printer was spewing out a copy. Harrison walked over and pulled the page from the feed as it came out. "Great. Now all I need is a ruler and a pencil."

"Ruler and a pencil?" Norton feigned indignance. "We're high-tech around here, Doc. Whoever heard of a ruler and a pencil—"

Harrison shot him a dangerous look.

"Try the top drawer of the desk." Norton grinned.

Harrison found them, balanced the printout precariously on top of a stack of folders, and found the intersecting point, which he circled. He held it up. "Now, anybody got a map?"

Ironhorse led the three of them to his basement quarters, a spartan, narrow room compared to the technological luxury of the scientists' offices. It was outfitted with little more than a government-issue metal desk, a phone, and at least a dozen different maps displayed on the walls. Ironhorse stepped behind the desk to stare at a giant wall map of the United States. "Show me that map again."

Harrison handed it to him.

"You're assuming they're still in the country," Norton remarked. "But there's no way we can be sure of that."

Ironhorse didn't turn around, just kept glancing from the printout to the map. "I'm sure. If they're still in the white truck, then they've got the entire army on the lookout for them . . . no way are they going to make it past the Mexican or Canadian border." He paused. "But there's something else. You know, the topography of this damn alien map looks familiar. I *know* this area." He stared at the wall map again, then stiffened. "Good God!"

"What is it?" Harrison tried to follow his gaze. Suzanne and Norton moved closer.

Ironhorse pointed and stood to one side so the others could see.

"Nevada?" Suzanne sounded puzzled. "Looks like the middle of nowhere."

"If the aliens consider it important," Harrison told her, "we'd be wise to do the same." He looked back at Ironhorse; the colonel seemed stunned.

"Damn straight it's important," Ironhorse finally said. "That's Nellis Air Force Base. They must be planning to overrun it tomorrow!" He stepped up to his desk and reached for the phone.

Harrison laid a hand on his wrist. "What are you doing?"

"Calling General Wilson," Ironhorse replied, easily

breaking free of Harrison's grip. He picked up the receiver and put it to his ear. "Someone's got to notify the commander at Nellis—"

"Why don't you think about it first, Colonel?" Harrison asked, trying to sound reasonable. "Like an alien would think. It doesn't make sense for them to attack an air force base right now. You said it yourself —without weapons, without resources . . . Even at full strength, even by surprise—their attack wouldn't stand a chance of success."

"Look what they did at Jericho Valley," Ironhorse said.

Harrison shook his head. "I think the terrorists did that—and the aliens overpowered the terrorists because they were *already* inside. You know what Wilson said—secrecy is of the utmost concern. What'll you tell them at Nellis? Be on the lookout for aliens? They'll think it's a crank call."

Ironhorse hesitated, then replaced the receiver reluctantly. "Okay. I guess that makes sense."

"There's something here we aren't seeing," Norton said thoughtfully, staring at the spot Ironhorse had indicated on the wall map.

"And we aren't going to see it," Harrison added, "until we learn to start looking at things the way the aliens do."

It was Saturday night at the Gold Mine, a bar and grill designed to look like a saloon dating from gold rush days. Both the exterior and interior walls were paneled with artificially weathered, unpainted wood, and the inside was adorned with sepia-tint photographs from the late nineteenth century, all of which worked to give the place that sterile, corporate-chain air of authenticity.

And because it was a Saturday night, the Gold Mine was packed with airmen from the nearby base. One of them, Airman Vic Giannotti, a sandy-haired, normally sober man barely six months past his twenty-first birthday, stumbled out into the unlit parking lot and gratefully sucked in air that was not two-thirds cigarette smoke. A few paces behind followed Doyle O'Connor, a ruddy-faced fellow squadron member who happened to be grinning from ear to ear at no one in particular. At the moment, Doyle was feeling no pain.

"Doyle." Vic paused and waited for O'Connor to catch up to him. Vic tended to get maudlin when he drank, and he and Doyle had just polished off three large pitchers of draft between the two of them. Vic had completely forgotten the fact that O'Connor was an arrogant ass that he'd never much cared for; now Vic was overwhelmed to the point of tears by the man's generosity. Not only had Doyle talked him into getting sloshed to celebrate Vic's first real "dear John" letter, but then Doyle had turned down the opportunity to go home with a cute-looking redhead.

"Doyle, ol' buddy . . ." Vic slung an arm rather sloppily over Doyle's neck in an inebrious embrace and pushed his face so close to his friend's that their noses almost touched. "Doyle, you've been a *gooood* friend. A great frien'. Bes' frien' inna whole world. I saw the look on your face when that redhead came up to you."

Doyle staggered a little under Vic's weight, then parted his thick lips to release an earth-shaking belch. "Well, hell, Vic . . . I got her number. Might give her a call later . . . after I'm sober enough to be worth something. Besides, we were celebrating your freedom from that—that bitch—what was her name again?"

"Donna," Vic said, becoming depressed again at the simple mention of the name. "Good ol' dump-'em Donna. Leaving me for a goddamn doctor. A goddamn doctor. Hell, the guy's *old*—practically thirty. What the hell's he got that I ain't got?"

"Money," Doyle reminded him. They looked at each other and broke into giggles.

"No-good money-grubbing bitch . . ." Vic gasped, not quite sure what he was laughing at.

Doyle struck an affected posture, pinkies crooked and raised high, and said in a shrill falsetto, " 'I'm dump-'em Donna, the money-grubbing bitch . . .' "

Vic began to laugh harder. Encouraged, Doyle trotted off into the dark parking lot, still mincing.

Vic ran after him. "Jesus, Doyle, stop it!" Vic giggled until tears ran down his cheeks. He couldn't seem to stop laughing—Doyle was just so damn *funny* . . . but underneath the cozily warm, whirling sensation of drunkenness, Vic knew he felt lousy. And tomorrow would be even worse: he'd have a hangover, plus the memory that Donna had dumped him.

The Firebird was in a remote corner of the parking lot; Vic liked to park it sideways, away from other cars, to keep it from getting scratched, and it worked: the Bird was a '75 and still in mint condition, and its two-year-old glossy black paint job looked like new.

"And heeeerrre's the car!" Doyle mimicked Ed McMahon, throwing out his right hand and stamping his foot in a "ta-daa" gesture.

Still recuperating from his laughing fit, Vic leaned against the driver's side and fumbled in his pocket. "Keys, keys, where are the keys?" Not there. Panicking, he patted all of his pockets—still no keys. "Shit, I've gone and lost them! We'd better go back inside."

On the passenger side Doyle grinned and jingled the keys at him. "They were in my back pocket, Vic, remember? You were gonna let *me* drive."

"Oh, yeah." Vic slapped his forehead clumsily. Doyle was right. After the first pitcher of beer, Vic had turned over the Bird's keys and proclaimed himself unfit to drive. But that was back before Doyle had started to drink the lion's share. No way was he gonna let Doyle get near the steering wheel of his precious Bird now. "You're right, Doyle ol' buddy, but I'm doing much better. Honest." Vic held out his hands. "C'mon. Pitch 'em over."

"Ready?" Doyle assumed the classic quarterback pose. "Here goes—Elway eat your heart out!" He launched the keys high into the air; they sailed over Vic's head and landed several feet away on the asphalt.

"Oops. Don't know my own strength."

"Not to get upset." Vic waggled a finger. "Everything is under control." He went staggering into the night after the keys. He quickly realized that the black leather keycase was impossible to see against black asphalt in the dark, and got down on his knees to grope for them.

"Hey, Vic, need a hand?"

"Naah." He patted the asphalt tentatively. After a minute his hand brushed against something. "It's okay, I found 'em!"

Vic reached out confidently this time. His fingers closed on something cool and slightly moist—almost oily. He grimaced. No telling *what* disgusting garbage was lying there in the bar's parking lot.

And then it moved in his hand, pulsed, flexed just like a muscle.

Vic opened his mouth to yell, certain he'd just grabbed hold of a snake. But the swift, crushing pressure on his throat made screaming impossible.

"C'mon, Vic," Doyle called impatiently. "We're gonna miss curfew."

TWENTY-SIX

Suzanne sat in what was now her customary place on the sofa next to Harrison; across from them sat Ironhorse in the leather chair. The after-dinner ritual of coffee in front of the fire had already become a routine . . . and God knew, Suzanne reflected, she needed routine, some kind of stability, some semblance of a normal, regulated life to keep from losing what shred of sanity she had left.

According to the ancient clock on the mantel, it was eleven-thirty; the others had long since gone to bed, including Norton, who had retired early, exhausted after a long day's work. But Suzanne was not in the least bit sleepy; how could she be, knowing that tomorrow they might face the aliens again? From the others' expression, she knew they felt the same.

Ironhorse broke the extended silence. His powerful shoulders hunched as he leaned toward Harrison. "I don't like this, Blackwood. Don't like it at all . . . going out to Nellis without an idea of what we're doing—just keeping an eye out for any stray aliens."

Harrison stared into the dying fire, his gaze steady as one hypnotized. Suzanne thought at first he hadn't heard the question, but then he answered slowly, without looking up, "They mentioned Nellis in their transmission for a reason, Colonel. Like I said before, we've got to start thinking like they do."

Ironhorse got up and went over to the fireplace to add more logs to the fire; clearly, he wasn't planning to go to bed anytime soon. He placed the logs carefully, leaving space between them, and fanned the blaze until the fire leapt up, encouraged. "You expect me to climb into the heads of those creatures," he said, glancing over his shoulder at Harrison, "you've got to give me something more to go on." In the fire's orange glow his profile seemed to Suzanne to take on an ancient dignity, the strong, determined face of a warrior contemplating the battle ahead.

Harrison took his time answering. "The invasion was incredibly well organized, efficient. Within a few days the entire world was on its knees." He looked up as Ironhorse returned to his chair. "They sent their trained military. They're soldiers, same as you. You tell me—how do soldiers think?"

A faint, hard glint of amusement crept into the colonel's eyes and faded swiftly. "We don't. I spent four years at the Point and fifteen more in uniform. I prepare. I stay prepared. And when the time comes to act, I don't think anymore. All I do is react."

"Okay, let's start there." Harrison sat forward,

resting his elbows on his knees. "You're their leader—react to your situation."

Ironhorse settled back in his chair and looked up at the ceiling. "I'd need good intelligence. Got to know your enemy. Communications—they already have that. Supplies—got to keep the troops fed. Weapons . . ." He trailed off and looked down at Harrison.

"Definitely weapons," Harrison said with a trace of bitterness.

Ironhorse nodded thoughtfully. "They don't have any—except for those handmade bolas and a few guns, but nothing that amounts to anything. That's their primary weakness."

"Which makes it our strength," Suzanne remarked softly. She'd read Forrester's files. She'd seen photographs of what those weapons had done. The two men looked at her as if surprised to see she was following the conversation.

"If I were their commander," Ironhorse said, "I'd make it top priority to get my hands on some weapons."

As the colonel spoke, Harrison began to look as though he'd just had a hideous revelation. Alarmed, Suzanne turned to him. "You okay?"

He nodded. "Something just occurred to me. Colonel, have you ever heard of Hangar Fifteen?"

Ironhorse shook his head.

"Of course you have," Harrison persisted. "Hangar Fifteen, the place where the air force stores all its UFO evidence."

Ironhorse's expression became skeptical. "You

mean Hangar Eighteen." He shook his head. "Forget it, Blackwood, that's a myth."

"No," Harrison replied with such total conviction that Suzanne believed him. "Hangar Eighteen is the myth. Disinformation, created by the military. Hangar Fifteen is the real McCoy."

"I don't buy it."

"Clayton Forrester did. It's in his papers. Colonel, I think now might be a good time to call General Wilson. Ask *him* if it's a myth."

Ironhorse rose and glanced at the clock on the mantel. "I will." His eyes narrowed threateningly. "But you'd better be right, Blackwood. The general won't appreciate my calling him at home." He strode from the room, leaving Suzanne and Harrison alone.

"And if you're right . . ." Suzanne turned to Harrison. "And the aliens are going to Nellis to recover their weapons . . . How will we be able to stop them?"

He stared grimly into the fire. "I don't know. But you've read Clayton's papers, Suzanne. You know what will happen if they get their hands on their ships, their weapons." He faced her, his eyes haunted, circled by gray shadows. He seemed to be looking beyond her at some horror that had taken place thirty-five years earlier. "No matter what it costs—we have to stop the aliens now, or we'll never be able to stop them at all."

The living room was warm from the heat generated by the fire, but Suzanne found she was shivering.

"What the—" Harrison said abruptly, and broke off.

362

Suzanne followed his startled gaze to the staircase leading to the upstairs bedrooms. She caught a flash of something pale and wraithlike retreating up the stairs; for an instant she thought they had both seen a ghost.

Harrison watched, too, then turned back to Suzanne with a worried expression. "She must have heard us talking, Suzanne. I think you'd better go talk to her."

"My God." Suzanne jumped to her feet, finally understanding. "Debi—"

Heart pounding, she crossed the room in a few quick strides and ran up the dark staircase after her daughter. She caught up to her at the doorway to Debi's bedroom.

"Deb—" She reached out a hand and touched the girl's shoulder in the darkness. Debi turned. She was dressed in the long white T-shirt that she wore for a nightgown, and even in the gloom of the unlit hallway Suzanne could see her face was pale and frightened.

"I didn't mean to snoop," Debi said in a thin, tremulous voice. "I couldn't sleep—"

"It's all right, chicken." Suzanne stepped inside the bedroom and snapped on the light. "Come on in. I need to talk to you." Miraculously, she managed to sound calm, but firm.

Deb followed her inside.

Suzanne shut the door behind them and sat down on the edge of the twin bed. The sheets and covers were thrown back in a twisted heap; obviously, Deb was telling the truth about not being able to get to sleep. Suzanne felt a pang of guilt; after what Deb overheard tonight, chances were she'd have many more sleepless nights.

"Sit down, Deb." She patted the spot next to her on the mattress.

Deb sat reluctantly, her tangled long hair hanging in her eyes; she swept it back carelessly. "What you were saying about the aliens"—she paused to look up at her mother with wide, pleading eyes—"is it true?"

"You know that I can't talk to you about my work, Deb. I made a promise to keep it a secret, and I can't break that promise, no matter what. I have to ask you to make a promise now too—a very serious promise. What you heard downstairs tonight—you must never, ever repeat it to anyone. People's lives depend on it."

"I promise," Deb said in a tiny voice. She looked so very small and scared that Suzanne was overwhelmed with pity for her.

"I'm so sorry you heard, chicken," she whispered, stroking the girl's hair back from her warm forehead. The last thing she ever wanted was for her daughter to experience the terror the rest of them took as a matter of course. "Even if I can't talk to you about what we're doing now—there's something that happened a long time ago—the history of something you should know about."

"This doesn't sound too good," Deb said matter-of-factly, screwing her face up.

"Why do you say that, chicken?"

Deb was scrutinizing her mother's expression carefully. "'Cause you're wearing the same expression as when you talked about the nuclear bomb." She paused. "Is this going to be about the alien invasion?"

Suzanne's jaw dropped. "Who told you about *that?*"

The girl shrugged. "Oh . . . Mrs. Stolz, our fourth-grade history teacher said something about it, even though it wasn't in our textbook. I think she got in trouble for it, though, because she mentioned it only that one time, and it was never on any tests. And Mrs. Pennyworth talked about it in one of our lessons. She has this really old book with neat pictures in it." Debi broke off, trying to keep her expression nonchalant and not quite succeeding. "Mrs. Pennyworth says she was good friends with Harrison's mother and father, and they were killed by aliens. I have the funny feeling these are the same guys you were talking about."

Suzanne's mouth twisted wryly at the thought that Mrs. Pennyworth was assuming Debi should know about the invasion without first consulting her mother —even though Suzanne now felt that the woman was probably doing the right thing. But from here on, she'd check with the older woman first before Deb was taught any more unauthorized subjects.

She smiled at her daughter with maternal pride. The kid was trying to pretend she wasn't afraid for her mother's sake, so that Suzanne wouldn't worry, but she knew that Deb had to be terribly frightened. "Look," she said, playing with a strand of the girl's long hair, "if you have trouble sleeping, you can stay in my bedroom tonight."

"Well . . ." Deb said casually in her grown-up voice, "maybe a change would help my insomnia."

"Insomnia? Where'd you learn that one?"

"Mrs. Pennyworth."

"Well, come on then." Suzanne rose and offered the girl her hand. "I could use a little company tonight to help my insomnia too."

Deb took her mother's hand. As they approached the hallway, she paused. "Mom?" The mature preteen was gone; Deb's voice was high-pitched, childish.

Suzanne looked down at her, concerned. "What's the matter, chicken?"

"Nothing. It's just . . ." Deb fidgeted awkwardly with embarrassment. "Well, I never knew that you were so *brave*."

Suzanne smiled. "You're a pretty brave kid yourself, Ms. McCullough."

Harrison lay down in the darkness on the strange bed and tried to sleep. His brain produced several perfectly logical reasons as to why he should do so: one, because he was exhausted, especially considering the number of naps he'd recently been forced to miss; two, because he needed to be physically and mentally alert tomorrow, and if he didn't get some sleep soon, he wouldn't be worth a shit; and three, because it had been almost eight hours since his last nap, and his body clock was going to get all fouled up if he didn't nod off soon. *So sleep, dammit. You've got to rest. After all, the fate of the entire civilized and not-so-civilized world rests on your scrawny shoulders.*

Yeah. Right. That was a great one for inducing relaxation. He squeezed his eyes shut, and again had the sensation of being pulled down into a black whirlpool of panic.

Harrison fought it, as he had when he was a kid, by

thinking of something funny. Eyes still closed, he did his best to recall every practical joke he'd ever played. What was the first one? Kindergarten, of course. Couldn't forget that one. The time he'd put the frog in Katie Seymour's pants, with gratifying results—though not so gratifying for the poor frog.

Then first grade, with Mr. Anderson, that tight-lipped horse's ass with the curious habit of plucking out his eyebrows and chewing on them. The old tack on the teacher's chair—not exactly original, but still worthwhile. Harrison smiled to himself at the image of old redheaded Anderson shooting straight up from behind his desk, his eyes round as quarters.

There, that was better. Everything was going to be all right; after all, Clayton would be coming out to the ranch tomorrow. Just like the old days. Harrison felt his body begin to relax. Now all he needed was inspiration for a practical joke to play on Ironhorse—after all this was over, of course, when Harrison would be a few thousand miles removed from the colonel—or the stiff-lipped Tom Kensington, who looked like a promising target. Something to do with the horse, or the girl; maybe he could get Debi's cooperation. He drifted off into darkness, his thoughts a confusing tumble of base-three digits and practical jokes.

Then someone switched on the light.

Harrison, darling, get up.

He bolted upright in bed, heart hammering so hard he clutched at his chest. In his momentary confusion it was all too easy to imagine he was five years old again.

"You were right," Ironhorse said. No apology. The

colonel stood in the doorway, still dressed in fatigues. His dark brows were knitted, his manner agitated, too agitated to register Harrison's terrified reaction to being wakened.

Harrison drew a shaking hand across his face. "I was *asleep*."

Ironhorse either failed or refused to get the point. He stepped inside the room and, without waiting for an invitation, sat down on the edge of Harrison's bed.

"Please," Harrison said sarcastically, gesturing, "come in."

The colonel got straight to the point. "I finally got hold of Wilson. According to the general, the government has had three of the alien ships mothballed since 1953. Care to guess where?"

"I already told you," Harrison said flatly. "Hangar Fifteen. You don't have to act so surprised that I was telling the truth."

Ironhorse grunted in grudging acknowledgment. "And guess where Hangar Fifteen is?"

"Nellis Air Force Base." Harrison smiled unhappily. "So my theory was right."

Ironhorse slowly shook his head, seeming overwhelmed. "Smack-dab in the middle. We've got to get to Nellis first thing in the morning, before the aliens do. If they get their hands on those ships—"

Harrison motioned him silent. There was no point in saying what they both already knew: if the aliens got to their ships, they would be impossible to stop.

TWENTY-SEVEN

It was normal morning activity along the flight line at Nellis Air Force Base. A typical day, the sun bright, harsh, superheating the tarmac until black heat waves glimmered against the near horizon. A squadron of fighters was lined up on the main runway; every few seconds one of them streaked up into the sky with an ear-splitting roar. Both inside and outside the hangars, repairmen were busy maintenancing helicopters and a couple of small prop planes. Every so often a jeepful of soldiers rumbled down the service road.

Everyday stuff, nothing unusual or suspicious at all, certainly not about the two airmen who strolled across the tarmac past a hangar toward a runway. Nothing unusual at all, except for the mottled purplish bruises that ringed each of their necks, or the slight clumsiness of their movements. No one noticed, and no one stopped them as they made a sudden detour toward two of the big troop-transport helicopters sitting on the outskirts of the runway and climbed into them.

By the time one of the workers heard the choppers start up and tried to yell out that the copters were scheduled for maintenance, not takeoff, it was too late.

Self-conscious and hot in camo fatigues, Suzanne sat in the driver's seat of the drab green Ford sedan and tried not to appear nervous. Think military, that was the key. She straightened and put her hands at ten o'clock and two o'clock—the ideal driving position— on the steering wheel.

Seated next to her, Harrison wore a uniform identical to hers and Ironhorse's. She could only hope it looked less ridiculous on her. Harrison leaned next to her and said under his breath and through his teeth, "Try to relax, will you? You look like you've got a poker up your—"

"Go to hell," she whispered, and looked through the open car window at Ironhorse as he walked up to the front of the commander's bungalow and saluted the base commander, General Arquette, a stern, jowly, gray-haired man who wore a carefully pressed blue uniform and the same cool air of confidence Ironhorse exuded.

Arquette returned the salute, then turned to narrow his eyes at Suzanne, peering in through the tinted windshield at Ironhorse's entourage. She swallowed, and did her best to look bored—but felt absolutely convinced that the general would never mistake her and Harrison for military personnel.

It was hot, and the car windows were all rolled down. Suzanne listened carefully to see what Arquette had to say to Ironhorse about his companions, but oddly enough, the general said nothing, just turned his attention politely back to the colonel. The two of them began to stroll the short distance in front of the bungalow.

As unconvincing as she and Harrison might be, Ironhorse was brilliant in his role. The man was a truly inspired liar; she would have to remember never again to believe anything he said. He walked next to the general, his hands folded behind his back, Arquette's aide a few respectful steps behind.

"I'm told the outlying areas of your base have ideal terrain for conducting my survival-training classes." Ironhorse's expression was far more pleasant and respectful than Suzanne had ever seen it.

But the general's expression was less than friendly; he narrowed his eyes suspiciously. "If I'd had advance warning," he complained, "I could have made some arrangements. This is most irregular."

Rather than become defensive, Ironhorse nodded sympathetically. "Know what you mean, General. It was last minute for us too." He glanced back at the aide, then lowered his voice confidentially. "Special mission coming up. Can't really talk about it."

Arquette's hostility melted instantly and was replaced by a spark of keen interest. He lifted one bushy brow questioningly. "South of the border?"

Ironhorse replied with a wink.

Arquette nodded approvingly. "About damn time." He gestured to his aide to come closer. "Let me have Captain Matthews here take you on your survey." They turned and headed back toward the Ford.

Suzanne tensed. If Arquette insisted on giving them a chaperon, the little masquerade would be over in an instant. She didn't even know how or who or when to salute. Maybe Ironhorse could bullshit his way into Nellis, but she and Harrison didn't know enough about the military to fool anyone, except from a safe distance.

She tilted her head to give a worried glance at the black metal insignia pin on her collar. Ironhorse had filled her in on the fact that the rank it indicated was that of corporal, but she couldn't remember which way the two little chevrons were supposed to be pointing. Right now they were pointing upward, and as Ironhorse and Arquette neared the sedan, she hoped like hell her rank was right side up.

But Ironhorse seemed totally unfazed by the general's offer. He smiled glibly and replied without missing a beat, "I appreciate the offer, sir, but it's unnecessary. I think we can find our own way." The smile widened. "General Wilson said we weren't to inconvenience you in any way."

"Well, if you need help," Arquette said, and walked him back to the passenger side of the sedan.

Ironhorse stopped at the rear door. "You'll be the first to know, sir. Thank you." He waited for a moment, then cleared his throat and tilted his head to glance pointedly at Harrison.

Suzanne caught the look, and nudged Harrison's combat boot with her own. "I think he wants you to open his door for him," she whispered.

"What?" Harrison turned to glance at Ironhorse over his shoulder. Apparently, the look on the colonel's face was enough to convince him, because he scrambled out of the front seat, came to a ragged attempt at attention, and held Ironhorse's door open. After the colonel crawled in, Harrison slammed the door shut, then retook his own seat in the front of the Ford.

General Arquette bent down to peer into Ironhorse's window. "Always glad when the air force can lend you army boys—and gals"—added as a patronizing afterthought at the sight of Suzanne—"a helping hand." He lowered his voice to address Ironhorse. "Keep me apprised. Love to get a piece of that mission."

"Will do, General," Ironhorse answered cheerfully, then settled back in his seat and addressed Suzanne, his tone becoming sharp. "Get a move on, Corporal. We haven't got all day."

She raised an eyebrow at that, and exchanged irritated looks with Harrison. Obviously, the colonel was relishing his role just a bit too much. Time to put him back in his place. She started up the Ford and jammed her foot down on the accelerator.

The results were satisfactory. The car lurched forward, slamming Ironhorse in a most unmilitary fashion against the upholstery.

She waited until they were out of Arquette's view to snicker. Harrison wasn't quite so reserved—he turned around and laughed aloud at the colonel, who didn't seem particularly amused.

"Hey," Ironhorse said indignantly. "What was *that* for?"

Suzanne blinked innocently up at him in the rearview mirror. "You *said* to get a move on, Colonel. I thought I was doing just that."

Harrison was grinning over his shoulder at Ironhorse. "I think it's Dr. McCullough's subtle way of saying she doesn't appreciate the way you bossed us around."

"I had to, or it wouldn't have looked right," Ironhorse protested. "And you're supposed to open the door for an officer. And by the way, Blackwood, the next time you come to attention, remember this—" He said it rapid-fire, like a marine drill sergeant barking out orders (and loving every minute of it). "Stand erect, heels touching, feet at a forty-five-degree angle, fingers curled, thumb to index finger, touching the seam of your pants. Now, to salute—"

Harrison gave a disbelieving smile as he shook his head. "Knock it off, Ironhorse. Call me a conscientious objector if you want, but if you think I'm going to go to all the trouble to remember *that,* you're crazy."

"Admit it, Colonel," Suzanne said. "You en*joyed* giving us orders."

Ironhorse frowned and was about to deny it, but something made him change his mind. "Well . . ." A grin spread slowly over his face. "Maybe just a little."

* * *

Ironhorse directed them through the hilly terrain, a mixture of scrub pine forest and desert, down a dirt road to a remote, quiet area where a lone hangar sat, bordered on its rear flank by sparse forest.

"Stop here," the colonel ordered although they were still several hundred yards away.

Suzanne brought the Ford to a smooth stop. The hangar door was closed, and as far as she could see there were no signs of life, only the occasional thunder of a jet passing overhead. "Looks harmless enough."

Ironhorse climbed out of the car—this time without waiting for Harrison to open the door—and went around to the trunk. Suzanne glanced over at Harrison. "What if we're wrong? What if they're not here after all?"

Harrison's mood had abruptly become somber. "I hope to God we're wrong, and they're not here, and yet, at the same time, I have to hope that we're right, and they are."

She nodded. If they weren't there, she and her two companions would be safe . . . but an opportunity to stop the aliens would be missed. She moved to open the car door.

"Come on, Corporal, move it," Ironhorse called with more than a little sarcasm.

Suzanne climbed out, and Harrison followed. Ironhorse had already opened the Ford's trunk and was pulling out equipment. He handed Harrison a holster which held a Beretta. "Here, Blackwood. You're going to need this."

Harrison drew back and shook his head.

Ironhorse sighed, disgusted. "Fine. I'm sure the aliens will respect your disapproval of guns."

"Harrison . . ." Suzanne put a hand on his arm. "We have a responsibility to stop them here. Extreme situations call for extreme actions. If the colonel and I are killed, you are obligated to stop them."

Harrison stared reluctantly down at the weapon in Ironhorse's hand, his expression one of distaste. "All right. This once. But I don't like it."

"We'll be sure to make a note of that," Ironhorse said. He pulled the Beretta from its holder and held it where Harrison could see it. "I've released the safety and cocked it. All you have to do is aim and fire."

"Aim and fire," Harrison parroted.

"Just remember one word, and you'll be okay," Ironhorse told him. "BRAS."

"Bras?" A whimsical expression crossed Harrison's face. "I had no idea the army was this much fun."

Ironhorse nodded. "That's right, BRAS: breathe, release, aim, and squeeze." He demonstrated with the pistol, then handed it and the holster to Harrison, who slipped it on. The colonel reached into the trunk again and brought out another holster, which he proffered to Suzanne.

"No, thanks." She nodded at the equipment case still in the trunk. "I've got something even better in there."

"Let's hope so," the colonel muttered. He handed the case to her, and another satchel to Harrison, then slammed the trunk shut. Together, the three of them made their way toward the hangar.

* * *

In a clearing not many miles away, the troop-transport helicopters had landed, and were in the process of being boarded—to all outward appearances by the members of Delta squad, who climbed the metal steps with heavy, awkward movements . . .

TWENTY-EIGHT

The old World War II hangar built of whitewashed wood on a steel frame was sizable enough to accommodate modern jumbo jets. In the hangar's huge sliding metal door, which could be pulled aside to admit aircraft, was a smaller, human-sized entrance, which allowed personnel simpler access. At the personnel door Harrison carefully checked the wires he'd attached to the card key and computer pad, then spoke into the transportable phone. "Norton? Still there?"

"All set on this end, Doc."

"Give me ten seconds, then fire away." Harrison removed the receiver from his ear and attached the acoustic couplers to the phone's earpieces and mouthpieces. His hands trembled only slightly—not fear of what he knew faced him inside, Harrison told himself sternly, but relief that they had managed to arrive at the hangar before the aliens. Next to him, Ironhorse and Suzanne watched, the colonel casting an occasional worried glance over his shoulder at their unguarded flank.

The lights on the wired-up keypad began to blink furiously in random sequence as Norton's Cray worked to break the security code. Some primitive, illogical part of Harrison's brain—the limbic system, he decided—prayed for the door *not* to open, while the rational part of his brain prayed it would.

It did. The door clicked, and with a painful creak swung outward. Of course; the hinges were probably rusted. The place had most likely been sealed for some thirty-odd years. Harrison quickly pulled the wires away and stuffed them and the portable phone into the nylon satchel.

He entered a few steps behind Ironhorse and Suzanne and closed the door behind them. Almost immediately, he was tempted to reopen it. The air inside was stifling, musty, dead after years of being closed up. He stood in the dark, suffocating warmth and fought the temptation to yield to claustrophobia. The door would have to stay closed—couldn't risk advertising the fact that they were there. He fumbled in the satchel for his flashlight. Next to him, Ironhorse snapped his flashlight on and found a wall switch, and the few soft, dim spotlights illuminated the windowless hangar.

There was a collective intake of breath as they saw the ships. Three of them, each one an eerily lovely thing with an irregular, flattened-disc shape. To Harrison's eyes, it most resembled a giant obsidian manta ray, its wings sloping obliquely downward on either side, as if the ray were swimming. Where the ray's eyes should be sat a translucent green dome from which proceeded a metal filament, atop which sat a great red eye—now dull, though Harrison had seen it glow hotly right before it lashed out with the laser beam that killed his parents. He understood it now to be a sensing device, a periscope of sorts that also doubled as a weapon.

The ships rested, delicately balanced on the edges of their downward-curved "wings." They had no wheels, no legs, no supports of any kind; Clayton's best guess was that they traveled on an electromagnetic "cushion." And they were huge—the size of a large passenger plane but broader and shorter—as huge and as frightening as they had appeared when Harrison first saw them as a child; time had not managed to diminish their size or the impact of their terrifying beauty.

Harrison took a staggering step backward, momentarily overwhelmed by hatred. If he paused much longer, he would lose his composure, be unable to do what he had come to do. He walked up behind Ironhorse and Suzanne, who stood—faces tilted up, gaping—and caught their elbows.

"We've got work," he said. They both came alive as if awakened from a spell. Harrison removed a flashlight from his satchel and moved past them toward the closest ship and shone the beam on it, searching along the smooth underside for the switch Clayton's papers had said would be there. He found it, pressed it, and waited. The metal, which appeared opalescent black-silver in shadow, almost white in direct light, felt sharply cold beneath his fingertip, despite the stuffy warmth of the surrounding air.

The ship rumbled. In the center of its underbelly a hatch opened, a ramp dropped.

Ironhorse's black eyes darted over at Harrison. "Blackwood . . ." His expression was one of distinct discomfort. "You sure this is the best way?"

Harrison's skin crawled at the sight of it, but he forced himself to take a tentative step toward the ramp. "Maybe not the best way, but the only way. According to the research, these ships produce an electromagnetic shield that can withstand a direct nuclear blast." He glanced at the colonel. "I don't much care for it myself."

Ironhorse stared back at the ship and nodded unhappily. "Okay . . . after you, Blackwood." He gestured with a strong brown arm.

Harrison swallowed and started walking up the ramp, Ironhorse at his heels.

"Don't be long," Suzanne called after them, an urgent note in her voice.

Harrison's fear was quickly lessened by his curiosity. The ship's interior presented many puzzles. For one thing, the interior seemed unnecessarily spacious. Most of it was not partitioned into rooms, except for a small area Harrison decided was the head. There was no color, but every possible shade of gray, and almost no furniture to speak of, except at the pilots' stations, three podiums that faced a long control panel—a counter built of smooth white metal, interfaced with a soft, yielding material Harrison couldn't identify. The panel (he kept thinking of it as the dash) was perfectly smooth, and he could see no way for the controls or what he took to be computer terminals of a sort to be manipulated.

Ironhorse swept the room with the flashlight beam, his expression becoming more and more puzzled. "How the hell are you supposed to fly these things?"

Harrison shook his head. "No one ever figured it out. Clayton—Dr. Forrester speculated that somehow the aliens used brainwave impulses. The pilots' brains were probably directly hooked in to a navigational computer."

Ironhorse shuddered.

Harrison reached into the satchel again and gingerly fished out the slab of explosive and the timing device. Distastefully, he proffered them both to the colonel. "Here. You're the expert in this department." He gestured at the panel. "I'd set it over there."

Ironhorse took them from him and set to work, sticking the plastic on the underside of the panel, at the far end.

"If you don't mind," Harrison said, peering over the colonel's shoulder, "I'll just go ahead and get the other ships opened up."

Ironhorse almost grinned, his eyes focused intently on what he was doing. "What's the matter, Blackwood? Don't think I know what I'm doing?"

"I trust you implicitly, Colonel. But let me put it this way—I'm no longer needed here, am I?"

Ironhorse shrugged. "Guess not. Get out of here."

Harrison walked back down the ramp, trying to ignore the wobbliness his knees had taken on. In the middle of the shadowy hangar, Suzanne knelt, engrossed in her examination of what looked like a tankful of oxygen. Harrison strolled up behind her, sure that with all the noise he made coming out of the hatch, she heard his approach.

There she was, working hard, unafraid, determined to stop the aliens even if it meant her life. He was suddenly overwhelmed with the need to tell her how much he admired her, how damn glad he was he made Ephram hire her, how thankful he was that she got Wilson's help, how impressed he was with the calm way she risked herself now . . . and how, if they ever made it out of this mess alive, he wanted to repay her in some way.

Instead, he peered over her shoulder and nodded at the pressurized tank. "Think you'll be needing that?"

She nearly jumped out of her skin. She leapt to her feet, nearly knocking the canister over, then stared up at him with that distracted manner she had when she was working.

"Warn me next time you sneak up, okay?" She glanced down at her equipment and said in answer to his question, "I hope not. There was no way to test it on a live subject, so I have no way of knowing if it'll be effective."

"Suzanne," he began desperately, not knowing exactly how he intended to begin.

"What?" She knelt back down to adjust the pressure on the tank.

"I just wanted to say . . . if we both manage to make it through this alive—well, I wanted you to know that I . . ."

She frowned quizzically up at him, which made him even more tongue-tied.

"I was trying to say that I . . ."

"One down, two to go." Ironhorse emerged from the ship and slapped Harrison on the shoulder. "Come on, Blackwood, get a move on."

"Shit," Harrison said.

"What?" Suzanne blinked. "Harrison, what were you saying? Something about if we both survive . . . ?"

"Never *mind*." Disgusted, Harrison shook his head. "If we survive, *then* I'll tell you." He didn't turn around so he wouldn't have to see the sneer he knew Ironhorse would be wearing.

"Did I interrupt something?" Ironhorse's tone was all innocence.

Harrison went straight to the next ship without answering.

They set explosives in the next two ships without incident, and climbed out of the third ship to find Suzanne waiting anxiously for them. She stood clutching the tank, a worried expression on her face. "We need to get out of here. I think someone's coming."

Ironhorse cocked his head to listen. "Helicopters. Two of them."

Harrison peered uncertainly at the hangar entrance. "How do we know if they're good guys or bad guys?"

"We don't," the colonel replied. "But considering what we're doing, it doesn't make much difference. Come on—we'd better take cover."

Ironhorse dashed to a far dark corner and hid behind a stack of cobweb-covered wooden crates.

Suzanne and Harrison followed and crouched down, Suzanne sandwiched between the two men. The thumping of the chopper blades grew louder; they had landed, Harrison guessed, just outside the hangar entrance. *Stay calm. We were probably spotted by some airmen on maneuvers, that's all.*

"How much time?" he asked the colonel.

Ironhorse held his watch in front of his eyes and squinted at the digital display. "If we're not out of here in ten minutes, we get to be part of the fireworks." His face was grim.

A sound: someone trying unsuccessfully to open the door. This was going to be bad. Suzanne was squeezed so close to Harrison, their shoulders touched. He could feel her tense next to him.

He whispered in her ear, "Look, I was just trying to say before: thanks for believing me. I can't tell you what your help has meant to me."

She looked at him and tried to smile, but her eyes were wide and frightened. He realized that his own fear had eased in the face of his concern for her and her daughter.

"Look, I feel terrible about this," he said truthfully, too low for Ironhorse to hear. No point in holding back anything; speak now or forever hold your peace. "My own hope was that Debi wouldn't have to go through what I did."

Her expression warmed at that; she managed a weak smile. "Maybe she won't. Maybe that's just air force people out there."

He smiled back, encouraged. "Maybe. And if we *do* make it through this—"

The metal door exploded under a hail of bullets, shrapnel flying into the hangar, scattering across the floor. Harrison ducked lower and squeezed his eyes shut. Next to him, Suzanne trembled . . . or was that himself?

"Shit," he breathed, but it was drowned out by the explosion. He raised his head cautiously and peered through the spaces between the crates. Soldiers were filing into the hangar. His initial reaction was relief— so they'd be arrested by the air force. He could deal with that.

But then he noticed the uniforms were wrong. These guys were army, not air force . . . and as he watched, he saw that some of the men's uniforms were torn and stained with congealed blood. One of them, obviously in charge, turned his head to survey the room . . . and revealed a face half shot away, a red, pulpy mass of dried blood, muscle, and cartilage. Harrison looked away, sickened.

"Jesus," Ironhorse whispered. "My men. Those are my men." He moved as if to rise; Harrison reached past Suzanne to lay a restraining hand on the colonel's forearm.

"Not anymore," he said softly.

The soldiers divided into three groups, each group heading for a ship. With intense relief Harrison realized they didn't suspect anyone else was in the hangar. Maybe there *was* a chance to make it out alive.

The three huddled behind the crates, not making a sound, until the last soldier made it onto the last ship, and the hatch closed. And then one of the ships began to hum; its metal began to pulse, dark silver alternating with hot white. Harrison glanced, terrified, at the red targeting eye. Still dull—but the minute the aliens activated their sensing devices, they would discover the three humans hiding in the darkness.

He leaned forward to whisper to Suzanne and the colonel. "We've got to go *now*—before their ships sense us." He got up and ran, half crouching, toward the entrance, staying in the shadows along the walls. For an instant the memory of thirty-five years earlier threatened to overtake him. *Suzanne. Think of Suzanne. Got to be sure she makes it out okay....*

The thought steadied him. He glanced over his shoulder to see Suzanne following, carrying the heavy tank, with Ironhorse bringing up the rear. As he watched, the colonel stopped suddenly, his expression stunned. Harrison followed his gaze. Blocking the entrance was the soldier with the blown-away face, who raised his M-16 threateningly at the escaping trio.

"Reynolds," Ironhorse whispered, then: "Gordie? Don't shoot." He spread his hands in a gesture of friendliness. "Gordie—it's me."

Gordie was unimpressed. He took aim.

Swiftly, Suzanne stepped forward and pointed the tank's nozzle at Gordie; she closed her eyes and turned away as a cloud of gray mist enveloped the soldier.

None of them moved as Gordie dropped the rifle, coughed a few times, staggered forward, and fell.

"It worked!" Suzanne cried, exultant. "My bacteria worked! We can use this on them!"

Gordie coughed again—then, before they could make it past him, began to crawl toward the dropped rifle.

"Better recheck that formula," Harrison told her. He swung the satchel of equipment in a wide arc and struck the fallen soldier on the head—with absolutely no effect whatsoever. Gordie moved relentlessly toward the gun.

With an expression of hardened pain, Ironhorse lifted his own rifle and took aim.

He didn't have time to shoot. Gordie fell forward, his back arching as a convulsion gripped his entire body. His skin began to bubble and swell until it burst, spewing pus and blood and decaying tissue—what was left began to dissolve into an obscene, vile puddle of ooze. Beneath, something dark and living writhed, struggling to free itself.

Ironhorse's mouth twitched slightly as he fired— once, twice, three times, until the thing ceased moving and lay still. He looked up at Harrison and Suzanne, his face terrible. "Let's get out of here."

They ran through the open personnel entrance. Once outside, Harrison gulped in the fresh air and began to run toward the helicopters. The colonel caught him by the arm, almost yanking it from the socket. "No! They expect us to head there! This way!" Ironhorse took off for the open field, beyond which lay the cover of the forest.

"Jesus," Harrison whispered, stopped dead by the horrifying familiarity of the scene. The open field, the pursuing ships . . . The nightmare was becoming reality again . . .

"Come on!" Suzanne came up behind him and grabbed his hand tightly. "They're coming! Run!"

She gave his arm a hard jerk, pulling him off balance. Harrison stared at her without comprehending at first—then descended into terror, and ran.

Behind them came a tortured groaning sound, the sound of the huge hangar doors sliding open for the first time in decades. Running wildly, Harrison glanced over his shoulder to see a bright beam—the alien death ray—streak out from the hangar's interior. The helicopters outside glowed a brilliant, painful orange and burst into flames that quickly extinguished themselves, leaving only smoldering, blackened skeletons.

The sight of it made them run harder, crazily, both of them fighting to keep their balance on the uneven terrain. Harrison's breath came in ragged, sobbing gasps. Well ahead of them, Ironhorse disappeared into the cover of the forest.

The air was filled with a deep, ominous hum. At the sound, Harrison's skin began to tingle. He looked back again to see a lone ship sail gracefully through the open hangar doors, past the smoking remains of the choppers. It paused, hovering a mere twelve feet from the ground . . . and its great red eye began to rotate, searching for the intruders.

The shelter of the forest was only a few yards away.

And then Harrison stumbled over a large rock and lost his balance. Suzanne struggled to hold on to him, to keep him moving, but lost her grip on his hand. He fell hard, facedown, onto the sparse grass.

He pushed himself up and looked over his shoulder.

The ship was gliding closer. Harrison felt the hair on the nape of his neck rise.

Harrison, no—

He looked in front of him. Through wisps of smoke that drifted over from the incinerated helicopters, he saw Suzanne stop running and cry out his name, her hazel eyes large with terror, the tendons on her white neck standing out like cords. She was starting back to help him to his feet.

Harrison—

No, Suzanne! He waved her on, tried to scramble to his feet. *Run—*

But she froze, her eyes wide and terrible, focused on the approaching ship.

Behind them the great eye paused as it found its target.

Harrison dropped back down and covered his head as the ship fired.

Xashron was filled with exhilaration to be at the controls of a ship again, with Xeera and Konar on either side of him.

"Prepare to destroy their vessels," he ordered, and waited while the last soldier pulled open the hangar doors before dashing back into the sister ship. "There is no point in allowing them an easy escape."

Xeera peered into her viewer, her human form hunched over. The host bodies were awkward, since the ships were not scaled for them, but there had been no time to exit them. "Door open, Commander."

In a weak voice Konar relayed the targeting informa-

tion to Xeera, who was poised over her control panel. Konar sighed and rested his head against the panel.

Xashron eyed him with concern. There was no better place for a soldier like Konar to die than at his post, but they could not afford to lose their targeter now. "Are you able to perform your duties, Konar?"

"Yes," he replied weakly, but was barely able to raise his head.

There was nothing to be done about it; Xashron turned to Xeera. "Fire."

Xeera complied. "Helicopters destroyed; but instruments indicate that the humans are fleeing by foot in the direction of the forest."

Xashron glanced at his unsteady officer. "Target them, Konar."

Konar struggled to do so. "Targeted, Commander."

"Fire."

Harrison felt searing heat skim across the top of his head; for one horrible second he was afraid to open his eyes, afraid of what he would see.

And then he heard Suzanne scream. In front of them a tree exploded in a blaze that faded quickly to blackness. She ran to him, pulled him to his feet, and together they dashed toward safety. Harrison turned to see the targeting eye rotate again, focus on them, and stop as it prepared to fire.

Strong hands grabbed him, pulled him into the protection of the forest behind the cover of a small rise. Suzanne, still fiercely clutching his hand, was dragged along with him.

"Down!" Ironhorse barked.

Harrison dropped onto his stomach and craned his neck to see over the rise. Their pursuer had stopped; gracefully, the other ships floated out from the hangar to join the first, and the three jockeyed into a triangular formation. Slowly, the deadly triangle made its way toward the humans cowering in the forest.

"Well, *shit*," Harrison said, bitterly disappointed. It was the only word that summed up the situation, and at the moment he very much understood why on flight recorders recovered from fatal plane crashes the last words of the crew the instant before impact were invariably of the four-letter variety. Now only Norton and poor Clayton would be left to fight the aliens: would they be able to find others to help them?

Harrison glanced over at Suzanne, who lay next to him, her eyes squeezed tightly shut. "I'm sorry, Suzanne," he said lamely. "And awfully sorry for Debi. I didn't mean for this to happen."

She opened her eyes to look at him, the corner of her mouth quirking with wry resignation in the midst of her fear. "Oh, what the hell." She shrugged cavalierly. "At least it's for a worthy cause. But don't apologize, Harrison. It's hardly your fault. Frankly, I think you're a truly good man."

"I hate to interrupt the love fest," Ironhorse said dryly, "but don't make out your wills just yet. It's just about ten minutes." He glanced from the approaching ships to his watch. "Three . . . two . . . one . . . *now!*"

Nothing happened.

* * *

Konar struggled against unconsciousness. His wounds from the human firearms had been extensive, and he had lost a great deal of bodily fluids, which left him weak. So weak that he was aware of the human host struggling to reclaim the body that Xana had permitted him to use.

He obeyed Xashron's order to target the fleeing humans once more, then slumped over his panel to rest. One arm dangled down and brushed against something unfamiliar, foreign—a lump of malleable material with wires and a small mechanical device stuck to it. He stared curiously at it for a moment, then consulted the host brain—a female named Urick, with an incredibly forceful personality. Urick had some military knowledge, and recognized the substance immediately: plastic explosives.

When Konar digested what this meant, he struggled to lift his head, to cry out a warning to the others.

Urick did not let him.

He was weak and dying, too weak to fight her, and in a sheer burst of will she took ascendancy and held him there, silent, in his position, not even allowing him to bend down and remove the explosive.

Urick, too, was weak and dying, but her determination was strong, and the explosive was her chance for freedom, for an end to her torment, to the twilight half-death she endured.

In her brush with Konar's mind, she realized that the explosive would end more than her torment alone. She knew little of the aliens, but she had glimpsed the destruction envisioned in Konar's dying brain. Perhaps her hopes of revolution had been naive, narrow-minded, unrealistic; perhaps she had failed in what she set out to do in Jericho Valley, but she would not fail now.

There's more than one way to save the world.

"Konar?"

Alien gibberish; deep, harsh, grating sounds, but somehow Urick understood that they were speaking to her.

"Konar—" *The one named Xeera leaned forward to peer curiously at her.* "Answer. What are the coordinates of our targets?"

Urick laughed silently. Konar was dying; Konar could not give the coordinates if he wanted to, and Urick would not let him if he did. She glanced down at the timer; there were only seconds left.

The other, Xashron, in the body of a strangled young soldier, rose from his post next to her and moved toward her. "Konar—obey your command, or I shall call one of those below to replace you." *He leaned over Urick, brushed against the edge of the panel. Something made him glance down, and see the explosive stuck there; the eyes of the dead soldier widened.*

"No!" *From the terror on his face it was clear the alien understood. He reached forward with human hands to tear it from the panel, to destroy it.*

Konar was dead, and Urick was dying now that his alien strength was leaving her. With enormous effort she rose and fell forward onto Xashron, forcing him to stagger backward, away from the panel. She was too weak to stop him, but she could try to slow him down until—

The timer reached zero.

Liberation, my friend.

The world exploded into a painfully beautiful fireball.

Harrison clicked his tongue in disgust. "And *you* said you were an explosives exp—"

The first ship burst into a ball of dazzling light, followed swiftly by two more rapid-fire explosions. The force of the blast made the ground shudder; Harrison covered his head with his arms as debris rained down from the sky.

Bits of metal stung as they pelted his back. Long after the shrapnel stopped falling, he stayed facedown in the grass, arms shielding his head.

Silence. Then someone touched him, gently, on the shoulder. He lifted his head and saw Suzanne. She was sitting up, bits of grass clinging to her dark hair. "Harrison," she said huskily, smiling, but her mouth twitched as if she were holding back tears. "Get up, Harrison. It's all right. It's over."

Harrison, darling, get up—

It's over.

He heard the words without understanding them, and pushed himself to his knees. For a moment he stared at her, then tilted his head back to gaze up at the silent sky. The ships were gone; what was left of them lay scattered in twisted heaps of wreckage for as far as Harrison could see.

The sense of relief was dizzying. He reached for Suzanne and gave her a fierce, grateful squeeze. "You're all right. Thank God. Thank God." He laughed softly at the sudden absence of terror and released her.

Ironhorse gave him a joyful slap on the back that nearly made him pitch forward. "We did it!" The colonel grinned toothily. "Son of a gun, Blackwood! We did it!" He held out a hand and pulled Harrison, then Suzanne, to their feet.

"We did it all right," Harrison said, his joy tempered with the memory of past sorrows as he studied the wreckage littering the field.

"It's all over," Suzanne repeated to herself, gazing back at the hangar entrance. "Thank God it's all over."

He stared at her. She was white-faced, dazed, still in shock. He was overwhelmed with relief that they had not been killed, that they had destroyed the ships before the aliens had recovered them, but his relief darkened as an unwelcome thought began to repeat in his brain: *It's not over. Not over at all. It's barely begun. . . .*

EPILOGUE

For the first time in years Harrison went to bed and slept a dreamless eight hours. By the time he was wakened by a knock on the door, sunlight was filtering through the curtains of the bedroom window. He sat up stiffly and blinked at the clock on the nightstand: seven-thirty, but it took him a minute to figure out whether it was morning or evening. He was still dressed in the army uniform; he hadn't even taken his boots off, had just fallen onto the bed without pulling down the covers and gone immediately into a deep sleep.

"Harrison?" Mrs. Pennyworth called softly on the other side of the door.

"Yes?" he croaked. His throat was parched and sore.

"There is an important telephone call for you. Dr. Jacobi."

"Jacobi—" he muttered, confused. Why on earth would Ephram need to talk to him? And then, with a start, he remembered: Clayton! With the stress and excitement, he had completely forgotten that Clayton should have arrived at the ranch yesterday at the very latest. Something must have happened.

"You only need to pick up the telephone by your bed," Mrs. Pennyworth told him. "I transferred the call for you."

"Thank you," Harrison answered abruptly, and swung his legs over the side of the bed. He reached for the telephone on the nightstand and spoke into the receiver, totally awake and very worried. "Ephram?"

"Harrison," Jacobi said quietly, and something in his tone told Harrison with horrible certainty exactly why he was calling.

Harrison leaned forward on the edge of the bed. "Dear God, Clayton—"

"I'm so sorry, Harrison." Jacobi's voice was gentle and full of sympathy. "I found him day before yesterday. He'd had another heart attack." He paused, and continued with some difficulty. "We rushed him to the hospital, but he never regained consciousness. I was with him when he died early this morning."

"This morning," Harrison repeated, having difficulty making sense of what Ephram was saying.

"I would have called sooner," Ephram continued apologetically, "but I knew you couldn't have come to see him . . . and he wouldn't have known you were there anyway. The doctor said there was no chance of his waking."

"It's all right, Ephram," Harrison said blankly, hardly realizing what he was saying. A heavy numbness had settled over him, making it difficult to breathe or think or speak. There was an odd, painful tightness in the back of his throat that made his eyes water. "You're right, I couldn't have come. But thank you for staying with him."

Jacobi was silent for a while. "I want you to know," he said finally, "that I found him in his office, with all those other files he had wanted to give you. I'd spoken to him the night before, and he sounded better than he had in years, like the old Clayton. Being useful was the best medicine of all for him; I know that he was very happy just to be back at the Institute."

"I think so," Harrison whispered.

"I'm taking care of the arrangements. Clayton didn't want any fuss, but I'll call later and let you know. If there's anything else I can do—"

"Nothing. Thank you," Harrison said. "Thank you for everything, Ephram."

He placed the receiver back in its cradle and stared at the telephone for a long time. There was a need to grieve, and he would not deny himself that; yet at the same time, he felt an odd sense of relief. Clayton's suffering was over, and he had died in his office, surrounded by stacks of his precious files.

Remember, he died a long time ago. . . .

He undressed, got into the shower, and wept.

Suzanne poured herself another glass of champagne and settled back in her place on the couch to enjoy the modest celebration: Mrs. Pennyworth had baked a pie for dessert, which was set out on the coffee table along with a sterling silver coffeepot and a bottle of Piper Heidsieck Kensington had brought up from the wine cellar. Next to her, Debi was stuffing herself on the remains of her second—or was it her third?—piece of apple pie, but Suzanne didn't discourage her. She felt too relieved, too indulgent, and a little giddy from the glass of champagne and the euphoria. Everything was going to be all right. The ships were destroyed . . . the aliens were no longer a real threat. All that remained now was a simple clean-up operation, finding the few aliens that remained. And then she and Deb could go home.

In a way, she'd be sorry to leave the ranch—in a way, she'd found a home there—but she also knew she had, like Harrison, found a home at the Institute as well. She glanced over at Harrison, who sat quietly at one end of the sofa, holding his flute of champagne. He hadn't touched it, and seemed oddly withdrawn. His wildly fluctuating moods still mystified her. Of all of them, he had the most right to be celebrating now.

"Your apple pie is the best, Mrs. Pennyworth," Debi mumbled with her mouth full.

Mrs. Pennyworth smiled, pleased. "Why, thank you, Deborah. If you like, I can show you how to make one."

A kind offer, Suzanne thought, *but I doubt we'll be around long enough for you to do it.* She wasn't looking forward to breaking the news to Deb that they'd be leaving soon—the girl would be heartbroken about leaving Spirit.

Kensington frowned at Debi. He was only feigning displeasure, Suzanne realized in her expansive, generous mood. Underneath his stern exterior, the man had a wry wit and seemed genuinely fond of Debi. "Aren't you going to thank me too, young lady?" Kensington arched a gray brow. "After all, *I* picked the apples."

Deb giggled. "And thank *you*, Mr. Kensington."

Mrs. Pennyworth rose and began clearing away the empty dessert plates.

"Here." Deb rose, swallowing the last bit of pie. "I'll help you, Mrs. Pennyworth."

"What a kind girl." Mrs. Pennyworth winked at Suzanne. "I think she really wants to learn how to make that pie." The two of them carried stacks of dishes to the kitchen as Kensington went over to tend the fire.

Ironhorse, dressed as usual in fatigues, took a sip of his coffee. He had refused to join the other adults in a glass of champagne. "General Wilson is taking care of the Joint Military Forces Board of Inquiry," he said after Debi and Mrs. Pennyworth were well out of earshot. "I'm told—unofficially, of course—that the board is predisposed to lay all the blame on an unnamed terrorist organization."

Norton, next to the colonel, snickered and studied the fire through his champagne. "Actually, that's probably a whole lot closer to the truth than they'll ever realize."

Ironhorse nodded, and gazed into the fire.

Suzanne set her glass down on the table. "Well, I for one am glad this is all behind us." She turned to Harrison. "When this is all over, I'd like to continue to work with you—that is, if you still need a microbiologist. I figure there's a lot of analysis yet to be done on the aliens, and with Uncle Hank's help—"

Harrison regarded her with weary, bloodshot eyes. "What makes you think it's going to be over anytime soon?" His voice was soft, but there was a hostility beneath the surface that confused her.

She was a bit taken aback by his attitude. Somewhat stiffly, she replied, "Excuse me, but I seem to be laboring under the notion that destroying the three ships constituted a major victory. A number of aliens were killed—and now they won't be able to recover their weapons." She glanced at Ironhorse for support. "Isn't that right, Colonel?"

Ironhorse looked down into his coffee to avoid meeting her eyes. "There are an awful lot of barrels still missing. The army was never able to track down the tractor-trailer rig. I counted twenty people who boarded that ship, but there were more than three hundred barrels stolen from Jericho Valley."

"But they can't get to their ships or weapons now," Suzanne persisted as a cold sense of despair slowly began to settle over her, replacing her exuberance. "That was the real danger. And as soon as they contact their home planet again, we'll be able to find them and stop them for good."

"It's unlikely that the three ships warehoused at Nellis were the only three ships in existence," Harrison countered quietly. He took a swallow of his drink as if to draw courage from it for what he had to say.

"I know we're all tired, exhausted, ready for this thing to be over with. And I'm not asking anyone to stay." He stared into her eyes with a gaze so intense she wanted to look away. "God knows, we deserve to celebrate something. But—oh, hell, maybe I shouldn't talk about it now. I'm sorry. I'm ruining the party." He stared down into his champagne.

"You've already broken the mood," Suzanne said flatly, "so you may as well say what you were going to say."

He didn't look up. "All right . . ." He sighed and squared his shoulders. "We already know the aliens are capable of inhabiting human bodies—the perfect cover, which allows them to roam freely, and makes them extremely dangerous. Plus there are probably other ships. And Jericho Valley wasn't the only place where the alien barrels were stored. There were lots of other places, other barrels."

Suzanne stared at him, aghast, unwilling to understand what she had just heard.

Harrison's lips stretched into a thin line as he waited for his words to sink in. "Clayton Forrester was not privy to most of the locations," he continued after a pause. "There aren't hundreds of barrels, Suzanne—there are hundreds of *thousands* of them, and we don't even know where they are. Most of the documents relating to their location have long since been destroyed." He drew a hand wearily across his eyes, then shook his head. "I'm sorry . . . I wish it *were* over. But I'm afraid it's just beginning for us."

The room fell silent.

In the comfortingly dark recesses of the cavern, Xana regarded the other two members of the Advocacy with disdain. They had just received another message from the Mor-Tax Council, this one a stern, almost threatening message which berated them for their defeat and reminded them that the Earth had to be prepared in less than a year's time for the arrival of the colonists.

It was all bluff, and Xana knew it. The Council could not touch them from such a great distance, and if the Earth were not prepared when the colonists arrived, what would be done about it? They would not kill their own soldiers as punishment.

Of course, they might take action against the Advocacy, but Xana no longer cared . . . at least, not for the moment. She was still grieving over Xashron's death at the hands of his human enemies, and could not be bothered with concerns about her own safety.

Horek, the idiot, seemed surprised by the Council's anger. "We were told the humans were primitive, unintelligent creatures," he said, trying, as usual, to defend his mistakes. Always ready with twenty-seven excuses, that was Horek. "But they have proven themselves unexpectedly clever. And without our ships—"

"Enough of your whining, Horek!" she snapped. "With or without our ships we will find a way to defeat them. They may be clever, but their cleverness cannot save them. We will improvise."

404

"*As long as we meet the deadline,*" Oshar remarked mildly.

"*We have no choice,*" Xana replied heatedly. "*Our fellow colonists are on their way. Earth will be prepared for them when they arrive.*"

And by the Power, she swore silently, it would, for in her sorrow she had but one thought: to find those humans responsible for Xashron's death, and to take her revenge on them.